SALVAGED HEARTS
The Hearts Of Emerald Bay

SYDNE BARNETT

Flame & Fiction LLC

ISBN:

eBook: 979-8-9903198-2-0

Paperback: 979-8-9903198-4-4

Cover Art: Shanoff Designs

This is a work of fiction. Therefore, the stories and characters in the novel are fictitious. All names, characters, companies, places, events and occurrences are fictitious. Any similarity to real persons, living or dead, or actual places or events is purely coincidental. Public bodies, institutions, or historical figures mentioned in the story serve as a backdrop for the characters and their actions, but these are wholly imaginary.

This book contains mature themes and is only suitable for readers 18+

To the girls who prefer their humor like their wine: dry, bold, and leaving a lasting impression.
Alice is for you.

Author's Note & Content Disclosure

Hello there, dahhling, thank you for joining me for Alice and Greyson's story. These two absolutely *consumed* my life, and I hope you love them as much as I did. *Salvaged Hearts* can be read independently, but if you get to the end and are just dying for more of the Rhodes, check out their lighthearted parent series, *Nomadic Rhodes*, for Rhyett, Jameson and Elora's stories.

Happy Reading!

As always, your mental health matters, so here are the content disclosures for this book. The themes in *THOEB* are a bit heavier than their predecessors, but you should still end the story feeling like you spent time with the Rhodes.

The following trigger list *_does_* contain spoilers, so if you're not worried about something specific, please keep that in mind before proceeding.

This story contains but is not limited to:

Military/mercenary themes, violence, harm to an animal, foul language, toxic family, and explicit sexual content. Mention of (no on-page 1st person content) human trafficking, murder, abortion, and an abusive parent.

The team works to keep these as comprehensive as possible, but if we missed anything distressing, please feel free to email us at flame andfiction@gmail.com.

RHODES FAMILY APPENDIX

The Rhodes family is made up of twelve rowdy siblings, many many cousins and a handful of 'pseudo-siblings'. And before you say what everyone is thinking, yes, families that big do exist. I married into one ;)

*For simplicity's sake, I've **only** listed those mentioned in **this** book.*

MILO RHODES
Dad, retired captain of the *Rhodes Away*

JUNIPER RHODES
Mom, keeper of the chaos, deliverer of epic hugs and warm food.

I. JEANNE
Eldest sister, world-traveling surgeon, divorced, location unknown. Spontaneously appears on family text thread, usually around the holidays.

II. RHYETT
Eldest brother, entrepreneur, current location St. Pete, Florida. Adorably—some would say obnoxiously—optimistic. He has a daughter—Quinn, or 'Quinny'—with his wife, Brexley.

III. JAMESON
Captain of the family fishing boat, located in Mistyvale, AK. Engaged to Noel McShane. Bestower of sardonic witticisms and tough love.

IV. ELORA
New York City-based life & business coach, author, public speaker, and soon to be reality television host. Newly married to Broderick Allen, with a baby on the way. Designated family know-it-all and planner of events.

V. AXEL
Fisherman, single, currently in Mistyvale, AK but travels for the winter. Equal parts sunshine and sarcasm.

VI. PAXTON
Pro quarterback for the Windy City Wolves in Chicago, single. Gazelle-like focus on his career, hates the cold.

VII. HADLEE

Travel blogger and influencer, single, location unknown. Aka, Hurricane Hadlee due to a propensity for chaos.

VIII. ALESSANDRA
Aka. "Alice", assistant to the CEO of Hart Investments, currently in Emerald Bay, CA.

IX. FINNEGAN
Aka. "Finn", digital nomad, we think he's in New York? That could change tomorrow though. Quietest of the twelve.

X. LEIGHTON
Twins with Kaia, waitress, currently staying with Alice in Emerald Bay.

XI. KAIA
Twins with Leighton, hair and makeup artist, currently in Mistyvale, AK but comes to Emerald Bay for the winter. Lover of all things beautiful.

XII. MAVERICK
Attending college in Washington. Bogarts the good tunes, sympathy crier.

"PSEUDO-SIBLINGS"

Max—Best friends with Elora, Hadlee and Alice, right hand to the CEO of Jorogumo defense. Travels as much as an authentic Rhodes, single, impeccable taste in both clothes and booze, currently in Mistyvale, AK.

Two Weeks Notice
ALICE

The methodic clacking of Greyson Hart's keyboard came to a stuttered stop as he dragged those hazel-green eyes off his screen and to my face. Blatant confusion lined his brows as he studied me, evidently intent on finding some sort of tell. He wouldn't. I'd been rehearsing this moment for the better half of the last year. The confusion on his face was more satisfying than it likely should have been as he asked, "*What?*"

I smiled sweetly, refusing to rock on my heels like my nerves were begging me to, and set my resignation letter down on the sleek marble top of his desk. Sliding it across the polished surface, I repeated, "I quit." Tapping the manilla folder, I added, "Please accept my two weeks' notice. I've compiled a list of the internal candidates I believe are best suited to replace me."

To the untrained eye, the man before me would seem unaffected. But, as everything was with Greyson, the devil was in the details. Buried below severe daddy issues, a misguided sense of injustice only an entitled trust fund baby could have, the heart of a wounded soldier, and about a decade of emotional constipation was the tiny line between his eyes, the subtle bob of his Adam's apple and an audible swallow that said this was—*somehow*—news that took him by surprise.

"We have a contract, Alessandra," he murmured, flicking up my letter as he leaned back in his armchair. One slick, heather brown loafer caught the glint of the window light as he crossed his ankle over a knee.

"We do," I agreed, folding my anxious hands behind my back as I straightened my spine so he couldn't see them wringing. "And it ends in two weeks' time. I will not be re-signing on for another term." *Oooh, I got a jaw flex*—that was about as unhinged and out of control as Greyson got, and some petty, vindictive sliver of my soul was squealing in victory as his eyes abandoned my face in favor of the paper in between his fingers, canting his head as his eyes flew across the page.

"Two years, two promotions, and two weeks' notice? How very ironic." The words flowed with the same svelte ribbon he used in his meetings. The man thrived on control and very little else.

Control of the schedule.

Control of the team chat—of when we submitted our work, of his own infuriating and unwavering discipline.

He was the only man I'd ever known to get quieter when something pissed him off. No matter how high the stakes were in a negotiation, Greyson's strength was concealed in his silence. His unwillingness to yield and to hold the line with a steady, unaffected facade. All skills I'm sure he picked up during his years as a Navy Seal.

Two. Years. For *two years,* I shared air with the man across from me—known to my family by a myriad of unflattering names, none of which were anywhere in the ballpark of *Greyson.* Hartless. Fuckface. The fire-breathing dragon. For two years, I bit my tongue and took it up the ass daily. Frankly, at this point, the literal option sounded like a walk in the park compared to the grueling torture that had been serving *Hart Investments* for the last twenty-three months, fifteen days, seven hours, and forty-nine minutes. *But who's counting?*

Like the irritated, telltale twitch of a cat's tail, he drummed his fingers on the arm of his chair before expelling a breath that sent my anxiety climbing. Greyson leaned forward, setting my letter on the marble between us before bracing his forearms on the desk, broad hands clasped together in the perfect image of composure.

He nodded at the chair opposite him and gave me a curt, "Have a seat, Ms. Rhodes."

Dammit. I knew I should have waited until four fifty-nine. Refusing to let him see the volcano inside me just waiting to explode, I spooled myself into the chair, with only the slick black expanse of stone as a barrier between us. Crossing my ankles, I leaned onto the desk to mirror his position. Those intense hazels locked on me a beat before a more pronounced *v* carved the olive skin between his eyes.

"Permission to speak candidly?" His request threw me so far off guard, all I could manage were two perplexed blinks and an unsure nod. The man gave orders—he certainly didn't *ask* permission to eviscerate me on the regular. Like a child in the principal's office, I shifted my weight in my seat before reminding myself that I would no longer squirm for Greyson Hart.

I'd held my own here. Challenged him. Advanced our projects. Saved deals that were half-sideways. I'd become a pillar of the department despite his blatant disapproval. He would not intimidate me *now*. Permission granted, he continued, "You've been moving up the ladder here, Alessandra. Aggressively for someone your age, with your...background." *My background.* For pity's sake, the man hadn't held back when I'd interviewed for Oliver's department—his younger, actually humanoid brother—a few summers back. Told me there was no way some *country bumpkin* would cut it in the big leagues. What part of *third-generation Alaskan fishing family* said I'd grown up throwing hay bales? And if I had, how in the hell would that disqualify me? *Elitist prick.* That lovely analysis was leveled about ten minutes before Ollie brought me on board, anyway.

And how was it that every single person in my life could get their head around the fact that I preferred being called Alice—his brother and niece included—but he insisted on using my full name?

Somehow, not three months after Ollie brought me on, I was transferred into Captain Hartless' direct clutches. And the bastard hadn't let go since.

"What inspired the sudden disregard for your prior efforts?"

Swallowing, I stepped into the wet blanket facade of a personality that was obligatory in the corporate climate and explained, "My vision for my life no longer aligns with your expectations of my performance."

"*My* expectations?" he asked, the tiniest quirk of his head the only indicator that his perplexed tone was authentic. "Please, tell me which expectations contradict your...*vision*."

I wanted to burst out laughing. I *wanted to* tell him that repeatedly calling me while I stood with my big sister as she got married was so far over the goddamn line he couldn't even *see* the line anymore. My older sister and her now-husband painfully pined for decades before finally taking the plunge and admitting what so many of us saw coming for years. Instead of enjoying the kismet caress of the sun on our skin as they exchanged vows in our perpetually cloud-shrouded hometown, I was praying to all that was holy that nobody else could hear the unending vibration of my cell. I wanted to tell him that his barging in on my first date in three years and calling a mandatory meeting was such a ridiculous display of entitlement and a severe lack of boundaries that his mother should be ashamed. I wasn't sure what I was born to do in this world, but it certainly needed to be more important than covering up a grown-ass adult's mistakes.

Instead, I weighed the reality that there were few men west of the Mississippi who held as much influence as my boss and simply said, "I'm sorry to admit I am no longer an adequate fit for the position. My work-life balance has become a priority that the demands of my role will not responsibly accommodate."

"Would it sway your decision if I assigned an assistant?"

My head snapped up from where my eyes had settled on the white veins in the marble, and my throat tightened. Was he... pushing back on my decision to quit? The formal request was more a nicety than actually asking for his permission. "An assistant? For *your* assistant?" He gave the briefest of nods, and I quirked my head, "Why would you do that?"

An invisible fishhook snagged the left side of his mouth as something like disbelief sparked in his eyes. Greyson ran his fingers through his chocolate hair, freeing an uncharacteristic stray from the meticulous style I'd grown so accustomed to seeing. When I saw him for the first time, I was struck by how gorgeous the Hart brothers truly were. You always see men like them in magazines and plastered over social media—especially American royalty like the Harts—but they don't often live up to the hype in person.

But...not Greyson.

If anything, he was *more* breathtaking in person. At least, right until he opened his too-pretty mouth with his too-straight, too-white teeth and told me I'd never make it in Emerald Bay. Just like that, the broad shoulders, sharp jaw, strong brow, and thick head of dark hair lost their appeal. Mostly, it stayed that way. Only the occasional navy suit that hugged his biceps a little too tightly or the unfortunate run-in on the beach where more skin than clothing was on display reminded me that he was more than adequately attractive beneath those walls. Or, you know, moments like this, where he looked the tiniest fraction disheveled—*human*.

"Turnover is expensive, Alessandra. We've invested a great deal into equipping you to do your job effectively and consistently, and frankly, I find your company far less grueling than most during mandatory travel days. Replacing you is a rather cumbersome task, so if I can simply assign a pawn to lighten your load— "

I laughed—I couldn't help it. It was strangled and somewhere in the ballpark of a Chihuahua sneezing, but it was a laugh.

Greyson leaned further back in his chair, crossing his arms over his chest. "Something entertaining, Ms. Rhodes?"

"I just...I think that was the closest you've ever come to complimenting me, Mr. Hart."

A flicker of insult crashed through his eyes before vanishing just as quickly. "Surely that's an exaggeration. You've been my right hand for the last—"

"Twenty-one months."

"Right."

"I think the last time you affirmed my efforts was after I found the plagiarized content in Molly's blogs, and you told me I made 'a decent cup of coffee'."

"You make a more than adequate espresso."

"Going for two in as many minutes?"

Where a laugh should be, a frustrated furrow took root instead. "Well, what do you think?"

"About the coffee or the assistant?"

"The latter." Hands braced together below his chin, he stared me down. *Right. Back to business faster than we detoured.* There was a human male inside that robot somewhere. I just no longer cared to find him.

"As I said before, thank you so much for the opportunity and the experience here at *Hart Investments. This is my* two weeks' notice," I rephrased the statement. Because it was a statement. I wasn't pleading with the man. "Unless you'd prefer I leave immediately? I would understand—"

"That won't be necessary," he gritted out. "Your assistance in finding and training your replacement would be very appreciated if you're willing to lend us a hand."

"Of course. This should expedite the process," I replied, nodding to the folder between us. His throat bobbed.

"Well. Thank you for compiling candidates. As per usual, that was above and beyond."

Confused, I stared across the desk at what appeared to be a sincere face of neutrality. I had to get the hell out of here before I lost my gumption. "I, unfortunately, have somewhere to be. If you'll excuse me." Standing, I headed for the door, only to have his voice freeze me on the threshold.

"Purely out of curiosity, what are your aspirations from here?"

I turned back to face him, but before I could answer, he continued.

"Your name has become synonymous with *mine,* Ms. Rhodes. Which means unless you intend to share that hand for espresso for a living, I don't see anyone in our circle risking a slight against our name by bringing you on. As it is, our confidentiality agreement renders you virtually useless to our competitors beyond—"

"Bringing them coffee?" I chirped, still refusing to grind my teeth. His shrug reminded me why I had to get as far away from Hartless as humanly possible. Perhaps I'd join my siblings, Elora, Finn, and Paxton, on the East Coast.

But I loved it here. Loved the year-round sun and the yoga studio within walking distance from my condo. Unease stirred in my belly. The Harts held 'investments' in nearly every sector of the business world—financials, media, public relations, sports teams, bars, restaurants, hotels, and high rises. You name it—they dabbled in it.

Much like his father, Greyson had a habit of forcing out or buying up shares in the companies that crossed them in ruthless takeovers that left his enemies unemployed and fleeing the city with their tails between their legs. He'd rehab the business, then sell it for profit in a matter of years. I might call him Hartless, but the industry knew him as The Titan.

Surely, he wouldn't be so petty for someone as low on the totem pole as me.

Clearing my throat, I clarified, "I don't intend to compete with you, Mr. Hart. I'm certainly not going to violate the confidentiality agreement, even if I were placed with a competitor. As for being known in your circle, I think that I have proven to be an invaluable asset, not a hindrance. Should someone be concerned with crossing you, I'm sure you could put in a call on my behalf to clear up any confusion."

"Could I?"

Don't squirm, don't squirm, don't squirm. That intense gaze, beguiled by an arched brow, would not make me cave. "Well, it's you they'd be worried about offending, correct?"

"I don't have time to hash out your future employment with my rivals or associates, Ms. Rhodes. I'm afraid leaving *Hart Investments* is leaving the industry you just clawed your way into."

Refusing to let him see me clench my jaw, I lifted my chin, slapped on a smile, and said, "I have plenty of connections back home and could use a little quiet."

"What a waste of talent, retreating to that island when you've laid roots down here."

"With all due respect, Mr. Hart, laying roots requires spending enough time out of the office to plant them in the first place. And, seeing as you video chatted me during my last OBGYN appointment, I can assure you I have nothing in this city holding me back." Heat scaled my neck and face like ivy up a brick wall. That was certainly the boldest I'd ever been with the man.

"I wouldn't be so sure of that," he muttered but glanced at his watch like he always did when he was uncomfortable. "I'll see you on Monday, Ms. Rhodes." And with that dismissal, he turned his attention back to his computer, leaving me staring daggers at the man who'd done nothing but make my life miserable for the last two years. *No more.* No more would I settle for a job that paid well but sucked the soul from my body. Irritated, I turned to leave the room, but his last statement hung like a guillotine over my head.

I wouldn't be so sure of that.

What on God's green earth did that mean?

GREYSON

"WELL, THAT'S A FUCKING SHAME," a tiny voice, muffled through a barrier, crept into my office the moment the door closed behind my assistant. I chuckled under my breath and shook my head, pushing my wheeled chair back. Turning, I bent to the cabinets in the hutch behind my desk and pulled one open.

"Mattie," I growled, staring at my niece, where she'd crammed herself into the tiny cupboard. She was too big, really. It was a wonder how she even folded herself in there like human origami. For as long as she'd been mobile, she'd always been searching for cubbies. Places to hide, I supposed. Couldn't exactly blame her. Rolling her eyes, she set her paperback on the black sweater over her chest and glared my way as I added, "We've talked about this."

"The cupboard is a perfectly adequate space to study," she stated flatly. *Ten going on nineteen, apparently.* This girl had always been too bright for her own good. She ran laps around my brother by the time she could articulate.

Odd, but brilliant.

It took all my years of training not to crack a smile when she lifted the novel and adjusted her book light. With an exasperated sigh, I snatched it.

Examining the cover despite her protests, I scowled down at *The Hobbit* before turning my glare in her direction. "I wasn't talking about hiding in corners, Mattie. I was talking about your trucker's vocabulary."

Hazel-blue eyes rolled like loose marbles as she lolled her head my way, extending her expectant hand. "Come on, Uncle Grey, Dad's still in his meeting."

"And where are *you* supposed to be?" I carefully marked her place, although what a ten-year-old was doing reading Tolkien, I didn't understand. Shouldn't she be into Judy Bloom or crime-solving dogs or something?

"I have a fever," she announced victoriously, curling her little fingers as if I'd return her contraband. The book thudded against my marble desk, earning a groan of protest from a mutinous-looking pre-teen. Kneeling beside her, I swallowed my smile as she reared back, meeting the unforgiving back of the cabinet and muttering another curse as I set my wrist against her perfectly temperate forehead.

"What'd you do this time? Hot pad in your locker?"

A wicked smile curved her little mouth when I sat on the floor beside her. "Hand warmers," she admitted, tucking her light brown hair behind her ear.

"*Christ*, Mattie."

"And you're worried about *my* mouth?"

"I'm not ten."

"Nona would have your——"

Brows raised, I clamped my palm over her mouth, shaking my head. "You were saying?" I flicked open the other cabinet door so she could at least be exposed to proper ventilation, then leaned against my desk.

For a solid ninety seconds, we stared each other down. My niece was unwilling to compromise why she'd—yet again—gotten herself sent home, while *I* would not let her continue to get away with this cycle. Finally, evidently sensing impending defeat, she sighed, resting her head against the wood surface as she scratched behind an ear.

Wrinkling her freckled nose, she confessed, "They were going to make us dissect frogs today."

"Ahh," I murmured with a nod.

"And Mr. Koraski paired me with Fisher."

The downside to being born with more brains than anyone knew what to do with was being pushed grades beyond her age. Her parents had to make the impossible decision between allowing her to be intellectually challenged or socially accepted. Bullies were always wretched in middle school, but especially so when you were two years younger—and a good head and shoulders smaller—than your peers. When I was a kid, a little asshole named Dalton had ceaselessly tormented me. Hocked into dumpsters like yesterday's trash. Blindsided by right hooks coming out of the locker room. It wasn't until I outgrew the bastard in high school that I could finally fight back.

Fisher was Mattie's Dalton. His assaults weren't physical, but he loved to torment her, steal her things, or dump chocolate milk on her on picture day. It was his daddy's fat wallet that kept him at *Emerald Prep*.

Sighing, I asked, "That hasn't improved since your dad met with the headmaster?"

She shook her head, explaining, "Fisher's just an angry kid, but that doesn't mean I want to deal with his bullshit."

"*Mattie*," I growled, and she rolled those stubborn eyes again.

"Ugh, sorry. I don't want to deal with his asinine behavior while he projects his unhappiness on me. *Happy*?"

"That you have the vocabulary of a thirty-five-year-old divorcee? Not really."

"So. What are you going to do?"

"Talk to your daddy——"

"About *Ms. Alice*, Uncle Grey."

"Oh, that." Great. I was being patronized by a ten-year-old. With a resigned sigh, I smacked my head on the wood desk leg, studying my ceiling. The perk of your best buddy being four feet tall was the lack of pretense for composure.

Alessandra Rhodes. If you'd asked me two years ago whether she'd still be working for *Hart Investments*, I would have unequivocally said on a cold day in hell. Everything about those big grey doe eyes and too-young face said Emerald Bay would chew her up and spit her out. But within days of my stubborn asshole of a brother offering her a position, she'd assimilated with the staff—memorizing not only their names and their children but dietary restrictions and important life events like a pretty little walking *Hart Investments* encyclopedia. After that, she'd doubled the productivity of her team.

Then she did the impossible. She won over my Mattie.

That alone was all the testament of character I needed.

Despite being nothing but a royal prick, Alessandra sidled up beside me at the first gala she attended, having memorized the roster like she'd been born into high society rather than some desolate rock in the Alaskan sea. Drink in hand, she'd hovered at my elbow, a demure smile on her gorgeous face as she subtly supplied the name of each attendee before they reached us, along with their spouse and a random fact about their work or whose kid was graduating from whatever university. The woman belonged in investigative work, not marketing.

With allies, enemies, and people of interest, I could spout off stats for days, but the same diligence seemed wasted on B-list attendees at stuffy soirees. At least, it did before Alessandra. But the show of goodwill landed us accounts like only Ollie had ever managed.

It was at that point that I stole my brother's acquisition for the PR team. *My* team. Me, more specifically. Because the woman looked like a cartoon princess but had the mind of a goddamned shark. A mind I'd used to my advantage for the last…well, twenty-one months, as she'd so aptly pointed out.

"That is unfortunate news, isn't it?" I said, looking down to find my niece had rotated out of her hiding space, planted her black, unlaced Converse on the floor, and braced her chin on her knees. At least she still looked tiny. Innocent. I knew better.

"I thought she was your prodigy." Even as she said it, those blue greens narrowed, like she knew— "That's wrong. *Apprentice?*"

"Protégé, kid. You were thinking of the word *protégé*."

"P-r-o-t-e-g-e. Someone guided by an older, more experienced person." I chuckled at her memorized recitation, reaching forward to ruffle her hair, which earned a defiant wrinkle of her nose. She ran her tiny fingers through mussed strands and demanded, "So, what's your plan? You seemed pretty confident she wouldn't end up leaving."

"Ms. Rhodes doesn't know about our most recent acquisition."

"Like, a company?"

"Like, an asset."

"Hmm, what kind of asset?"

"Talent."

"Like…a new player?" Heart Investments was the umbrella above the empire this pint-sized genius would inherit, but we owned a decent share of the West Coast when it came down to it. My father—for all his faults—and his father before him had built a dynasty to pass down the line. I might have denied my heritage for the better portion of my adolescence and into my twenties, but it was Matilda entering the world that made me first set aside my resentment and realize if I dropped the ball—walked away—it likely wouldn't keep running long enough for her to step into her place at the top. Mattie and her baby brother Beau were the only reason that Ollie and I didn't sell everything.

Everything except for our football team, the *Emerald Bay Bombers*. Our most recent acquisition. Ollie bought it on his thirtieth birthday after a humiliating run of losses. His first action as owner was canning the arrogant coach. The second was bringing in our cousin to run it. The program had improved a bit in the two years since, but this trade would be his magnum opus. *This* trade was going to make waves, not just in the media but in the rapport of our guys, and in the team's strategy. Because he'd just pushed our new coach, Nico Sartori, into stealing *Windy City's* star quarterback. America's Prince Charming. The prodigy kid. With an arm like a canon and an unshakable head on his shoulders—much like his little sister— hopes were soaring that he'd rally the team. Be the difference we needed to return the Emerald Bay name to its former gilded glory.

Miming ringing a bell, I said, "*Ding, ding, ding.* You got it, kiddo."

"Why would Ms. Alice care about a new player?" She blinked in confusion.

I expelled a long breath, pinching the bridge of my nose. "Because I wasn't going to tell her until it was finalized, but Coach Sartori just made the biggest trade in team history. We're about to sign Alessandra's brother, Paxton, for a five-year contract."

2

No "Sir" For You

ALICE

The soft hum of after-class conversations picked up while I rolled my mat into a tight little tube Saturday evening. My younger sister, Leighton, nudged my elbow when I sidled up beside her, grinning over her tan bare shoulder, her frizzy, nearly black hair tamed into a long fishtail braid down her back.

"You wanna go grab drinks with the girls after we both shower?"

"You know, a bubble bath is calling my name," I answered, shaking my head.

She gave me a knowing look of sympathy, head cocked like a puppy. "Still stressed?"

"A bit," I admitted. "Relieved too, though. I can survive anything for ten days." Ten more workdays. Ten more days until I would walk away from the illustrious corporate career I'd always thought I wanted.

"You really want to head back to Mistyvale?" she asked as we walked between the other women in our Pilates class.

Shaking my head, I replied, "No, not really. I love it here. The sun, the beach, the—"

"Lack of snow," she guessed, grinning as we both fetched our bags from the cubbies against the far wall, moving on muscle memory. This little fitness studio had been my one haven in these last few years, if only because our phones were required to be turned off when I came in the door.

"Yes," I admitted, lolling my head back with a groan.

"Can't fault you there," she said, rushing ahead to push open the door for me, the heat of a Southern California spring instantly embracing us. Leighton and her twin, Kaia, had come down the first winter after I moved to Emerald Bay. Kaia would pop in every winter and wait out the worst of our Alaskan weather, but Leighton never left. She fell in love with the boardwalks and collision of cultures, just like I did. And truthfully, I didn't mind the company. Growing up as the eighth of twelve siblings, chaos had been an omnipresent vein of my existence, marbling through every childhood memory. Between our litter of kids, a plethora of cousins, and a prominent line of respected fishing captains, there wasn't a citizen of Mistyvale who didn't know the Rhodes name.

In the months I'd been here alone—save for the spontaneous drop-in visit from my nomadic siblings and friends—I'd missed the chatter of voices, the huddle around the coffee pot first thing in the morning, the support during trials, and even the ceaseless ribbing. Big family dynamics seemed synonymous with sarcasm as a love language, but I'd grown to love it. Missed it desperately when my only company came in the form of a snake plant. I would have loved a dog if my schedule would responsibly allow one. Maybe I'd finally get myself that Morkie I'd always wanted.

But their constant banter was why I didn't bother to pull out my phone as it vibrated in my bag on an endless loop. Between Greyson and his bottomless list of needs and our siblings and their spouses' constant chatter, my notification list was in a perpetual state of overwhelm. The obnoxious orange message count would send me into a spiral if I opened the screen now—the expectation of responding to all of them exhausting just to think about. It could wait.

"Do you think he's bluffing? Wouldn't hiring someone from the inside of a competitor's organization be an asset?" I asked as we started walking down the street, the quiet hum of traffic now mindless background noise.

"I mean, you signed an NDA, so it's not like you can run around swapping trade secrets. I can't see why your perspective wouldn't be considered an asset."

"Maybe that's the conflict—that I *could get* into trouble if I said the wrong thing?"

When silence was my answer, I looked up from where my eyes had fallen to the sidewalk, only to come to an abrupt halt when Leighton wasn't beside me. Whirling, I found her gaping down at the phone in her palm. "Did you know about this?" She breathed.

"Know about what?" I demanded, panic slicing through what little Zen our class had just spent sixty minutes instilling in me.

"Sissy, look at your phone."

"Leigh, what the hell is going on?" When I pulled it from my bag, I *did* see an astronomical count in that little orange bubble, but when I opened the messages app, it was ninety percent the Rhodes Family text thread. "Is this some kind of joke?" I demanded as heat coursed through me, my temper flaring behind my eyes as I scoured through my siblings' sequential freakouts.

JAMESON

Pax, my man. Congratulations on the trade.

MAVERICK

Hell yeah.

But also, can you please stop setting impossible expectations? My coach thinks just because I'm your brother, I'll walk on water or some shit.

FINN

Woah, man. Congratulations. That's an enormous change, though. You ready to leave your guys?

RHYETT

Warm weather, Alice and Leigh in town, and two hundred and fifty million on a five-year contract sounds like a fucking deal to me.

ELORA

Already ordered Emerald Bay Bombers jerseys for Brod and me. Family reunion for Pax's first game?

HEART IN MY THROAT, beating a drum of denial inside my arteries, I panic-scrolled up to the top of this chaos, where Elora had nonchalantly dropped an article into the thread with a colorful 'Congratulations' gif. Hand flying to my mouth, I blinked down at the headline before clicking the icon to follow it.

Sure enough, national news was blasting Paxton's name like some kind of sports messiah, Bombers fans celebrating like just Paxton's presence would magically restore the team to its former glory.

I wouldn't be so sure of that. Greyson's parting words from last night planted in my chest as fury burned in my veins. He knew I was about to get more family in town when I'd told him so confidently nothing was holding me in the city. Fucking bastard.

Pax wasn't *just* family; he was my friend. My closest big brother. Only two years older than me, he'd been Hadlee's and my protector growing up and the only reason bullies ever backed off. Despite being showered in fame for the last decade or so, he hadn't turned into a colossal asshole. Aside from Elora, he'd made the most effort of my siblings to check in, to follow my career, and to have my back on days when Hartless pulled his usual bullshit. He visited often in the off-season and video chatted when he couldn't. And they'd just traded him from his home of the last *eight* years.

Ollie and Hartless now owned my brother's career.

I glanced back to the screen as the thread auto-scrolled to accommodate the deluge of messages.

JAMESON

Jesus, that's a hell of a number. Don't blow it all in one place.

PAXTON:

Can you imagine?

HADLEE

A castle in the Scottish highlands.

MAVERICK

I was thinking a San Diego mansion, and an endless parade of punt bunnies.

ELORA

Maverick Rhodes, you kiss our mother with that mouth?

MAVERICK

Oh please, sis. Like you don't know what guys talk about in locker rooms.

AXEL

Holy fucking shit, bro. Congratulations.

On the trade and the punt bunnies *winking emoji*

ELORA

Boys.

HADLEE

Honestly, there are ladies in this chat.

AXEL

Really? I can't see any. Let me know if you find them, and I'll mind my manners.

PAXTON

Fuck that.

MAVERICK

I think that's what El is discouraging.

PAXTON

No, smart ass. I ducked out of the 'punt bunny' scene in college. Too much drama. If you're smart, you'll do the same thing.

MAVERICK

Coach picked me up for my speed, not my brains.

KAIA

Oh, we know.

ALICE

Were you planning to tell me about this before or after you came to town?

MAVERICK

Ouch, Kai. Ouch.

PAXTON

Nothing is official until it gets signed, sis. Didn't want to get your hopes up if it was going to fall through.

JAMESON

You retiring at the end of this?

PAXTON

That's the plan. One last big swing. Bow out before my body breaks.

RHYETT

As someone who's about to hit thirty-eight, I'm worried you're over-anticipating what your body will do by thirty-five.

ELORA

Bullshit, you big baby. Keep up your supplements, PT, and yoga, and you'll be fine, Pax.

ALICE

Please call me in a bit.

DEEP CLAWS of overwhelm made my vision go foggy, my head throbbing as I forced myself not to panic. This was fine. This didn't actually change anything. Yes, it would be nice to live within driving distance of my favorite brother. I know you're not supposed to have favorites, but I couldn't help it. That didn't mean I needed to stay trapped with *Hart Investments*. Greyson was bluffing. Throwing a tantrum like a toddler, trying to manipulate me into staying.

Your name has become synonymous with mine, Ms. Rhodes.

The asshole didn't own me. I wasn't his, and with a resume like mine and carefully honed interview skills, I'd land a solid position in no time. I'd just put Ollie down as my reference—he'd vouch for me.

Hell, how many women had *two* bachelor's degrees under their belt?

Damn his name. Damn *him* for thinking my brother's position would change my mind. Had he drafted Pax in some ploy to keep me under his thumb? To ensure loyalty the way that banks and employers kept people indentured with long loans as an indicator of stability? Like if I had something important entangled with the company, my loyalty would be stronger?

Leighton and I made the walk to the bar in a thick silence as my brain ran in circles and my temper grew, but when I made to drop her at the door, she grabbed my hand. I tried to hide that I was shaking. "You sure you don't want to come in? I'll buy you nachos?" she asked hopefully.

"Thanks, but I'm good. I want to pretend my boss didn't just purchase our big brother and hide in a rom-com for the next twelve hours until I have to go in and face the music."

"Alright. I'll see you in a bit?"

Nodding, I gave her arm a little squeeze and promised, "See you soon."

"Love you," she added, pulling me in for a hug.

"I swear I'm fine," I said with a laugh, squeezing her back. "This changes nothing."

"Okay."

"Okay! Love you, too, you weirdo." Even as I turned away, it didn't look like she believed me. I wasn't so sure I believed me, either.

The navy embrace of night had wrapped around the city by the time I made it back to my apartment building. I hustled up the stairs and into my home, relieved for once that it was empty. I'd never lived in a space this beautiful before—the condo had been my gift to myself a year into my position under Greyson, and it was perfect.

Walking distance to both my gym and the beach, modern in design with sleek lines and glass windows, it was exactly what I'd always pictured when I thought of life in the city. Could I even afford this place with a job outside the corporate world? Did I want to? Or was it time to refocus on my roots and start fresh somewhere new, with something humbler and more reminiscent of my coastal upbringing?

Glowering at the margarita mix I kept in a pretty glass canister on the counter against the slate backsplash, I went to the cabinet and pulled out my favorite authentic tequila—something we stocked up on whenever we made it over the border. Too lazy to pull out the blender, I just poured myself a shot and knocked it back. The second went down smoother, and I curled my lips as I set down the glass.

This changed nothing.

The heat of tequila crashed into the frustration in my veins, and I snatched my phone. Before I could think better of it, I pulled up my thread to Greyson—something I'd never electively initiated.

ALICE:

Were you planning to tell me we drafted my brother?

THREE DOTS APPEARED AND VANISHED, and I paced around the island before the text finally bounced into my inbox.

GREYSON

Good evening, Alessandra. It was scheduled to come up in our weekly briefing tomorrow as a courtesy.

ALICE

This is why you were so certain I wouldn't want to leave my position.

GREYSON

I thought it might be an incentive to stay. Yes.

ALICE

Is that why you drafted him?

GREYSON

Oliver, Eli, and Coach Sartori oversee the team. And the term you're looking for is traded, not drafted.

ALICE

So, this has nothing to do with my position working for Hart Investments?

BUBBLES APPEARED AND VANISHED, but my mouth popped open when *Greyson Hart calling appeared* on my screen.

Figuring that I wouldn't be his employee for long, I slid the button to answer. "Good evening, Mr. Hart. I didn't expect a phone call."

"I didn't expect a text from you."

"Yes, well, I was a little caught off guard by the news. Truthfully, I would assume you would share information like that directly, as you prefer to be in front of any potential fallout."

"Potential fallout?" he asked skeptically.

"You can't assume I'm particularly comfortable with this."

"On the contrary, I thought your brother's presence in the city would be *of comfort* to you. Congratulations to your family, by the way. You must be so proud."

God, that patronizing tone made me want to stab something. Preferably that obnoxiously pretty face. "Yes, thank you," I said flippantly, rolling my eyes. Before I could ask my questions, he was speaking again.

"I was calling for clarification, as tone cannot be conveyed via text. Your last message could be interpreted in a few ways, and I wanted to see which you meant it in."

I pulled in a long breath, trying to decide how to navigate this. "I just wanted to make sure his position isn't compromised by my leaving the company."

"The two events are unrelated."

"Okay. So, this trade didn't have anything to do with ensuring my loyalty to *Hart Investments*?"

A dark chuckle rumbled over the line, dripping in condescension that perfectly foreshadowed the next words from his mouth. "Don't flatter yourself, princess." Before I could balk at his use of the word *princess*, he went on to add, "Paxton Rhodes is the winningest quarterback in NFL history. His accuracy is unprecedented, his players worship the ground he walks on, he just led his team to his second Super Bowl win, and Oliver has been biding his time waiting for the *Wolves* to max their cap so he could add him to our lineup for years now. I assure you, it's entirely coincidental that his little sister has been *fetching* my *coffee*."

My mouth fell open as I blinked into the starless void through my windows. It was an accurate representation of how efficiently he'd just emptied my chest of any trace of confidence.

Fetching. His. Coffee.

Don't flatter yourself.

Well. The man certainly could remind the peasants of their place in fifteen seconds or less. I managed to keep my voice steady enough to utter a two-word response. "I see."

"I had intended to share congratulations tomorrow morning as a courtesy of our working relationship, but the vultures in the press somehow got their hands on the briefing before it should have posted. Mr. Rhodes signs the papers tomorrow afternoon." When his statement met a wall of silence, he cleared his throat.

"You're quiet. Is there something else you want to say, Ms. Rhodes?"

Go fuck yourself? Deeming that unprofessional, I swallowed and said, "No. Thank you for the clarification. I'll see you at the weekly briefing." *No "sir" for you.* So be it if my only form of vengeance could be enjoying stripping the formality from our dynamic.

"Have a good evening, Alessandra."

With the subtle click of the line disconnecting, I slowly lowered my cell to the counter.

June could not come fast enough.

GREYSON

I STARED at my phone for a beat before muttering, "Fuck, Greyson," then sighed and slid it into my pocket.

I'd gone too far. I knew it the moment the words were out of my mouth, but my irritation with the accusation in her tone got the better of me.

From the beginning, I'd decided that pushing her away was the only option. Had always been the only option. I couldn't afford to like a woman that beautiful, lest she become a more glaring distraction. Liking her would complicate things. *Liking her* would *compromise* her.

Confused about the vernacular or not, Mattie hit the nail on the head when she called the woman my protégé. I'd certainly intended for her to fill my shoes someday. I needed her to familiarize herself with the ins and outs of the business in order to look after them once I turned my attention to more pressing ventures or was taken out of commission. Alessandra's workload was heavy because I *needed* her to feel the burden of it before she actually assumed the role I'd planned to offer her in a few short months.

Obviously, the approach backfired miserably. A fact that was more disappointing than it had a right to be.

Perhaps that played into my frustration tonight. Knowing that the most valuable asset in my arsenal was about to walk away, and I'd be back at ground zero, hunting for a mind sharp enough to step into our COO's shoes—losing Tiffany was bad enough, but to lose her and Alessandra within months had a headache forming with the promise of many hours of tension.

I was still rubbing at my temples, wishing I could go back five minutes in time, when an elated squeal and blur of purple caught my attention. "Uncle Grey!! You came!"

Plastering a smile on like I didn't just shoot myself in the foot, I turned to face a beautiful, beaming Mattie as she sprinted for me. She might only come up to my ribs, but my niece took up space like the heiress she was born to be.

Wearing a fitted light purple costume and pink tights, hair wrestled into one of those military-tight buns with some little flower thing wreathing it, she hurdled for me. I'd just knelt, arms wide, when she collided with the force of a tiny train. This was her fourth year in the Emerald Bay Ballet, and while Ollie and his ex, Carly, had initially signed her up, hoping she'd gain balance and coordination, she'd really learned to love dance.

I just loved that it made her happy. She was a tricky kid to keep that way.

"*Of course*, I came. Did you think I'd forget?"

She gave a one-shoulder shrug. "You had that art thing, too," she explained with more understanding than any ten-year-old should have.

"Wouldn't miss it, kiddo." I resisted ruffling her hair, reminding myself she had yet to step out on that stage. Although it appeared to be waxed to her head, so maybe it would've been fine.

Mattie's bright, beaming face made up for the irritation on my Uncle Reggie's when I told him I would *also* not be making it to the Art Museum's gala tonight. "She's ten. She won't even remember these childish recital things once she takes her place here," he'd grumbled.

But I remembered.

So did Ollie.

And Mattie had twice the brain I ever did as a kid.

Reginald Hart was…old fashioned, to put it lightly. Quick to please but just as easy to anger, he'd stepped in to guide Ollie and my unexpected transition into leadership when Dad was killed in that accident.

To my chagrin, he was currently our acting Chairman of The Board despite attempting to hold the position from the sidelines. As the senior member of our family, Reggie expected our generation to hold ourselves to the same scrupulous standards he and my dad had been held to, our feet forever to the fire.

Growing up, I would have killed to have either of them show up to support me at a single football game or hockey match. Ollie and I both vowed to be different for his little ballerina, even if it killed us.

When Beau was big enough for hobbies, we'd have his back too, whenever humanly possible. But if we could both buck up and take our spaces in a company we never wanted for the little girl that changed both our lives, we could certainly carve out three hours on a Saturday evening.

It was with that end in mind that I crushed her against me as she giggled, throwing her head back as she attempted to wriggle free. "Good luck out there tonight. I'll be the one whistling."

"Uncle Grey!" she scolded. Her next words were rapidly hissed, "You can't say good luck the night of a performance!"

"What? I thought that was just theater."

"We are in a theater," she pointed out as if it were obvious.

"My bad. Break a leg, or tear a tutu, or whatever you say in dance."

"*Merde!*" Oliver's voice had me glancing up to where he was standing with our little bruiser on his hip. Beau was—fittingly enough—the perfect image of his namesake. Dark, tousled curls sat over olive skin and glacial blue eyes. He was built like a little tank, still holding onto that squishy toddler look.

"Fun fact. Merde means shit in French. But the ballet uses it to ward off bad luck," Mattie stated sagely, not noticing as my brow arched.

Glaring at my brother, I muttered, "And you wonder where she gets her mouth." Like it wasn't bad enough that she swore in one language, Ollie taught her in at least two.

"Oh, *I* don't wonder anything," he argued, leaning forward with a bright smile to wrap me in a hug, which I returned quickly. Giggling ballerinas sprinted past us in a cloud of hairspray and glitter as some woman came over the speakers to usher our dancers back to their teachers.

"Hey, big man!" I said as I straightened, giving Beau a squeeze.

"Hey, Unca' Grey."

"Beau is very excited to see sister dance," Oliver supplied with a smirk, though my nephew already looked too *exhausted* to be here. *Me too, kid. Me too.*

We walked Mattie to her room and then quickly found and filed into our chairs in the amphitheater, where Beau immediately began bouncing on the spring-loaded seat. Kid couldn't hold still if his life depended on it.

Glancing around, I sighed when I didn't spot that ridiculous black-and-white hair. My brother's ex had one chunk of her onyx hair bleached nearly silver. I didn't understand the statement, but it made her easy to spot. "No sign of *Cruella?*"

"And there won't be," Oliver muttered, elbowing me in the ribs. His go-to way of telling me to shut the hell up. But Beau wasn't paying us any mind at the moment. "Spa week," he added in explanation, though it only made me loathe her more. Some humans shouldn't have a right to procreate. Mrs. Hitler, for example, probably should have just swallowed.

Carly was another one. If it didn't help Carly, it didn't happen. End of story.

I could never regret her swindling Ollie into her life because it gave us these two, but they deserved so much more than she would ever give them. Deserved more than a couple of brothers who could wield keyboards like weapons but had no clue how to raise half-decent humans.

"Can't say I'm shocked," I muttered, crossing an ankle over my knee as I leaned back in my chair to examine the recital program. A moment later, the lights dimmed, and the music began as the director of the academy took her spot at center stage, and the evening began.

When Matilda's class finally took their turn, I found myself more emotional than any man should be while watching ten-year-olds spin and leap across a stage. But that little girl, putting her whole heart into her first solo, was solely responsible for my being here to witness it in the first place.

In the months after the accident that flipped my world upside down, her big, expectant eyes, quirky kindergarten anecdotes, and absolutely absurd knock-knock jokes made me remember how to smile.

As she leaped over the center of the stage with her little chin lifted and hands outstretched like a proud purple bird, I remembered her leaping in front of me before spinning to grin back with that cherub's face. Egging me on—first in that damn wheelchair, then on the crutches. Hell, it was Mattie who decided it was a game to keep my cane just out of reach, forcing me to move my rickety ass between PT appointments. Not even her daddy could've kept me on this side of death like she did.

I wasn't Nona—not a Sunday mass kind of man, to her devastation—but Mattie made me wonder if there really was a god out there. A god that knew Ollie needed a reason to get his shit together and that I would forget how to smile and need someone to teach me again. Some benevolent being that sent us Mattie.

By the time she pranced off the stage, my eyes were a little misty, and I frankly jumped at the opportunity to excuse myself into the hallway when my phone started buzzing.

Jackson Reynolds calling…

My old captain called for three reasons, but only one of them was good.

Nerves clipping my voice, I answered, "How'd it go?"

"How the hell are you too, asshole?"

"I'm at a ballet recital, dick." Honestly, where we came from, these were endearments between brothers.

"Say hi to Oliver."

"Will do. You gonna answer my question?"

"We fucking did it, Commander." Jax was the only motherfucker allowed to call me that these days. He seemed to enjoy needling me with it at any opportunity.

My heart ratcheted up. When you lose the ability to do the saving yourself, living through your guys is the only way to keep your sanity. Or at least, it was for me. Glancing around the mostly abandoned brick corridor, I asked, "Yeah?!"

"Everybody's home safe." His words had me blowing out a breath I'd been holding since his name popped up on my screen. Every face of every man who put themselves on the line for our cause flashed through my mind. *Home safe.* My shoulders relaxed, and I leaned into the nearest cement block wall.

"How many?"

"Twenty-two."

"Jesus Christ," I breathed, my chest constricting as I processed that.

Twenty-two lives. Twenty-two victims saved. At least not everything about being a Hart was a nightmare. Our resources, at the very least, could make an impact. Feeling lighter and not wanting to be missing when all the dancers came out to bow, I managed a curt, "Thanks for the call, Jax."

"I'll be in touch."

"Anytime."

3

Is Something On Fire?

ALICE

Monday morning, I took extra time contouring my cheeks and styling my hair into a glossy sheet of straight chocolate strands before adding the fiercest winged eyeliner I could manage. I was no Kaia, but it was impressive, regardless. While I sat with my coffee at the kitchen counter, I pulled up Instagram, smiling when the first picture was of Ollie and the kids at what looked like a recital. I gave it a like and a quick comment congratulating sweet Mattie. Perhaps the only thing Hartless and I had in common was how much we adored Matilda.

She was a quirky little kid, but her spontaneous appearances in the office, around Greyson or Ollie's houses, or whatever resort we piled into when the board had mandatory appearances out of town had become something of a game for us.

When the Harts beat me into estates, I was wise enough to look for hidey-holes, and if I was first into the rooms, I'd wriggle under a bed or behind a curtain like Big Bird. She always found me with a glare at my simplicity but giggled anyway.

I had no doubt she'd end up as the first female President of the United States if that's what she wanted.

Holding myself a little taller after a night with the latest Lucy Score—a gift from my brother's fiancé—and a bath hot enough to turn me into soup, I gathered my bag and keys and headed out to conquer Monday.

I couldn't put the roof down on my Bronco in the morning without destroying my meticulous hair, but I'd packed my beach stuff in the back and would one hundred percent be taking advantage of the sunshine tonight. I put on *Weaker Girl* by Banks and let her voice guide me through the city until I pulled into the parking garage beside our building.

Car locked, I flipped my pepper spray into my hand to make the walk through the garage and out into the sunshine—a habit my big brother Jameson had insisted I acquire the first time I left home. Thankfully, I'd never had a reason to deploy it. That gratitude faltered a step, although the click of my heels stayed steady as nerves shot up my spine when I spotted the two men loitering around the corner.

It wasn't all that unusual for paparazzi to linger when big news had broken in the Harts' world, but I had a sinking sensation in my gut. Tightening my hold on the canister in my hand, my thumb flipped the lock when one of them looked up and not-so-subtly nudged his friend when his eyes found mine. Lifting my chin, I eyed the entrance and then decided just to leave a bit of a berth around them. Ollie, Reggie, or Greyson would deal with them when they arrived.

Only, as I went to sidestep them, the first mimicked the motion. "Alessandra Rhodes?"

My eyes flicked to him before I thought better of it, giving me away, and I resisted the flinch that followed. What the fuck did he want with *me*? I ran my thumb over the rough edge of the lock on my mace and tried to walk by him, but his friend blocked my path to the door. I was about to step off the curb into the street when the second lifted his phone in my face.

Rearing back, I thanked all that was holy my voice held strong. "If you approach, I will engage. *Back. Off.*"

"Ms. Rhodes, we're here with *Emerald Daily* and thought you'd like to make a statement about the allegations against Greyson Hart."

My heart leaped into my throat. Turning his way, I scanned his face for a bluff but found a lifted chin, eyes sparkling with victory.

What fucking allegations? I hadn't heard shit about any allegations. And I all but ran the PR team.

"No comment," was all I said.

"This is going to be the story of our generation, Ms. Rhodes. The Titan of Emerald Bay embezzling from his own company? You have a unique opportunity to be the first quote to hit the web— you've worked with Greyson Hart for about two years now, correct?"

"No comment," I repeated, stepping into the road and skirting past his buddy as the first one barked a laugh.

"A word to the wise, Ms. Rhodes. Burn the bridge before you go down with the ship."

Nice jumbled analogies, you idiot.

I sucked down a breath when security buzzed me into the building, my heart booming against my ribs and throat. They were so damn certain, but…

My instincts were reeling.

Roiling.

Revolting.

Nothing about his comment resonated with my intuition.

While Hartless was a complete prick *to me*, this company was his life—his family's legacy—and he loved nothing in the world like he loved Ollie and Mattie. He might have the personality of a rattlesnake, but…I couldn't picture a world where Greyson would intentionally hurt Mattie or the empire he fought to preserve for her. And stealing from Ollie and their shareholders would undoubtedly destroy their plans for her.

She was why he lived and breathed this business. Why he was the first person in the building—second only to me if I was feeling spiteful like I was this morning—and the last to leave. Hell, I'd driven by well after midnight on a Saturday and spotted his illuminated office window—like a lonely beacon in the darkness.

In a full storm of cognitive dissonance, I rushed to my office, dropped my things, and made my way to his, finding it mercifully empty. The thing about being his right hand for the last two years was that there were few aspects of his life I didn't have full access to. His passwords and accounts were all locked in a vault inside my mind. Bluntly, there were few personal parts of his life I wasn't uncomfortably privy to.

I just stared at his sleeping computer monitor for a moment, fighting through a tsunami of denial in order to think of this pragmatically. Growing up as the middle of twelve had its benefits—like being able to read situations better than most because I was used to gauging *thirteen* other people when shit was going down. Years of bruised ego might've encouraged me to tell Hartless that karma was a bitch and to kick rocks. The bully on the playground was finally getting laid out by somebody bigger.

But…that honed gut instinct said this accusation was baseless.

God damn my conscience.

Blowing out a heavy breath, I woke the monitor, mentally going through the crisis protocol as I keyed in his password. Never in my wildest dreams over these last few years would I have ever assumed I'd be going into war mode for Greyson.

Three buttons on the desk phone had me ringing up Ollie—we'd need him in here either way—and a few rapidly pressed keys on his computer would have security headed my way. The Harts would need them to get through the paparazzi without an incident. Maybe the Capitol entrance would be a better plan.

Despite gearing up to give him hell today, I prayed for Ollie,

Beau, and Matilda's sake that our only problem would be a brewing defamation case.

Sliding my phone from my bag, I pulled up my best friend's thread and fired off a text. Never in my life had I been more grateful the man had used his geeky childhood tendencies for good, and now worked in cyber security. Hopefully, it would get me what I needed and quickly.

ALICE

Morning, Maxi. I'm phoning a friend.

MAX

What game show are we winning?

ALICE

Heart Investments. Can you talk? Work your magic and make it a secure line.

MAX

Let me get coffee, and I'll be yours.

GREYSON

"THIS IS TREMENDOUS NEWS, and I don't understand why you're not celebrating," Reginald—Reggie—Hart was a regal, sixty-year-old embodiment of the term 'old money'. My uncle could balance an impressive number of hats, but none were labeled *subtlety*.

He looked like a kid on Christmas morning…sans the silver hair and tube of extra fat around his middle. Closer to suave Santa, I corrected internally. Despite his clear glee, my stomach had been in knots for the better portion of the last thirty-five hours. After leaving the ballet, it wasn't Jackson or Matilda on my mind, but my own patronizing words hurled at my assistant that weighed me down. I didn't often feel the need to apologize for the ruthlessness Harts were known for. Only one of those was applauded in our family, and it wasn't the former.

"I'll celebrate when the contracts are signed," I countered flatly, turning the page on my paper as our driver took a gentle turn onto the business strip of the city center. My eyes scanned over black ink on flimsy pages, but I couldn't absorb any of it. I was too preoccupied with running my own words on a wheel in my brain.

My watch buzzed, and I rotated my wrist to see it as Reggie continued to gush over Paxton Rhodes.

The name made my teeth grind after my conversation with her Saturday night. *Everything* made my teeth grind after that night.

I may not have put stock in her when she interviewed, but seeing her working was a whole different game. For example, my passcode had just been used to access my computer, and according to the display screen, it wasn't even seven in the morning. Only one other person knew those codes.

Fetching my coffee.

Christ, I was as bad as Ollie insisted I was.

Irritated, I slammed the newspaper closed and set it aside as Reggie filled me in on our final starting line for the season. His son, and Ollie and my favorite cousin, Eli, was the department head, so Reggie was always up to speed on the goings on. While entertaining, football was way below my pay grade. I plucked a few stray dog hairs from my navy-blue jacket—my four-year-old Shepard was why I had lint rollers stashed in every office, vehicle, and gym bag. His companionship was fantastic, but it came with a perpetual furry sweater I didn't care for. My watch chirped again, and I glanced at the face.

"Interesting." I hadn't actually meant to say it aloud, but… Alessandra was running through our numbers. Hell, that was below *her* pay grade. I had accountants and bookkeepers for that. Over the years, my mind had concocted at least a dozen fantasies of things she *could* be doing in my office at the crack of dawn, but none of them would make HR happy with me. Which is precisely why she'd always been—and would always be—off limits.

I tapped the icon for our head of security, bringing my phone to my ear.

His groggy voice told me I woke him. Good. Civilian life was making him lazy. "Is something on fire?"

"Morning, Mike. Can you check the footage of my office for me?"

"Christ, it's early," I heard the shuffle of feet and tapping of keys as he yawned, "Everything alright, sir?"

"Just humor me."

"You got it, Commander."

"We've talked about this." We had. A dozen times, at least. Which is why I knew what his next words were about to be.

"Old habits die hard, sir."

"Well, kill it already. I'm not your Commander. I am, however, still your superior." I'd only just earned the rank four months before the accident. Maybe his perpetual endearing use of it wouldn't bother me so severely if I'd been his acting Lieutenant

Commander for a longer period of time, but as it was, I hadn't earned it.

A decade served with the Navy Seals—ironically, the more pleasant alternative to submitting to my father—was cut short by some idiot getting behind the wheel drunk. All that work *was gone* in an instant. One man's selfish impulse wiped my father and my chosen career off the face of the planet in a heartbeat. I wished it was the first time fate had struck our family, but it seemed in addition to our wealth, we bore a curse to die young.

Which led me here, in the back of a town car with my uncle in his stuffy suit, running the company I never wanted. It was only Mattie that forced me to step into my place. However, I quickly realized I could use the resources two generations had built before me to fight the evils of the world from…a fresh vantage point.

He chuckled and then asked, "What am I looking for, *Mr. Hart?*"

"Anything unusual."

"Alice is busy at your desk. A few photographers out front—I assume for the Rhodes announcement. I see nothing out of place."

"Good. Thank you, Mike."

"Feeling paranoid today, sir?"

"Not anymore. Be in soon."

"Looking forward to it."

Before I had a chance to question my suspicion, Reggie was asking, "Why are you checking security?"

"Anxious," I grunted in response, my forehead aching with the depth of the furrow between my brows.

"Get in a good workout. That always helps."

I pursed my lips and nodded my head. Never mind that I'd been so pissed off after that call that I couldn't sleep or that I'd woken up today to a message from my source from the local news station telling me they were about to run a story investigating me, but she didn't know what for. Only that she'd be in touch.

All this on the same day Alessandra was poking through my files? It couldn't be coincidental.

That was the question that dominated my thoughts as we finished the ride into the office, my fingers tapping over my phone screen as I checked through emails, our chat channel—anything that could indicate what she'd searched for at seven am Monday morning. Nothing. I couldn't see anything that would give her a reason to inspect our books. But in the last two years, if I learned anything about Alessandra Rhodes, it was that she was as unequivocally intentional as I was.

That's why I was nodding with a painful kind of resignation when Mike called me right back. *Trouble.* This spelled trouble.

Swiping to answer, I managed one word. "Yeah?"

"Sir, we've got a situation at the entrance. It's on the sidewalk, so we can't boot them. I can have security escort you past them or——"

Reading his next thought, I asked, "Is the Capitol entrance clear?" We were positioned in the historic section of downtown, on the network of underground evacuation tunnels leading to and from the Capitol building. Rather inconvenient should the bureaucrats need to evacuate, but fantastic for avoiding the press.

"Yes, I sent Carlos and Wade over to meet you."

Smiling at how well he knew us, I said, "Thank you, Mike. I'll see you soon."

"Heading in now, sir."

WHEN I REACHED MY OFFICE, I expected Alessandra to be sitting at my desk. What I *didn't expect* was for Ollie's glum face to look up at me with a little two-finger salute. My brother never——and I do mean never——was in the office before me.

What I expected even less was that as I leaned against the doorframe to watch her work, she growled, "Your firewall is bullshit."

"Pardon?" I nearly choked on my saliva. Had I ever heard her *curse* before? To keep from laughing, I looked at my sleeve and plucked a long black hair from between the fibers of the fabric. Ollie stifling his own certainly didn't help.

"It took Max under sixty seconds to walk me through it. *That's bullshit*, Hart. You, of all people, should have a system that's ironclad."

"I'm sorry. Who walked you through what?" My irritation was poorly concealed, but what the fuck was she doing poking holes in our system?

"*Max*. He's a friend. Ollie has his information. He'll get our tech up to date. Trust him with my life. The same can't be said for whoever set up your security system."

"*I* set up my security system," I responded dryly.

The corner of her pink lips pulled up as her eyes flashed to me again, keys slowing. "Like I said."

What the fuck? Pursing my lips, I stepped inside and closed the door softly behind me. Was she having a stroke?

So help me, if my brother let that laugh escape the hand he had clasped over his mouth, I'd smack him upside the head.

"I suggest you explain yourself, Ms. Rhodes. This is peculiar behavior, even for you."

"Even for me," she grumbled. "I'll show you peculiar."

"Are you drunk?" I asked, flabbergasted by the one-eighty in her usually reserved personality.

So softly I barely deciphered her words, she grumbled, "On freedom."

"Freedom?" I repeated, entirely out of the fucking loop. Something I was neither accustomed to nor remotely fond of.

"From you," she muttered, shrugging her shoulder before turning the computer monitor toward me. "Seeing as all I've accomplished in the last two years of dedication is an adequate latte, I no longer feel the need to earn your respect. I'll be out of here in no time, and you're clearly not a reference for future endeavors."

I winced and started, "Look, Alessandra—"

"No," she cut off my protest, shaking her head as she held up her hand, "thanks for making it perfectly clear what I've contributed to this company. I no longer feel remorseful leaving, as any bimbo with two brain cells will be able to successfully fetch your coffee."

"Alessandra, I—"

"Don't need to explain anything about our conversation, but don't be offended when I put Oliver down as my superior."

Ollie shrugged, adding, "You have my ringing endorsement. But uh, let's move this along, Rhodes."

"Move. *What*. Along?" I snarled before jamming my eyes closed and hating myself just that much more. Tone and tact were two skillsets I'd never particularly mastered outside the boardroom.

"You're going to be real glad you still have me and Tiff both working this week," she muttered.

"Alessandra, answer my question, please." The way those gray-blues snapped to me, scowl carving her pretty face at my use of the word please had me feeling like an absolute douche.

"Had an interesting conversation this morning," she explained casually, leaning back in my chair as she folded her arms over her chest.

In my experience, power lay in silence, so I turned to lean against the desk, sliding my hands into my pockets and feigning disinterest. "Oh?"

"Reporters ambushed me on my way in today to ask if I wanted to make a statement regarding the embezzlement allegations leveled against you."

Every drop of blood in my body turned to ice. There it was. The niggling anxiety in my chest. "I'm not embezzling."

"I assumed." And yet, her eyes were narrowed on me.

"Really?" I drawled, hiding my surprise that she wouldn't immediately *assume* the worst in me.

"You're a shitty boss, but you came home for Mattie."

"True," Ollie agreed from where he was now bracing on his knees in the corner.

I shot him a glare before looking back at her and demanding, "Explain."

"Why would you do all of that just to rob her of her future? You're not exactly subtle about the history with your father, so you didn't come back for him."

"Let me get this straight. You didn't believe the press, and yet here you are…digging?" What she believed she'd find, I wasn't entirely sure.

A wry smile stretched her lips. "Trust but verify."

Unblinking, I flatly asked, "Are we in a Cold War, Ms. Rhodes?"

"You tell me," she countered slowly before glancing at the screen. For someone who played an impressively convincing doormat for the last two years, she certainly held her ground, her chin raised and shoulders back. It was only the momentary line between her brows as she glanced at the monitor that gave away her uncertainty, but it vanished as quickly as it appeared. *She knew something.*

Jaw clenching, I didn't respond before Reggie slipped in the door, worry lining his austere features.

"Morning, Reginald," she chirped as I straightened to my full height, hands still in my pockets. "We're almost done here."

Irritation quickly replaced confusion as he looked from Alessandra to me. "What in the hell is going on? You just abandoned me before I'd exited the town car."

"Ms. Rhodes here had a concerning run-in with some members of the press," I supplied. When her eyes flew to mine, I gave her a nearly imperceptible shake of my head. *Not here,* I willed her to understand. I turned to my uncle and added, "She alerted me to the incident during our drive to work, which is why I had Mike hop on security, but I wanted to make sure she was okay myself."

"Oh, Christ, I thought something was terribly wrong." Then, he had the afterthought to ask her, "Are you alright, Ms. Rhodes? Did they touch you?"

"No, sir." Her focus met mine. Which was why the cold bead of sweat dripping between my shoulder blades was the one point of contact I had with my surroundings until she breathed, "I was checking with Mr. Hart to see how he'd like to proceed."

Relief slid through my veins as my mind spun through options like a roulette wheel. Keeping a monotone, I explained, "Evidently, the scavengers at the *Emerald Daily* have forgotten how inconvenient a defamation lawsuit is and are looking to sling accusations my way."

Reggie collapsed into the formal leather loveseat shoved against my office wall behind a deep green leafy plant that I believed Alessandra had dubbed *Brenda*. With a fatigued sigh, he demanded, "At what point will they find a new target? Haven't we exhausted them by now?"

"Evidently not," Alessandra responded, leaning back and crossing her legs primly, eyes boring holes into my profile.

"What are they attempting to hit us with now?"

"Not us," I corrected. "Me."

Reggie's eyes slid to Alessandra as she said, "They were looking for a statement about an embezzlement case against Mr. Hart."

"What embezzlement case?" He snapped, turning his full focus on me, dripping with disapproval.

"There is no embezzlement case, Uncle Reggie. You can confirm with legal. Nothing's been served. They're blowing smoke. My insider gave me a head's up something ugly was coming down the line, but I didn't know what." Admittedly, this isn't where my mind went. They could be going after Jax's and my operation, and that idea was somehow worse. Likely, it was that sphere I needed to look at once we had damage control lined up.

Reggie pursed his lips, staring me down for a beat before turning Alessandra's direction. "Ms. Rhodes, please excuse us. This is a family matter."

Alessandra lifted her stare to mine expectantly, her shoulders relaxing when I obliged.

"She stays."

Reggie shifted uncomfortably before shooting a less-than-friendly glare in her direction. "This isn't a subject I'm comfortable discussing in front of the help."

"*Reggie,*" Ollie scolded, sounding just as aghast as I was.

My skin heated. Not that I had a right to be aggravated on her behalf when I'd been more heinous not thirty-six hours ago. Her irritated scoff was punctuated by something that sounded a lot like "Apple. *Tree.*" But as she rose, snatching her discarded blazer as she moved past me, I grabbed her wrist, holding her in place as her face snapped up.

"I trust her," I declared simply. The words were for our Chairman, but my eyes locked on hers. "My office, my reputation, my right hand. Ergo, she *stays.*" There was no room for negotiation in my tone—or the implied order that passed between her and me—but just for good measure, I added, "Alessandra has been spinning PR slip-ups and fixing media messes for this company for the last few years, and does it with the brutal, unforgiving finesse of a Hart." Her eyes widened before she smoothed her expression out. Lifting my gaze to my Uncle's, I continued, "The Martinson scandal?" I waited for the realization to dawn on his drawn face—one of our clients had made the stereotypical fuck up that resulted in scandalous private surveillance photos with a hooker a year back. "Alessandra was the mastermind behind making that go away. If there's smoke, she's the one that will find our fire."

For the briefest flash, I thought he looked impressed, but that assumption was dashed as he said, "With all due respect to Ms. Rhodes and her finesse for *faking a* deep fake, I don't see how her skill set will help diffuse an allegation this serious. We need to call a war room."

"With all due *respect*," she practically hissed the word, "I already have. Our security, legal counsel, forensic accountant, and PI are due within an hour. The rest of the board will be in by noon. I have a third-party cybersecurity contact on standby who has already signed our NDA. Our contact at the *Daily* will be here at two."

It was damn hard not to smile at that. She still hadn't removed her wrist from my hold, so I gave her an approving squeeze. Someone had been paying very close attention while we put out prior fires. But Reggie wasn't done.

"As for a *PR spin*? What in the hell do you think *she* can come up with that would overshadow America's most eligible bachelor being accused of robbing his own company? The only thing that could make a splash big enough to swallow *that* would be a royal wedding," he jabbed with a graveled laugh.

I gingerly released Alessandra's wrist, relieved when she didn't flee. Her eyes were calculating when I glanced down to where she stood beside me. Not scared. Not accusatory. Like the wheels in that pretty head were turning a million miles a minute. It was mesmerizing to watch, and as those blue-grays landed on me, churning with intensity, I realized I'd stopped listening to my uncle in my attempt to decide if she was truly an ally.

Tuning back in, I heard him jab, "Seeing as the last time you were seen with a woman other than your cousin was before your father died, and those gossip rags have been speculating whether you're a closet gay, I don't think you have that option. As for today, if we're about to have a board meeting, I need to prepare."

"The last five years' internal audits are in your inbox, as is the *Daily's* salacious history targeting your family," Alessandra said matter-of-factly. Now, *that* expression on my uncle's face was respect. She seemed to see it too, explaining, "If you're proficient at anything in a family my size, it's organizing chaos and herding cats. I keep files like my life depends on it."

"Ours might," Ollie muttered under his breath as Reggie reassessed my assistant.

"Thank you," he begrudgingly murmured. Despite his bigoted traditions and distaste for the middle and lower class, there was nothing my uncle took more pride in than our family name. It's why he kept the bad blood between him and my father under wraps. Reputation superseded justice. That was precisely why I was hoping he would be on my side for this.

"Let's reassure the board, dot our I's and cross our T's, and I'll get it handled," I said firmly, shifting away from my suddenly-ballsy-as-fuck assistant and walking to open the door, gesturing for Reggie to cross the threshold. "The board is going to expect you to be ahead of this. Now, if you don't mind, I need to consult with my head of PR. This is nothing new—certainly nothing we can't make go away."

My uncle practically growled in frustration. He shook his head as he pulled out his phone, but he surprised me by getting right in my face as he stepped through the doorway. "You better know what you're doing, boy. This is no joke."

"Am I laughing?" My response was pointed. But his perpetual refusal to acknowledge the value I added to this company and treat me like a child was exhausting.

Blowing a harsh breath out of his nose, the man stalked from the room. Hopefully, he'd use a bit of that temper to sort out what the hell was going on.

When I closed the door and turned to lean against it, Alessandra was watching me skeptically from where she was braced on the desk.

"You really called a war room?"

She crossed her arms below her chest. "Am I your barista or your PR wizard? You can't seem to make up your mind."

"I'll take that as a yes?"

"They'll be here shortly. She CC'd me on everything," Ollie answered.

Narrowing my eyes on her, I asked, "Why are you helping me?"

"I'm not."

"Certainly had me fooled." I stepped into her space, but she didn't bother to shift. Didn't so much as glance away.

"I'm helping Mattie. You just so happen to hold the strings to her future. If there are allegations between her and making the impact I know she's destined for, I'll squash them before I leave next month."

Nodding, I studied her long frame, where she was still braced against my marble desk. Nerves in my throat, I asked, "What if I was guilty?"

"Are you?" She challenged below a skeptical brow.

"Of many sins."

That remark earned a sly smirk and scoffed, "And this one?"

"No." I ignored the subtle spiced scent that had driven me mad for the last two years and instead studied her, looking for a slip in that harsh mask. Christ, she could guard her thoughts.

"Then I can protect her future with a clean conscience," she said simply. "Besides, it's the job."

"I'm touched."

"Don't be. It isn't for you."

"Regardless."

"I need to gather our packets from Paul before the meeting, so if you'll excuse me," she said, motioning to the door. I nodded and tracked her movements as she left. Ollie whistled, low and long.

"Sure glad she doesn't look at me like that."

"Like what?" I muttered, slowly sinking into my chair to massage my temples.

"Like she wants to fuck you or kill you, I'm not sure which."

"Perhaps she's a praying mantis."

"Both is good," he chuckled.

"Not going to ask me if there's validity to this?"

"Would you ask me?" he countered. I didn't need to answer—he knew I'd never. "Somebody is trying to crucify you, Grey."

"Yeah, and I'm going to find out who." Bringing my phone up, I glanced at the clock. I had a few minutes before I needed to take my place at the head of our table. Clicking Jackson's icon, I brought it to my ear, relieved when he answered on the second ring. "We have a problem."

4

March To The Gallows
ALICE

"Look, Mr. Hart, I challenged their sources, but there's not a single reporter worth their salt who would give those up. I bought you twenty-four hours while the editor reviews things. *Maybe* forty-eight if we're lucky. That's the best I can do. I'm sorry."

"Thanks, Stacy," Grey muttered, voice uncharacteristically soft. He wasn't defeated, per se, but it was as close as I'd ever seen him get. It was oddly unsettling, especially with the entire board focused on him where he still sat at the head of the table.

"Of course. Call me when you know where you're going with this. I've got your back."

"Appreciate you," he said as he stood and leaned forward to disconnect the line.

There was a high probability there had never been a more perfect example of the phrase *you could hear a pin drop* than the silence that followed. Greyson braced one arm beneath the other, covering his mouth as he stared at the conference phone.

It lingered for far longer than comfortable, everyone having evidently said their piece before we called Stacy. Greyson was the one to finally blow out a harsh breath and declare, "I will, of course, be stepping down until the internal investigation confirms my innocence."

A throat cleared from the enormous flatscreen mounted on the wall where the four out-of-state directors stared back at us. Emmaline and Ellington, Greyson's cousins, were together in one frame, looking uncharacteristically rattled. Like an advertisement for their mother's Norwegian bloodline, the siblings bore matching blond hair and blue eyes. It was only the subtle golden undertone in their fair skin that hinted that any trace of Hart had snuck through their genetics. Their concern was the kindest emotion on the screen—the others sharing some kind of skeptical anger, evidently directed at Greyson. I couldn't blame them, of course. Their asses were all on the line today.

It was the baby of the empire to raise her voice. "I believe that's preemptive, Greyson. Prepare for that, but I don't think you should bow down until allegations are leveled, and perhaps not until they're presented with proper evidence."

"It would be protocol—"

"To suspend you in the face of proper charges, yes, but I agree with Emmaline," Ellington cut Greyson's protest off. "We have the advantage of starting the investigation now, but that doesn't mean you need to bow out for some baseless—"

"He could interfere," snapped Malachi, the chief of HR. "This is an unfortunate formality that we need to adhere to so Reggie can assure stockholders we've been thorough if and when the allegations come to light."

"Right, but him running away looks guilty," Ellington argued.

"It looks pragmatic," Reggie countered on the tail of a pained sigh. "Fearless leader or not, he is the one being questioned and, therefore, the one who should cooperate with any investigation."

Greyson's eyes met mine for the briefest flash, like he was attempting to communicate silently. The bastard was in luck, though, because whatever it was he had buried in his personal system, I hadn't been able to touch it. Suspicious? Yes. Expected from someone of his caliber? Also, yes. As for my intuition? I didn't think whatever files he had beyond company borders were any of my business. As long as he wasn't siphoning off the company, I didn't give a shit what kind of trouble he got into in his off hours.

"I have nothing to hide from you—this company is our legacy. Trust me when I tell you, death would be more appealing than betraying what we've built here. If me lying low is what this ship needs to endure the storm coming, that's what I'll do," he stated matter-of-factly.

Unable to believe the fact that I was about to aid the man who had given me gray hairs before thirty, I cleared my throat. "I think lying low is a poor strategy, given the baseless accusations. I think the company has to follow the expected protocol to ensure both shareholders and the public that we're doing our due diligence and that we don't have a corrupt king leading this empire, but Greyson should do anything but lie low."

"With all due respect, Ms. Rhodes, we should defer to someone more experienced," Reggie interjected, glaring at me like his eyes could tell me to *shut up* when his surroundings didn't permit it.

"I'd quite like to hear her finish," Tiffany countered, a soft smile playing on her lips as she glanced between me and Greyson, who gave me one curt nod of approval.

Clearing my throat, I continued. "Lying low screams, 'Something is wrong.' Continuing on with your life—making public appearances on behalf of *Hart Investments* or your favorite charities and entertaining the press with exclusive interviews because you need their support *now* more than ever—will encourage the public to see you as innocent."

"Just carry on, business as usual?" Ollie asked.

"Outside the office?" I clarified. When he nodded, I did the same. "Yes. As for the family," I looked at Ollie before glancing quickly between the surviving Harts, starting with Emmaline and Ellington, then to Reggie, and then his wife, Vivienne, before finishing my thought. "Being seen with them on personal time will be just as invaluable because it tells the public they don't believe the accusations and trust you implicitly."

"I agree," Tiffany declared, a subtle, smug smile on her face as she studied Greyson. Something unspoken passed between them before she looked back at me expectantly.

"Then why is he stepping down?" Emmaline pressed.

"Valid question," I said, hoping to encourage her to keep throwing her voice out there. "It's temporary. The internal investigation is just to CYA, as is his brief vacation from corporate life. From there, we all turn our attention to a multi-layered press tour to shine a light on the real Greyson Hart."

"Oh, he'll *love* that," Ollie muttered sarcastically from behind the fist he was propped against. Greyson shot him a glare as Ellington snorted on screen.

"He doesn't have to do much," I added, suppressing a smile at his expense. "I already have our girls ghostwriting stackable content we can send to our trusted media contacts."

A sense of bewilderment filled the room as everyone turned their attention to me as if they had never bothered to notice my presence in the corner before today. Only Greyson, Ollie, Emma, and Ellington looked nonplussed as Greyson held a hand out in my direction as if to say, 'I told you so.'

Swallowing, I added, "Oliver, would you be comfortable with us featuring Greyson at one of Mattie's events?"

"Of course," Ollie answered, nodding like I shouldn't have even asked.

Simultaneously, Greyson barked, "*Absolutely not.*" When Oliver's and my eyes snapped to him, brows arched, he cleared his throat. "I'm not exploiting a child to protect my image."

"She's a Hart," Ollie hedged gently. "Her birthright puts her in the spotlight, no matter what, Grey. She's destined to be loved and loathed at the whims of the press, and they already run her name through the tabloids. At least this would be a narrative we could control."

Remaining silent, I looked between the two brothers as Greyson wet his lips before insisting, "No. I'm not comfortable putting her in their crosshairs."

I nodded, knowing him well enough to recognize when a fight was lost. "That's fine. I have a half a dozen other angles already in the works."

"I still think he should wait for the article to run before stepping down," Emmaline pressed. She was a senior at the same university in Washington that my baby brother Maverick attended but held herself like she'd been sitting in on these meetings since infancy. Groomed to perfection by two generations of Harts. Her blood bought her seat, but her mind bought everyone's focus.

It was our COO, Tiffany, who blew out a harsh breath with a counter. "I understand what you're saying, Ms. Hart, but if we do it now, it looks like we're ahead of the storm. Should we wait and do it after—"

"They can use our hesitation as evidence of a bias and run additional articles about the company's nepotistic nature shielding *an American prince* from criminal investigation." Aside from The Titan, that was their favorite moniker for him. "The reporters will have documented speaking to me—along with several other staffers —today, which means delay or not, the clock is ticking." Yet again, the entire board stared at me like I'd grown a second head, but Tiffany nodded solemnly. Yes, you self-important motherfuckers, I've been sitting in this room for two years, taking notes for Greyson.

"Protocol would dictate that security walk you out, Grey," Reggie announced morosely as anger oozed from his pores, peppered brows dipped in the middle. Vivienne was watching with silent fury, although I wasn't sure if it was in defense of or directed toward her nephew.

"That's way overkill."

"It doesn't need to be a march to the gallows."

"I thought Ms. Rhodes said it should look like we believe he's innocent."

The room exploded in a storm of protests, and I watched as they increased in outrage. How he could be such an ass and inspire such unwavering loyalty was beyond me. Clearing my throat, I offered, "I'll walk him out through the evac route."

Only, I wasn't the only one with the thought, my eyes snapping to Ollie and then to Mike, our head of security, as they said the same thing.

Nodding, Greyson ground his teeth before saying, "I'll grab my things." As he prowled out of the room, he looked more like a man preparing for battle than one doing the walk of shame.

I'M NOT sure what I expected to find when I emerged from Greyson's home office, but it was probably in the ballpark of him looking pissed while brooding on the back terrace with his phone in his hand. What I certainly hadn't expected was a shirtless Greyson with his admittedly delicious ass in the sand, building an impressively tall, albeit crumbling, sandcastle with Mattie and Beau.

It wasn't the first time I'd seen the man with his guard down, but it was unexpected, given his current circumstances. It also wasn't the first time I'd appreciated all the hard lines of his honed body or that bright flash of his understated smile before remembering who exactly I was ogling. Kicking myself, I looked to my feet before glancing around to find Ollie jamming to One Republic's *I Ain't Worried* where he worked the grill. They'd dismissed the staff for the day to clear the house for candid conversations. NDAs or not, the more people in the know, the more likely we were to have a leak.

The day had been long. Made longer when Max called and told me he needed me to plug the USB he was sending via courier into the Hart House network. Stacy would plant our talons in her company's as well. Her loyalty to the Harts could end her career, while mine was protected despite my imminent departure.

Under Ollie's authorization and Max's signed nondisclosure agreement, we'd started digging and searching for holes. I'd watched the man take down corrupt senators because their sons were girl-friend-abusing shitbags. If anybody could get us answers for what we were up against, Max could.

Sidling up next to Ollie—who was, mercifully, fully clothed—I peered over his shoulder and grinned at the lobster tails on the grill. "Still impressed you know how to cook."

He shrugged. "Always hated having people in my house. Learning was a given."

"Fair. How's he doing?" I asked, glancing out toward his brother.

Shaking his head, Ollie said, "I dunno. Didn't say much on the ride home."

"He's in his head?"

"The depths of it, apparently."

As if on cue, I watched Greyson bury himself in his thoughts, staring unseeingly down at the sand for a long beat before Mattie leaped at him, and his reflexes jerked him into action to catch her.

Sometimes, I hated that my mind seemed hard-wired to defend the truth, no matter who benefited. Because the man on that beach was just an uncle. An uncle who would do anything to protect the kids now attacking him in a synchronized assault that knocked him backward into the sand. And through all our days spent enduring each other's company, I couldn't fathom him betraying them.

Captain lifted his black and gold head from where he watched them on the patio sectional before giving a low 'woof' from his chest. He leaped off the couch, stalking into the house a beat before the bell rang.

"I got it," I assured Oliver with a hand on his shoulder before following our canine companion to the front door.

I opened it to a second courier with a slim package already outstretched. After thanking him and signing, I glanced at the box to see my name printed on the label with *Jorogumo Defense* on the sender's side. *Max.* Peeling the box open, I tilted it to pour the contents into my palm, only to catch an old-school flip phone.

"What the fuck?" I muttered, turning it over in my fingers a beat before the thing rang. A chill coasted over my spine before I brought it to my ear.

"Who are you with?" Max's authoritative baritone came through clear as a bell the instant the line clicked to life. Glancing over my shoulder, I checked to make sure the Harts were where I left them through the wall of windows overlooking the ocean.

"I'm alone."

"I have good news and bad news."

"Shoot," I said, watching as Greyson dove into the ocean to escape his tiny assailants.

"Suit Daddy isn't stealing from the company. Not as far as I can tell, and I'm kind of the shit." Max snorted at his own joke, and I couldn't help but smile.

"Okay, what's the bad news?"

"There's malware buried on his network, and you're not going to like who put it there."

5

The Hellcat

GREYSON

The sound of my name pulled my attention back to Hart House through the hysterics of my niece and nephew. I had Mattie flung over my shoulder as she beat her defiant fists on my back and Beau tucked under my other arm like a massive football.

Alessandra looked entirely out of place in her curve-hugging black pencil skirt and heels at the border of the beach and pristine grass, looking at me like I was a dead man walking. Fitting. That's a bit of how it felt.

Giving the kids one last snuggle, I sent them running across the sand toward my brother, who was waving a lobster tail between tongs like a summoning. I shook the water from my hair and closed the distance, enjoying how she refused to let her chin or eyes drop from where she'd lifted them to hold my gaze. Her arms crossed beneath her chest defensively.

"Can we talk?" was her curt request as she held up a towel that I accepted with some trace of amusement. She hid discomfort well, but her mask wasn't impervious. She was always uncomfortable when I was casual.

Deciding to be a gentleman, I dried quickly before draping it around my shoulders to cover up a bit. Business mode that happened to be on the beach.

"What'd you find?" I asked, tone level.

"Not here," she clarified.

I quirked my head. "It's as good a place as any," I countered.

"I called in a favor at *De Luca's* for you, and we have a reservation in thirty minutes."

Studying the harsh set of her expression, I narrowed my eyes.

De Luca's was our family's favorite restaurant. My mother's cousin owned the place; it was our go-to for celebrations and funerals. Her harsh façade made this outing feel like the latter. But the firey fight in her eyes had me nodding in acquiescence.

Because the fight hid something worse that I didn't want to be the cause of.

Fear.

The ride to the restaurant was made in a heavy, contemplative silence. Occupying the second-row captain's chairs in the SUV, Alessandra kept her attention on the city, passing her heavily tinted window while I kept mine on her beautiful profile. I would miss this infuriating woman when she left. I would miss her sharp observations and proactive anticipation of what we needed as a department and company. She was the only assistant I never wanted to forcefully remove from my office, car, or home. I'd miss that too.

But first, we had to survive the scandal to come.

When we got to *DeLuca's*, I rushed around to beat Arthur to her door, holding it open and extending a hand to help her out. Her nose was so often glued to folders, tablets, or her phone as she navigated my life like the co-pilot I hadn't realized I needed. It was an unspoken protocol that she didn't even notice anymore.

Greetings were exchanged with familiar staff members before we were led not to my usual booth in the back but to the private party room fit for thirty. The long tables greeted us, ominous in their empty finality as we were led to the two lone place mats at the head of one. Neither of us sat. For a moment, I contemplated her chosen location.

Private for conversation. In my family's restaurant so the press wouldn't be permitted back, and surveillance wasn't a concern. But public enough that she knew she was safe.

She wasn't just scared. She thought the information she was about to deliver was worth killing for. Or valuable enough to destroy her over. I had a sinking suspicion it might just be. But there wasn't a country on the planet where Alessandra Rhodes would be *my* collateral.

The lights were left low, and a hush settled over the space when the hostess closed the sliding doors behind her. Alessandra hovered behind her chair for a beat before crossing the space and clicking play on the stereo, which stirred to life, opera filling the speakers.

When she returned, she stood behind her chair and blew out a long breath.

Motioning to the banquet table between us, I declared, "You have the floor, Ms. Rhodes."

Never one to beat around the bush, she breathed, "Tell me what you know about *Obsidian*."

The world…stopped. The fucking bravado of this brilliant, infuriating woman. There it was. I knew there was a chance but clung to hope she hadn't dug far enough to find the information hidden inside codes within codes.

I just needed to know how much she knew. "I'm sorry. About *what?*"

"Don't play games with me, Greyson." She leaned forward to brace herself on the wood surface, and I did the same. "You're on their list for crucifixion, and we're either a team or we're not. Answer the question."

Interesting choice of words. "Whoever this *Obsidian* is, why do you think I'm in their crosshairs?" I watched as recognition dawned in her eyes. I'd used the same term to explain why I didn't want Mattie involved in my rescue.

"I won't pretend to have information I don't, but give me a day or two, and I'm sure I'll find it." That was confidence, turning those molten gray eyes to stone. She would, too. If she kept digging, she wouldn't stop until she had her answers. It's what I admired most about this woman. "You could expedite the process by bringing me up to speed so I can decide how to protect the company from this."

"Tell me what you think you know," I countered.

She gave an irritated huff before saying, "My source only recognized their code because he's clashed with them before. He didn't bother to tell me their alias, but nothing good can come from getting tangled in their web, Greyson."

"What makes you think I'm tangled in this *Obsidian's* web?"

"The fact that they have spyware in your network was the first clue."

Well, that was news to me. Jax was going to lose his fucking mind.

I wasn't tangled in *Obsidian's* web. *I was the spider.* They were *my* prey. Only, if she were correct, they'd snuck a spy past my defenses.

"The fact that they seem to be going after something with the code name *Thunderstrike* was the second. Communicating via shifter code inside an anagram was a little amateur, but it was buried pretty deeply." God damn, she'd just lit a match, and she didn't even know it. She must have seen it on my face or sensed it somehow because her own spider's smile stretched her lips. "*Okay.* What do you know about *Thunderstrike?*"

She was already tangled in this. Alessandra and whomever she'd enlisted to help her had just stumbled into a war she knew nothing about. A war fought in the shadows by men who refused to stand by complacently while innocents suffered.

This would change everything. She had no clue that she'd just changed the trajectory of her future. *I* didn't have a clue how to keep it from touching her. Slowly, tracking the way her throat bobbed, I rounded the table. Answering honestly, I said, "Classified."

"You're a civilian again," she pointed out, rotating her back to the wood so she could keep me in front of her as I closed the distance.

Flashing a roguish grin, I said, "To your knowledge."

"Medically discharged," she argued.

Narrowing my eyes, I barked, "Did you run a dossier?"

"I have good friends," she simply supplied, lifting her chin to glare at me as I towered over her.

"Max."

"For starters."

For what felt like an eternity, we just stared each other down. Her chin jutted out in defiance as I caged her against the table with my body, a hand braced on either side of her. She always smelled like those chai drinks she brought on Fridays. It was infuriatingly sweet. My proximity had me setting my jaw while I stared down at her. It didn't seem to distract or intimidate her in the slightest, anyway. Some distant part of my mind dragged up the fact that she had *six* brothers and was near the tail end of the lineup. Fishermen, construction workers, football players. This girl *would* be tough as nails.

Figures. Keeping my tone level, I warned, "Don't go digging for answers you're not ready to find."

"Stop assuming you know what I'm capable of accomplishing."

Voice low, I asked, "Who replaced my demure little princess with a hellcat?"

"*What?!*" She burst out laughing, and I relaxed at the sound. Relieved I'd dissolved a bit of that concrete wall, I sighed and turned to pace, slowly making my way to the other side of the table before palming my face.

"What a mess."

"You supposed to kill me now or something?"

Insulted, I glared over at her. "I'm not a hitman."

"Max knows where I am and is waiting for my call."

"*I am not a hitman,*" I snarled, irritated that she thought so damn little of me.

She shrugged unapologetically. "*Thunderstrike. Obsidian. Blackwater.* There's a vibe about it."

I couldn't argue with that. "How deep did you get?"

"Not much farther."

"Still too far. *How* did you get that far?"

"There are many things you don't bother to learn about the people you view as beneath you."

Clenching my jaw, I lifted my head to study her. There wasn't a trace of apology across her face. "You think that's how I see you?"

"You think you've given me a single sign it's not?"

Fuck. "I deserve that."

A wry smile curved her wide mouth, mischief sparking in her eyes. "I can keep going if you want the full tally."

"That won't be necessary." I already felt like a sack of shit. But even these last twelve hours of unhinged Alessandra had me loathing the two years of wasted frustration where camaraderie should have been if she wasn't so damnably tempting.

"Maybe I wouldn't feel like quitting if I'd found my voice sooner," she mused, humor tilting those pillowy lips.

"What changed?"

"I quit," she supplied, "and found out I dedicated ninety hours a week to being your beverage girl."

"It's like you ran out of propriety with no notice."

"It hadn't gotten me where I needed, so I'll try not giving a shit instead."

Chuckling darkly, I shook my head. "I appreciate you digging, Alessandra, but you have to stop. You already went too far."

"Look. I'm not going to pretend to know anything more than I do. But this isn't good, Greyson. Whatever you've tied yourself to with these dark web groups," she shook her head. "Max is better than most government trolls, but—"

"Then why doesn't he work for them?"

Her brows winged up as shock softened her eyes. "Not all men can swear fealty to a government we all know is corrupt—to leaders that can change at the drop of a hat. Max isn't one to kneel to anyone who hasn't earned it, and even then, it would be a cold day in hell."

"So, he risks prison time to do it freelance?"

"Define prison. Being indentured to a government you may or may not believe in doesn't sound all that different."

She had a point. "If you care for him, you'll tell him to stop looking."

"Even if he does, if this allegation draws government attention, the feds won't."

"I know," I breathed, watching her for any hint at what was going on inside that mind of hers. "Luckily for me, my assistant is a wizard at spinning the media to eat out of her invisible palm."

She smiled softly, evidently accepting the compliment. "You better pray—*for Mattie and Beau's sake*—I can come up with something more tempting than the fall of America's prince."

HER WORDS EMBLAZONED themselves into the flesh of my mind. Although I was no threat to her, she was too bright to allow me to give her a ride home. Insisting her big brothers would throttle her for even considering it—not that I expected her to run and tell them anything. I believed her when she said she'd keep our conversation between us and Max.

Her diligence elicited a warmth—like pride—in my chest. Even if it were misplaced, I'd have to meet these brothers of hers someday. I didn't have a sister, though I supposed the closest thing was our cousin, Emmaline. But I could only hope to train her and Mattie just as thoroughly to look out for themselves.

This *Max* of hers had arranged for a driver to pick her up from *De Luca's*. I'd have to do some digging and see if I could get a full name, although if he was smart enough to hack through government-fortified defenses, prospects of his legal name being easily located weren't encouraging.

Arthur was waiting at the curb when I stepped out of the restaurant, and I called Jax to bring him up to speed once I was safely tucked in the back. But I couldn't slow down and process until I was home, alone on the back terrace overlooking the ocean.

If *Obsidian* knew who was funding our mission, it would only have been a matter of time before they came after our mercenaries. Worse yet, what we did—while known—wasn't strictly speaking...*above board*. The United States government might use us like any tool in their belt, but should attention turn our way, we would receive no aid from them. It was our hides on the line if the law came knocking. We were disposable. I had no intention of being the next Wagner Group executed by an enemy militia because our government couldn't acknowledge our existence.

If Alessandra and Max left a single trace that they knew more than they should...they'd just become throwaways, too. She'd either be ruined or have to testify against me.

A chirped notification had me pulling my phone from my pocket where I stood on my balcony, hoping the crash of the Pacific held answers my office didn't.

Despite her well-thought-out location, someone managed to snap a photo of me leading Alessandra out of the banquet room through the front window. The article was yet another story speculating about a secret love affair. The vipers had been using our consistent appearances together to spur on rumors for the better portion of her twenty-one months with me. She'd never so much as wasted a breath dispelling the tale, treating the paparazzi like gnats —irritating, but not worth her time.

Kind of...*kind of like a Hart.*

I straightened from my place against the railing, pacing before making my way to the stairs and down onto the beach, where I stripped to my boxers in the concealment of night and dove into the ocean. Nothing cleared my head quite like salt and sea. Only, instead of the soothing rush of the pulsing ocean, my ears replayed the last twelve hours.

Reporters ambushed me on my way in today to ask if I wanted to make a statement regarding the embezzlement allegations leveled against you.

Somebody is trying to crucify you, Grey.

Tell me what you know about Obsidian.

Even if he does, if this allegation draws government attention, the feds won't.

You better pray I can come up with something more tempting than the fall of America's prince.

The only thing that could make a splash big enough to swallow that *would be a royal wedding...*

The last time you were seen with a woman other than your cousin was before your father died...

Gasping for breath, I hauled myself from the surf because no matter how hard I swam along the shore, the mess just swirled behind my eyelids.

Dried and dressed, I snatched my phone and read the rest of the article, which included prior images of us in Paris and Rome and an extensive list of the galas I'd paid her to attend beside me. Of course, according to the article, she was there as a romantic plus one, not an obligatory one.

You're born either loving or hating the media when you grow up in the limelight. I was the latter. I loved my privacy. I wanted nothing to do with status or show. Which left them to speculate however they wanted to about whomever was in your life. If you decide not to humor the vampires of society with endless interviews, you learned better than to go poking around the fairytales and accusations they weave around your name like invasive vines destined to suffocate the truth with their imagined reality.

But when I finished the article, a psychotic idea struck. One I would inevitably regret, but it might hold merit. Curious to see if I had a leg to stand on, I did the one thing I promised never to do.

I googled myself.

"DO you still have the paparazzi images of us in Barcelona? The one at the theater festival?"

"Make yourself at home," Alessandra scoffed, gaping as I stormed past her into her sleek condo about two hours later.

"We were drinking wine," I snapped my fingers, attempting to draw the details out of my memory bank. For this to work, it would have to be as convincing as unhinged. "It was the trip you met my golf buddy, Ashcroft, and his wife on."

When I whirled to face her, she glared at me with equal parts confusion and irritation. Was that...*insult* in her parted lips? "I *remember* the theater festival, Greyson," she patronized with an endearing level of condescension. "They named the damn amphitheater after you, and *I helped you cut the ribbon*." She enunciated every word like I was an invalid.

"Good. Right," I nodded, turning to pace as she reluctantly closed her front door. She wore loose plaid boxer-style shorts and an oversized *Guns N' Roses* T-shirt with the neckline cut into a V that left it hanging off her shoulder in an obnoxious temptation. The woman had the most decadent golden skin I'd ever encountered. Forcing myself to focus on the insanity unfolding in my mind, I asked, "But do you have the images in your delightfully anal little archives?"

"They are *not* anal. They're *efficient*," she bit out before knocking back her red wine and following me to her kitchen island. "And you know I catalog everything. Why?"

Nodding, I blew out a heavy breath. Why'd the old prick have to suggest a royal wedding, of all things? And why the hell did the ploy have merit?

I studied Alessandra as she glared back at me, still awaiting answers I couldn't give. She self-consciously pulled the t-shirt back over her shoulder after setting the glass on her waterfall marble counter.

"You know, Greyson, this is *exactly* why I quit," she snarled.

"Because I think your systems are anal?"

"Because you think it's acceptable to burst into *my home* with obscure questions about an event we attended sixteen months ago, at ten-forty-five on a Monday night when I work at eight tomorrow. You could have just sent me a text."

"Trust me when I tell you I couldn't send this over any form of unsecured communication. And time is of the essence." Finally forcing myself to stop the incessant pacing, I turned to study this woman who'd worked her tempting little ass off for me for two years straight. She glared at me with the skepticism my late-night outburst no doubt deserved.

"Why are you staring at me like that?"

"Because I have four people on the planet I actually trust," I admitted candidly before shrugging. "*Three*, if minors are eliminated."

"Okay…?"

"You're one of them."

For the first time since I came into her space, she looked… surprised. Her gray-blue eyes rounded and then narrowed like she was waiting for a punch line as she lowered onto the bar stool across from me.

"I had plans for you, Ms. Rhodes—plans you ruined submitting your notice. I appreciate your diligence in protecting Mattie, but you have interests at stake you know nothing about. This means at some point, once your loyalty was undeniable, you would have gotten answers to every question, which I'm sure is now planted in your irritatingly sharp mind."

"And now?"

"*Now* you've unintentionally implicated yourself, and I need to…*adjust* some things to ensure you're safe."

"And this plays into the allegations?" An ordinary woman would've run screaming from the room, but not Alessandra. No, she was still curt and to the point.

"It does now."

"You're infuriatingly vague, do you know that?"

"Yes," I answered. *Honestly*. The air conditioner kicked on with a whoosh and a hum as I added, "And my uncle is right."

"About not talking to *the help*?" she asked venomously.

"About the PR mess." When she didn't respond, we just studied each other. Some kind of muted kitchen standoff in negotiations that had yet to begin. "About needing something dramatic to keep their focus where we want it."

Uncle Reggie had been right about a few things but wrong about another. Pursing my lips as my mind attempted to maneuver pieces on the board, I finally swallowed my pride and locked eyes on the only non-relative woman the press *had* seen me with in years. The woman they'd been begging to get an inside scoop on.

Laughing at the insanity of it all, I smiled back at her. "Marry me, Alessandra?"

6

You've Cracked

ALICE

"*You've cracked*," I squeaked through some manic laugh of complete disbelief as I rocketed upright, bashing my knee on my counter in the process. I was too shocked to care.

"Maybe," he agreed, a rare, understated smile tugging at the corner of his mouth as if this was entertaining for him, but those hazel-green eyes remained locked on me. "Look, Reggie is an elitist snob, but he wasn't wrong about the story idea."

"You've gone *mad*," I insisted. "Certifiably insane. I'll call a shrink and book an appointment tomorrow morning." He tracked my movements as I paced across the room behind the kitchen island, bending forward to brace my hands on the edge of the marble as I studied him. Partially to catch my breath—mostly bent over while pretending you're fine, like you do after a long sprint—and partially because there was a high probability my knees would give out, and I wanted my best chance at not smashing my face in.

I was supposed to be unwinding. Recovering from what was inarguably one of the most stressful days in my career before a long stream of crisis mitigation that would likely be worse. Leighton was on the closing shift at the restaurant, which meant I was supposed to have a date with a book and a bubble bath, not earn an unhinged proposal from my boss.

Disconcertingly enough, he didn't *look* particularly unhinged. As a matter of fact, he seemed entirely too composed. Too steady as he tracked every shift of my weight. More breathless than I meant to be, I barked, "*What are you playing at?*"

"Not a play, Ms. Rhodes. You have to admit, we'd be good together."

"Did you fall off a balcony this weekend and land on your head?" I demanded, earning a rather satisfying deadpan. "You've done nothing in the years I've known you to indicate that I'm anything more than gum on your designer boot until you defended my merit to your uncle today. But I highly suspect that was because he was challenging *your* authority, not because he disrespected *mine*." I sucked down a breath, having released all my words in one rush of frustration.

"I'm sorry about my remark Saturday night. I was frustrated you'd throw away your talent."

"The *cost of replacing me* frustrated you," I argued. He rounded the counter so abruptly that I straightened from my place, braced on it, and backed up. Keeping as much distance between us as humanly possible. He seemed to catch how I interpreted the motion because he slowed, hands up as if to soothe a feral animal.

"I was frustrated that the *greatest talent on our team* was about to walk away and prove me wrong."

I scoffed. I couldn't fucking help it. This man was insane. Greyson Hart, America's prodigal son, had gone insane. People speculated when he walked away from a billion-dollar empire to enlist in the Navy, but something must've rattled his brain until it scrambled and fried because this was utter madness.

"You told me a country bumpkin would never make it in this city."

"And then I watched you work, and you proved me wrong. Finding you is undoubtedly the best thing my brother has ever done in his career." When my mouth popped open, but no words came out, his shoulders raised and fell with the strength of an exasperated breath before he continued. "Think critically, Alessandra. Do you truly think an *assistant* earns the salary you're allotted? Has access to the company's *financials*? Gets to sit in on board meetings with a voice just as valued as a division head?"

"When their boss makes more money than God, who the hell knows? The elite spend more on handbags than I make in a year." It was true. I'd seen them go for twice what I earned—and I brought in a very healthy six figures thanks to the man standing across from me in the middle of a nervous system collapse.

"Only the spectacularly pretentious ones," he grumbled with a derisive eye roll.

"And in case you couldn't tell by your Uncle's mini aneurysm, today was the only meeting I've ever spoken up in."

"That was a result of your own limitation, not mine."

Some hysterical lapdog-adjacent yip escaped me as I turned in a panicked circle like there was somewhere to flee. Unless I intended to break through the tempered glass wall of the condo building and free fall into the city where I'd meet an untimely demise, there was no exit.

His voice was close enough and gentle enough to send goosebumps up my spine when he spoke next, "Hear me out."

I whirled to face him, but my mouth dropped open when he was towering above me. "God, *make a noise*, you psycho!"

"You covered for me. With my uncle."

"And?!" I barked before I noticed something I'd never anticipated seeing on Greyson Hart's face. His eyes had softened. Some cousin to vulnerability flashed in those hazels before he seemed to blink it away at my retort. Regret sloshed in my belly.

He wet his lips, hard gaze like a brand across my face. "You didn't have to. You didn't even know what you were protecting, but you understood I didn't want it shared."

"It seemed like it had to be valuable information."

"And Reginald Hart is a valuable man."

"Reginald Hart is a self-entitled *prick*. You forget I've walked these circles beside you for two years now. I know where he places value."

"And what about his nephew?" He arched a solitary brow, chest rising as he watched my face. He was in tan slacks and a casual short-sleeved button-up that hung half open, hair disheveled as though he'd been running his hands through it on repeat.

"An entitled capitalist prince that loves his niece more than the air in his lungs."

He looked to his feet. "It's an obligation of those with power to look after those without it. She's my responsibility as much as Ollie's."

"Your peers vehemently disagree."

"Not all of them." He ran a frustrated hand through his hair, confirming my theory. I hated that I liked it that way—a strand falling across the tension lining his forehead. A fissure in the façade of perfection.

"Oliver aside?"

"Okay, well…most of them," he allowed with a cocky little grin. "So. Back to the topic at hand. What do you say?"

"Mr. Hart, I—"

"*Greyson*," he cut in. "Please, call me Greyson. Regardless of your decision here, you've known too much for too long to be so formal."

"Until this evening, I believed I was your coffee girl."

"Until a few hours ago, only three people knew about *Thunderstrike*. You went in looking for proof of the allegations and found something far more dangerous. Those communications were locked behind government-orchestrated security." He shook his head, adding, "You forced your way in in under twenty-four hours. You've yet to realize how valuable your mind is."

"Max forced his way in," I corrected.

"And leaders know exactly when to delegate so they can operate to their strengths. You've yet to realize what you could do with the right resources."

"And *you've* yet to explain what *Obsidian* or *Thunderstrike* is," I pointed out, my breath halting as his hand came to cup my elbow, eyes falling to where his skin met mine. Which, coincidentally enough, was now tingling with a rush of anticipation I would not be acknowledging. The way my hand came to wrap around his forearm was entirely involuntary. Whether I was holding him at bay or holding him to me, I wasn't even sure, and fear and arousal were way too similar in nature for my liking. Suddenly, my bare legs on display felt ungodly vulnerable.

"And I can't," he said calmly. "As it is, you've already implicated yourself in something I wanted you very, *very* far away from. So long as you can be forced to testify, you need to get the hell away from those files, Alessandra." As if in emphasis, he gave my arm a gentle squeeze.

Silence settled between us for a long beat, his thumb absently running over my elbow, even once I broke it. "You were a Seal." It came out somewhere between a statement and a question. He nodded once. "It's related to your time there?"

"Like I said, it's classified. Don't ask questions you're not prepared to have answered." He let those words simmer like a rich sauce, allowing the flavors of each implication to marinate in my mind before that edge to his voice sharpened. "You can't go back, Alessandra. There is no unhearing what will be heard. That being said, you would be an invaluable asset."

To a team I didn't even understand. Doing some kind of shady work he couldn't discuss with me. If it was classified, it had to be government-related. But if I was implicating myself...it wasn't strictly...*legitimate*.

From the little information I could gather before he showed up, it seemed the fire-breathing dragon was funding something rather... philanthropic. I thought of my Max, taking down corrupt politicians from within their own framework. I wondered if he'd specifically led me to something he wasn't supposed to know about but had seen, anyway.

So many questions. So few answers.

I was just a girl from a small town in Alaska. A girl from Alaska lucky to land a position with one of the planet's largest investment and media dynasties. A girl from Alaska who was about to walk away from said position. Did I...did I still want that? Did he actually think I could do more, or was he just covering his very rich, very fine, Armani-clothed ass? Using the strength of mouthwatering cologne and his towering, beautiful frame to scatter my sensibilities as violently as the bomb he'd just dropped.

I glanced at my watch, sucking in a steadying breath as his words tumbled through my mind, gathering momentum like a snowball. Mouth dry, I mumbled, "It's eleven, Greyson. I have a meeting at seven."

"Answer my question, Alessandra."

Jaw set, I looked up to him, that steady *stroke, stroke, stroke* of his thumb over my skin, sending pebbles across it. Christ, I was so grateful he'd never touched me prior—it would have been all I could think about. "Nobody will believe it."

"Here, google me," he ordered, unceremoniously tossing his cell phone to me. I caught it on reflex.

"I'm sorry?" I balked.

"Look at the screen. You search my name, and you invariably see yours as well. But if you add—"

"Romance…" I finished his sentence as I glanced at the populated search results he had open on his screen, my mouth falling open.

"You're the only woman they've snapped photos of beside me in *two years*. It won't be a hard sell." Scroll after scroll of search results confirmed what he was saying. Not just photos but articles and blog posts speculating that we were together.

"My *family*, for starters, would believe I was dead long before they believe I up and married you." My words earned a visible wince, but I couldn't stop. There were too many questions. This was just my first. "You were going to dig through my archives and repurpose those candid Barcelona images?"

He rubbed at his forehead like he could ease some of our reality away. "There was one of me guiding you through a door—hand on your low back." His eyes went distant, his head softly shaking, like he was searching through old memories. "Another where you took my hand stepping out of the car over a full gutter. So many on the UK trips. Even articles speculating back then. Multiples of you getting out of the car in front of my house. *Creeps*," he complained but shrugged begrudgingly. "Could benefit us now, though."

"We'd fake a photo with a ring and leak it ourselves," I concluded—correctly, based on his smirk and the subtle nod as he watched me. "It's still a scandal, Greyson. *Hotshot CEO runs off with his secretary*."

"You and I both know you're much more than my appointment setter. That's what Paul is for."

"My point stands—it's a cliché, but it will still make headlines."

"Headlines *I can live* with. Headlines that don't bring the feds poking around in my financials or lead them to my…extracurriculars. You could invoke spousal immunity should they come knocking. Plus, Stacy would make her career on this story," he said with great satisfaction. Stacy was the one reporter we could count on to fan flames or extinguish them when needed. We already knew we had her allegiance in this after today's call. "We'd be doing her a favor in the long run."

I covered my mouth, heart pounding just at the fact that I was considering this insanity.

"Unless you have an alternate diversion significant enough to draw media attention for a prolonged period, at which point I am *all* ears. An alternative plan wouldn't protect you with immunity, though. Should the law come knocking—you won't take the fall for me; you'd have to tell them what you know, which I hope is very little." He pursed his lips. "If you've got something else that could solve our immediate allegation problems…throw it on the table." His eyes dropped, a focused furrow pinching his brows. "But I think he was right. I think the royal wedding would swallow some baseless accusation—and we could draw it out."

"Speculations, confirmations, announcements," I concluded, sucking down a breath.

"Vapid parties and all the details around the wedding itself."

"The ring."

"The dress," he said, expression warming, no doubt as he realized I was playing along.

"Elopement or a big, televised fiasco sold off to the highest bidder."

"Elopement, obviously." As an afterthought, he explained, "I notoriously hate productions."

"Then, it would turn to the guest list." I hated that it made sense. Hated that he was right—the public would believe it as long as my family didn't light the building on fire.

"Your siblings would help with that."

"I'm not exploiting Elora or Paxton," I argued. "If—and I cannot stress the *if* enough—we even entertain this in some acid trip-altered reality, they only participate electively."

"We wouldn't have a choice. The media would write whatever they wanted to write. Your family has placed themselves in the public eye. They'll be seen. After the wedding, they'd talk photos and guest list—"

"Food and vendors."

"Where we honeymooned."

"Pregnancy speculations." When he glared at me, I added, "Tell me I'm wrong."

"You wanted months of content," he pointed out.

"And this would protect me from having to testify, taking down Ollie with you."

"We keep their attention. If we win in the court of public opinion, we win whatever game they're playing."

"Who cares about finances when they can talk tulle and chiffon?"

"Lobster or veal," he supplied, shaking his head. I tucked away his disappointment for later because my heart felt like it might bust through my ribs like the *Kool-Aid* man.

My mind was spinning, whirling with the overwhelm of so much new information, and my mouth opened and closed repeatedly. I turned for the windows again, needing space between us. Needing air that didn't smell like him—no doubt some pheromone-filled aftershave mixed with sea salt, designed to entice the women too smart to drop their panties the moment they saw dollar signs.

"I swear on my mother's grave, I'll treat you right. The prenup will be favorable. Enough to start fresh when this is over—hell, you could live comfortably for the rest of your life if you're smart with it."

Whirling on him, I demanded, "Are you trying to pay me proactive hush money to marry you for a media arrangement, Greyson? I don't think that sin is covered by spousal immunity."

He rubbed at the space between his brows, blowing out a harsh breath. "*My*, I've made one hell of an impression." Pursing his lips, Greyson closed the distance again, replacing his hand on my arm. "No. I wouldn't cheapen you that way. *I didn't mean it like that.* Although, the rich marry for less. People still sign away their daughters for business arrangements and status regularly. The women agree because of the privilege afforded them." He shook his head. "Never thought I'd be one of them. What *I meant* was that legally speaking, I would handle this like I would with any woman willing to dedicate her life to me as *my wife*. A standard prenup would account for you walking away fairly. Ask Ollie."

Oliver's ex, Carly, was the worst kind of woman. I wouldn't have been shocked if she poked holes in the condom to land a Hart brother, with how little she cared for Mattie or their son Beau. Like the traditionalist he was, Ollie married her while she was pregnant with Matilda, but when Beau was a few months old, she ran off. Sent a courier with divorce papers. Made out like Satan's mistress, with more money than most people would see in a lifetime.

Ollie got the kids.

My skin crawled just knowing someone could essentially sell off their babies for a few million—walk away with no care what became of the two human beings she brought into the world.

"*I'm not like her.* I don't need your money, Greyson." I weighed my words. "Beyond what I earn serving this company. *That,* I'll continue taking."

He smiled again. It was the most I'd seen on his face in anything but a focus-induced scowl. Perhaps it *was* a mental breakdown, after all.

"I know. You weren't particularly quiet the day you told your sister to *eat the rich.*"

My face flushed, but at the amused curve to his lips, I couldn't help but laugh before slapping a hand over my mouth to silence it.

"It's okay." The dark chuckle that emerged from him sent a flock of birds flying through my chest. "I spent three deployments saying the same thing."

I shook my head, chuckling despite myself. "What changed?"

"My spine was reconstructed with metal pins, and after the bitterness and rehab, I realized I could help more people with the resources my name garnered than the rifle in my hands."

"Hmm," I murmured, studying him and finding a carefully blank canvas of sincerity.

"Three years," he said abruptly. "I think that should be long enough to dispel any rumors that may surface." All the air in my lungs somehow squeezed into my cheeks before I blew it out in an endless stream as he went on.

"I mean this with as much respect as our respective positions garner, but I nearly killed you in two. Probably would've if I could get away with it. What makes you think I could possibly survive three?"

"This is different."

"Explain."

"You're not my subordinate. As my wife, you're my partner. You're not answering to me; if anything, it would be the opposite. As my wife, I don't have to pretend I don't find you maddeningly attractive. It would be expected that you would move in with me, that my drivers chauffeur you, all the normal privileges for your position would be afforded. And I would insist on an honorable prenup. It's my ass—my niece's legacy in this company—you'd be saving."

My swallow was suddenly painfully hard, but I managed. Brain stuck in a permanent buffering state after his words 'maddeningly attractive.' His flattery wasn't winning him any points. I refused to let it.

"I'm asking the impossible of you. A long con bestowed to an untrained civilian, essentially, but you would be given all the assets my wife deserves—to do with them whatever you want. Fund charities, go get a doctorate, or buy a Birkin bag, I don't care, frankly. It's the least I could do if you agree. I'm not a man prone to begging, so that's as close as I'll get."

"This is madness," I breathed, wrapping my arms around myself.

Unflinching, he said, "I know."

"As long as you're aware."

"Is that a yes?" He stepped a little closer.

Motioning between us, I stammered, "W-we'd have to sell this."

"Spent ninety hours a week together for twenty-one months, and I haven't sent you running with a severance check, so I think it's believable."

"I mean…PDA. People would expect it."

"Ahh," he breathed, a cocky smirk falling to the floor. I tracked his tongue as it wet the seam of his lips before he added, "The fun part." I squirmed, but he wrapped both of his warm hands around my arms, guiding our bodies together. "Do you find me repulsive, Alessandra?"

I will not squirm for Greyson Hart. When I just gaped up at him, his eyes flicked to where my hair stood on end in the trail of fire he was leaving on my arms.

"Then that's the fun part. As it is, I'm a notoriously private man and would never be one to flaunt my affections. Media expectations of your participation will be minimal unless you decide to instigate something yourself."

Despite the shiver up my spine, I sheepishly admitted, "My family calls you Hartless."

The tiniest twitch tugged at his lips. "Wonder where they got that idea."

"They think I can't stand you." Because I couldn't. Had been livid since the day Paul showed up to transfer me from marketing to PR, dropping me off in his office.

There was nothing—and I mean nothing—worse than telling a Rhodes we couldn't do something.

Greyson shrugged one shoulder, shirt straining against the movement.

"I'm a Hart. When you're born with a silver spoon, and the eyes of the world on your family, being hated is in the job description. I'll just have to spend three years earning their trust. On a positive note, you hating me keeps our boundaries pretty firm."

"The board will have a field day with this."

"Leave them to me."

"You'll regret this," I warned, feeling oddly emotional about how he'd respond.

He gave me a long, hard look, eyes pensive as he stared me down. Goosebumps crept up my arms when he gently lifted my shirt back over my bare shoulder, giving me a firm squeeze before saying, "Impossible."

"I'll drive you crazy—I paint and draw with charcoal while blasting oldies at all hours of the night. And I like things clean. *And* I have to work out every day, or I get stabby. *Especially* when I'm dealing with you."

"I'll clear out the guest room. I already sleep poorly, I have a housecleaner who comes daily, and there's a state-of-the-art gym in my basement."

"You can't be seen with anyone else—I can't live with the shame of some big, public affair. Of being your *Cinderella* story turned couldn't-keep-her-man."

Greyson deadpanned, lips pursed in irritation. "Have you seen me with anyone in the last two years?"

I blinked, realizing if he had to have a plus one, he paid me to accompany him to galas and events. It was why I'd missed Christmas with my family. My eyes flew wide. "*Are you* gay?"

His laughter bounced off the walls before supplying a light-hearted, "No."

"Then I don't understand." Hell, he was named the sexiest man in the country last year. Greyson Hart could have anyone he wanted, and they'd thank him as he kicked them out of his house.

He studied me, and that focused furrow deepened. "I've never been a casual hookup man. And...after Carly and Ollie...if I fuck someone, it will mean something to me. Frankly, having you around will ward off the vultures, which would be deeply relieving. A built-in escape hatch."

If I fuck someone, it will mean something to me... that was the part of the statement that stuck with me, and I cursed my ridiculous brain. What half-wit bimbo didn't look at this man and imagine what that would be like? I certainly didn't intend to be one of them. "You're not going to set the same rules for me?"

The rakish grin that stretched his cheeks this time made my toes curl. "If my wife cheats on me and is stupid enough to get caught, I'm doing my job wrong."

"It isn't real," I clarified when his answer sent fear skittering through my body, nerves wrapping a noose around my neck. His smile transformed and deepened into a real one that reminded me of my very first impression of this rendition of Satan in a suit. "Why are you smiling?"

"You said *isn't*." He wet his lips again, eyes lingering on mine. "Is that a yes?"

"Three years?"

"Quicker than *another* bachelor's degree and much more lucra-tive." Okay. Yeah. I was surprised he remembered that I had two under my belt. When I leveled a glare in his direction, even though I had to crane my neck to look at him, he finally wrestled that smile off his face. "Am I wrong?"

I could only picture this man in the sand with those kids, and Mattie looking at him like her superhero. *This was madness.* "I want a new title."

"How's the *head of public relations* until I'm confident you can step into acting COO?"

My mouth fell open until I could remember how to keep it closed. *Acting COO?* A satisfied kind of arrogance settled over his features when he rendered me silent.

"Told you that you're sharper than your peers." My mind was reeling, but Greyson wouldn't compromise a position so significant to prove a point or as a means to an end. As if reading my thoughts, he shook his head. "My promotion proposal was slated for fall when Tiffany retires from the position, but you jumped the gun with your resignation. Your performance today solidified her endorsement."

Eyes narrowed, I added, "I want a say in the company's charitable donations."

"As my partner, that's inherent."

"Partner?" I gaped.

"*Wife*," he emphasized, one eye narrowed comically. "You'll be a Hart—however temporarily. Unlike my misogynistic bastard of a father, I don't do trophies."

Because that made perfectly logical sense, I was clearly the one out of sorts. I was waiting for a punchline, but he just studied me, expression pensive, like he was trying to anticipate my next objection and get ahead of it. Scrambling for anything that would pop this balloon of crazy, I blurted, "You don't get to blacklist me when this is over. If I still want to leave the company, I get to work for whoever I want to."

"You'd be equipped to start and fund your own venture by the end of this, but should you choose to be someone's pawn, you'll have my blessing and a ringing endorsement for whoever you send calling."

Dammit. How did he think all this through so quickly? "Paxton keeps his deal, no matter what happens between the two of us."

He leveled me with a glare dripping in disdain. "That's a given."

Ignoring how quickly my mouth dried out as nerves and anticipation danced in my belly, I sucked down a breath. Took a shaky step back. "I want to spend Christmas with my family this year."

"Florida sounds superb." *Didn't expect him to remember that, but okay.*

"And take the whole *two-week* trip off work."

"Done."

"You're going to say yes to anything I ask for right now, aren't you?"

"Perhaps," he allotted, one arm propped like a shelf below the other so that he could brace his hand against his mouth. But I swore beneath his deceptively casual stance, another smirk twitched in his cheek. "Don't use your powers for evil, you tiny extortionist."

Oh god, I was going to regret this, wasn't I? Feeling spectacularly bold, I replied, "I still don't like you."

"I can live with that."

His smolder held my unblinking bewilderment, as unyielding as he was with any corporate conquest.

Three years. A place on the board and influence over billions of dollars in the philanthropic budget. The ability to understand what shield he'd taken up and hide behind spousal immunity should anyone come poking around. I could make a difference with these resources—Elora had just started a vocational school for women in Manhattan that could always use extra funding, and Jameson's fiancé, Noel, had started a foundation for victims of domestic abuse. There were so many causes I could aid with a last name like Hart. It might be the ultimate red herring of media manipulation, but the access he was offering me was…unparalleled. If we played our cards right, we'd preserve Matilda and Beau's future and keep the public's attention where Greyson wanted it. Hell, I'd been doing the same thing for his clients for years. This wasn't new—it was just personal this time.

Lengthening my spine, I extended my hand to Greyson Hart. Eyes glinting, he reached out to shake it, and life as I knew it flipped on its axis.

7

Nepotistic Sack of Overpriced Wine

GREYSON

It took a great deal of focus to hit my usual rep count the following afternoon. My mind locked miles away, staring at gray-blue eyes looking at me like I'd become a Cerberus. But that focus snapped away as Cap whined from behind my bench, and my brother burst through the door of the private gym in my basement.

"What the *actual fuck*, Grey?" With his usual spectacular finesse, Ollie stormed into the space, paying no mind to Captain as he lifted his head to observe us. With a grunt, I lowered the barbell onto the rack, sighing as I sat up. Inevitable, I supposed. This entire interaction was inevitable. He'd always been fond of the woman, which is why his next growled demand came as no shock to me. "Alice Rhodes?!"

"Evening, Ollie. Nice to see you."

He tongued a back molar, light brown eyes ablaze with a disproportionate anger. Like mine, Oliver had his hair cropped tight to the sides in a subtle fade but left longer on top. *Unlike mine*, he liked to leave his dark locks in disarray, swept off to the side, which meant it was hanging across his forehead as he glared down at me. Snatching the towel off the rack, he hocked it at my face, and I swiped it from the air before wiping the sweat from my forehead.

"What the fuck are you doing?"

"Will you shut up for a minute and sit down?" I drawled back.

"Fuck off, Grey. She's a good woman. Bright. Has so much untapped potential. She's wasted sitting in your office every day, and you have no right to drag her into your world."

"I know."

"You wouldn't know potential if it bit you in the ass," he growled, beginning to pace in a tight circle.

With a prolonged sigh, I watched him take four long strides to the perimeter of the mats and back. Refraining from making a quip about his lack of congratulations, I forced myself to unclench my jaw. "Are you done?"

"Have I broken your damn jaw yet?"

A devilish grin cracked through my control. I couldn't help it. Despite growing up in the public eye, we'd tousled like the best of them. Hell, it's what got us both into the training ring by high school because Mother decided if we couldn't turn off the instinct, we'd learn to control it. "You're welcome to try."

"Don't tempt me."

"I'll give you the first shot," I goaded, leaning onto my knees and watching the feral beast slow to a stop, nostrils still flared with anger as he set his hands on his hips.

"Seriously. What are you thinking?"

It wasn't really a question, but I'd answer him, anyway. "I'm thinking she found *Thunderstrike*." And just like that, Ollie's mouth snapped shut. His expression transformed from anger to fear in a heartbeat. Was it wise for my brother to be privy to the mercenary group I'd been funding since I was wheeled out of the hospital five years ago? Probably not. Was it even more ill-advised that he'd been on the inner circle of it on more than one occasion? Yeah. But Mattie and Beau were as much my collateral as his. Keeping him on the outs would only leave him in the dark in a situation I very much needed him to be illuminated on. One cannot deliver justice without taking risks. Our loved ones are the primary targets. This meant my brother being properly prepared and his family protected was just as essential as *me* being prepared. Studying the fear in his eyes, I said simply, "She won't say anything."

Temper palpably cooled, he reached up to loosen his tie, yanking at the knot as he begrudgingly lowered onto the bench across from me. Confusion sent those light brown irises somewhere distant a beat before he asked, "How do you know? She…is she…"

"Blackmailing me?" I guessed when his thought drifted off like he couldn't fully consider it. I scoffed. "No. Until yesterday, I would've said she wasn't capable of that."

"And now?"

I shook my head, blowing a heavy breath into my cheeks as my eyes widened. Nodding, I declared, "You always had an eye for spectacular talent."

"What does that mean?"

"She got through those walls in a matter *of hours*, Ollie. Jax set us up, and I couldn't even crack those myself."

"*Alone?*" He asked, his voice heavy with disbelief.

"Nah, not entirely. The guy she sent you to yesterday, Max, he helped."

"A…friend? That's more capable than the US government?"

"Laws don't dictate everyone, Ollie. Some people knowingly play in the gray."

"Christ." He palmed at his clean-shaven jaw, shaking his head. "I swear I didn't have a clue you had anything to find when I authorized her to dig."

"She went looking for evidence or a defense. I'm not sure which."

"You would never—"

I shook my head. "She knows."

"She hates you," he pointed out helpfully.

I leveled him with a glare. "Yes. Thank you for that. But she knows I'd never hurt you and Mattie."

"Where in the hell were they digging?"

"In the wrong places," I admitted.

"If you stuff a closet with skeletons, you don't get to pick which one falls out."

Hanging my head, I studied my hands for a beat. The skin was red, and my veins and tendons were livid with the exertion of exercise. Fuck, if that wasn't true. Our family had no shortage to choose from. It was how I knew about the evils of this world so intimately.

"You gonna explain how this ended in you *proposing* to your *assistant*—that's an HR nightmare, by the way."

"Do you remember what Uncle Reggie said yesterday in my office?"

"I cannot see how Uncle Reggie would approve of—let alone suggest—you marry an employee."

"He said that the only thing that might create a big enough media flurry to swallow the allegation case was a royal American wedding." I bobbed my head. "I don't think he's wrong."

His eyes narrowed for a long beat, and I just allowed the concept to linger as the cogs turned in his eyes. "And Alice is the only woman the paparazzi have seen at your side since before Beau was born."

Nodding, I chewed on my lip. "Plus—"

"Once you're married, she can't be forced to testify," he deduced. When I hesitantly brought my eyes to his, it was a deep analysis looking back at me, not judgment. Maybe a trace of fear. "And what the hell does she get out of this?"

"Protection. Privilege that comes with the last name *Hart*. My purse strings and a proper Christmas vacation? Aside from her love for Matilda, I'm not entirely sure why she agreed. She'll have a place on the board as my partner—a say in our philanthropic ventures."

"I don't see Alice being that easily bought off. She's so down to earth—doesn't care about *status* or *money*." The last two words were practically spat.

"I know."

"So, what's she doing?"

Shrugging, I answered honestly. "I'm not actually certain."

"Then how can we trust her?"

"Call it a gut instinct."

"Your gut instinct was not to hire her," he pointed out.

"Quite the opposite."

His scoff was of comedic proportions. "Is your memory that short?"

"She was pretty and naïve—why else wouldn't I have wanted her working directly under you, Ollie?"

"Oh, get fucked," he snapped, anger flashing in his eyes. "I'm not the one that just propositioned my employee. I've never crossed that line, and you know it."

"But if you were going to, it would take someone as beautiful as Alessandra."

"You're saying you were protecting me?"

"It was a rough year. Carly *made it* a rough year. I wasn't sure where you were because you wouldn't talk to anybody."

"Like you're any better?" He bit back. No. I wasn't. Harts didn't do big feelings. It wasn't proper. We just stuffed them down and snapped a lid over the containers. "And now? What's her play in this?"

"Hell, if I know," I reiterated. "She might throw me under the bus the moment Mattie can inherit. *I don't know.*"

"Not a terrible idea—I wish I'd thought of it first." That soft, melodic voice had both of our heads snapping sideways to where Alessandra hovered in the doorway. "As it is, we have another problem."

A mirroring figure appeared—minus a few years—with a scowl on her pretty little face. Her hair was darker than Alessandra's, but just as long, and it was swept back into a loose braid. With eyes nearly the same shade of slate gray, I assumed this was one of her million sisters. Which—at least judging by the hatred rolling off her in waves—was, indeed, a problem.

ALICE

LEIGHTON'S TEETH were audibly grinding as she stared down the Hart brothers, with determination in the set of her shoulders and fists clenched so tightly her knuckles were white. As if the two men in front of us couldn't erase us both from existence with a nod to a couple of well-placed henchmen.

"You don't have a problem; you *are* the problem," Leighton spat, crossing the distance as both men found their feet.

"*Leigh*," I scolded, but she paid me no heed. Nope. My baby sister was marching right across the space on a warpath.

"You can't just wave your wallet around and order people to give up their lives, you self-centered, nepotistic sack of overpriced wine."

Ollie and I both choked on our laughter. Judging by his prolonged coughing fit, he'd mixed a bit of saliva with his humor, and even as she glared at him, Leighton smacked him across the back like he'd inhaled a grape. Greyson shot daggers in my direction, but I just shrugged, hands up defensively.

"Don't look at *her*, you psycho; look at me," Leighton snapped her fingers, and I decided I'd never been so damn proud to be a Rhodes before. Adorable little psychopath. Growing up with eleven brothers and sisters had its trials, for sure. But she didn't even have the full story and was ready to soak this immaculate basement gym with gasoline and strike a match herself. My protests be damned. Hell, Leighton and Kaia had gone full-blown retribution on one of their bullies growing up, and he ended up leaving the school for the shame of it. We were all athletes—save for Finn—but it was the twins we could count on getting red-carded and going toe-to-toe with the refs. Authority had never been a qualifier for respect in her world, and I envied that as she jerked her hand away from Ollie when he straightened, leveling Greyson with a glare capable of igniting him.

With an exasperated huff, Greyson arched a brow, looking down at the infuriated little sprite all up in his business. "Ms. Rhodes, I assume?"

"*Leighton*, you entitled prick."

"Pleased to make your acquaintance." I swore the corner of his lips quirked if I wasn't kidding myself.

"Can't say the same. And you——" she spat, whipping her face to Oliver, whose cheeks were a little flushed. "What the fuck are you doing standing by for this bullshit? You're going to let him sink three generations of effort by extorting his assistant?"

"Sissy," I pressed. "It's not extortion if I agreed to it of my free will," I insisted.

Not taking her eyes off Greyson, her fists shaking at her side, she snarled, "I. Don't. Buy it. *What did you do?*"

It was Oliver's wide, amused eyes that caught my focus as he took a step back. "This one is fucking feral."

"Have you had your pet vaccinated for rabies?" Greyson asked flatly, eyes flicking my way, mask impervious.

"*Pet!?*" Leighton shrieked, and I snatched her arm, yanking her away from him as she cocked it back like she'd deck him right in that obnoxiously pretty face.

"I like her," Ollie declared definitively to nobody in particular.

"Oh, get fucked," she spat before whirling back on Greyson. "What do you have over her? *Huh?!* Because she won't fucking tell me. And there's no way on god's green earth that my sister would marry *someone like you* unless she was blackmailed into it."

"Huh," Ollie muttered. "That's what I said."

"And I can promise you—wait, *what?*" Her eyes turned back to Ollie, and I couldn't decide where to look. At calm, cool, collected Greyson with his deceptively unaffected facade, at Ollie, whose arms fought against the fabric of his suit jacket sleeves where he crossed them over his chest, or Leighton who did, admittedly, look a little feral as her fiery eyes landed on him. Her hand had subconsciously settled on the scar on her chest as her temper ratcheted up.

Ollie shrugged. "My first thought was he had something over her, and my second was—"

"That she was blackmailing me into it," Greyson supplied in a monotone, eyes boring holes into his brother. *They* didn't know what she did or didn't know. And judging by his expectant eyes on me, he needed me to fill in the blanks.

"I told her about the allegations," I admitted. "She didn't think that was substantial enough for me to agree to marry you. She left to kick your ass, and I followed."

The briefest nod escaped him before Greyson turned those eternally calm eyes on Leighton, who looked notably less likely to bite his face off. "Well. Alessandra, Leighton, would you please join us upstairs for a nightcap?"

"So you can poison us, you robot?!" Leighton interjected, earning a broader smile from Oliver, who took all of this in his usual lighthearted form.

"Yes, thank you. That's a fantastic idea," I said over her, elbowing her in the ribs. She shot me a skeptical glare but redirected her irritated huff at Greyson.

Motioning for him to lead the way, she hissed, "Fine."

APPEASING Leighton and Ollie was a bit like diffusing a bomb. Delicate maneuvers and gentler affirmations. Greyson and I kept locking eyes in desperate attempts to convey information without speaking. While I was battling a gradually rising sense of anxious nausea, he seemed to catch on to the fact that I hadn't told her about *Thunderstrike* despite the way it burned in my veins. His entire body relaxed back into the cognac leather couch he occupied across from us. More so when he realized I'd already made her sign an NDA before we came here. Like that was a sizable enough reassurance.

He was as relaxed as you could get in a sweaty set of gym clothes, staring down your very hostile, soon-to-be sister-in-law.

Everything about Greyson's life seemed stiff and uncomfortable. The gorgeous beach house—known in the community as Hart House—was full of strategically coordinated color but sterile with its lack of personality as though he'd had it staged by a designer. The furniture sat in precise angles, beautiful but intimidating in its pristine condition. Certainly bore no Friday night pizza stains or the forlorn remnants of a glass of wine that sloshed while laughing with friends. There were no scratches from Cap's nails or worn spots where someone clearly sat more often.

I hadn't ever really cared to notice before. At first, he intimidated me despite my determination to tell him to shove it where the sun didn't shine, and then because of my distaste for him. But sitting here now, observing the ostentatious floral arrangements that likely had a four-figure price tag and the art so meticulously chosen…the space felt empty. It checked all the required boxes of shelter and reputation without fully being embraced as a home. Perfect light blue rugs lined the pale, wide-plank flooring in the hallway, where tables sat below the artwork, but there were no discarded books or magazines, no rings left from full cups of coffee hastily set aside, or dents in the corners. It was like I'd wandered into a gallery rather than occupied space. As I stared up at some modern calamity of color framed in gold filigree, I felt…*melancholy*.

Because only a heart empty of life could exist in a space so…untouched.

I was still staring up at the chaotic slashes of blues and yellows where they harshly intersected against a canvas that seemed too white when Greyson stepped up beside me.

"They gone?"

"Yeah," he murmured. "I had Arthur take Leighton home. Ollie walked across the street."

I nodded, but his hand gently settling between my shoulder blades pulled my attention to his eyes.

"That's twice in twenty-four hours, Alessandra."

I knew what he meant. Didn't need to ask. I'd kept his secret *twice*, just filling Leighton in on the arranged marriage half of this fiasco. Pursing my lips, I returned my focus to the painting. "I have ten more of those to appease, Greyson."

"If you're going to back out, now's the time to do it."

Studying those abrupt splotches of color, I asked, "You think of an alternate?" When silence was my answer, I said, "Then let's do this. But be prepared; my older siblings are even more protective than the younger ones."

He blew out a breath adjacent to a laugh. "Thought she was going to take my jugular out with her teeth."

Smiling, my gaze fell to my feet. "I wouldn't put it past her. Don't forget that." When he canted his head as if to say 'noted,' I added, "I'm sure Ollie would do the same thing for you."

"Maybe," he chuckled.

Daring a glance his way, I found those evaluative eyes doing the same. "You two are tight."

"He'd assume I got myself into the situation and likely be correct. If I were wronged in some way, he certainly wouldn't approach it head-on like that."

"I assure you, the slowly destroy your life siblings just haven't arrived yet."

"Goodie. Something to look forward to." Every nerve ending in my body tuned in to where his fingers traced over my shoulder blade until he could gently squeeze my arm. "Come on. I have something I need to show you."

Greyson led me through the house in an uncomfortable silence, his face thoughtful, and steps unhurried across the soft padded throws. I'd been here dozens of times, but never when the air felt saturated with the weight of so many unsaid things. We made it to one of his guest rooms, and he gently threw open the door. "This can be your room. I had the house cleaner pay it special attention, and she stocked the linens in the bathroom."

That sickly sensation threatening me stirred my anxiety, a writhing monster beneath my skin.

My room.

Because I had to move into this big, sterile house. Struggling to swallow, I looked around the stunning, immaculate space. The wall to my left bore white floor-to-ceiling bookshelves that kissed the chunky coastal window frame with a view of the ocean wrapped around the far wall. There were a couple of hardbacks scattered between forced-feeling pieces of décor. To my right was the door to the sizable bathroom. Oblivious to my body revolting against me, Greyson explained, "Everyone but security leaves at night, so you can stay in here once they're gone. I figure you'll keep your belongings in the owner's suite with mine to ward off suspicions most effectively. But this will be your space. Use it as you wish."

My mouth popped open as I stepped onto the lush carpet. It felt criminal to be wearing heels in here, and I glanced at my feet as I looked around with my stomach in my throat.

My. Room. Oh god, I would be living with my boss, lying to the entire world about being with him. For *three* years. Oh, god, I couldn't do this.

Before words could form, that throbbing ball in my throat turned into something far more malicious, and I bolted for the ensuite bathroom. That slowly brewing nausea I'd kept at bay while we diffused Leighton became a roaring beast I could no longer contain in my chest.

"*Alessandra?*" He barked after me, concern thick in his tone. But I couldn't stop. I was going to puke. I was going to puke all over the luxurious carpeting in the room he set aside for me today. Bless every god or goddess or ruler of the universe because I made it to the pristine porcelain bowl as the contents of my stomach roared up my throat. Leighton was a dainty puker—a ladylike ejector. Meanwhile, I threw up like someone was performing an exorcism. It wasn't quiet. It wasn't neat. Everything hurt. It was like my stomach was attempting to blow the capillaries in my face. But as I heaved again, warm hands snatched my long hair off my neck and then gently stroked over my back.

"Jesus." Another sweeping motion over my shoulders. "I've got you."

I've got you. Greyson Hart was soothing me. Somehow, that awareness sent me heaving into the toilet all over again. I was going to die plastered to the side of my boss' toilet. What a shitty way to go. Pun intended.

A frantic laugh spilled from my lips as my stomach stopped its emergency ejection. His harsh fingers kept hold of my hair as I sat back on my heels, gently tugging through it, soothing me as I caught my breath.

"I'll find a different way to swallow the press. I'm not doing this," he muttered, finally releasing my hair, although his absence was immediately resented. At least when he was touching me, I didn't feel alone in this pool of panic. "You're free and clear; just do me a favor and don't go digging. This is all on me, Ms. Rhodes." Without another word, he vanished from the space, and I sat on his cool tile floor, staring unseeingly at the white plaster across from me. He hadn't been angry that Leighton was in the loop—hadn't lashed out that I didn't contain my sister/roommate. He'd just…dealt with the aftermath. Like he'd no doubt deal with the fallout of the impending allegations. But he—

He was standing on the threshold, observing me. Gingerly, he offered me a glass of water and a washcloth, and I accepted them both, studying the man I swore for two years that I hated.

Free and clear. I was free to bow out of this. Clear from the press. At least for now.

But he wouldn't be.

Which would implicate Ollie.

Which would threaten Mattie and Beau.

The press had to have *something*, or they wouldn't have approached me so brazenly, which meant that every tool was needed for this fight. And for our red herring to work, our news had to break before theirs did. Otherwise, they would dismiss it as a cover-up, and conspiracy theories would spread.

Could I do this?

"Come on, I'll take you home," he offered, extending a steady hand.

"I suppose, if this is to work, this just became my home."

"Alessandra, I mean it. Forget the plan. I'll deal with it a different way."

"The press is about to have a field day with your company one way or another. Let's give them something to talk about."

8

You Did Vow to Disembowel Him
ALICE

Wedding Bells for Billionaire CEO?

Love in the Limelight: Greyson Hart's Assistant Sporting Mystery Ring

PDA-filled Stroll Fuels Engagement Rumors: Is America's Most Eligible Bachelor Off The Market?

From Boss To Bride: Everything You Need To Know About Alessandra Rhodes

MAX

Looking good, beautiful. You gonna fill me in?

RHYETT

If you don't answer soon, I'm booking tickets. Pick up the phone, Alice.

ELORA

So help me, god, if you don't answer someone, I'm
going to have a stroke, sissy.

HADLEE

So. Uh. Congrats? Care to bring us up to speed?

MAVERICK

This certainly gives a new meaning to slaying the
dragon.

We leaked the first photo twenty-four hours after Leighton
barged into Greyson's basement with me on her heels, and my
phone had been buzzing ever since.

It was a meticulously arranged image, made to look candid with
grain and a slight blur, shot through a plant and patio table as we
exited the limo. Me, in a sophisticated white dress, hair professionally styled—a girl could get used to the decadence of being
pampered every day. Greyson wore a signature navy Armani suit,
the jacket tossed over his arm, where he'd unbuttoned his sleeves
and rolled them to the elbow. The top button of his shirt was
undone, giving him a dashingly debonair yet disheveled vibe that
generally came with being relaxed. Not that the man knew that
word. He sure pulled it off for the camera well enough, though.

Greyson's hand was at the small of my back, his eyes on the side
of my face with deceptive endearment, lips subtly upturned in a
cocky little smile. My left hand—now sporting the world's most
ridiculous sapphire and diamond engagement ring—was adjusting
flashy sunglasses that concealed the anxiety eating my soul for
dinner. Social media sites lost their mind, with speculations that the
rock was larger than Kate Middleton's.

Royal American wedding, indeed.

By the time Friday came back around, there wasn't a gossip rag
or newspaper worth their salt that hadn't printed headlines about
the illustrious Greyson Hart, speculating that he was the one who'd
put the rock on my finger. However, we'd yet to confirm to any

member of the mob of paparazzi now planting roots in the sidewalk outside our homes and office building.

The next step? An official announcement. Which was why I now had a posse of assistants working on my face and hair like a hive of freakishly proficient bees. Their mission? Wrangle my thick, two feet of hair into a posh updo I'd never electively don, paint my skin into the perfect vogue-worthy contour that would make me look more like a skeleton than a human female because pronounced cheekbones are a fashion requirement, not a sign of malnourishment. They'd also buffed away my dip nails because my usual bold fuchsia was too much of a statement, while French tips would supposedly tell the world this small-town Alaskan had some semblance of *class*.

I wanted to be mad as I was plucked, groomed, and tweezed within an inch of my life, but the publicists had been my idea, as had the photo at the bistro. I'd been spinning the media for this man's clients for years. Now, it was his turn.

The persistent buzz of my phone drew the first sigh from my lungs as my stylists—Lina and Sandra—leaned back to survey their handiwork. Lina arched a light ginger brow as she asked, "Need to get that?"

"No," I breathed back. I knew who was calling, and she wasn't about to stop.

"She's just going to show up," Leighton drawled ominously from where she was perched in one of two armchairs like an irritated cat. I was almost entirely certain she hadn't turned the page in her thriller in at least thirty minutes.

She knew the bulk of Greyson's proposal, though not the entirety. Whatever made *his extracurriculars* worth hiding below mountains of code wasn't likely something I wanted my baby sister involved in. Personally, I highly suspected some sort of mercenary operation, although what mission would twist Greyson Hart into such a tightly wound knot, he risked his family empire…I hadn't figured out. Even as it was—mysterious operation aside—Leighton didn't hide her disapproval, and I couldn't blame her.

Lying to our family? That might just kill us both.

Worst of all? She was right.

"Maybe," I amended apologetically. My eyes darted to Elora's name, where a picture of us from her wedding illuminated my screen. Our big sister was a formidable force of nature— entrepreneur turned business coach, turned best-selling author, and soon-to-be reality television host. We usually talked almost daily.

A *week* of radio silence would have her foaming at the mouth. A week of radio silence while the media created a frenzy around my alleged engagement?

I blew every scrap of tense air from my lungs to my cheeks. The fact that the woman hadn't flown across the country and barged in here in a gorgeous pencil skirt, three-inch heels, and a bold blazer was a freaking miracle.

"I know," I mumbled, bracing myself. With a pained sigh, I swiped my phone, slid the answer button before I could talk myself out of it, and brought it to my ear.

"*Alessandra Lennon Rhodes.* Where have you been?"

"Right here, sissy."

As if she didn't hear me, she bulldozed on, "What in the *hell* is going on? Mom, James, Rhyett, and I have been calling you for *four days*. Leighton only gives us one-word answers when she bothers to pop onto the thread and refuses to answer questions about this PR nightmare. So help me god, if that no good, narcissistic miscreant has had you in that office this whole week trying to cover up these bullshit rumors spurred on by his lecherous hand on your body, I will personally see to it that the fish are particularly well fed this week."

The longer Elora snarled, the broader Leighton's smirk inched up her face, making me think of *The Grinch*—you know, the cartoon version where his hair uncurls with his smile.

"Oh good," I breathed when she finally took a beat to inhale. "So, you've seen."

"The engagement fodder? *Yeah*. I think the entire country has seen—congratulations on the debut of your face on every news column in the nation, by the way. So much for keeping a low profile as his assistant. What the hell do these people get off on, anyway?" Before I could answer, she snorted, then scoffed, "*Never mind*. Nobody with a life worth living wastes their time following around people actually doing something. Pathetic batch of parasites. Now. Why didn't you tell me Greyson's been sexually harassing you for years? How have I not seen these photos?"

I grimaced but kept my voice even. "It's not harassment if it's consensual, sissy."

"*Consensual?!*" she barked, voice reaching a decibel only dogs could hear as she pressed, "Those photos were from years ago— your hair was half a foot shorter. What business could *your boss* possibly have *touching* you? Holding your hand? And *girl*—the hand on the lower back thing all the time? What the fuck."

As it turned out, we had multiple images to choose from in that department. I'd been so busy resenting the man I hadn't noticed how often he guided me through crowds while I dug through folders in my case or hashed out details of a campaign with our admin. "He was helping me out of the car, Elly."

"Helping you—" her protest was cut off by choking like she'd inhaled saliva, which honestly was probably close to the truth. This was all bad. What in the hell was I thinking, signing on to help him, much less *marry* the bastard?

"Relax, sissy. Stress isn't good for the baby." Low blow to use my unborn nephew as a shield? Maybe. But he might be the only thing to get through to Elora Rhodes-Allen on a warpath.

Still coughing, she bit back, "Neither is an auntie that goes AWOL when the press has a field day spinning bullshit about her."

Holding my hand up, I scrunched my face in a grimace, asking the girls for a minute. Lina and Sandra both walked away. Sighing, I responded, "It's not bullshit, sissy." The line went so suspiciously quiet that I double-checked to make sure it hadn't disconnected. When her voice came through again, it was in the territory of a growl.

"What's. Not. Bullshit. Alice?"

Was it possible for each sigh to grow longer and more exasperated than the last? Because this was just the beginning, and it was already exhausting me. "Look. I would've talked to you, but the media went crazy when they caught wind of things, and I wasn't sure how to tell you guys." Dead silence. Seriously, I needed a defibrillator for my phone. "It's real, sissy. The engagement, the ring." I eyed the monstrosity perched so proudly on my finger. Only Greyson Hart could discreetly get his hands on a national monument without notice. I'd fall right to the ocean floor if I went overboard these days. "Hell, I have to do extra reps on my right side to keep my muscle mass even…sissy?"

"Sorry, I'm looking at my calendar, but *no*, it's *not* April first."

"Very funny."

"*I'm* very funny. What are you playing at? Last month, you were drunkenly threatening his life at my bachelorette party because he wouldn't let you enjoy your trip home."

Leighton's delighted snicker from the armchair had my eyes snapping to her, and her glee earned an ensuing middle finger. Which, of course, sent her guffawing into her hands.

"And you and Broderick bicker like cats and dogs," I argued feebly.

"*Playfully* bickering with a man who loves and respects me is not the same thing as actively wishing another human would meet an unfortunate end for two consecutive years, and you know it."

"That's a bit of an exaggeration."

"You did vow to disembowel him."

Point taken. "Okay, so we got off on the wrong foot, but that doesn't mean we've stayed that way."

"Got off!? *Got off on the wrong foot?* Try six hundred consecutive wrong feet."

"Look, sissy. I can't stay on the phone——"

"Alice," she cut me off. "We're worried about you. You've gotta give us something."

Sucking down air like my life depended on it, I steeled my spine and declared, "Things change, El. *People* change. You and Brod are evidence of that. Now. I'm a twenty-eight-year-old woman, and did it occur to you that I might not be calling because I knew how you'd react and didn't want to dim the excitement of this chapter of my life with your judgment?"

I could practically hear her mouth gape in the silence as the lies bittered on my tongue. While guilt slithered through my intestines like a snake, I held to the statement's truth. Of all my siblings, Elora would be the hardest to convince.

Because, of all my siblings, *she* was the one I turned to to bitch about him most frequently. She knew better because I told her everything. Which meant I had to make it worse before I could make it better.

"Look, I appreciate that you want to protect me, but I'm not a baby anymore, and I can make my own decisions."

"Of course…Alice, you…you could've talked to me if things were changing. I…I just hope you know what you're doing. Blink twice if he has you held against your will."

"I'll blink twice if things go belly up, I swear. And then you and James *and* Pax can fly in and play vigilante all you want." Probably poor word choice, but that was an unfortunate side effect of just spitting out what was top of mind as panic and guilt did the horizontal tango in my chest.

"I love you, sissy."

"Love you, too." Slowly, I disconnected, steadying myself with a deep breath as I looked around at the exquisite bathroom Greyson set aside for me. Everything about this space was elegant. Luxuriously thick rugs adorned the marble floor that was so sparkly, I wasn't sure if they'd legitimately crushed diamonds into the stone, beautiful pale blue patterned drapes, and a view worth selling a few organs for. The ornate vanity was reminiscent of movies set in Cape Cod or Martha's Vineyard.

But it certainly wasn't *mine*.

I'd been enjoying the excuse of returning to my apartment every night, but that all ended tonight.

Tonight, Greyson's ridiculously expensive movers would bring in my things, and we'd officially confirm the suspicions we'd planted with an announcement of our own and a formal portrait on his expansive deck. Today, the performance of my life would begin. All I could do was pray I'd sell it well.

Women had married for less.

It's not like I had any legitimate prospects. I honestly couldn't remember the last time I'd been interested in a man. And the 'swipe right' scene was just not for me. In my experience in a world determined to label me as odd, solitude was a far more comforting companion than forcing on a mask to earn the approval of others, much less trick a man into loving the idea of you. Eventually, my facade would tire and crack, leaving him with the real thing. The mask could delay rejection, but it could never eliminate it.

Hell, I kept reminding myself that women had married for pettier reasons at the whims of men much worse than Greyson Hart. At least, that's what I was telling myself as Matilda emerged from a bathroom cabinet.

"Can we get pizza?" she asked as if Leighton hadn't just rocketed to her feet like she was prepared to bolt for her life. Mattie's spontaneous appearances had lost their effect over the last few years, although this one was particularly untimely.

"Aren't you supposed to be home?" I lamented without any real bite to my tone. If I was honest, her peculiarities were rather endearing.

She wrinkled her nose. "Nanny quit again."

"Mattie," I scolded. "What happened this time?"

"Don't look at me; look at Beau."

"Where is Beau?"

"Upstairs with Daddy and Uncle Grey." She shrugged nonchalantly before liquefying onto the floor like a limp ribbon. "*I need pepperoni.*"

"I'm sorry," Leighton blinked. "You're Greyson's *niece?*"

"Matilda Hart," she supplied dreamily before releasing a pent-up sigh and adding, "at your service. *Technically*, I'm asking one of you to be at my service because Daddy took my phone away again, and I need someone to order dinner."

I pinched the bridge of my nose, trying very hard not to burst out laughing at the ridiculousness of it all. Which grew harder as Mattie extended her little hand as if to shake, and Leighton accepted with narrowed eyes.

"Leighton Rhodes. I'm Alice's sister."

"I could tell by the nose. And the hair. And the skin. You have pretty skin in your family. Did you know that skin is the largest organ, yet it's the one most people neglect?"

"I did, actually," Leighton answered, a tentative smile stretching over her cheeks.

"And did you know that it absorbs toxins within thirty seconds? I think that's why middle-class housewives die so much—all the bleach and chemicals, you know?" Her little nose wrinkled with distaste despite her tone staying entirely matter-of-fact.

Chuckling, Leighton pulled her further onto the floor before hoisting her to her feet. "Well. That's a very intriguing theory. What other theories do you have bouncing around in there?"

"So many. But first, I'll show you the good pizza places online."

Leighton's laugh trailed back to me as she was towed away by the strangest preteen I'd ever had the pleasure of adoring. But my amusement was cut short by the figure in the threshold.

Greyson. Leaning against the doorframe in his signature navy suit.

"They seemed to hit it off rather quickly," he noted with amusement.

"Yeah," I agreed. "Leighton's always been awesome with kids, and she's never been easy to rattle."

"Mattie will love that." He pushed off the frame and stepped into my bathroom, which is when I noticed the long, slender black box in his hands, my stomach somersaulting. "I have something for you."

"Oh?" I managed, incapable of straightening my ducks. Truthfully, I wasn't sure I even had ducks anymore—just a whole blender of chaos in my skull. The entire scenario was still too surreal.

Me in Greyson's house.

Me, engaged to my boss.

Me, sitting on a pedestal, with professional stylists catering to my appearance, and Greyson Hart being kind for the sixth consecutive day because I finally—albeit unwittingly—had the man by the balls.

"I need you to promise me something," he said sternly, stepping behind me until our eyes locked in the mirror before me, his hands fiddling out of view with the subtle slide of cardboard and fabric.

"Another demand—*why, I'm shocked, Mr. Hart,*" I replied, bringing a hand to my chest. The irritation in his eyes was more satisfying than it should've been. He'd been nagging me all week to call him Greyson, but I liked it better this way. Regardless of the frustration that evidently earned a long, steady exhale as though that could replenish his control, his hands came around either side of my neck with a reverent kind of gentleness. I was still enamored that they were calloused, even though the man spent sixty hours a week at his desk. What was he doing in those off hours out of sight? Rough fingers softly slid over my clavicle, and my eyes found a delicate gold chain glinting in the mirror as he wrapped it around my neck to fasten it.

My fingers settled against the beautiful gold cross at its center. I'd never been religious, but the piece was intricately woven—art in the form of ancient sacrifice.

"You'll have to stop flinching when I touch you if people are going to believe you're in love with me, Ms. Rhodes."

"You're going to have to stop calling me by my last name, *Greyson*."

Chuckling, he gave the necklace a little tug. "Touché. Now, I need you to wear this, always. If something happens to me, it will lead you to the necessary answers." Gently, he skimmed over the line of my neck, hazel eyes watching my reaction in the glass as I fought back the need to close my eyes at the touch. It wasn't a flinch. Not that he needed to know that.

"I've never been one to pray to be saved."

"Some secrets are hidden in plain sight."

Curious phrasing. "Is it a tracker or something?"

"Or something." One hand settled on my shoulder, giving me a gentle squeeze, in prompting or reassurance, I wasn't sure. The other trailed back down my neck before he stepped away abruptly and waved in the stylists, who had just bustled into the bedroom beyond the doorway with coffees in hand. "Wear it for me?"

I nodded, unsure of the significance or whether my words would hold the gusto I needed. There were so many questions, so few answers.

Greyson lifted his chin to the girls before curtly greeting them, "Lina, Sandra." He wound one of my face-framing curls around his finger, and I didn't have to fake how my breath got trapped in my chest. "What exactly are we going for with this…look? *Prom?*" he asked, eyes on mine, which meant he didn't see how both of their faces drained of color before their mouths caught up.

"Timeless," Lina exclaimed, then added, "Sophisticated."

"Elegant?" Sandra supplied, hopefully, more a question than an answer.

He grunted, the sound blatantly displeased. When I turned to face him, his expression was pensive. "Let's tone it down, shall we?"

"Tone it down?" Lina squeaked, rushing to set her coffee on the counter and reclaiming her tools as if donning armor for battle.

"I'm not my father," he stated firmly. When two sets of round eyes blinked back at him, he clarified with a sigh, "This is giving first lady, White House *Barbie*. Nothing brings me to my knees faster than this woman with her hair down. Let's ease up on the Skeletor cheekbones, and I'd like to see the freckles over her nose. I happen to love that she's not waifish." Gently brushing a knuckle down the side of my face, he smiled softly, evidently unaware that my entire body was tracking that point of contact. "She should look like herself."

"Yes, sir," Sandra blurted, diving for the sink like her life depended on it. I guessed in this world, keeping Greyson Hart happy might be the same thing.

"Of course!" Lina promised, immediately shoving her hands into my hair to start pulling pins. "Sorry, Mr. Hart."

"You'll make it right," he assured with a gentle smile. The man walked from the room like he hadn't just sent three grown women scrambling for their composure.

Albeit mine was the result of a very different kind of fear.

GREYSON

THE FAMILIAR RASPY laugh of Lucas Riviera broke through the conversations of my staff as they rushed about readying the venue for our engagement party the following week. Luke was a detective—one of two people outside of the operation who knew the full scope of what *Thunderstrike* did. He'd started as an adversary and, within a few months, had grown into a friend as our relationship became one of mutual respect. He was also why city brass would monitor the engagement party alongside my security personnel. As though he'd checked off every box on the list of stereotypes, the man strutted into my building like he owned it, wearing a black leather jacket. His hair was slicked back, and his button-up strained over an extra twenty-five pounds in his belly, which he swore he would lose—thus refusing to update his wardrobe.

I'd been working with the man for three years, and neither had changed.

"Hart! You son of a bitch," he barked, announcing his presence to my entire staff as they prepared for the evening. The man didn't have a subtle bone in his body, but he was shrewd and had integrity wreathing every action. I studied his open body language and the slow smile stretching his stubbled cheeks. Sincere enough. Opting to return his greeting, I handed back the seating chart the event planner had been explaining and turned to meet his approach. Yanking me into a one-sided hug and slapping my back, he said, "I had my suspicions, but you are one tough motherfucker to read."

"We kept it quiet for obvious reasons," I simply supplied, jerking my head toward the bar, where they'd ensured my favorite bottles were well stocked. "Whiskey?"

"Nah, man. Thank you, though."

"I insist," I said, settling a hand on his shoulder. Stockily built, Luke was all of five-foot-eleven but took up space like a brick wall. "Let me get you something."

"Unless it's a cola, you're outta' luck. Just got the lay of the land from Mike, so my guys are up to speed."

"Good deal." I motioned toward the open terrace, overlooking the putting greens and beach below. "How have you been?"

"Better than I deserve. Gotta say, I expected a call before the press caught wind."

"I intended one, but things…escalated."

"You knock her up or something?"

"Nothing like that." It was in that precise moment that Alessandra stepped onto the balcony from a side room like an ethereal dream. At five-foot-ten, she towered over most other women, bustling to get things in order. A curve-hugging white lace dress highlighted sinfully feminine lines; her long sheet of shining chocolate hair was straight today with salon-level perfection. My gold necklace adorned her skin for seven days running, much to my satisfaction. She wore it obediently through public appearances, dinners, private evenings with our publicists, and countless meetings. I'd noticed her study it a time or two, but if she'd noted anything peculiar, she'd yet to say anything.

I just wished she'd emerge from her rooms every now and then. It was like a ghost haunting my halls—food not where I'd left it in the fridge, the occasional pair of shoes by the door, but otherwise, a heavy silence had filled the space once the movers left. She attended our meetings and spent longer hours at the office to which I was dying to return, but she seemed to have decided avoiding me was the answer.

No wife of mine would spend her days hiding in her home. It would have to change, but it didn't seem like she'd make it easy on me.

Sharp gray eyes surveyed the greens, the decor being meticulously placed, then softened to return smiles as staff recognized the queen in their midst. She held herself like royalty—unbothered by her height and sure in her observations. If she gave a single flying fuck about status, the woman would wear wealth exceptionally well.

That was one thing that caught my attention. Alessandra didn't speak unless her words held value, kindness, or humor. Didn't act unless she was certain. It's why I knew that if anyone could pull this off with me, it was my begrudging right-hand woman. She could hate me all she wanted; it didn't negate that she was damn good at her job and even better at trusting her blunt intuition. Which, luckily for me, had at least hinted that I was innocent and, somehow, despite her distaste, worth helping. "Sometimes, you just know."

"She put up with your stubborn ass for the last two years, I guess that's as good as it gets." Luke chuckled darkly, but my eyes tracked my soon-to-be partner as she slowly studied the preparations across the ballroom, as if she had taken notes of the details naturally. "Damn, Hart. You got some drool on your chin. Gotta say, I don't know how I didn't see it before. You're so obvious."

His observations didn't sit well with me but worked in our favor.

Jerking my head toward the open double doors, I said, "Come say hi."

"Not in the habit of taking orders."

I deadpanned. "Stop your bitching and come say hello under a new pretense."

"You could've used charm school, asshole."

"Know a lot about that, do you, Rivera?"

"The chief of police has more niceties than you do."

"Which is why he deals with the public, and I don't," I supplied.

He snorted. "Thank god for that. The irony of you in PR will never get old."

"Don't get used to it. That will be Alessandra's role shortly."

"Now, who the fuck is *Alessandra*?" His low chuckle ran nails down an invisible chalkboard. "That some backward pet name thing you have going? You're the only bastard I've heard full name her."

"Because she's mine and deserves a title as elegant as she is."

"Jesus Christ, you've got it bad." His sentiment made me realize exactly how much conviction I'd put into those words despite the way they sounded absurd in my ears. *Mine*. I'd never had a person that felt like mine. "This whole time?"

"No," I answered honestly. "But it's rare for me to underestimate someone, and she's bested me at every turn. If you'll excuse me." With that, I abandoned Luke to make a beeline toward the most intelligent woman in the room, where she'd been cornered by the event planner outside. Her smile was nearly blinding as she laughed, listening to the woman's concerns. Eyes full of stars, Alessandra glanced at me across the terrace and through the ballroom, a timid smile growing as I approached.

For a moment, as my staff hurried to step out of my way, and vendors carrying teetering platters and décor rushed to do the same, I wondered what it would feel like to have someone look at me that way authentically. For a woman to light up because I was walking toward her. She was convincing, wearing her role well, despite what I assumed was a brutal clash of her morals.

Her need to help and her hatred for dishonesty.

As she'd predicted, her family hadn't taken the news well. Less so when our official engagement photos released.

The fan favorite was an image of her standing beside the rail of my balcony, with me crowding her against it. We were both laughing. I could still feel her body nestled against mine, feel the slight shake of her hand as she settled it on my chest and looked up at me under too-thick lashes. Could remember exactly how fucked up I felt knowing I was about to derail this young woman's entire future for my own benefit.

I'd meant what I said. She was wasted as an assistant. Wasted in my company at all, to be frank. At least her new title was more fitting. But it wasn't enough.

Alessandra Rhodes was the master of a mind destined to bring men to their knees. I'd known it for a while now but wasn't sure how or when I'd get to use it. Her ability to appease debutantes and executives with an arsenal of personal knowledge was just a parlor trick.

As I watched her laugh, the sun bouncing off her warm complexion, I remembered that some corner of my mind had logged away the fact that her touch didn't make me want to hide.

Women and I had a turbulent history. Frankly, I'd take the snake every time if I had to choose between sticking my hand in a rattlesnake hole and braving the dating world.

But Alessandra didn't want my money. Didn't give a shit about the fact that I bore my father's last name or was now at the head of an American empire. She'd been honest in her distaste for me as I offered her a world most women would kill to get a foothold in. Her help was contingent on my innocence and my determination to provide for my niece's legacy.

And I'd been waiting for the opportunity to see if my fascination with her faded. Only, as I finally closed the gap on the terrace, I realized not an ounce of it had dissipated. The woman was immune to status. I just had to pray her steadfast morality would also apply to our cause.

Clearing my throat to announce my presence to the vendors chatting with her, I stepped into their circle, hands tucked into my pockets. "Apologies, ladies, but I need to steal my fiancé for a moment before the crowd arrives."

Her gaze on mine overshadowed their pleasant laughter, even as both women gushed their understanding with, "Of course, Mr. Hart," and, "So happy for you, Mr. Hart."

"Thank you both," I said, nodding and shifting into her space as her throat bobbed, big gray eyes looking up to mine. My hands wrapped around her biceps, our bodies pulling together as I sensed the scrutiny of so many eyes on the couple of the hour. I hated few things as much as I loathed growing up in the spotlight. Thirty-five years, and that hadn't changed. I couldn't imagine what it felt like to her, being thrust into it so suddenly. "You alright?"

Tone saccharine-sweet and smile cemented in place; she prattled on at a speed that put auctioneers to shame. "I can't move my face for fear of wrinkling the layers of cosmetics; there is a small knife disguised as a bobby pin tearing the skin from my scalp where they put this barrette in; your stylist put me in heels as if I needed to be *taller*, four people have asked me if I'm pregnant which either means they're socially incompetent or this dress makes me look fat, and my big brother called to tell me not to throw my life away and that men get lost at sea all the time."

I disguised my laugh by sipping my whiskey and hiding the expression behind my glass. She reminded me of Mattie. "This new blunt side of you has me wondering if the demure woman in the office beside mine ever existed."

The spark in her eyes and the subtle crinkle beside them said this smile was authentic. "The doormat was an expected pretense."

"And the ball buster?"

"A survival tactic. You have to know what you're signing up for. You might have big house energy now, but wait until I'm manic because I chugged pre-workout."

"Have you always spoken so candidly?"

"No," she admitted, cocking her head. "Spent most of my life silent. But look at where that got me."

Engaged to a Hart. That fact was instantly reduced to a sentence instead of a godsend. That should irritate me, but it didn't. Actually, I was rather amused.

Her belongings had been moved and sorted for her, and her car upgraded to a limo with a driver or her pick of Teslas, luxury SUVs, or sedans. Clothes had been neatly folded, sorted, and put away by a staff that sang her praises because she memorized their names and made eye contact while they talked to her. A private chef occupied her new kitchen five hours a day. And she dismissed it because her reality was arranged rather than stumbled into with some tacky meet cute like the books she read. I knew countless power couples who'd started out as mergers rather than romances. Leave it to Alessandra to make it seem outrageous.

"You move like a god damned greyhound," Luke noted, finally catching up with frustration carving his strong brow.

"And you shuffle like a bulldog." I pointed out, earning an honest to god giggle from Alessandra and a glare from Luke as he ran a hand through thinning brown hair. "Alessandra, you remember Detective Rivera?"

"From the Sullivan case. Yes, of course. Nice to see you——"

"Luke," he cut in." Please call me Luke. We're friends now, Mrs. Hart." His use of the moniker sent her cheeks flaming, a timid smile on her face as those eyes dropped to her feet. "I'd blush if I was crazy enough to marry this guy, too," he teased, hooking his thumb over his shoulder toward me.

"You underestimate your friend if you feel that way," she countered, words taking me by surprise. Perhaps she'd wear this role better than I even anticipated. That or she hated me less than she let on, which would be preferable given the proximity we'd be in until this mess was resolved.

"I'm not in the habit of flirting with men—might give people the wrong impression," I stated, eyes only for her. I liked the smile my stupid, understated joke earned. Liked the way those blue-grays ignited with amusement. The way some long-buried flame in my chest seemed to wake in response.

"Wouldn't want to feed the stalkarazzi fodder."

"Of course not," I agreed, smiling as she did, knowing full well our entire arrangement was designed to do exactly that. It had been our plan, of course, to leak one morsel of gossip at a time. The ring. Perfect photo announcement. This party. Wedding date speculations. She had each piece timed precisely.

"Ahh, there's Mike. I'm going to go coordinate," Luke cut in, pulling our focus as he nodded to us in turn. "Congrats to you both. Really. Thrilled about the news."

"Say hi to Marie," I replied, reaching out a hand in thanks.

He shook it quickly. "Will do, Hart. Will do."

Alessandra looped her arm in mine when he'd gone and angled us toward the venue entrance. "Why do I feel like there's more than one reason you reintroduced me to Detective Rivera."

"Because trust is challenging to find within government institutions, and he's one of the few you could safely turn to."

"Ahh," she said simply, as though that made perfect sense.

We stepped through the expansive double doors onto the ballroom floor as a coastal breeze shifted her silky hair. Gently tucking a side behind her ear, I slid my arm out and down to her hand. "Tonight will be a whirlwind," I noted, squeezing her fingers gently.

"Nothing we're not used to."

"Except you'll be the center of their focus this time."

"I can handle myself."

"I know," I agreed, nodding. "Tell me I have a phone call waiting in the office if you need an excuse to leave."

"You don't need to look out for me."

"But I will," I countered. Abandoning my hold on her fingers, I ran my own up the length of her lace-shrouded arm. "And Alessandra, one more thing."

"Yes?" she asked softly.

"The dress fits you beautifully. You're a mirage in ivory. *They're asking* because they can't fathom a woman as kind as you would take pity on a man like *me*."

"*HAVE YOU NO SENSE OF DUTY?*" My uncle's snarled demand pulled my attention from the cuff link I was fastening. With guests set to arrive any minute, I was well past the curtain call and needed to make sure I pulled my weight tonight. Alessandra looked radiant, so I needed to attempt to match.

We'd made it through week one of this charade virtually unscathed, save for a lecture from the head of HR, an ungodly amount of paperwork, and out-of-pocket comments from basement-dwelling internet trolls.

Still no whisper of the allegations that pigeonholed us in the first place.

Perhaps ignoring Reggie's calls all week wasn't my brightest choice, but the man had *just* touched down in Paris the day after the board meeting. We should have been free of him for a few weeks yet.

Door slamming behind him, Reggie tore into the room like the devil himself. It took every ounce of my control not to audibly sigh as I flicked my eyes up to his very dignified stomp through the bathroom of "the groom's suite" in the venue.

He looked like a petulant toddler with raging cholesterol and a high likelihood of an aneurysm based on the pulsing vein in his forehead.

"Evening, Reggie," I drawled, arching a brow as his face flushed a promising shade of tomato.

"Don't *evening me*," he growled, snatching my cell from where I'd discarded it on the counter. He swiped up the screen before feigning shock. "Oh, so it does work, and you just didn't deign to answer."

"It's been a busy week." My even tone somehow elicited another shade of crimson in his face. That's the thing about maneuvering egotistical pricks regularly: the sooner you can regulate your emotions, the sooner you own every hothead in your proximity. My Uncle included. For fun, I reached for my other cuff link without shifting a muscle in my face.

"I'll say," he spluttered. "Such an absolute disgrace. This is *not* what I meant in that office last week."

"If you came to my engagement party to protest, I do believe the minister will request objections at the ceremony. For now, I'm a bit preoccupied fastening this."

"You little shit."

"Care to help?" Glancing up to him in the mirror and seeing that seething scowl, I arched my brows and added, "*No?*" I shrugged, refocusing on my sleeve while maintaining a careful mask of calm.

Reginald and Carlisle Hart were birds of a feather. Mean when drunk—which was often—and convinced they were god's gift to business. My father and his brother were likely two of the bastards who coined the term 'shark.' How either of them secured the cherubs they called wives, I couldn't comprehend for the life of me.

My indifference obvious, he opted for a new tactic, leaning onto the counter and crossing his arms over his chest. "You've betrayed everything your father and I worked for. That your *grandfather* worked for."

"The company is currently sailing at record profit. Employee retention is at an all-time high. Stock is selling for double what it was before Dad died. If you're making a point, you're doing it poorly." Finishing the second cuff, I straightened my spine, adjusting my collar in the mirror as he sputtered in fury.

"I said Royal wedding. *Royal*, Greyson. *Not rabble.* What were you thinking?"

The first drip of cortisol took a swan dive off a very tall cliff into my bloodstream. Keeping my breathing steady, I raised my eyes to glare in his direction. "Lower your voice."

"We raised you better than this. Ollie demonstrated just how easy it is for some whore to open her legs and destroy your foundation, but you're just going to run off and do the same thing?"

"Lower. Your. Voice." Mine had dropped into some kind of growl. Likening Alessandra to Carly was a vile overstep. One had brains, drive, integrity, and class, and one was a bottom feeder with impressive synthetic tits.

"You might've gotten too big for your britches the last few years, but don't you forget how quickly you could throw this all away to get your dick wet."

Pinning him with a glare, I bit back, "If you can't control your mouth, I am not beyond having security escort you out. Personally, I think the board has enough on their plates this week, don't you?"

"*Head of PR*," he scoffed. "You decide to mock that title before or after you had her on her knees for you?"

Anger has always been the easy solution. The effortless solution. A weak man can mask their anger as strength, using brute force to intimidate their way through life. A weaker man would have grabbed him by his fat throat and put him in his place.

Power is found in control. *Strength* exists in the chasm between animal instinct and self-discipline.

And so, I breathed.

No matter how much I wanted to silence him.

I would not throat-punch my uncle…even if he deserved it. "I will not have you ruin this for my bride, but before you spew more vile words, do consider that your great niece is likely stashed inside a cubby somewhere, hearing every single thing that you say."

His lip curled. He loved Mattie, but even that might be a stretch in my attempt to bring him to heel. "Start talking."

"Not much in the mood for conversation. The ballroom will be full of willing participants shortly, however."

"Is this a game to you?" he demanded, clearly infuriated by my lack of outburst.

"I don't waste my time with cheap entertainment."

"Greyson," he scolded, shoulders slumping in a sudden wave of exasperation. "A man of your stature cannot just run off and marry his assistant. Suitable alliances are forged for years—and with people of equitable caliber."

"What do you know of Alessandra's *caliber*?" I asked, sliding my hands into my pockets and turning to face him.

"That she has none," he hissed. "You're squandering your one opportunity to elevate our name. To merge with an empire just as advantageous as ours." He threw an arm back at the bathroom door.

"What is this, 1312? We don't need to marry for advantage. You're being ridiculous."

"And you're being shortsighted. That girl will never fit in here."

"*That woman* is the first to look at me for me and not our name. She has more than earned my respect, and if you could think logically instead of flying off the cuff when I step outside the lines of your plan for me, I think you'd love her, too. And, I'm not sure if you've noticed, but I don't fit in our circle, either."

"All the more reason to select a woman who *thrives*. Let her plan your parties and forge relationships. *She*—" he wielded the empty glass in his white-knuckled fist back toward the ballroom, "was raised gutting fish and *bonding* with *bears*. She doesn't belong here. Never has. Never will. *Marrying her* shows me just how little you think of our previously pristine family lineage."

"Alessandra possesses more substance in her left pinky than those brainless inflatables parading around in their daddy's jewels will ever have."

"Alessandra, much like Carly, is after a favorable prenup, my boy." This time, his ice clinked in his glass as he pointed it at me. "That's what all of them are after."

"She's different," I ground out, trying to breathe away the red clouding my vision.

"That's what they all say," he scoffed, tossing his free hand up, face spectacularly red.

"Reggie!" I barked, desperate to keep the rapidly dissolving hold I had on my temper. "She *is* different. All those things you criticize are traits I happen to adore. She grew up humble—which, unfortunately for me, means she's far more impressed with a work ethic and dedication to family than she'll ever be by a fat wallet or name in print."

"I should have known when you kicked me out of your office that she had her claws in you," he sneered. "You're both subtle, I'll give you that." He shook his head, upper lip curling. "Once she carries your seed, she'll turn tail and run. These lower-class women are overpriced surrogates, nothing more."

Lunging into his space, it took all my control not to smash his face in. One hundred easy ways to kill a man and none of them could get me out of here in one piece. Not with the bustling venue just outside the cracked-open door.

I wanted to growl like some kind of beast and shove his head through the nearest wall. *Needed to*. My hands started shaking as my body geared up for a fight that couldn't come. Instead, I sneered down at him, relishing in my extra four inches as I used his lapel to yank him closer before straightening it as I gritted out, *"Get. Out."*

"Excuse me?"

"Uncle or not," I growled, dusting invisible lint from his shoulders before sliding down his jacket and giving it a quick tug. "Chairman or not. You will *not* come into my venue, insult *my bride* and my judgment, and then indulge in *my* food and booze. Get. Out."

"Mark my words," he declared, jamming his sausage of a finger into my chest. "You'll regret this. This is a mistake." He threw up his hands as he walked away. "I can't stand by and watch you marry some gold digger filling your head with lies."

"Then don't."

"Excuse me?"

"Don't *watch*, then," I over-enunciated every word, satisfied as his nostrils flared. He looked a breath away from dropping dead, and not for the first time, some cruel, vindictive part of me wished he would. His absence would certainly make my life easier. "I didn't have an invitation printed for you anyway." I shooed him away, teeth still grinding. "If you'll excuse me, I have a party to attend."

9

The Help Talk

ALICE

It was the engagement party of my nightmares.

Every little girl grows up dreaming about *Prince Charming* whisking them away to live their fairytale. Even those of us who were closer acquainted with mud, briny water, and the reek of fish than we were designer bags and pools of silk.

My teenage visions looked like a mountaintop meadow overgrown with violet lupine. A handful of friends and family gathered in the tall, wild grasses of Mistyvale, overlooking the black rock cliffs and the rumbling gray ocean below.

As for an engagement party? If we bothered with the formality, it would've been greasy burgers or a fish fry in the local pool hall, filled with my siblings, cousins, and so much laughter that my cheeks hurt.

Instead, I was passed from one insufferable blue blood to another, like the latest commodity in a ballroom, more social statement than venue. The miles of shimmering white and gold marble reflected ostentatious chandeliers where they dripped diamonds like collected spring rain.

But this demand for my focus was just the beginning. The first wave of guests, clamoring for any morsel of gossip they could say they had first. No wonder these events were always open bar. You'd have to be inebriated to enjoy it.

Desperate for a break, I excused myself to the bathroom and skirted around the perimeter of the social melee. Luckily for me, years of being a nobody made me exceptionally good at evading their eyes, and I slunk into the hallway without being noticed. As the eighth of twelve, I was used to being the one nobody thought twice about.

Jeanne and Rhyett were always the high achievers, casting shadows so long none of us had a chance to compare.

Jameson always got into trouble, while Elora *had* to be the center of the show and the loudest voice in any debate.

Axel had been a super easy kid until he saw the attention they got compared to the rest of us. His life was notably better once he started boxing and playing hockey, but he'd always been the one smiling while he self-destructed.

Paxton was the athlete from the time he could toddle. Come to think of it, I was pretty sure El said he took his first steps with a ball in his hand.

This left Hadlee, me, and Finn as awkward middle children. We were so preoccupied with trying to make life easier for our over-whelmed mother that our actual personalities got lost in translation.

The twins were the spunky ones, and Maverick took the title of the designated family baby—i.e., spoiled rotten punk.

The perk to being the forgotten 'easy' daughter was that I was just as easily forgotten in crowds. I dipped my chin and melted into the chaos, dodging bodies like traffic cones as I navigated the hallway.

All the air left my lungs in tandem with the tension in my shoulders.

I'd made it halfway back to the ostentatious bridal suite when a familiar raised voice caught my attention. *Reggie.* Of course, the old ass would fly back from France just to make an appearance.

With a sigh, I glanced around and spotted the groom's room door cracked open. As I inched closer to discern his words, my breath caught on my ribs like lace on barbed wire.

"I said Royal wedding. *Royal*, Greyson. *Not rabble.*"

Who the fuck was he calling rabble? My family might have built our legacy on the backs of blue-collar men, but they were the best men I knew. Far better than the entitled children masquerading as adults in that ballroom. Where I came from, not a soul in town didn't know the last name Rhodes.

"*What were you thinking?*"

"Lower your voice," Greyson uttered in an unaffected monotone.

"We raised you better than this. Ollie demonstrated just how easy it is for some whore to open her legs and destroy your foundation, but you're just going to run off and do the same thing?"

"Lower. Your. Voice."

The bridge of my nose burned as my mouth fell open. Frozen outside the door, I wrapped an arm around my ribs as my other hand pressed to my lips. *Come on*, I pled internally. *Say something.*

"You might've gotten too big for your britches the last few years, but don't you forget how quickly you could throw this all away to get your dick wet."

Nope.

That was enough for me. Repulsed, I reared away from the door, glancing around and relieved to see the hallway was empty. Briefly warring between opening the door to tell off the piece of shit that sat at the head of our board and fleeing, I landed on the latter.

My eyes burned as I retreated to the bridal suite on the quietest steps I could manage in these ridiculous heels.

Rabble.

I wasn't naïve enough to believe the respect our family name garnered in Mistyvale would translate here, but I hadn't realized how easily I would be equated to trash after years of serving their company.

My hands flew to my mouth the moment the door closed behind me. Leaning my back into it for support, I closed my eyes and pulled in a long breath.

Reginald Hart did not deserve my tears. Neither did Greyson, for that matter. In no universe would either of them have the satisfaction of seeing me rattled. I pulled in breaths until my hands stopped shaking, used the restroom, washed my hands with the water set on the coldest setting, and steeled my spine.

There was no going back now—we were already public knowledge. With that in mind, I returned to the party.

Over the next few hours, countless selfies were snapped with forced, chic smiles. These men might look like they'd been peeled from the pages of magazines, but like Reggie, they countered the appeal with a general lack of consideration for anyone or anything but the bottom line and who they could swindle to advance it.

The women, in my humble opinion, were even worse. Like Oliver's ex-wife, they were out on the prowl. In a room full of modern-day kings, they needed only to trick one into bed, get lucky enough to carry their baby, and saving face would come with a healthy check and an NDA, *after the paternity test, of course.*

Their exhausting vitriol about dress size, the latest designers, and Emerald Bay's most eligible bachelors—including either oblivious or tasteless remarks about *my brother*—had run me out of patience in the first hour. The second had me rooting for the Brioni-wearing man boisterously bickering with a brunette snake in Prada heels that cost more than most Americans' paychecks. But their entertaining scuffle ended when security escorted them both out, much to my disappointment.

Pity, Greyson had said. What an interesting choice of words. One that made more and more sense the longer I was in a room with people who suddenly believed I was their peer rather than an underling to bark orders at and then forget just as quickly.

Much like the day of the photo session, Greyson had dropped the compliment, lifted my hand, and pressed my fingers to his lips with chivalrous formality before turning and vanishing into the organized chaos of party prep. It would have been the picture-perfect shot if a camera had been around. Some corner of my brain noted that he'd said it *without* an audience. The idea of it being authentic was even more haunting than hearing him claim *nothing brings me to my knees faster than this woman with her hair down.*

But then…why didn't he defend me? The man had me more confused than a zebra confronted with a referee.

While I'd been attending the notorious Hart brothers' parties beside Greyson for years, he was right; this *was* different. Being here as his assistant had been like wrapping myself in an invisibility cloak —not worth their time or energy. But the cloak had been stripped away, and I stood there in my lace dress, and the admittedly beautiful Jimmy Choo's Greyson's stylist selected, suddenly in the spotlight.

Everyone, no matter their social bracket, was clamoring for some nugget of information—about me, my family, the relationship with Greyson, how he proposed if we'd set a date or picked a location.

I was a small-town girl at heart with a huge family.

Our relationship developed slowly, during long nights spent poring over contracts while sharing pots of coffee and trips overseas, but it came to a climax last year in Paris.

He proposed on our favorite beach, and his German Shepard, Captain, wore a bow tie.

Women I'd met dozens of times at galas and luncheons suddenly deigned to remember my name as they attacked with mind-dizzying persistence.

"Oh, I bet your gown will be beautiful," Julianne gushed, looking a little worse for wear after one too many glasses of champagne and a recently finalized divorce from husband number three. "Delilah Jean is absolutely to die for," she added with a hiccup, not seeming to notice—or care—as she steadied herself on my forearm. "And Grey wouldn't allow you to buy off the rack, after all."

Grey. I hated that she felt comfortable enough to address him by his family's nickname.

"Of course not," Camilla added authoritatively. She was the daughter of an oil baron, her southern twang alive and well, no doubt aided by the martini sloshing in her hand. She eyed me up and down skeptically before adding, "He'll have a bit of work cut out for him, I'm sure, just bringing you up to speed."

It was a simple fact. Not slung like an insult but still insulting in her simple patronizing assessment and a passive-aggressive reminder of my status. Legally speaking, I was engaged to one of the wealthiest men in the country, and yet I'd never felt more like scum.

I pursed my lips, canting my head before saying, "Some men aren't in the habit of finding women to work on so much as falling for those whose depth exceeds a pothole." My smile grew as her confusion did. Probably shouldn't have said it. But honestly. How many insults should a woman turn her cheek to before standing up for herself?

Rabble.

Has Greyson scheduled your boob job yet? A-cups are so 1999.

Oh, I have a surgeon that can do something about your nose.

Your face is pretty, just much too long.

Have you considered adjusting your smile?

A fisherman's *daughter?! My, who knew Grey would like someone so…rustic?*

These two had been aggressively chipping away at my flaws for the better half of the last hour while pretending they were thrilled to see me. Frankly, I'd had enough.

Jealous.

I knew they were jealous, but *they* had no idea what they were so green over. Their assumptions were laughable given my scenario and even more ridiculous given how comedically unappealing Greyson found the socialite dating scene. I might not like the man, but at least I knew he wouldn't fall into the clutches of one of these vipers.

"I'll see you around, ladies," I chirped in a saccharine tone, mimicking the obnoxious fluttering finger wave I'd been on the receiving end of all evening. Sighing my irritation, I turned away, downed the last of my vodka tonic, and wove through bodies toward the bar, ignoring eager smiles along the way. If I thought high school was catty, it had nothing on these rabid heiresses. Evidently, a man's merit was entirely dictated by the money in his wallet rather than the heart in his chest or razor edges of a mind worth exploring.

Reaching the bar, I smiled at tonight's bartender and wiggled my glass in hopes of a refill. His nod was like a life preserver. I clung to it, quite certain we were about to become *very* close friends.

Suddenly, I didn't feel so bad about Greyson's promised alimony. That thought was interrupted by a slick black tux hugging a slender body with a rather smug, albeit handsome, face attached to it.

Money might not buy happiness, but it certainly bought jaw lines and rhinoplasty just fine. The inhuman perfection around me was like a blinding mirror focused on my unacceptable pore size and prominent Mediterranean nose. I'd never cared about it until I was supposed to pass as one of them.

The suit extended a hand.

"Evening, Ms. Rhodes. Royce Ashcroft, pleased to meet you."

Eyeing the blond man before me, I recognized the smile, then the eyes. He'd shaved off his *GQ* beard in favor of defined lines of shadow. We'd hovered around each other at a few dozen events like this over the last couple years, including that trip to Barcelona. Auctions, mostly. I bit back the fact that he hadn't been pleased to see me until I had a title like 'future Mrs. Hart' to care about. Instead, I smiled up at him—all tan skin and fair blue eyes—and extended my hand to take his as my mind rifled through the folders of the who's who in Emerald Bay.

"Royce! Nice to see you. How's Miranda?"

Surprise glittered in his eyes for a breath before he smiled. "She's wonderful! Pregnant with baby number three. She would've been here but was afraid she'd be hugging the porcelain throne."

"Awe," I cooed, sliding my hand away when he lingered longer than necessary. "Congratulations, you two. I hope she feels better soon."

"Thank you! Any future Harts we should know about? Cassy is just big enough to be in love with babies." *Cassy.* His second-born daughter, I remembered.

Did these people only marry for status or breeding? Royce was the fifth person to ask a question along these lines since the evening started. I was beginning to doubt the words Greyson had left looping in my mind and fought the urge to look down at my stomach to check for a muffin top.

"Not at the moment," I answered, forcing a laugh. "Though I'm sure Greyson will have plans as soon as things are official." Was that puke climbing up my throat at the idea of carrying my boss' babies? Yep. Yep, it was. On second thought, a favorable prenup sounded fantastic. Get enough cash in my wallet to pick up, change my name, reconstruct my face like all of these glamorous, glittering sociopaths, and vanish into the void somewhere they didn't have social media.

"Oh, I'm sure he'll get right to work," he said with a wink. "I know I've kept Miranda busy."

This was my idea. This was *my* strategy. The parties, the slow drip of information to prolong the media buzz and keep their eyes where we wanted them. That didn't mean I didn't have to remind myself of it in every single conversation I had tonight. Looking past his shoulder, I scanned the space—both irritated and relieved, when I spotted Greyson looking equally miserable across the room, chatting with a couple of day traders.

"Hopefully, those vapid piranhas haven't been too brutal on you tonight," he added, glancing down to his hands, where they wrapped around a glass of what I assumed was Greyson's favorite Macallan. "Miranda was a preacher's daughter when we met. Did you know that?" When I just shook my head, he smiled softly, nodding as he stared into the single malt like it was a time capsule. Eyes reminiscent, he said, "I was the big bad party boy that corrupted the innocent princess. At least, that's how her father would tell the tale."

"I'm sure you were an upstanding young man," I teased with a smirk. The comment earned a low laugh and a smile that split his stubbled cheeks.

"I was a *scoundrel*. But…I fell hard and fast for her. Been proving myself to her and her family for seven years now." He knocked back his drink. "I guess what I'm trying to get to is that this—" He shrugged like he was lost for words as he motioned vaguely around the room, "*life* of ours. It's an adjustment if you didn't grow up with the rest of these trust fund babies. Go easy on yourself. You'll find your way." Okay, so maybe I'd misjudged Royce a bit. "Welcome to the circus, Ms. Rhodes."

A throat cleared behind us, and we both straightened, turning to find Greyson, his hands in his pockets in that effortlessly superior stance only the wealthy could pull off. "Getting to know my bride, Ashcroft?"

Royce chuckled, smoothly transferring his glass from one hand to the other in order to shake with Greyson. "She's lovely, Greyson. Congratulations to you both."

"Thanks," Greyson replied, voice uncharacteristically clipped. "How's the missus?"

"Miranda is pregnant with their third," I supplied. Reminding Greyson of important names had been a predominant part of my job description. Who knew my weird talent would also equate to job security?

"Congratulations to *you*, then," Greyson said smoothly, sliding an arm around my shoulders to tuck me against his ribs. I forced myself to relax into his warmth, wishing the heat of him and mouthwatering cologne was a sincere comfort in this shark-infested water. "Boy or girl?"

"Surprise this time," Royce shrugged. "Figure we'll let the tiebreaker keep us on our toes."

"Very old fashioned. Patient. I applaud you. I know this one would need to know the moment it was possible," he declared, giving me what was likely meant as a playful squeeze but felt like a possessive reminder of who I was here with. "She likes to plan all of the details out. Keep control of whatever she can."

That's fucking rich coming from you. Instead of vocalizing my sincere thoughts, I amicably agreed, "That's true." Because he wasn't wrong

—I would want to know so I could prepare—I just didn't appreciate his tone.

"Well, Ashcroft, say hi to Miranda. My bride and I are needed elsewhere."

"Will do. Congratulations again," Royce repeated, raising his now-empty glass in a symbolic salute. We turned to leave, but he added, "Oh, and Alessandra, do be careful with who you open up to. You'd be shocked how quickly a server will blab confidential information for a few hundred dollars."

I'd barely nodded when Greyson laughed and pulled me across the room. Royce's warning was still turning circles in my mind when we slid into the cool limo with its low lighting and lower music. Scooting away the instant the door closed, I glanced out the window, breathing a sigh of relief that our first performance had come to a blessed close. Which, of course, was when Greyson decided to hit me with a one-two punch.

"Cozying up to rivals won't win us any points with the press."

Blinking, I jerked my face back to his. "Excuse me?"

"Ashcroft. He's a buddy on the golf course but a rival outside it. You'll do well to remember that."

"He was the first person to treat me with any ounce of dignity, but your opinion has been noted."

"Trust no one in these circles, Alessandra."

"Does that include you?" I asked under arched brows.

"Depends on what your objective is. If you intend to see this arrangement through to fruition, then I intend to be the best alliance you can make in your lifetime. But if you're going to publicly indulge in dalliances that create new media fires for me to extinguish, then I would go with no, Ms. Rhodes. Because I won't cover for you when they chum the waters if you're planning to dishonor my name."

My jaw popped, it dropped so suddenly. A headache was blooming behind my eyes as my heart rate escalated. "Are you fucking serious right now?"

"You know first-hand what an image of you on the arm of another man would do to this campaign."

"I wasn't on his arm, and Royce is married."

"Royce?!"

"He has a first name."

"Marriage means nothing to these people. You understand that, don't you? It's an alliance. A piece of paper bartering for allegiance in business."

"Just because *you're* buying a bride to cover your ass doesn't mean that everyone is. I highly doubt a preacher's daughter advanced Royce's place in this social circle." The hum of the motor filled the silence as we rounded a corner, Greyson scowling out the window across from us.

"This needs to be precisely executed, is what I'm trying to say."

"Then say *that*. Don't insinuate I'm not doing my part because I just entertained the vapid musings of plastic sex dolls and feral men who would happily befriend me to get to you for the last three hours."

"Don't trust them, either."

"I wasn't born yesterday," I snapped. "Contrary to the selection of breeding mares available in those walls, I actually have two brain cells to rub together and know when someone isn't acting in my best interest."

"Well, that's a relief."

"You approached me, not the other way around. I highly suggest *you* don't forget that."

"Like you'd let me," he scoffed petulantly.

"What's that supposed to mean?"

"You don't show your face unless it's obligatory—you don't even eat dinner with me."

"That wasn't part of the deal."

"You'll have to do more than the bare minimum to satisfy the arrangement, Alessandra."

Ooh. I wanted to knock him the hell out. "The terms of our agreement are simple, although I'm happy to get a translator to re-outline them if you need clarification, though I doubt you want to involve another party, no matter how ironclad your contracts are. I sold the story. All night long."

"We're going to need a deeper understanding of each other—beyond our scandalous office romance and fictitious European proposal—to pull this off."

"You might," I countered, crossing my arms over my chest. "I know *plenty*."

His eyes narrowed. "Coffee to creamer ratio isn't exactly what I was going for."

Grinding my teeth, I argued, "How about exactly how many pins in your spine required you to be medically discharged after the accident that killed your father? Or the fact that there was a criminal investigation to follow, where they proved you weren't at fault but never found the driver who was? The only reason they believe he was drunk were the open containers in the totaled vehicle he left behind."

"Those facts are public record—"

Maybe so. But I was on a rampage and wasn't about to slow down. "You're allergic to shrimp and crab but can eat clams and lobster. Your first girlfriend was named Jenilee. Your high school sweetheart, Selene, was the one woman you claim to have loved. You're the oldest of three boys, but a drunk driver killed the youngest while he was still in elementary school. Your mother blamed his loss for the strained relationship between you and your father, although the logic behind the fallacy evades me. Your why in life is Mattie, shortly followed by Beau, who was named for your late brother, and if you absolutely had to choose a third, it would be Oliver. *Oh*, and I don't think you want me sharing this tidbit, but you never orgasm inside a woman—condom or not—because your Uncle Reggie told you not to sire any inheritance-stealing bastards. I guess Oliver didn't get that speech or didn't particularly care. I'm not sure which."

"You don't know what you're talking about, Alessandra," he ground out.

"*You forget* yourself when I'm around, Mr. Hart. But *the help* talk. And you and Ollie aren't as quiet as you think you are when you're too busy being men to realize I'm there. The perk of playing the pretty doormat is that everyone underestimates you—nobody bothers to notice when you enter a room. But don't preach to me about learning my subject. I know you inside and out, Mr. Hart. That's the job."

"What is wrong with you?" he snarled as the car slowed around familiar bends in the road.

"You. It's *been* you for two damn years, and I'm insane for thinking I could tolerate you for more."

"You're insufferably condescending."

"And you're arrogant and self-centered. You mock me as though all I've learned in two years under your supervision is your coffee order, but I highly doubt you could supply mine in a pinch. You don't bother to learn rudimentary things about *the rabble* that serve you. We're so far below your pay grade I'm shocked you bother to learn names, although maybe that's generous because you haven't bothered to learn mine. So, I suppose you're right. We need deeper communication if this is going to work. But it's not me—or the men I talk to—that you should be concerned with."

I was out of the car before the driver had it in park.

10

Just Call Me Belle

ALICE

The thirteenth floor was unusually busy on Monday morning. The smell of burned coffee greeted me with my first step off the elevator. People were bustling, copy machines chugged out daily reports, computer keys clacked at astounding speed, and voices buzzed through the large, open work room. The thing I admired most about the Hart brothers was their dedication to the idea of a team—although they certainly weren't a part of ours.

Office walls all glowed white to reflect the sunlight that streamed in through oversized windows. Twin staircases led up to the over-hang where the executives were tucked behind walls of glass that made the entire space feel like a fishbowl. Sleek modern desks lined down the center, each facing the other so co-workers could pop around their monitors for conversations. They were all electric and could be raised to stand or sit as they worked to accommodate better ergonomics or even exercise balls for those who struggled to focus sitting still. Gorgeous modern artwork splashed color across the walls, keeping with our coastal city. Framed, signed posters of our star football players lined the bathroom hallway in bold emerald green, gold, and black.

All touches I attributed to Oliver's part in the family business. I'd seen pictures of the outdated eighties decor they'd inherited, and the dingy space was a far cry from the environment I'd walked into a few summers back.

But all of those progressive pieces of company culture did nothing to dull the abrupt cutoff of conversation as I stepped in between the lines of desks and monitors. A hush settled over the desks like a wet blanket tossed over a fire despite my smile. A smile that went rigid under their scrutiny.

Just like that, I was no longer a peer. I was one of *them*.

I was going to be a Hart. Surely, a handful of them thought I'd slept my way to my position, which was more frustrating than it should have been. And what had been camaraderie two weeks ago —sharing jokes at Greyson's expense and planning summer concerts together—had been replaced with fear and furtive glances. *Great.* I hadn't even thought about the fact that the very few friend-adjacent relationships I had in this city would vanish when I was publicly declared *his*.

"Morning, Paul," I greeted as I finally hit his desk at the back of the room outside of the executive's offices—mine included. He was the first person to both meet my gaze and smile.

"Morning, Alice! How are you, beautiful?" I shrugged, but the attempt at nonchalance wasn't fooling Paul. He'd been with Greyson for years before I joined the team and had been one of my earliest allies in this overwhelming building. He offered me a sympathetic smile before saying, "Give it time. They'll get over it the moment some new juicy scandal arises."

Nodding, I mumbled, "Thanks."

"Oh. Your *betrothed,*" he overenunciated the word just for emphasis, a devilish smile curling his slender lips. "He asked me to tell you to see him in his office when you arrived."

"Thanks, Paul," I said as I walked past him, holding back the groan that climbed up my chest. Hesitating at the foot of the executive stairs, I realized he wasn't supposed to be here, but I clamped my teeth shut on the question that almost flew from my mouth because, his fiancé *would* know why he'd broken his hiatus.

Dammit.

I hadn't seen him since the limo ride fiasco after the engagement party. Spent the weekend with a too-smug Leighton, who still wanted me to call the whole thing off for the farce it was. A farce coming to a head quicker than I could possibly prepare for. There was no way to have a royal wedding ready in a matter of weeks, but we'd decided a secret intimate elopement with 'exclusive' photos offered to Stacy and her paper was just as good. We'd leak secondary images to a second source and stoke the scandal of celebrity obsession for extra diversion.

But that meant this was my last week to walk away before things became infinitely more complicated. Rather than going to my end of the hallway, I walked directly into Greyson's office. Those hazel greens landed on me the instant I filled the doorway, clutching my bag in one hand and coffee in the other. With a pained sigh, he motioned for me to close the door. All too eager to comply, I slipped into the room, but the heavy click of the latch behind me felt more final than I'd like.

"Morning, Mr. Hart," I said, sitting when he motioned to the chair across the desk.

"One moment," he said curtly, tapping away at his keys. While par for the course, it was still maddening, my irritation already rising. Maybe too much history sat between us to pull this off after all. It wasn't that he'd said anything spectacularly dickish in the car Saturday night—though his refusal to defend me to Reggie spoke volumes—and it wasn't unusual for him to wrap up a last-minute email after calling me in for a meeting. Yet, the pretense of a relationship—transactional as it may be—made all of the Heartless-isms that much more agitating.

"I have a very full agenda today; perhaps I should come back at a more convenient time."

"Stop it," he ordered, not moving his eyes from the screen that was rapidly filling with little black letters.

"Just communicating the requirements of my day, *sir*."

"You know what you're doing," he growled, clicking the enter key with theatrical finality. Fingers laced behind his head, he leaned back in his chair and crossed one ankle over the other. God must have had one hell of a sense of humor if he thought putting the personality of a rattlesnake into a package like that was appropriate. Begrudgingly, my brain hashed out whether or not he was pretty enough to make up for being so callous. The arm porn currently on display beneath a slick button-up with sleeves rolled to the elbow wasn't helping the logic win out.

Luckily for me, he opened his mouth again, quickly reminding me why he was only as beautiful as a poisonous plant—luring you in with bright colors and silky petals only to send you heaving into the bathroom toilet if you were dumb enough to take a taste. "Where've you been?"

"Home."

"No. I was home." A lone arched brow accompanied inflection-less anger. "You were not."

"You can't be serious."

"As a heart attack." He leaned forward, bracing his forearms on the desk as he clasped his fingers against the marble surface. "We argued about how best to keep up appearances. Do you think running off for forty-eight hours is an appropriate response?"

"Leighton came down with the flu, and I went home to take care of her," I supplied sardonically.

"I have doctors on staff for that."

"I appreciate that, but I don't throw money at my problems when I have a heart that can solve them. Besides, Leigh was fine—thanks for asking, by the way—but the media doesn't need to know that."

He nodded, lips pursed as he let that sit between us, stewing like a pot of soup about to boil over. "When you agreed to this, I didn't realize you intended to make it as miserable as possible."

"I didn't realize you'd be a territorial caveman, either. I guess we both misjudged the other. *Shocker*." I deadpanned as he did the same. It would've been funny if it were anyone else.

"You know, I miss the version of you that you lured us in with over the last two years."

"Of course you do," I sighed, leaning back and peeling at a bit of orange stuck under my artificial nail. "She had the personality of a desk lamp."

"Did you ever think I would've been more eager to put you in a position of leadership if I'd known you could hold your own?"

"Did you ever think that's not synonymous with being a *dick*?"

That little twitch of his lip brought me way too much satisfaction. In a matter of weeks, I'd shown him the ugliest, meanest sides to me, and he found them *entertaining*.

"If we're suddenly in the habit of shooting it straight together, answer me this. Are you in or out? Because I can't tell."

"I said I'm in."

"Words take only a tongue, but commitment requires compounded action over time. Are you all the former, or do you possess the latter to see this through?"

"I *said* I'm in," I growled, lifting my chin.

"Then act like it," he countered, leaning back. "As it is, no one close enough to leak to the press will believe a word of it. What bride runs off after her engagement party? I have staff. Staff who knew your bed was never slept in. Who probably think it's odd you're keeping your own rooms, despite my justification that we're taking a break until we say 'I do.'"

I opened my mouth—once, twice—but snapped it closed. I knew he was right, even if the idea of climbing into his bed at night made me...simultaneously a bit flushed and nauseated, like I'd caught a nasty stomach virus.

But that didn't diminish my irritation with him. "I want to be treated as a partner, Greyson, not a subject."

"And I expect my wife to be in her own bed, especially after a disagreement."

"Ooh, *quick*," I said sardonically. "*Demand* I join you for dinner."

"The staff will expect it."

"Just call me Belle," I muttered, not dropping our locked gazes, which granted me the pleasure of rendering him confused. This time, I couldn't help but laugh, "Oh, come on, think about it."

He narrowed his eyes on me. "Did you just liken me to a cursed beast?"

Smirking, I shrugged as if to say 'obviously.'

"I'd argue, but aside from Cap, I am alone, and we do have a library. If you'd like, I can gift it to you to really cement the picture."

Aaaand, I was smiling. How the fuck did he do that? When we both blew out a sigh in unison, laughter naturally followed.

"Ollie was right," he muttered, palming his jaw. "I hate when he's right."

"About what?"

"That this would be harder than I anticipated."

"Duh," I replied unflinchingly.

"You say that quite casually for someone who also signed on the dotted line." He palmed his face before muttering, "We don't even know if this marriage will even be adequate enough to keep the sharks in the water we chummed instead of feasting on the embezzlement story."

"It will," I assured, my gut set on that as reality. "The public is enamored with romance. White collar assholes being assholes isn't really news when they have juicy theories and celebrity pregnancy speculations to sink their teeth into."

"They're really sticking to that?"

"Why else would I marry you in a shotgun wedding?" Okay, so my smirk might've been a bit devilish. To my eternal amusement, he returned it.

"Okay. So, we're doing this."

"We're doing this."

"The second photo run prints tomorrow."

"Rumors of our plans release on Wednesday."

"The jet leaves at nine am on Thursday."

"By Saturday night, I will—legally speaking—be your wife."

A dry chuckle shook his shoulders as he smirked. "I'm going to have a wife."

"That as hard for you to believe as it is for the rest of us?"

"Thought I'd stay single forever out of spite." Something heavy and vulnerable slithered through his words and had me shifting in my seat. Before I could follow that up, he added, "I think it's appropriate to keep public appearances in the office professional, but we need to give the media more to buzz about."

My stomach did a full backflip. Forcing bravado, I said, "Welcome to the fun part. But Greyson…" When he looked up at me, I dipped my chin and asked, "What are you doing here?"

"It's my office."

"Right. But you're not supposed to be here until the investigation is over."

"My fiancé didn't have a chance to come home while caretaking for her sister," he said morosely as he rose from his chair to round his desk, "and I needed to see her." Greyson leaned against the edge of the marble, his gaze softening as it locked on my face. Gingerly, he tucked my hair behind an ear, lips quirking when I sucked down a breath. Concern pinched his brow as he dropped his eyes to his lap before looking at me, more seriously this time. "And something she said has been eating at me."

Yikes. Where to start? My harsh reminder about his unplanned retirement from the Navy? Callously listing the facts surrounding the deaths of his father and brother with the care of baseball scores?

Hartless or not, my words unleashed in anger had stuck with me all weekend.

"You overheard my uncle in the groom's suite?"

Oh. That. When my eyes dropped to my hands, where I was peeling at my cuticle, his hand snapped out to gently grip my chin, lifting my eyes to his stony hazels.

"Nothing he said holds even a grain of merit, Alessandra," he promised, shaking his head. "Not a word."

My lips parted and then closed. Twice. What could I say to that? "I don't expect you to defend me to your family, Greyson. This isn't real."

"I'm not sure how much you heard—"

"Enough," I cut in.

"But I'm unspeakably sorry you had to hear any of that. The man is vile and bitter and hates that despite his position, he holds no real power in my life beyond being an inescapable, insufferable nuisance. You are only his most recent in a long line of targets he knows will cut me the deepest."

Jerking my chin from his hold, I argued, "You didn't seem particularly bothered."

"Because murder is illegal and therefore highly inadvisable with witnesses," he stated firmly. I breathed a little laugh, wishing he sounded less sincere. "Plus, gratifying his vitriol with an emotional response only gives him what he wants—proof he can still get under my skin. That he has some ounce of control."

He slipped from the desk to kneel in front of me, big hands coming to cup my face. How does one breathe with their boss on his knees, holding you captive with pained puppy eyes? *You don't.*

"But I'm guessing you were smart enough not to subject yourself to more of his venom and left before you heard me dismiss him. He won't be receiving the wedding details until after we're home. You deserve better, Alessandra. I'll see that you have it."

"We need the family unified," I stammered, loathing the waver his words put in my voice. Greyson's brow pinched with something like pain before he smoothed it over.

"I need my wife to know I won't tolerate anyone disrespecting her, least of all *my family*. I never meant to be the one to rattle you," he said with a gentle shake of his head. Deftly smoothing my hair behind my ears, he added, "Ashcroft is clever. I enjoy his company on the golf course, but I don't trust him with you. In retrospect, I can recognize how my actions were perceived. That wasn't my intention." When I just nodded, he softened his expression, making sure my gaze was locked on his as he wrapped my fidgeting hands in his, keeping me from peeling my fingers raw. "You are now the most desirable woman in any room—socially as well as physically. Don't forget that."

The rest of the week went off surprisingly smoothly as we coordinated details and kept things business as usual in the office. Home was much the same, and I took his words to heart. I even gave in and started sleeping in his room, but that presented its own challenges, all of which I chose to ignore.

The hidden blessing of his freakishly robotic life was that outside of his in-home staff, not a soul speculated anything out of the norm with us only holding hands in public. On his request, my wardrobe was restocked with boujee clothes that all fit me like gloves, although I absolutely combed through the donation totes until I could fish out my ratty sweats to hide for pajamas. Who the hell wants designer butt floss on under silk nighties? Not this girl, that's for sure. Though something was empowering about walking into Greyson Hart's bedroom dressed in the aforementioned silk night things and watching a dark-haired Adonis squirm. But waking up and discovering that your subconscious thirsty-bitch brain had transported you across the thirty-eighth pillow parallel and into the warm embrace of your *maddeningly-attractive boss* was…less than ideal. After that first night, I opted for my big brothers' *Grizzly Grind* sweatshirt, or Paxton's college jersey in lieu of the delicate unmentionables that had been sourced for me. Besides, us Rhodes were a proud bunch, and like hell was anyone throwing away anything that celebrated our family, especially each other's achievements. The fact that Rhyett built the best coffee shop on the island and that Pax played pro were highlights for all of us. I might not get to see them regularly and certainly didn't pop into the family text thread as often as I should've, but that didn't mean I wasn't just as invested in them as the others were. It was just…a lot to process all the time.

By Thursday night, I was primped professionally, draped in a

Grecian-style dress that matched the color of the Caribbean Sea crashing against my ankles, with butterflies in my belly. Most of my siblings weren't able to cover the distance with basically no notice, but my parents, Leighton, our sister Elora and her husband Broderick, Paxton, and our oldest brother Rhyett, along with his wife, Brexley, and daughter, Quinn, were all due to arrive tomorrow morning, and *that* had my intestines tying themselves into many, many knots. Lying to staffers and reporters was one thing, but my family would be entirely different.

Mattie and Leighton were building castles with little Beau in the sand while Ollie watched on from a pretty blue lounger, his tattoos peeking out of his open shirt. His preferred photographer and Stacy, the reporter, would be here in a matter of minutes, and we had to paint the picture of the perfect American family.

I felt Greyson approaching before I heard him. The man was like a planet I'd unintentionally begun orbiting when I transferred to his office. That familiar gravitational pull had me turning over a shoulder, the sand squishing beneath my toes and rubbing against the pretty gold jewelry they'd given me in lieu of shoes like some life-size doll.

Fuck. Me.

The man was sinful in a suit, but airy white linen pants and an open, lightweight button-up that exposed his tan torso, his gorgeous, meticulous hair a bit windblown? I could blame the fact that I was ovulating, but the reality was this man was walking sex appeal—all lean lines and a smattering of dark hair over a few stray, speckled scars. Some paradoxical tug of war between hero and the billionaire he was born to be.

But those hazels—now a warm gold-green in the bouncing sunlight of the beach—caught my attention. Maybe it was the intensity. Maybe it was just the fact that they were trained on me with some concocted fire in them. His beeline through the gentle surf led him straight to me, and every scrap of air in my lungs rushed from my ribs as he scooped me into his arms and settled his forehead against mine.

Oh. Dear. God.

He smelled *edible*, with his breath hot on my face and his warm hands on my bare back, just above where the dress cut across the curve of my ass.

"What are you—" I started to ask, but with my current lack of oxygen, the words weren't even audible before he unintentionally cut them off by moving one hand to my neck, pushing away the strands sticking to my skin in the summer humidity.

"You can't tell me that's not how a bride wants her groom to greet her when she wears a dress like that."

"Greeted—" I whispered as my heart raced up a dozen flights of stairs, impossible goosebumps winning out against the persistent sun on my skin. Hormones be damned because those fuckers don't know the difference between healthy chemistry and performance.

"Your sister is here early," he calmly announced, entirely oblivious to the fact that his thumb stroking over my pulse point had me ten kinds of flustered. "With her husband. They seem to have shared a ride from the airport with Stacy."

"Stacy," I panted. *Panted*. Like a dog in heat.

"Our reporter," he reminded me, but every synapse in my brain was occupied by his nose tracing the end of mine and that methodic circle his thumb kept drawing over my carotid artery. My head was a tilt-a-whirl of warring logic and attraction when his next words ghosted over my mouth, "You should probably touch me back, Belle."

Blinking, it took a solid four pathetic pants for my brain to buffer what he'd just said to me. *Belle*. Like the beauty to his beast. I was just bursting out laughing, my hands flying to his chest, when a familiar voice cut through the solid wall of water that was Caribbean air.

"Alice!"

"Oh, you're good," I admitted breathlessly, turning to face the music. Greyson didn't take his hands off me, instead leisurely shifting me in his grasp, his hand staying in a possessive hold around my neck as his other palm found its way to my belly, pulling my ass against his groin as my eyes found El and Broderick, hands clasped between them as they descended the beach with cautious eyes. Pulse suddenly a ten-pound hammer, I forced in a breath and looked up at him over my shoulder with what I hoped would pass for adoration.

"Thanks for the warning."

"Thanks for wearing the dress," he whispered, nuzzling against the side of my face like I wasn't already on the brink of folding like a damn lawn chair. I couldn't remember the last time someone held me like that. Hell, I wasn't sure if anyone had *ever* held me with the possessive intent of Greyson Hart.

Each hammer of my pulse was a reminder, chanting 'not real.' *Not real, not real, not real.* This was a business arrangement, at best. Like two warring kingdoms, although mine had nothing to offer beyond an adequate face and average body. Belle, trading her freedom for the betterment of her family. Only, I was saving Mattie's and walking away like a very well-paid sex-less hooker.

Forcing my eyes back to the beach, I slid free from his disconcertingly appealing hold on my body, pulling up my dress to keep it free from the splash zone as I rushed to meet them in the middle.

"Elly," I breathed, practically collapsing into her open arms as

Broderick chuckled knowingly behind her. I'd grown up with Brod in our house—he was best friends with our two oldest brothers—so he was all too acquainted with how close us sisters were, even if we upset each other. "You came!"

"Hey, sissy," she chirped back, crushing me against her. "Of course."

"Don't squish baby," I protested.

"Baby Allen is well insulated in there," she laughed back. Still, I pushed her away to examine her still-flat stomach. She was only a few months along, and with this being her first, there was no sign she was incubating a tiny human. Even her skin was still glowing, although maybe that was just humidity.

"You don't have a single pound of insulation on you," I argued. It was true. El was a little brick house of honed muscle. Long dark hair and gray-blue eyes, just like mine.

"He might've had to make do with organs for cushion, but I promise he's fine. At least, according to the doctor. Now. How's his auntie?"

"Spectacularly stunning in blue," Greyson's low voice cut through the space as gently as a guillotine, the gooseflesh pebbling across my skin again. *Damn hormones.* Elora shot him a glare that lesser men would cower beneath, but Broderick—ever the gentleman—stepped in, extending a hand as the warm umber skin around his brown eyes crinkled with his smile.

"That she is," he agreed as Greyson accepted the gesture of goodwill. "Broderick Allen, nice to meet you in person, Greyson."

"The pleasure is all mine. You're the professor?" Impressed with his recall, I smiled between the two of them as my new brother-in-law nodded.

"Guilty as charged. We're not as boring as we sound, I swear."

"Debatable," I teased under my breath, laughing when Elora pinched my side.

"Mr. Hart," she said cordially, not bothering to reach for him. I pinched her back. With a huff, she reached out a hand and added, "Thank you for hosting us this weekend."

"My pleasure."

Expression unflinching, head held tall, and tone dripping with promise, El said, "We'll see about that."

Broderick cleared his throat as Ollie, Leigh, Mattie, and Beau sidled up beside us. Grinning at a curious-looking Mattie, he asked, "Who's this sweetheart?"

Somehow, Greyson not only *survived* the next forty-eight hours of relentless inquisition but managed to win over my family. Well—Brod, Pax, Rhyett, Brex, and baby Quinny.

Elora could give Elsa a run for her money with her ice queen routine. She might back my decisions, but under no uncertain terms would she be showing Greyson anything but the wrath he'd face if this ended poorly.

I loved her all the more for it. That unyielding loyalty.

Growing up, it was always my four towering, big brothers that warded off dates, but in reality, they all should've been afraid of El and Leighton. However, even Leigh wasn't immune to the relentless charm of the Hart brothers despite her valiant effort.

I blamed Mattie and her adoration for them.

But between gifts in their rooms, a menu to accommodate Brexley and Quinn's new dietary restrictions, and a bar stocked with my father's favorites, Greyson expertly whittled away at the image of *Hartless* and started to carve a new picture in their minds in the blink of an eye.

By Saturday afternoon, my six-four daddy had unshed tears in his gray eyes as he handed me over to my groom with our feet planted in the scalding sand, and if I was unmistaken, both Paxton and Rhyett were dabbing at their eyes as we exchanged our vows. The laptop live stream stared back at us with nine screens—eight of my blood siblings, plus Max. Their love for me somehow warmed my chest while guilt clawed into my belly.

But the moment Greyson turned on me with a sun-kissed smile, stretching his cheeks and wrinkling the skin beside those warm green eyes, sent my world rocking. He played his part too well as he finished the ceremony with his expertly written vows, a slight shake to his hands where they held the paper. Mine had been handed to me Thursday night—no doubt a gift from his speech writer.

"Hello, *Mrs. Hart*," he whispered huskily after the minister pronounced us husband and wife. As that rasp worked over my skin, my body forgot. Forgot it was a role as he stroked a big palm down the side of my face to the frantic click of camera shutters, whoops and cheers of my mother, Leigh and Mattie, and the applause of the guys.

"Hello." I smiled back as he pulled my body to his. Nobody could ever accuse Greyson of not knowing exactly how to handle a woman. Just his touch on my waist sent my nerves soaring. *Brilliant bastard.*

With his adoring fiancé mask firmly in place, he tucked my hair behind my ears, slowly cupping my face with his big hands before bringing his lips to mine.

It started slow.

Hesitant.

All too aware of the audience witnessing our first kiss. Damn, I should've thought of that. Should've thought to practice in case we sucked at this. But Greyson didn't need practice. No, the man claimed me right there under the sun on an island bearing his last name.

But as my heart raced and heat blossomed in my belly, I pulled the air from his lips and filled my lungs with his scent.

Before I realized it, my hands were on his exposed skin, nearly clawing at the buttons still holding the fabric together. Relishing in the tickle of his chest hair against the pads of my fingers. *God, I loved chest hair.*

Greyson's hands slid through my long tresses, knotting my hair around a fist as he angled my chin up for him. Years of pent-up frustration channeled through to this moment—a war between wills, a clash of lips, tongues, and teeth.

Tender turned demanding.

Pretense turned feral as he pressed my lips apart, and I opened for him, melting under the southern sun and urgency of his mouth against mine. If the company was his kingdom, *this* was his battleground. A king on a conquest. Judging by the possession in his hold, I was the prize.

It's said that we do everything…like we do *everything*, and while Greyson's initial movements were as calm and calculated as his ability to conquer any boardroom, they gave way to something…*primal.*

He wrapped an arm around my back, locking me to him as our family applauded with two claps to each soft growl of the ocean. The hand on my neck angled up to grip my jaw possessively, angling me just so. His tongue plundered all sense from my brain as he took what he needed from me, returning more fervor than I could've asked for.

Much too soon, he robbed me of that tantalizing demand when Paxton barked, "Get a room!" to a small chorus of laughter and Oliver's slightly less boisterous, "Seriously."

But he only pulled back far enough to catch his breath as I saw something I never imagined in Greyson Hart's eyes: *panic.*

11

Do They Ever Shut Up?
GREYSON

The Fam Damily:

NOEL

Congratulations Alice & Grey! The photos are beautiful.

JAMESON

A heads up would've been nice.

NOEL

What James means is we wish we'd been able to get there, but we're so happy for you guys!

HADLEE

You made a beautiful bride, sissy!

Someone kiss her for me.

AXEL

I'm with James. What was with the rush?

MAVERICK

And the hush-hush?

MAX

I'm happy if you're happy, Alice. Suit Daddy *better* make you happy.

cracks knuckles

BREXLEY

It was beautiful, and I kissed her for you, Hads!

KAIA

Congrats guys! Ignore the boys; men are stupid.

BRODERICK

Thanks, Kai.

KAIA

Most men are stupid.

MAX

Having attempted to date them for the last decade, I agree with Kaia.

LEIGHTON

Home safe.

AXEL

All jokes aside, I'm happy if you are as long as he treats you right.

BREXLEY

It was so thoughtful for Grey to make sure there was food for me and Quinny. This new no-dairy thing is brutal.

PAXTON

Oh, is that why you were puking Sunday morning?

BREXLEY

middle finger emojis

PAXTON

laughing emojis

JAMESON

Wait. What?

RHYETT

Baby, the cat's out of the bag.

PAXTON

Or the BUN is out of the oven.

BREXLEY

Technically, the bun will stay in the oven until New Year's.

MAVERICK

MORE BABIES!!!

BREXLEY

If god loves me, that will not be plural.

MAVERICK

ONE MORE BABY!

BREXLEY

Much better. Thanks, Mav.

ELORA

Sorry, my head was back in the toilet. All that airfare
was not great for the morning sickness.

AXEL

Wait. Is sissy's eggo preggo too? Is that why Greyson
put a ring on it?

GREYSON

You do know that Rhyett added me to this chaos you
call a text thread, don't you?

MAVERICK

Hahaha excellent. Putting you down as my emergency
contact in case I ever need bail.

PAXTON

Two seconds in, and you're asking for favors from the
new billionaire brother?

MAVERICK

Like he didn't know that was coming. There are twelve
of us. 12!

PAXTON

I've been dethroned so easily.

MAVERICK

Billion with a B, Pax. That trumps M.

PAXTON

Fucking ruthless, Mav.

GREYSON

I have attorneys on retainer. Don't exploit that.

JAMESON

We have a family attorney, thanks, though.

BRODERICK

My dad could use a break, I'm sure.

GREYSON

In the habit of getting into trouble?

HADLEE

Questions you should ask BEFORE you pop *the* question.

AXEL

Wait. He never answered *my* question. Is this a fertilization epidemic or something?

ELORA

I think we would know if Alice's eggo was preggo.

ALESSANDRA

You all suck. No. I'm not a human pod, thank you very much. Like that's the only reason a man would marry me?

AXEL

Let's be real. That's the only reason a man would marry anyone.

JAMESON

Speak for yourself, kid.

RHYETT

Yeah, agree to disagree, man. I had my ring before I knew Brex was pregnant with Quinny.

BRODERICK

I wouldn't have cared if your sister ever wanted kids; I needed her to have my last name.

AXEL

gagging gif

Very happy for you all.

But I'm not gay. That emo stuff ain't in my wheelhouse.

JAMESON

Dude. That doesn't even make any sense.

ALESSANDRA

JFC, could you all be any more embarrassing? Can you maybe not make my husband regret this before we're even off the island?

HADLEE

Awwwwwe, you said 'my husband.'

ALESSANDRA

Generally, that's what the white dress and exchanging of rings means, Hads.

HADLEE

It's just cute, that's all. Alice the menace is all
grown up.

MAX

You did see that spread in Time magazine last year,
right? How our girl held out this long is beyond me.

GREYSON

The infamous Max. We meet at last.

MAX

Greyson Hart knows my name.

fainting gif

You taking good care of my girl, Mr. Hart?

GREYSON

She's not your girl anymore, Maximus.

AXEL

You misspelled Maxipad, but okay.

MAX

middle finger emojis

That's where you're wrong, Mr. Fancy Pants. She'll
always be our girl.

FINNEGAN

Welcome to the family, Grey. May the force be
with you.

"CHRIST, DO THEY EVER SHUT UP?" I asked when keeping up
became impossible. By the time I read a message, a new one popped
up. It was my fifth year running a billion-dollar division in our
family conglomerate, and the Rhodes family text thread was overwhelming as fuck. Like some kind of radioactive artifact, I hocked
the device onto the plush ivory leather of the seat across from us on
our private jet.

Alessandra snorted in an entirely unladylike manner, kicking her
bare feet up on the chair beside my discarded nuclear bomb. It was
oddly adorable. Everything about this infuriating, brilliant woman
was. She'd taken my control in a blink and crumbled it in her dainty
little hands like the walls I'd built were constructed of sand and
paste, not stone and mortar. The memory of her curves wrapped

around me, her thigh slung over my groin, in nothing but a flimsy silk negligée, was permanently carved into my mind.

I was raised to be a gentleman. But there was *nothing* gentlemanly about the way my palms buzzed or the primal images all of that smooth skin on display planted in my mind. She'd taken mercy on me after that first night, constantly climbing into bed in something that hung off her body, but I kept waking to my fingers settled on the strip of silky skin where those oversized hoodies rode up through the night. My perpetual morning wood a not-so-subtle salute to the goddess in my bed.

The goddess now grinning at me mischievously as she shook her head.

"Not unless their mouths are full, and even then, that's debatable. You see why I never have my phone on me outside office hours."

"They do this a lot?"

"All. The. Time."

"And twelve weren't enough, so you just...added Max?" I recalled, trying my best to grapple with her insane family line.

"He's the easiest of the bunch, believe it or not."

"His family terrible or something?" That was the only explanation I could think of that would entice parents to add another mouth to feed to the dozen they'd intentionally created.

"Nah, wonderful, actually," she chuckled affectionately. "But he connected with El, Hads, and me in elementary school, and we just sorta...kept him, I guess. Jameson and El helped him come out to his family during his senior year in high school. His dad is Japanese, and his mom grew up a fundamentalist Christian. She's not usually over the top, but it scared him to talk to them alone, you know? Only child, so it was kinda' us against the world."

"That was pretty solid of them."

"Yeah. He's definitely the suffer in silence type."

"Still," I blew out a quick breath. "How do you keep up?"

"I don't," she admitted with cartoon-wide eyes, wiggling to settle deeper into her seat, the Hart family crest peeking out from behind her hair. Hair I was desperate to touch again, to wrap around my fist and remember exactly how sweet she tasted.

We hadn't talked about that kiss since the wedding. Hadn't talked about the smaller signs of affection we exchanged over the weekend while her family was around. If it wasn't for the fact that I'd created a game out of earning her blush or a delicious hitch of her breath, I would have thought I imagined it. The spark between us on that beach.

I hadn't always been the monk the media knew me as. I'd had women. Not a ton. But I knew what it was to kiss a beautiful female, to feel them yield beneath my touch. To earn their submission.

It had never been like *that*.

I needed more. Not that I could say that.

Circumstances would demand a caress or kiss from time to time, but the last three days were proof this would be a torturous three-year sentence. She just *had* to be the most breathtaking creature I'd ever laid my hands on.

The text thread still lit up my discarded screen, and guilt had set in my bones for the second time since this began. Because most of her siblings seemed legitimately pumped about the union, but it brought my focus back to what she was saying.

"They'll be quiet for weeks at a time and then randomly pop off like this. El, Pax, and I talk a lot, but the rest..." she trailed off, looking more than a little guilty.

It was already challenging enough to keep a regular-sized family informed.

We had all the necessary resources, and I still couldn't fathom electively having a dozen children. "I'm suddenly glad it's just me and Ollie."

She shrugged, an endearing little smile on those full lips. "Eh, they're not all bad. Chaotic, but they come through when it's needed. Nobody can rally like a Rhodes."

"Kinda like your sister cornering me Friday night to threaten everything I love?" When Alessandra blanched, turning to me with horrified eyes, I chuckled. "She certainly loves you. Don't take that for granted."

"She *didn't*," she gasped.

"You just said you two are close."

"Well, yeah, but she—"

"Promised to destroy me if I hurt you, so you'll have to dump me and run off with the love of your life when this is over and save my balls, alright?" When her gaze fell to her lap, brows tight-knit, I reached over to hook her chin with a finger. "Hey."

"Hey," she echoed back weakly.

"You were phenomenal this weekend." My words elicited the prettiest little flush in her neck and face, some pathetically male part of me wondering if I'd feel the heat of it against my lips. "Perhaps consider an acting career. I know a few directors I could introduce you to."

She blew out a disbelieving breath. "That sounds like hell."

"Millions per film, adoring fans. Just *awful*."

"Haters scrutinizing every aspect of my existence from my hips to my home."

I ground my teeth. Because that was the reality for those of us in the public eye, no matter what arena we played in. The price of great privilege was disproportionate attention and the judgment that followed. There are no right answers when the internet feels entitled to the details of your life.

Deducing where my mind went, she chuckled morbidly. "They already are."

"So far, they've mostly wondered who your sun dress was designed by."

She snickered, looking sheepish under that pretty pink tint. "2017 Target?"

"The socialites will hate that."

If anything, that idea seemed to please her. "But the middle class won't."

"True." I sat pensively for a long moment before adding, "You can be whoever you choose to be at my side, Alice. Shake up the status quo if that brings you joy, or blend in if you'd rather. I think there might be more than one reason our paths have collided." Somewhere along the way, her mouth popped open, something between confusion and awe on her face. Equally curious and concerned about where I'd befuddled her in that statement, I asked, "*What?*"

A gentle, feminine slant pulled on her mouth a beat before she tucked her lower lip between her teeth. My weekend had been occupied by trying *not* to imagine the feel of that pillowy bottom lip between mine. Of trying not to cross our boundaries and scoop her into my arms after she fell asleep. Instead, I'd just studied her as she rested, away from the scrutiny of her family. Where the focus lines faded from her forehead, and her dark lashes rested against high cheekbones. Her beauty was suffocatingly captivating, like a flame before it consumes you.

On a heavy inhale, eyes on her lap, she murmured, "You called me Alice."

Secrets, Sand, and Sunset Vows: Inside Greyson and Alessandra Hart's Intimate Elopement

ASIDE FROM THE extra day off on our family island and the predicted social media storm that followed our exclusive four-spread wedding coverage, the next few days went smoothly.

Better than that, actually.

My bride ventured into the kitchen the night we got home with a box tucked beneath her arm, looking a bit sheepish.

She broke the silence with an offer. "You strike me as the kind of man that would enjoy a little *Risk*."

"An inevitability of being in business," I agreed, smirking as she rolled her eyes, closing the distance to where I was reviewing a high-profile client's quarterly plan on the couch. She plunked down beside me and set the box on the cured driftwood coffee table with enough enthusiasm that Cap raised his head from where he rested in my lap. He wasn't a tremendous fan of being apart and had been even more glued to my hip than usual. She unfolded the board and began counting out players. While every inch of my brain urged me to finish looking through our strategy, some corner of my being demanded I humor her. Acknowledge a gesture that felt like…an offering of sorts. "You play a lot?"

"In a family our size on an island that's almost always rainy, cheap home entertainment is a necessary commodity."

"I take that as a yes?"

"Define *a lot*," she challenged, smiling as she emphasized the phrase. Cap smashed his cold, wet nose into my palm the instant I stopped petting him, my focus on her as she added, "I will warn you; don't ever play Elora. She eviscerates the best of us."

"We'll have to see about that."

"Feeling cocky, Greyson?" Greyson. I loved the way this woman said my name like a challenge.

"Confident," I corrected.

"Isn't that just a euphemism for the same thing?" she asked, narrowing her eyes…*playfully*? There was definitely some level of amusement staring back at me. I liked it more than I strictly should've. As it was, it was day one of nine hundred and eighty-five before we would stage our inevitable split. Perhaps a way to kill time was precisely what we needed.

"Cocky men can't walk their talk."

"*Oh*," she scoffed. "And you can?"

"I'm not in the habit of gambling unless I know I can win."

"So, *you knew* I'd say yes and not report you to HR?" Judging by the satisfaction in her subtle smile, she'd been dying to bring that up for a while now. "Logic would lend to the idea that I could've turned around and added another headache to your heartbreak."

"Okay," I allowed. "I don't gamble unless it's worth the risk."

That glorious pink colored her cheeks as her gaze dropped to the board. "Then let's play, Mr. Hart."

"I'm also not prone to showing mercy," I teased flatly.

"Like I'd ever request it." She arched one lone brow before demanding, "So? Prove it."

It turned out that Alice was a far more calculating opponent than my brother or cousins had ever been. She could've given my dad a run for his abundance of money, which was why it was absolutely no surprise when she knocked on my home office door Thursday morning.

"You got a second, boss?"

"For my wife? Always. Come in, beautiful." I'd say about anything to earn that blush, I realized. She quirked a brow, smirking like she knew exactly what I was doing...and didn't seem to mind. Stepping inside, she quietly shut the door behind her and sighed as she eased into the chair across from me. "That sounds good," I drawled sarcastically.

Her eyes shot skyward as she sighed, "The article is live."

"Now would be a great time to specify."

"*The allegations* went live this morning," she explained, glancing to her phone and reading aloud, "*From Wedded Bliss to Financial Crisis:* Hart Investments *CEO Greyson Hart Accused of Foul Play.*"

"Ahh, that." I echoed her sigh as I leaned into my chair, lacing my fingers behind my head. No doubt our surprise engagement had delayed their game plan. "Are we changing our strategy?"

"Nope, I already messaged our journalists." It had been Alice's idea, after all. It made sense that she would get to pull the trigger. "The first leak will hit blogs tonight, and the next three will launch over the next few days."

"Counter articles?"

"Through editing and ready to cause a buzz."

"Follow-ups?"

"Exclusive interviews will stagger out over the next four weeks. We have pregnancy speculations and trouble in paradise on standby." Like a commander reporting to their captain, she stated the facts without much in the way of inflection. No one would look at the sinfully sexy vixen in front of me and ever expect such a calculating, cunning mind to accompany it. I'd just married my best weapon, and the world had no idea she'd already been unleashed. "Your investigators now have names and sources?"

"They're in the thick of it."

"Good. Your name was cleared this morning, so Reggie just needs to make his statement, and you'll be back where you belong. Do you want me to do anything else?"

Nodding with a smile fit for the genius I was about to unleash, I ordered, "Burn it down."

The smile that overtook her face was devious, to say the least. She didn't look scared. The allegations weren't flustering her this time around. We had layers of defense, not the least of which was a team of attorneys and private investigators already digging into every corner of the business to search for anything Alice or I may have missed.

We'd prepared, we'd placed our decoys, we had a story that should draw their attention. She knew it as well as I did. At least judging by the spark in her eyes to accompany that smile.

"My pleasure."

Unseen Photos from Greyson and Alessandra's Clandestine Nuptials!

Star-Studded Surprise: Hail Mary Hero, Paxton Rhodes, and Reality TV Host Make Waves at Private Wedding!

Undercover Romance: Sneak Peek into the Billionaire CEO's Hush-Hush Wedding!

From Best-Seller To Bridesmaid: Elora Rhodes-Allen Spotted At Sister's Secret Wedding

An avalanche of articles was posted in magazines, papers, and blogs over the next forty-eight hours, with more scheduled on a drip over the following weeks, and while I knew Alice didn't particularly care for exploiting her siblings' growing fame, she hadn't forbidden a single tool in her arsenal.

I was studying one of the 'leaked' wedding photos we'd supplied of the three Rhodes siblings, laughing around our beach bonfire Saturday night, and couldn't help but smile.

Her sister was laughing—an arm draped around Alice's shoulders—and Paxton was grinning, looking at ease as he watched the fire towering over her other side. But it was my bride, in a dress Leighton called 'Mediterranean BoHo'—whatever the hell that was—smiling down at her hands like she did when she was nervous or contemplative, that my eyes kept tracing.

Stunning.

A blind man wouldn't even deny that. Not with the kindness in her voice or the generosity she showed, even to the cursed beast she claimed made her life miserable. She'd seen the threat to my company as unjust, and regardless of her feelings about me, she couldn't stand by and let it threaten the people we both cared for.

"Will I see you at Paxton's welcome party?" Oliver's voice tugged me from the screen, and I discreetly clicked the exit window.

"Nice knock, asshole."

"Nice open door, prick."

Chuckling, I shook my head but waved him in. Despite the low-level buzz around the embezzlement allegations, Alice's plan had worked—the public was focused on us, which meant the board okayed a public statement of my innocence, backed by their internal investigation. It felt damn good to be back in my office and even better as my brother sauntered inside it.

Of the two of us, Ollie had always been the wild one. Classic middle child syndrome that miraculously outlived Beaumont through years of adolescent hell-raising and college days spent chasing skirts rather than A's. Everything he did, he did with a lightness I both envied and cherished. Envied because I never tasted it, and cherished because I'd fought so hard to preserve it. The best part about an angry drunk of a father was that it didn't take long to know exactly what would piss him off, and like I'd waved a red flag in front of a bull, his temper zeroed in on me.

If it meant I was the one that was never enough, and my brothers went undetected, it was worth it.

That's the thing people don't realize. Addiction doesn't know a class. Just because the man could function ten hours a day didn't mean he didn't hit the bottle when he walked in the door, freeing the demons in his head in the process.

We thought after Beaumont died, he'd sober up, but he dove deeper into the bottle. Uncle Reggie and my mother picked up the slack.

It was that hard-fought-for innocence that my brother embodied as he flopped into the chair opposite me, kicking his feet up on my desk like the heathen he was. Mattie might be ten going on thirty, but Ollie was thirty going on ten.

"So? Are you coming to the welcome party? Alice says she'll be there." Paxton was due to arrive within a matter of hours, so naturally, Ollie and the team would give him an Emerald Bay welcome this weekend. I glanced at the time and blinked, palming at my face. I hadn't realized how late it had gotten. Alice headed home ages ago.

"Wouldn't miss it," I promised with a yawn, shutting my laptop and turning to power down the curved monitor beside it.

His scoff had me glaring up at him. "Right. Because you're normally a party guy."

"They're less annoying now that women won't be flinging themselves at me." I stood and pulled my suit jacket off the back of the chair, throwing it on in the next motion as Ollie smirked my way.

"That's what you're telling yourself?" When I just arched a brow, he widened his eyes like I was an imbecile. "Dude. Something about being vetted by one of their own…women are nasty. They get way more forward once you're married."

"What?" I growled, almost choking on my spit.

"Yeah. I don't know—something about knowing you're worthy of a commitment."

"That's so fucked up," I muttered, reaching forward to pull him to his feet. He begrudgingly humored me, following my lead out into the hallway. Ollie and I always shared the car if we wrapped up at the same time. The perk of buying up land and developing the neighborhood yourself was getting to pick your next-door neighbors. Ollie and the kids were across the street, and I was sandwiched between cousins and Nona, not that we'd see her until snowbird season. "How are the kids?"

"They love the new nanny." Surprise sent my brows lifting as I glanced his way. With rolled eyes, he clarified, "*Beau loves* the new nanny."

Chuckling, I said, "That's what I thought."

Pushing the elevator button, my brother glanced back at me, shaking his head in exasperation. "She's gotta stop running them off."

"Sure it's not *Cruella* at fault?"

Ollie grimaced, running a hand over the back of his neck. "Between the two of them, I swear. We're going to end up shipping in an unsuspecting Au pair."

"Desperate," I noted, smiling as we stepped into the elevator.

"Desperate times," he countered as the doors closed. "I don't want to crush that willpower—she could run a country someday, you know? There's not a dictator on the planet that would want to fuck around and find out against Matilda Hart…" Somehow, he managed to recap her entire school week between the thirteenth floor and the car. By the time we slipped into our seats, he moved on to Beau, who seemed just as intelligent as his sister but a little more conventional in the personality department so far.

Arthur guided the car through familiar turns, and I relaxed into the seat, breathing for the first time since getting back into the office. I was still enjoying the view of my eyelids when a chill danced down my spine, forcing me to straighten. Unease had me pulling out my phone, but the screen was free of notifications…well, aside from the *Fam Damily* Rhodes group chat, which was insane. Alice was right. That sucker would stay muted.

Oliver's eyes zeroed in on my phone as his story came to an end. "You expecting someone?"

"No, I just got nervous out of nowhere."

"Almost home. Nothing from security?"

"Nothing," I confirmed, though it did little to ease the tension in my chest. We hadn't even hit the driveway when Arthur rolled down the divider.

"Mr. Hart, would you like me to call security?"

Adrenaline shot through my system as I saw what he was surveying through the windshield. Alice, looking twelve kinds of pissed off in her perpetually prim, composed way, wearing a skintight pair of yoga pants and an athletic top, was cornered by the dead-men-walking paparazzi.

Bolting from the car to the muttered curse of my brother, I made a beeline for them just in time for her to ask if he had a life. But I slowed as I neared the edge of our gate. She stood tall, her head high, as she looked down her nose at the motherfucker I wanted to smash with his camera.

I snagged my brother by the elbow as his momentum carried him past me. Because Alice was speaking in the sickliest, sweetest, serpentine tone, and I found it sexier than sin.

"I would tread very carefully if I was in your shoes." A patronizing lift of a brow, like she was looking at a bug she'd stepped on. "I certainly wouldn't be daft enough to challenge the safety of *my husband's* home. Careers can be ended in moments, and lives destroyed much faster." Damn, the confidence in her words had pride lifting my cheeks.

"Are you threatening us, Ms. Rhodes?" The second of three asked.

"It's *Mrs. Hart.* And I'm telling you to remove your hands from Greyson Hart's wife before he erases your name from the face of modern media. Assault and harassment charges would be the least of your concerns."

Straightening, I realized the first dead man did, indeed, have a hand wrapped around her wrist, anchoring her in place. *Too late, motherfucker.* She was right. Nobody touched what was mine without paying with their peace of mind.

This pile of shit would be lucky to see daylight as a free man again if I had anything to say about it.

The desire to use that zoom lens around his neck for some complimentary tooth extractions had my voice near a growl as I said, "*My wife* is correct." All three of them spun to face me, but Alice only smiled, like she knew I'd come for her. "What you do next will determine the forecast of your future, so I suggest you *step. Back.*"

12

Freddy Kreuger

ALICE

Freddy Kreuger brought to life would have gotten less of a jump scare out of the reporters standing sentinel outside Hart House than Grey did. Shoulders sagging while my heart still hammered like a bass drum in my ears, I locked on to irate hazel eyes. He leisurely scanned from the meaty hand that had been wrapped around my wrist a moment before to the man he appeared to be preparing to murder, based solely on the unfiltered fury in his eyes. I'd seen his version of *nuclear*, and it was a terrifying silence that promised the swift destruction of entire family legacies.

This was so much worse.

And I'd never felt safer in my life.

Beside him, Ollie had his phone angled at us, and a shit-eating grin on his face that made me think of Axel. Like these three idiots just fucked around and were about to find out. The men faltered, scrambling to remember why they'd accosted me in the first place and lifted their cameras. The curl on Greyson's lip had them staggering back a step. All but the first, who snapped a photo.

Greyson charged at him. It wasn't like a bull or like the idiots in movies. No, these were slow, calculated steps, somehow made predatory, though his hands casually slipped into his pockets. There was an ease to his movements as he prowled toward us, his smile breaking free the moment the idiot stepped past the gate. Four members of his security team were hustling down the driveway.

"You know," he drawled, smirking now that he had the man on his property. *Smart.* "I keep thinking the press can't grow less intelligent, and yet, here you are, proving me wrong."

Attempting to regain control of the situation, the first blurted,

"Greyson, what do you have to say about the recent allegations you're stealing from your shareholders?"

"It's Mr. Hart to you. And you're being arrested for trespassing on private property, harassment, and assault," he announced as that wolfish smile grew.

The man scoffed. "You can't arrest me."

"Citizen's arrests are a perfectly normal occurrence," Greyson said dismissively before motioning to the four looming men approaching. "These gentlemen will keep you company until the police show up. I assure you, they're well on their way."

"That wasn't assault," the man barked in disbelief. It was the first time Greyson's gaze fell on me.

"Alice, darling, did this man touch you without consent?" Swallowing, I nodded. He didn't change his tone as he asked, "Did you feel that this man was attempting to coerce or intimidate you by laying hands on you?"

"Yes," I breathed. My hand absently rubbed the tension from my chest as I caught my breath. Pressure was building in my head like a thunderstorm brewing on the horizon. Greyson's jaw visibly clenched as his gaze went razor sharp, turning to the man in question.

"This is bullshit," the guy barked. It was about then that I noticed the police cruiser pulling up, which meant security had likely called them before Greyson even arrived.

"And did you, or did you not tell him to stop and leave you alone?"

"Yes."

"Did he?"

"No."

Victory curved his mouth as he turned back to the man now frantically surveying the trap he'd unwittingly set for himself. "You'll be grateful the police handle this their way." With a curl of his fingers, security came down to surround the man who'd grabbed me. For a moment, I thought he might swing, but then he thought better of it—whether it was the size of Greyson's guys or Oliver still poised with a camera, I wasn't sure. Greyson's livid scowl turned on the other two. "I'm feeling generous, so I'll give you a heads up. This gate," he pointed up to the beautiful Hart House entryway, "is protected by copyright. If your stalker photographs of *my wife* include her running by it, you'll be sued for copyright infringement. If I were you, I'd turn over those memory cards."

"You can't be serious," idiot number two blurted.

Grey shrugged as if it made no difference. "Find out for yourselves. But neither you nor your employers have a better attorney than my architect." The gleam in his eyes told me he would be funding said attorney. He'd enjoy it, too. When he held out his hand, idiot three rushed to surrender his SD card. With a sigh, the second followed suit. "Good boys. I suggest you get off my property, but I am sending you a message for your posse of imbeciles. My *wife* is off-limits. Touch her again, and you won't be pleased with the results. Understand?"

I thought they got the memo based on the speed with which they backed off the driveway. With security dealing with police and the paparazzi running off with their tails between their legs, his attention turned to me. Greyson closed the gap in an instant, crushing me against him. Shock rendered me momentarily immobile, but in the next instant, I was hugging him back.

"I'm sorry, beautiful," he murmured against my hair. "So sorry."

"I'm okay," I assured, though I wasn't sure if it was more for him or me.

He pulled me back, refusing to let go as he looked me over before lifting my hand to examine my wrist. "Are you?" He asked, a livid tremor in his tone. "He didn't hurt you, did he?"

Bewildered by his concern, I shook my head. "No, I don't think so." A quick internal inventory told me all was well. "Just…startled me. They haven't been that aggressive with me."

"You weren't mine before."

"No," I agreed, swallowing hard. Hearing that possessive edge to his voice solicited an unwelcome rush of warmth through my body. Memories of that beachside kiss assaulted my brain as my eyes traced his parted mouth. "I wasn't."

"What were you doing out alone?" he asked, snapping me back into the moment.

"Clearing my head," I supplied, now irritated. Not even Greyson Hart would be telling me I couldn't go out alone.

"I can't protect you if you're off the property," he murmured breathlessly, hands raising to cradle my face, momentarily disarming me. "Not if you run off alone. The city isn't safe for you, baby. Never really was, but especially not now."

"Mr. Hart, a word?" With a shaved head and a day's worth of scruff, an officer about Grey's height dipped his chin as he approached us. Looking more concerned than accusatory—which was a relief, to say the least—he glanced between us, giving me an apologetic grimace. "Are you okay, Mrs. Hart?"

Nodding shakily, I allowed Greyson to guide me over to the man as he plucked a pen from his front pocket.

It was only once we'd given our statements and Greyson waved off the police cruisers that we finally headed inside. A wall of fatigue hit me as the unexpected adrenaline crash knocked the strength from my limbs. Swaying a bit as I steadied myself, I caught Greyson's concerned hazels.

"You okay?" he asked, tone still gentler than usual.

"Yeah, I think I'm just…tired. My body overreacted, and the adrenaline is wearing off now."

"Your body getting ready to get you out of a bad situation isn't an overreaction," Ollie pointed out as he kicked his shoes off in the entryway. "I'll go make us some tea. What do you like?"

"That's awfully thoughtful of you. Thanks, Ollie."

"Yeah," Grey said, not sounding very thankful at all. "Thanks, asshole," he grumbled, making me laugh even as my head spun. His brother's grin made me make a mental note to keep Axel far away from him—the two of them would *only* get into trouble. But…something was wrong. A familiar disconnect between my mind and body had me chewing my lip.

Blowing out a breath, I kicked off my shoes, not flinching away when Greyson reached out a hand to steady me. The concern in his eyes had me bristling as I straightened, pulling in a long breath.

My body had always been prone to flooding more anxiety into my bloodstream than was strictly warranted. As a teenager, I'd been convinced someone was breaking into the house while the guys were playing football, and I was home alone, and before Max and El got to me across our tiny town, I'd already broken out in hives.

Fear seemed to elicit weird symptoms—like I internalized the stress, which is why the familiar, slow-moving, glittering spots filling my vision had me cursing under my breath.

"Alice?" Expensive-looking checkered socks stepped into my vision, and I realized I was staring at the wide plank floors, attempting to blink away the floating shimmer in my eye. Instead of vanishing, the little spots grew like tiny worms or some kind of ameba, as they inched across my vision. When he spoke this time, Greyson's tone had turned urgent. "*Alice?*"

"I, um—" There was a chasm between my brain and my mouth, making words suddenly impossible to form, the glimmer bacteria burning into my vision as an ache pressed against the back of my eyes. "Not today," I whimpered, swearing as I jammed my eyes closed. It was the heat of his broad palms stroking up and down my arms that had me peeling my eyes open, reluctantly attempting to focus as more of my vision was gobbled up by the aggressive migraine rapidly consuming my world.

"What, Alice? Talk to me."

"Do you…um…do you have coffee?" Each thought was more fragmented than the last, and I felt myself cling to his forearms like my life depended on it. I heard him snap his fingers and the shuffle of feet while I just tried to will away the blind spots blocking his face from view. I needed to get to the bathroom and quickly. Episodes that hit this hard and fast almost always came with a visit to the porcelain throne.

"Can you get her some coffee, please? Black and hot. She likes it just shy of scalding."

"And…um," I closed my eyes, willing my brain to function, "Ibuprofen or Excedrin or something?"

"I uh—I'm sure there's something—*did he hurt you?*" He hoisted my hand to eye level, and through my kaleidoscope of brain fuckery, it looked like he was examining my wrist. If the strobes would stop flashing at me, I could see if he was as terrified as I thought he looked. "Ollie, call Doctor Eastman."

"No, Grey," I protested, squeezing my deathtrap on his forearm tighter as his face came in and out of focus through what was now about half my vision. Not for the first time, I wondered if this was what going on a bad trip was like. "I'm okay, I just…I get migraines with aura."

"*What?*"

Oh god, was that panic *in his voice?*

"I'm losing my vision," I explained, trying to isolate the pain in my head and not allow it into my voice. "The faster I get down a strong painkiller, the easier this will be, okay? If I don't get them down quickly, I can be out of commission for a day or so, and I'm more likely to vomit. If any of the staff happen to have a cold cap in their car or rooms, those are…amazing." It was getting physically hard to speak, the pain was so searing.

"Jesus, okay. What else can I do? God, I should have killed that motherfucker," he growled, pulling me against his chest and cradling my head into the cranny of his neck. Something between a giggle and a whimper escaped me.

He was…*soothing*. The ache suddenly slamming against my skull had to compete with his palm wrapped around my face like he could shield me there. I focused on the subtle stroke of what I assumed was his thumb over my cheekbone as fast footsteps approached from the direction of the kitchen.

"Preston," Grey's voice rumbled against my ear, "bring every painkiller we've got to my room so she can tell me what's best."

"You got it, sir; I'll head right up with water," a male voice said. *Preston?* Had I met a Preston? Feeling entirely separated from my body, I wrapped my arms around his tight waist, turning into his torso and bowing against him. Dear God, the man's body was solid. Reassuring.

"I've got you," he breathed. For some damn reason, those three words had tears welling in my eyes as searing pain slammed against them again to the rhythm of a metronome. My heartbeat, I realized. "Can you walk?"

"I'm so sorry."

"Please don't apologize. I got you into this mess."

I was too afraid to shake my head, instead asking, "Can you please guide me? I can see about half...uh—my upper left is still okay." I held my hand up to the side where I still had a good chunk of sight. Fear rocked through my body, and I had to beat it back. I'd had these since I hit puberty, and now was not the time to panic. Fuck that. I was better than that.

It didn't matter that I was in Greyson's house or that it was *my boss* soothing me with long strokes through my hair. *Husband*, my inner bitch corrected sardonically.

This wasn't new, she reminded me.

But it never seemed to be less startling to suddenly be deprived of such a critical sense, especially as pain slammed against my eyes, around my cheekbone, jaw, and teeth.

"I've got you. Wrap your arms around my neck."

"What—" my question was cut off as he scooped me into his arms, moving gently for his usually abrupt nature. "What are you doing?"

"Taking care of my wife."

"*Greyson.*"

"*Alice.*"

"Put me down." Even as I said it, I leaned into him, tightening my hold and soaking up his mouthwatering scent.

"I will."

"On the floor."

His low chuckle warmed my bones. "Nice try, Mrs. Hart." Someone rushed past us, and I heard a foot hit the bedroom door a breath before he was gingerly placing me on a plush comforter. "Hang on, I've got you," he repeated, and I felt him rearrange the linens as I soaked up the darkness, pain easing when the light of the hallway no longer assaulted me. But it would get worse before it got better. So, so much worse.

A moment later, half of Greyson's face was in my view, and he was trailing warm fingers down my arm to cup my hand, bringing it up to place pills in my palm. "Here, water," he urged, pressing a cold glass into my other hand.

As I tried to adjust past the flashing lights to see the cup, his hand guided the other up to my lips. I popped the pills in my mouth —three, if my thumb was correct—and knocked them back with the water.

Mission accomplished, I eased down onto the luxurious feeling mattress and melted into the safety of something solid beneath me and the surrounding darkness. Closing my eyes, I cursed the strobes but tried to remember the breathing techniques I'd learned over time.

"You get them a lot?" he asked softly, concern thick in his voice.

"Not so much anymore. Mostly when I'm stressed."

"Those days Leighton called in sick for you?"

"I thought she talked to Paul," I whispered, the sound of my own voice like nails on a chalkboard.

"There are very few things Paul doesn't tell me." He ran a soothing hand across my forehead, and I leaned into the touch. "Now, relax, baby. You're safe." I nodded against his skin, unwilling to admit my grief when his touch vanished. Something about pain this acute robbed me of my logic, leaving in its place the most intense terror of being abandoned.

Being trapped in a body that spontaneously renders you helpless is a special kind of hell.

Eyes closed, still trying to unclench my jaw, my ears strained at the rustle of fabric. Stiff fabric, by the sounds of it. There was a soft thud and muffled footsteps and then the mattress dipped before those warm fingers returned to draw a sigh of relief from my lips.

More soft footsteps proceeded a less graceful landing on the bed, and I smiled when Greyson said, "She's alright, Cap." There was the undeniable whine of his Shepard a beat before his heavy weight landed on my legs. My fingers found fur and then the cold wetness of his snout.

"You're both ridiculous," I giggled weakly. "Thank you."

"Harts take care of their own," Greyson supplied simply. The soft kiss against my forehead had to be imagined. But he was stroking soothing lines across my face. "You confirmed that today."

"What?" I whimpered.

He huffed a soft laugh before saying, "You were a Hart in true form today. I don't think I've ever seen something as sexy as you telling those reporters to get off our property."

I nearly choked on my laugh, wincing as the pressure of it slammed into my forehead. "You're hilarious."

"I mean it. You'd think you grew up dispersing those assholes. You wielded our name like a blade."

"Even a dog fights back when provoked." Some distant part of my mind registered his use of *our* name.

"Well, *your fight* was sexy as fuck. I'm so sorry it cost you." When his claim pushed me to argue, but the pain sent me wincing instead, he demanded, "*Rest*, Alice. Preston's bringing up coffee any minute." I nodded softly and let his reassuring touch lull me toward the promise of sleep.

Sleep buried the pain. Sleep was the *only* safe space. But his soft voice caressed my senses, keeping me on this side of consciousness because his next words hung heavy, like a confession. "This is agonizing, Alice." Somehow, I believed him and could hear pain in that familiar timbre. "Why didn't you ever tell me?"

"Hmm," I murmured, working to find my voice as that *pound, pound, pounding* assaulted my head, my eyes, my ears, and my spine. "Why didn't you ask?"

I WOKE up to the dull throb of lingering migraine, relieved to find my vision restored when I opened my eyes, though they loathed the slice of light from the ensuite bathroom, like a blade directly across my brain.

Greyson's room was at least twice the size of the guest suite he'd designated for me. The curtains were still closed, a glimmer of light cutting through.

Still in my workout clothes, I stretched, inventorying the tension in my head and neck and feeling lucky it hadn't been a bad one. Puking once in front of Greyson Hart was one too many times, thank you very much.

"Hey, pumpkin," Leighton's groggy voice warbled into existence as she sat up beside me, rubbing her eyes in the gloom. "You okay?"

"What're you doing here?" I croaked, trying not to make any sudden movements as I came to.

"Grey called, silly. Told me what happened with the paparazzi bastards and that you went into an episode after."

"What time is it?" I asked, entirely disoriented with the sunlight still coming through, though I felt like I was peeling myself from a comatose state.

"Slept through the night."

Wincing, I slowly sat up, rubbing at my aching face and hoping I didn't give thanks too soon as my stomach flipped. Greyson called my sister—likely had her brought over—because I had a migraine?

I've got you.

Harts take care of their own.

I should have killed that motherfucker.

Damn, the man was on a roll of disarming sweetness. Evidently, a woman in crippling pain was Greyson's weak spot.

"I'm not sure what you put in that man's morning cereal, but he paced like a feral tiger all night."

"What?" I stammered, thinking surely I misheard her.

"I don't think he slept, sissy. Every time I woke up, he was checking on you, or pacing the end of the bed. You'd think you were laying on the brink of death in the ICU for how frantic he was."

Barely blinking, I hadn't wrapped my mind around what she'd said when a knock on the door announced Greyson as he stepped into the room. On a whoosh of breath, he said, "Alice." Beelining to the bedside, he asked, "You alright?"

I glanced between him and Leighton. She nodded softly as if encouraging me to talk to him, before excusing herself to the bathroom.

"Thank you," I breathed, my hand coming to settle over the cross on my clavicle. It was then that I spotted the furry, anxious Shepard slinking into the room behind his human and settling at his feet.

"For what?" he asked gruffly, tone still quiet.

"For taking care of me."

Silence settled between us as he nodded, bending to rub Captain's ears. "Dr. Eastman will be by this afternoon to check on you."

"They're just migraines, Grey. There's not anything they can do."

"There was nothing *just* about that, Alice. There's nothing *just* about randomly losing your sight in crippling pain. She's the best. If anyone can get you answers, Dr. Marnie Eastman will. You need to tell her everything when she gets here."

Throat tight, I went to answer, but the words died on my tongue. He was…taking care of me in a very bossy, intrinsically Greyson way. "Thank you," I breathed. He gave a curt nod, evidently satisfied that I'd cooperate if nothing else. He rose and then patted the bed to prompt his doggo to take his spot at my feet.

"Rest, my clever Belle. The beast will leave you be."

13

A Rather Tempting Kitty
GREYSON

"Are you stocking a battlement?" Alice laughed later that day, shaking her head shallowly as I showed her another stash of pepper gel. Her movements might've been stiffer than usual, but at least she was smiling. We had pepper gel in every vehicle, and after last night, I'd ensured she had one in every purse and gym bag, as well as on her keychain, insisting she take one running. Gel would be more effective than her canister of pepper spray and had less of a chance of coming back at her on the wind.

She didn't seem to understand the lengths I'd go to to keep her safe yet. She would.

"Focus, Alice. I never want you feeling so scared for your safety that you send your body into shock like that." *Helpless.* That's how it felt watching her fight an invisible battle buried in her mind. Not even money can buy answers if they don't yet exist.

Dr. Eastman hadn't had much in the way of encouragement. Much like Alice had warned me, the study of migraines was evolving slowly, and I wasn't even open to considering some *experimental* medication.

To see my fierce girl crippled in that kind of pain was a hell I didn't know existed until she voluntarily fell into my arms. I might not be able to make her brain avoid short-firing, but I could equip her to function through her fear. That was what we learned first as Seals. Powering through the kind of terror that gripped your marrow.

I hadn't slowed down to think too hard about when and how she became *mine.* The devil on my left shoulder told me the moment she'd sauntered into our offices in that tight dress and fitted blazer with stars in her eyes. But the guy on the right? He kept reminding me she hadn't chosen me—*this*—beyond appeasing her conscience. Maybe our kiss during the ceremony tricked the chemicals in my brain into thinking I had some claim to her beyond that, but that's all it was: a trick.

Her words were on an ever-present loop in my mind. *Why didn't you ask?*

To her, I was still the asshole that signed her paycheck.

Her amused sigh brought me back into the moment, focused on those grey eyes as she said, "I am focused. Pepper gel *is everywhere*, and window breakers are on the keychains and in the center consoles of every car. First aid in every glove box, with a comprehensive kit in the mud room."

Throat aching, I nodded. Ollie and I ordered everything we could get our hands on to have in the house for her, but I didn't want to combat crippling headaches if we could just avoid them. If fear was her trigger, we could take steps to dismantle it.

"Good girl. Now, come on."

"Come *where*? Greyson, your tour has been thorough."

Her irritation was welcome if it meant she was prepared. Was it a little overboard to show her all my emergency exits in this house? Hopefully. However, with my involvement in *Thunderstrike*, she needed to know a plan for each scenario.

I slid my hand against hers, threading our fingers and trying not to focus on the way her breath hitched.

Okay. Coercing a woman I found positively breathtaking into an arrangement like this was likely my least intelligent move to date. But as she wrapped her fingers around my hand, I found I didn't very well care.

Because she just...fit. Here. In my house. Where my doctors fussed over her labs, and my staff was frantic to ensure the cartoon princess had whatever she needed.

They already loved her—this doe-eyed, silky-haired, brilliant brunette now rolling her eyes but following me, nonetheless. As we came around the corner, she smiled at Marianne, one of the housekeepers, and I watched her entire face relax the moment we were out of sight. She was still in pain and trying to hide it.

"Greyson," she groaned. "Where are we going now? I'm exhausted. It's Paxton's party day, and I want to nap before we get ready."

Stifling my smile, I said, "I have someone I want you to meet."

As if on cue, a cheery baritone barked, "Hart! Where the fuck are you?"

Her eyes flicked to me, and I grinned, calling back, "We're coming. Hold your fucking horses."

"Oh shit," she giggled, "he is human."

"What?"

"Didn't know you could swear," she noted dryly, a silent smirk threatening her lips. Her humor could so easily be mistaken for indifference, but I was starting to get a feel for it.

"Oh, come on."

"Mr. Serious all the time," she said, puckering her lips and pinching her brows as she dropped her voice mockingly. I was still shaking my head as our hallway dumped us back into the foyer.

"This asshole?" Retired Captain Jackson—A.K.A. Jax—Reynolds was standing in my living room in unlaced motorcycle boots, his blond hair slicked back, hands casually stuffed in his back pockets. Fucker had gotten bigger while I was stuck behind a desk. "Nah, he's a *crack-up*."

The thing that won me over about Jax was the fact that he always had something sarcastic to say, even in the shittiest of situations. The more time I spent around Alice, the more I thought the two of them would hit it off.

"Motherfucker," I said by way of greeting, grinning as I slipped my hand from Alice's and opened my arms. He immediately came in for a hug, clapping my back as I did the same.

"*Pinman*, how you been?" he asked, pulling back. The guys closest to me had given me the nickname after the surgeons put me back together with pins, plates and rods. Jax shot that trouble-making smile in Alice's direction as his eyes did a far too thorough scan for my liking. Alice was not the kind of stunning that could be missed. "I hear congratulations are in order. Though I'm a little chapped, I wasn't cool enough to be invited."

Yeah, the way I wrapped her little waist in my palm and pulled her into me was possessive. Not even gonna apologize for it. "Jax, this is my beautiful bride, Alice. Baby, this is Captain Jackson Reynolds."

"Jax," he corrected, shaking his head reproachfully. "Call me Jax."

Her smile was a bit too eager, and she was way too damn quick to take his hand.

This was a mistake.

"Nice to meet you." To me she added, "You didn't tell me we had company coming, *honey*." Everything about the pet name sounded alien and I had to stuff back the laughter in my chest.

"'M not *really* company," Jax dismissed. "An unfortunate necessity, by the sounds of it."

Curious gray-blues landed on me, obviously unsure of what to say or expect. Giving her a little squeeze, I said, "Jax is the second of my four and has agreed to be your personal bodyguard until things quiet down in the media."

"Oh, that's not necessary," she breathed, a bit panicked.

"Absolutely necessary," Jax and I responded in unison.

"Starting tonight, at the party," I added, bracing for her push-back. As expected, her eyes narrowed.

"I am not going to walk around with a tail at my brother's welcome party."

"Ill-advised unless it's a costume party," I said, smirking, holding her gaze even as she glared at me. Jax brought out the punk eighteen-year-old enlistee in me better than about anybody else. Just for fun, I slowly dragged my eyes over her chest and the exposed column of her neck. "Though I think you'd be a rather tempting kitty."

Yep. It was official; I would say anything to make her flush like that.

"*Okay*," Jax drawled teasingly as Alice bit her lower lip, eyes dropping to her feet. "Do y'all need to get a room, and I can come back later, or you gonna give me the lay of the land?"

"Come on, asshole, we'll bring you up to speed." As we turned to guide Jax through Hart House, I lowered my lips to her ear and whispered, "Careful, little Belle. Keep blushing like that, and it will be hard for me to keep this a gentleman's agreement. You'll give a man the wrong impression if you let his words affect you like that."

Her throat bobbed audibly before she whispered back, "I'm not responsible for your lack of mental fortitude."

"No," I agreed, "but you are responsible for whatever thoughts had you biting down on your lip just now."

"I'll take the numbers for the producers you promised. If my performance has you convinced, maybe I am better than I thought," she said smugly as she lifted her chin. But the blood coloring her cheeks didn't lie.

"Maybe," I allowed, smiling as I straightened. "Or maybe you remember exactly what that kiss felt like on our beach." I certainly did. It was all that occupied my mind during waking hours. "What did you say before the wedding? Welcome to the fun part."

FORMAL ALICE WAS a vision no man could overlook. But casual Alice was infinitely more appealing. When she styled herself, she left her skin glowing, the light pattern of freckles over her nose was accompanied by a subtle pink like she'd spent too much time in the sun today. Maybe we had. One of her ridiculously flowy sun dresses was draped over her curves, hanging off her delicate shoulders. Half of my evening had been spent wanting to unwind the Roman-looking sandals wrapped around her calves or run my fingers over her bare collarbones.

I'd always found it fascinating the way she morphed into the socialite culture like the best of us; but she did the same thing in an event tent packed full of towering football players. Her shoulders were more relaxed, her smile a little less posed and more flirtatious, and she laughed a bit louder.

She was still the quiet one in most circles, always watching, rarely instigating, but just like she did with tycoons and politicians, she'd memorized a few stats on key players, making more than one of them take a step back to reassess her.

Paxton was just as at ease. If he was intimidated coming into a new team—one owned by his new in-laws, at that—he didn't show it.

It was the tight end with his hand between my wife's shoulder blades that told me we'd had enough socializing for the evening.

Abandoning my conversation with her brother and one of his most dependable, soon-to-be linemen, I rotated to her, pulling her into me and relieved when the idiot removed his hand with the sense to at least look a bit apologetic. I wasn't sure exactly when the feeling of her in my hand became so necessary, but I'd have to think about it later.

"Haven't seen you eat anything in a while, baby. Wanna grab a bite?"

"Would love one," she answered a beat before I brought her mouth to mine. This wasn't a beachside wedding, wasn't the place to claim her, but god dammit, if her taste didn't consume every inch of my being. Her pliant submission beneath my palms was exactly what I'd been needing since we left the island. Pulling away was a feat in itself, but at least every player in her radius had seen who she belonged to.

Jax, who'd been obediently hovering behind her without being overly intrusive, locked that navy gaze with mine. My dipped chin was enough of a dismissal for him to hang back as I led her away from the group of players and their significant others and over to the buffet of food.

Handing her a plate, I asked, "Having fun?"

"Yeah," she admitted, a note of surprise to her tone. "I haven't spent much time around your guys, but they're entertaining. I think Pax will enjoy them."

"Swell," I said simply, nodding at the chafing dishes lining the white tablecloths. We made our way down the line, filling our plates as the party rushed around us. Relief washed through me when she wandered out of the tent and into the burgeoning dusk. I might've been born into this dynasty, but that didn't mean I enjoyed the obligatory events any more than she did. Selfishly, I was sick of sharing her focus with a lineup of brooding athletes. The prepared ocean-side bonfires down below would be a breath of fresh air.

"Oh my god," she gasped excitedly, pulling my attention from the faces of partygoers to the light in her eyes. "Are those S'mores?!"

I chuckled. "Ollie has the pallet of a toddler, so I wouldn't be shocked—" but she was already making a beeline for the table between the grass and beach. Vaguely, I was aware of Jax trailing behind us and glanced over my shoulder to see him with his own plate of goodies, nonchalantly making his way across the lawn. Good man. Sure enough, this table was full of supplies to make S'mores, and Alice was cheerily stacking them on a fresh plate.

She was cute when she was excited, even if she was trying to downplay it for appearance.

Fire no longer raging, plates cleared about half an hour later, she reached over and snagged a metal roasting stick before stabbing it into a marshmallow.

"Remind me not to piss you off."

She grinned mischievously, "You don't grow up on a boat and not learn how to use a blade."

"Do a lot of stabbing?"

"Fireside?" she clarified, her brows shooting up as she strategically lowered herself onto the ground and hovered her marshmallow just over the coals, slowly rotating it. "Yeah. We spent the bulk of our summers in Mistyvale down on the water. Not a lot to do in town, so we'd all build fires nine feet tall and burn away the summer nights." Her smile grew more authentic and endearing, eyes going distant as she reminisced. I grabbed my own marshmallow and joined her. "My big brothers and dad taught me how to build the perfect fire and when the embers were ready to use. We'd roast bratwurst and fill our bellies on skewers of veggies, then Rhyett, Jameson, and Brod would break out marshmallows and spooky stories."

"Hmm," I murmured. When her eyes widened, I said, "It sounds absurd, but I wish I'd grown up like that."

"In some backwoods fishing town?"

"Bonding as a family," I clarified.

Her brows knitted together. "You and Ollie are tight."

"Now," I admitted. "But when you grow up two steps removed from doing all the things, you miss all of the…"

When my words wandered off, she blinked, studying me before finishing, "Connection?"

I sighed, admitting, "Yeah. It's not the same when your father *pays* someone to make you oven-roasted S'mores with ritzy Swedish chocolate and some ridiculous French wafer. God forbid you dirty your clothes actually enjoying the damn thing, bringing shame to the family name."

"You and Ollie don't do that to Mattie and Beau."

"No. We've made a point of letting them be kids."

We sat quietly for a long stretch as she processed all of that, but then a sheepish smile lifted her cheeks. "Your marshmallow is on fire."

"Fuck," I grumbled, yanking the stick upright as she burst out laughing. I blew the flame out like an oversized candle. She was covering her mouth when I lifted my eyes from the charcoal exterior. "You can laugh, you know. I can handle it."

Forcing her face straight didn't stop her chin from wobbling with the humor begging to go free. Her teeth dug into her lower lip, and I tracked the moment as she carefully freed it. "Nah, I'm fine."

"It's pretty pathetic," I admitted dryly.

"*No*," she scoffed. A little giggle broke free before she teased, "Poor rich boy can't roast a marshmallow." Before I could respond, she'd rolled her eyes and pulled up her golden-brown, puffed sugar ball, blowing on it like a textbook example. "Here," she said, taking pity on me as she reached over, but instead of discarding my destroyed disgrace of summer dessert, she curled her nails around the lower lip of it, and slid off the crust in one smooth motion, revealing a gooey ball of melted confection. She blew on it, though I'm sure her fingers were protesting. "You can use it like that or roast it again." With that, she popped the charred crust in her mouth. "I kinda like 'em burnt anyways."

Shaking my head, I questioned, "Twice-roasted marshmallow?"

"Exactly."

Glaring at her, I slowly lowered it back over the embers. It's not that I *couldn't* cook outdoors; I just hadn't spent much time out here since I came home. Who had the time for this? It didn't help that she was *sinfully* distracting, even now, as she sandwiched her prize between crackers and chocolate.

"The real trick is to wrap them in foil afterward and set them back by the fire. This will do for now," she explained, setting her sweets on the edge of the pit.

"Really?" I pressed.

"Really," she confirmed. The chatter of the party and crash of waves seemed to vanish when the woman smiled. I'd always seen her beauty. Been painfully aware of her curves and those intense eyes. But I hadn't ever seen her quite like this. Apparently, I was staring more intently than appropriate because she asked, "What?"

"I like it when you smile."

"Could've fooled me."

Ouch. "Wouldn't have been appropriate to tell you that as my assistant."

"But it is now that you married me like a mail-order bride?" A few weeks ago, I would have thought her tone was abrupt, but now...? *She was teasing me.* That subtle curve of her full lips? That was Alice having fun. Finding humor in our ridiculous setup.

"I believe calling you my wife buys me the privilege of appreciating you." I dropped my eyes to my twice-roasted marshmallow as she skewered a second, refusing to humiliate myself by screwing it up again.

"For centuries, that title would buy you the privilege of heirs, too. Are we following all the customs of ancient nobility?"

"Luckily for us both, I have no interest in heirs. Ollie has successfully secured the family line."

"The media will call for my head if I don't give them a mini-Greyson. Force us to divorce for the good of the nation."

That concept had me scowling at the fire as I rotated the rod in my fingers. "I'll make a public statement that I'm infertile." Maybe vasectomy advocacy was a thing? Everyone always left or died anyway; not much of a point in considering the alternative. The last thing I needed was more potential collateral—the kind that would bring me to my knees, that I'd burn the world to save.

"*Greyson,*" she giggled, shaking her head as she added, "it was a royalty joke."

"Fine, but I don't want their scrutiny on you." I looked up right as she pulled her second masterpiece from the fire and mimicked the motion, catching mine on just this side of too-toasted. "It would paint you as a saint for staying with me. Couldn't hurt."

"You really do have to think of everything through the lens of the press."

"I *loathe* them."

"I would, too, if that's how I grew up." She nudged my hand, and I looked down to see the now-melting S'more she'd set by the fire. "Here. Mistyvale special."

"That's yours," I argued.

"Shut up, *husband*, and eat my dessert." She took my laugh as the opportunity to pop the corner into my mouth. Begrudgingly, I took a bite, shaking my head as she smiled a victorious, feline smile. She ran her thumb over my bottom lip before pulling back and taking a bite from the same S'more.

I took my time looking her over—that satisfied smile as she closed her eyes, soaking up the flavor. But all I could think was that chocolate was the last thing I wanted to be eating with Alice Hart's exposed thigh on mine. Watching her throat work should not have been sexy, but all I wanted to do was slip my hand between those creamy thighs and slide my way up as I ran my lips over it. The only melted chocolate I wanted to eat would have been off her pebbled skin. Her words didn't dissipate the need she planted in my body as she asked, "See, it's better fireside, isn't it?"

"You look gorgeous tonight." All I could see was this woman in the flickering firelight. Her tentative smile, the glimmer in her eyes. The chocolate smeared on her lower lip. Like she'd done to me, I brought my thumb up to brush it away before popping it between my lips to suck it clean. Her mouth fell open in surprise, and need ate at my sense as her eyes tracked the movement, the long line of her neck working in the harsh firelight.

And then she closed the distance, sending any other thoughts skyward as her sugary lips crashed into mine.

14

I'd Prefer You Didn't and Said You Did

ALICE

Despite the million and one offerings, I hadn't had a drop of alcohol tonight.

Nope, I was stone-cold sober, mesmerized by the lines of his chocolate-smudged lips when I kissed Greyson as if my life depended on it.

His hesitation lasted only a moment, and then something between a purr and a growl rumbled in his chest, and the man moved. Still vaguely sticky hands came down on my arm and neck as he rotated to face me on the bench, lips moving in sync with mine. I couldn't bring myself to care.

Because Greyson Hart was kissing me back with just as much frenetic energy as I was throwing at him.

Each movement was urgent. Each kiss was a little harder, a little rougher, a little more demanding than the last. Part of me had hoped it had been a fluke—my reaction to him on the beach that day. Evidently not.

One warm palm dropped to my thighs, and as his fingers wrapped around my leg, a satisfied rumble emanated from his chest when I parted them for him. Heat bloomed from my thighs to my neck, every inch of my body responding as he devoured me.

At some point, it swapped from my kiss to his. Taking me captive bit by delicious bit. Grey set the tone, the pace, the intensity, and I was so far from complaining as my breaths grew ragged. Somehow, he straddled the bench and hoisted me onto his lap in the next movement. Just like that, he took ownership of this kiss—of my body.

I loved it.

Legs parted, I settled over his groin, wrapping my calves around his back as his legendary strong arm got an entirely new meaning.

Dizzy and panting, my hands finally raked through that perfect head of dark hair as his free hand slipped under the flimsy sage dress I picked up downtown, and a whimper escaped my lips. Every glance, every internal admission that he was as obnoxiously beautiful as the magazines claimed, every subtle hand at the low of my back, and bickering match came back.

Only the memories didn't send me running. I'd spent years of denying the truth of it. Under all the animosity, I—at least physically—wanted what I couldn't have. And we finally hit the boiling point.

Because he was right here.

Not only could I have him—*I did*.

Greyson's thick, straight hair was silky between my fingers, the powerful lines of his back like a handle as my fingers dug into his muscles. Strong fingers pressed into my legs until he wrapped his hands all the way around my thighs, inching higher. I needed him to. Needed those fingers to release the ache coiling in my core. Needed his mouth to ravage me entirely.

Breaking the kiss, Greyson kept our foreheads together, heady breaths filling my senses as he said, "We do this at your pace, baby." When I nodded, he accepted my next desperate kiss before saying, "This wasn't part of the plan. We can't erase intimacy once it's started."

"Shut up and kiss me," I breathed back.

His brief smile would have been infectious had he not swallowed mine in the next heartbeat. "That all you're looking for, princess?"

"For now."

"And later?" Another bruising collision of lips and teeth, his fingers tightening their hold on me, sending a fresh wave of lust through my body. Triumph rolled through me as his cock strained against his pants. For years, his infuriating self-control felt like a prison wall, trapping the world away from the man. The Titan, in all his glory. For it to falter because of me...*that* was intoxicating.

"Our house is full of football players," I pointed out.

"Our *yard* is full of football players," he countered before pulling my lip between his and giving a teasing pull.

"The staff's laundry room entrance should bypass that."

"Ahhh," he rumbled, "You *were* listening."

"I'm always listening, Grey," I panted.

"I fully intend to use that to my advantage."

"Only an idiot wouldn't."

"Alright, clever girl, lead the way."

I gave one quick nod before stealing his mouth, then unwinding, embarrassed to remember this beach was probably well within view of the partygoers despite the setting dusk. Grabbing his hand, I led us down the beach at what I hoped would be seen as a leisurely pace but was probably much too rushed to be so. Glancing over a shoulder, I checked to make sure no one was watching—save for a smirking Jax, who nodded in apparent farewell—and led him through the tall beach grasses toward the side path the staff used.

"You have the most exquisite ass," he declared conversationally. Choking on my laugh, I glanced over my shoulder to find a satisfied curve to his lips, eyes scraping over my body. With a shrug, he added, "Always wanted to tell you that."

"Might've caused an HR issue."

"Maybe," he agreed, smirking. A stabbing pain shot through my foot, and it was mostly Greyson's hold on me that kept me from falling as I jerked back.

"Ouch!" I barked, scowling through the near darkness at the arch of my foot, exposed by the sandals they'd picked for this outfit.

"What?" He breathed, concern heavy in his tone.

"I stepped on something—" My words turned into a whoop when he scooped me right off my feet. "You intend to make a habit out of this?" I questioned with a laugh.

"Five years of PT finally paying off," he said with a coy smile. "Now, if you could stop getting into trouble, I have other skills I'd like to demonstrate with these hands." Grey carried me through the laundry room entrance and into the kitchen, where he promptly placed me on the counter. Standing between my legs, I gave him a little squeeze with my thighs, keeping my hands where they were looped around his neck as he brought his mouth to mine.

Slow. Meticulous. As if we had all the time in the world, and nobody would notice our absence.

"Alright, give me your foot."

Snorting, I shook my head as he pulled away. "Oh no, you're one of *those*? I should have known." His only response was a sardonic glare that would put all of my brothers to shame collectively. I burst out laughing, but the sound cut off abruptly when he dropped to his knees, hands on my thighs. "Oh," I breathed. "You're one of *those*."

"Do you know how badly I want to dip under this damn dress and taste you?"

Dead. I was dead. Six feet under and seeing nothing but stars. Somehow, despite all of that, I managed to shake my head. The intensity in his eyes had my belly doing flips, every inch of my body alight with his touch, the need he'd built on that bonfire bench.

There wasn't enough time to contemplate what changed or when—maybe it was the way he defended me and took care of me, or perhaps this was all a long time coming; I just knew I wanted this man on his knees for me.

"For two years, you've tempted me with these flimsy little things, always prancing around the office, swishing your hips as you walk away," he growled, hands on my legs. Nonsense, of course. "That outfit you wore to the Kentucky Derby had me so bent out of shape I took an ice bath when I got back to the estate." We'd taken that trip to network with a new acquisition. I remembered the blush dress as well as the back of my hand because I'd never felt so…feminine. Unexpected tears welled in my eyes.

"I don't understand," I admitted. Why the hell did he remember that?

"Sometimes, you keep threats at arm's length."

"And I'm a threat?" I breathed, the words barely audible as he moved both hands to the leg in question.

"To my sanity and our working relationship? From the day you sat at that table with my brother."

It felt like the mental anvil you left in a confession booth, shrouded by sworn secrecy, heavy as though I'd pried it from him.

Impossible, my brain argued. I'd been a gnat buzzing too close to his impeccable hair for years. An annoyance. Not temptation.

Taking his time, Greyson grazed those firm fingers down my leg until he hit the leather straps wrapped around my calf. Eyes never leaving mine, he drew one away and then the other.

His lips twitched as he unwound them bit by bit. "Attraction is a cruelty when circumstance prohibits it." Sentence punctuated by an audible wince, he grimaced down at my foot, sucking all that sex appeal out of the space as he muttered, "Christ, what'd you do?"

With a pained sigh, Grey rose, straightening to his full height and moving for the sink, where he washed his hands thoroughly, eyes drifting my way from time to time. All I could manage was remembering how to breathe. He ducked out of the kitchen, muttering about the mud room, leaving me to my own company for a moment.

Suddenly acutely aware of the stinging in my skin, I glared at the slice across my foot. Dark crimson leaked in a steady stream, and I glanced over to my now stained heather brown sandal.

"Dammit, I liked those," I complained, earning a chuckle from Grey as he reentered the room with a first aid kit in hand.

"I'll buy you a dozen. Just sit still."

"*There's* Mr. Boss man," I drawled dryly.

"Shut up, you like it," he teased.

Did I? *Oh god, I might like it.*

He didn't leave me a whole lot of time to think that through because he lowered to his knees again and had me wincing as he examined it. The disgruntled wrinkle in his nose made me grimace in anticipation. Instead, I leaned back on my palms and decided to stare holes into the ceiling.

"You always want to live in California?" he asked as he slid my dress up and tucked it under my body weight.

"No," I answered honestly. "But when you grow up in a town like Mistyvale, it's kind of an *anywhere but here* philosophy."

"Noted," he said simply. "Avoid the last frontier." There was a searing sting and a tug that had my eyes watering.

"It's not all bad," my voice came out a little tighter.

"Had your heart set on marketing?"

"It sounded fun."

"With your analytical mind, I would've taken you as a data analysis girl."

"*Boring.*"

"But you're good at it."

"It lacks the human interaction I wanted."

"Past tense?" he asked casually as another stabbing pain shot through my foot, and I bit my lip to keep from whimpering.

"Turns out I'm exceptionally good at protecting grown men's egos," I teased.

When Greyson stood, I released the breath I'd unwittingly been holding, only gasping in enough air to answer his questions. "The best distraction you could think of was interview questions?"

He licked his swollen lips before shaking his head gently. "No, but the other one wasn't particularly conducive to watching what I was fishing out of your foot. Would've been a hard mission to accomplish with my head between your thighs."

Fucking troublemaker. "Thanks again."

A solitary brow arched. "Again?"

"First, my head. Now, my foot. What the hell was in there, by the way?"

He huffed a chuckle. "Shell. Broke into little fragments—I'm sorry I couldn't get 'em all at once." He tossed the pieces into the sink with a little sandy clink and then rewashed his hands before stepping back between my legs. "Can we pick up where we left off?"

"I have a feeling I'd prefer you didn't and said you did."

Mouth popping open, I whirled toward that familiar teasing tone, and tears flooded my eyes for an entirely new reason.

Max, in all his glorious, dark-haired, impeccably styled *Max-ness,* stood on the threshold. My momentary annoyance at being interrupted vanished as quickly as it appeared. Flying across the space, I hurled my arms around his neck, breathing a sigh of relief as he lifted me off my aching foot. Grey cleared his throat, and as I peeled away, I was embarrassed those tears had escaped down my cheeks.

Palming at them, I said, "Grey, this is our Max. Maxi, this is my—"

"Handsome, empire-crushing *husband*," Max finished with a devilish smile, his brown eyes glinting as he rotated my body to his side.

My watery laugh betrayed exactly how stressful these last weeks had been. Whether or not I let myself acknowledge that.

Greyson stepped forward, his expression softening as he extended a hand. But it was his next words that threw me off my axis. "Welcome to the Hart family, Max."

AFTER THAT, the evening passed by in a blur of martinis and more fancy food. Only this time, Grey was Velcroed to my side as we led Max around until we found Paxton hanging out on an enormous outdoor sectional with a handful of his new teammates, all shootin' the shit.

His words, not mine.

To my simultaneous disappointment and relief, I did not end up sleeping with my husband.

Instead, I passed out on his shoulder when the house had emptied of all but our four collective siblings. Evidently, Leighton accepted Arthur's offer to drive her home around midnight, which left Grey, Pax, Ollie, and Max getting to know each other. At some point, I woke up, rubbed at my eyes, knocked back Grey's glass of water, and curled up like a cat on his lap.

The man slept like that. Sitting up. On his back patio, with the roar of the ocean as our lullaby. Or at least, he claimed he slept, though the dark circles under his eyes had me questioning that.

When I demanded to know why he didn't wake me, he simply supplied, "You looked peaceful."

Those were the words in my brain as Jax turned our SUV into the business district. Hell, those were the words in my brain as I made myself a latte in the break room. I'd just poured a pretty little foam flower—a byproduct of your big brother giving you a job in his coffee shop—when the telltale chatter of women spilling the tea broke through my hypnosis.

I turned to find Rory and Hollyn rounding the corner. Up until the whole engagement fiasco, I would have said these two had been as close to friends as I'd made in the city. Nothing substantial—

mostly weekday coffees or lunches. But their silence these last few weeks spoke volumes.

Apprehension made my feet feel uneasy, so I smiled at them. Hollyn, with her wild auburn waves, caught my eyes and grinned back. "Well, if it isn't Mrs. Hart herself."

"Morning, ladies. How you been?"

"Not as good as you, by the sounds of it," Rory responded, tucking her mousy brown bob behind her ears.

Before I could formulate a coherent response, Hollyn gave me a roguish smile as she put her lunch in the fridge and said, "I gotta say. You had me fooled. I thought you hated Greyson."

"Hate and love are very dear companions," Rory pointed out, smiling playfully my way, "Aren't they, Alice?"

I thought about how quickly those years of sworn hatred vanished beneath the caress of his skilled fingers. His reassuring words while I hid from the daylight.

"Doesn't she know it," Max drawled as he came in behind them. He was tagging along today to fill Greyson's open three o'clock, acting as a consultant for our cybersecurity. It felt a little like bring a friend to school day to my nostalgic little heart. Grinning, he said, "But damn, if you two don't make one hell of a couple."

Hollyn's navy eyes roved over Max, and I couldn't help but chuckle. *In her dreams.* Even if he swung that way, I wouldn't let him within a mile of her. Max and I avoided fair-weather friends like the plague. Either you were all in or out with us, and I liked it that way. Quality over quantity was perfectly fine with me.

"I mean, you're both so generous; it just makes sense," Rory pointed out helpfully, shrugging her shoulder like that would be a given.

I actually had to stop myself from cackling at that description.

Okay, yes, he'd been disproportionately kind *to me* since we struck our deal. But I was his wife on paper, ally personally, and now a necessary roommate. The last few weeks aside, *generous* wasn't the word I'd use to label Greyson Hart. He conquered businesses like it was a sport and was fearless when it came to slicing off dead branches so new ones could grow.

Ruthless? Brilliant? Strategic? All yes. Generous? That had yet to be determined.

He viewed me as his responsibility now—of course, he'd look after me. Yes, the physical chemistry could scald my organs, but that didn't entirely erase two years of irritation...did it?

Seeming to sense my internal aneurysm, Max asked, "Now, this I gotta hear. Alice played this whole thing close to the vest. What do you know of Grey's generosity, Ms..."

"Rory," she supplied with a cheeky smile, happily rushing to take his hand. He introduced himself to both women as the two of them led us out of the break room and into the fishbowl.

"I'd like to hear that myself," I said, flashing what I hoped was a demure smile.

She jerked her chin at Hollyn, explaining, "I mean, he does all kinds of thoughtful things. For starters, her Aunt worked for the company, too."

"Worked?" Max clarified. Suddenly, I had a knot in my stomach and looked around to make sure nobody else was within earshot. Staffers were busy at their desks, Ollie was laughing by the printers, and Greyson was pacing the length of his office, gesticulating with his hands like he was on a rather heated phone call. I peeled my eyes from *sex in a suit* and turned back to my present company.

"Trish was diagnosed with breast cancer last spring. Stage four-b. Before the summer was up, she had used all her sick days. She'd only been with the company for a few months before they found it." She cleared her throat, looking a bit uncomfortable, and explained, "Mr. Hart kept her full salary rolling while she went through treatment and told her to stay home and heal."

Eyes watering, I didn't fight my sympathetic smile. "God, I'm sorry to hear that. Why didn't you say anything?"

She gave a one-shoulder shrug. "It wasn't my story to tell, but he paid her full salary right up until she passed away after Christmas and then called my uncle and insisted on covering the cost of the funeral. When Uncle Brad went to arrange a payment plan with the hospital, they told us it had been taken care of. Greyson refused to confirm it was him, but I mean..." she shook her head, tears welling, "who else has that kind of money?"

I turned my head up to his glass wall, smiling weakly as he made his way through the door to overlook his kingdom. "He never told me that," I admitted gently.

"Not his story to tell," Max echoed sagely. "Not so Hartless after all."

"No," I breathed, locking eyes with the man now leaning on the balcony and offering a smile I hoped he knew was authentic. "He's not."

"*Heartless*," Rory giggled, breaking the wall around us. "Clever."

MAX SET his *fourth* espresso down with a little clink, leaning back to stretch his arms over his head. Grey had joined us for an hour so that Max could bring him up to speed before he had to excuse himself to sit in on a meeting with Oliver and Reggie. I would never understand how he tolerated the man as well as he did.

The wink he'd shot me as he slipped out the door had me smiling into my fist, elbow propped on the table as Max narrowed his eyes on the screen again.

"Keep your pants on in the office, Alice," he teased.

"Shut up," I countered with no real bite to it, leaning back to fiddle with the cross hanging around my neck.

"You wear it on your face—that's not *my* fault. You've been the smitten kitten since he walked in the door after lunch." Max had been busy assessing our security holes all day, jotting notes down on his laptop for things to change and ways to fortify the company. Pieces of it were understandable with my limited experience, but others went right over my head. "Am I one of the third-party consultants you guys will skewer if those reporters make a comeback?"

Rolling my eyes, I said, "Obviously. Top of the lineup."

"Excellent. We live for drama."

"But for real. What do you see?"

"Security aside, nothing overtly concerning beyond what we discussed."

"And on our personal servers? Any elusive trusts or shell companies?"

"Still skeptical even after you jumped in his bed?"

So close, but so far. A pang of need shot through me as I remembered the feel of his solid body between my legs last night. "Love covers a multitude of sins, but even marrying into it, I'm not naïve enough to pretend a family like this doesn't have secrets."

"Eh, nothing we want to discuss unless we're home."

I nodded, sliding the cross along its chain as Max tracked the movements. "Good."

"What is that?" he asked, canting his head.

"What is what?"

"The cross around your neck."

"Well, Max. There's this entire demographic of our population that believes the son of God—"

"Fuck off, smarts," he said, throwing up a middle finger. "The necklace. That's the one from Grey?"

"Yeah, why?"

With a jerk of his chin, he asked, "Can I see it?"

"Sure?" I responded, more a question than an answer. Handing it to him, I added, "I've wasted hours of my life looking for a seam or an SD slot and came up empty. I'm sure it's some kind of tracker," I shrugged, "but otherwise, it's just a necklace." His glare was intended to silence me, so with a sigh, I complied, watching as he thoughtfully rotated it in his fingers. Equally frustrated and curious, I asked, "What are you looking for, you weirdo?"

Running a thumb along the long edge, Max narrowed his eyes. "Yahtzee," he breathed and broke it in half with a flick of his thumb.

"*Hey*——" I croaked, but my protest was cut short because my cross wasn't a pendant at all.

It was a flash drive.

15

Shiny Little Euphemism
GREYSON

When Arthur pulled up to Hart House after work and hopped out to open my door, Jackson was walking Max out, both of them grinning.

It was rather unnerving, like a couple of creepy ass clowns. That sensation intensified when their focus turned on me.

"Evening, Max," I greeted as he closed the gap with a hand outstretched. Jax retreated into the house behind him.

Grasping forearms, Max said, "Greyson, thanks for having me. It's been a pleasure working with her."

"Awfully formal tone for someone I've taken shots with. Anything I should be concerned about?"

"Nah, I just…hadn't ever got to sit with Alice while she did her thing."

The smile threatening my composure was entirely authentic. "She's amazing."

"She is. I knew that part, though."

"Where you headed?"

"I've got a date," he answered with—at least from what I could tell—an uncharacteristically sheepish grin. "Day trader in the city."

"What's his name?"

"Kyle Walbherg. You know him?"

"Can't say that I do."

"Well. Wish me luck. I'll have your analysis and action plan back by Monday," he promised, giving a salute of a wave.

"Appreciate it. You staying in the city?"

"Yeah, I think I'll give you two your space for the night."

"Don't be silly. She adores you. Besides, there's plenty of room," I said, arms wide to emphasize the front of the house. Opening the car door, Max turned over his shoulder, that creepy smile back on his face.

With a wink, he said, "You're gonna need it."

"What's that supposed to mean?" *Mischief.* That was what the smirk across Max's face was. Because smirking in answer to a question wasn't unsettling as fuck. "Max? *What's that supposed to mean?*"

His Uber driver closed the door behind him and, with a vague nod in my direction, circled the hood to get into the driver's side. Without another answer, they descended the drive, and I was left staring up at my house, wondering what in the hell they'd gotten into today.

I was a trained Navy Seal, for god's sake. I didn't get to be scared to go inside my own damn house. Terrifying though she may be, Alice was five-foot-ten, and I was pretty sure I could take her.

With a fortifying breath, I shoved open the front door and found the entire space...quiet. Dark. I wandered to Alice's room, where she liked to draw or paint as the sun set. *Nothing.* Easing the door closed behind me, I headed for the kitchen. *Nothing.* Balcony? *Nada.*

"Alice?" I called as I wandered into the dark dining room, only to find it empty, and deciding Jax must be hunkered down in the security room. When I finally reached our room, I hesitantly opened my own damn door like an intruder, which is when I heard her...*singing.* Given the acoustics, she had to be in the ensuite bathroom.

Never in the two years she'd worked for me had I been given any indication the woman could sing. And she *could* sing. Beautifully. So well that I leaned into the door when it clicked shut behind me. Just to steal another moment. I didn't know what she was singing—something about finding peace in a place with black sand. But her words lulled me onto the edge of the bed, sitting in silence to soak up the pain buried in her voice as I loosened my tie.

Pain I prayed I hadn't put there.

Charcoal, paints, music... Alice hid the heart of an artist behind data and strategy.

I was just yanking my second shoe free when her pitch changed, my ears straining for her footsteps and instead hearing the clink of metal as something zoomed through my peripheral. Tracking the flash of gold, I found the cross necklace I'd given her beside me and snapped my head up, turning to watch Alice step into my room wearing nothing but a white bath towel wrapped around her still-damp body. Long tendrils of dark, wet hair hung over her shoulders. Her song, naturally, stopped.

"I told you I didn't want your money, Greyson."

She knew. She knew *enough.* Voice level, I countered, "But there are circumstances where you might need it. Dragging you into this…" I shook my head. "You're my responsibility in this."

Like two predators sizing each other up, she prowled into the room, eyes locked on me. Wrapping the necklace around my fist, I brought the cross to my lips, bracing for whatever her reaction would be. Ever since that day in the office last month, this woman had held the ability to break me. There wasn't a world where I could look at her like collateral, which meant she undoubtedly had the upper hand here.

I might be the face of the company, but Alice would be the one calling the shots.

"Were you ever going to tell me?" she asked softly. To my surprise, when she reached the bed, she nudged my knees apart and stepped between them. Breath flying into my lungs, my hands fell to settle on her hips. Grateful for the feel of her. The soft give of her body beneath the fabric. The heat from her shower.

Of all the reactions to what was contained on that flash drive, I had to admit this was not the one I expected.

"Grey, answer me. Were you ever going to tell me about *Thunderstrike*?"

"Why didn't you ask?" I parried the question with one of her own.

Scowling, she ran her teeth over her bottom lip, and I beat back the desire to do the same. "I did."

"Why didn't you ask *again*?" I clarified. Smiling when she went pensive, I explained, "We haven't had the time to confront all of this."

She blinked before sucking down a breath. "Touché, Hart."

Pride brimming through, demanding I smile up at her as my hands tightened on her hips, I asked, "So?"

"So?" she echoed back.

"What were you singing?"

Her eyes went wide with surprise, and then she laughed. "Borders, by Kalandra."

"It was beautiful. Your voice is beautiful."

"Thank you. But, stop it."

"Stop what?"

"You know what you're doing. And *Thunderstrike is* like Blackwater. Now. What part do you play?" she volleyed back. When I just stared up at her, willing her to vocalize what she suspected, she stated, "You're hunting predators. On a global scale."

"No," I said simply, smiling when her lips twitched. Running my fingers from the soft fabric of her towel, I ventured up and over to bare skin, encouraged when she closed her eyes, sucking down another controlled breath as goosebumps erupted over her arms.

"You're *funding* men who hunt predators." Her fingers twined in my hair, slinking an inch deeper between my legs as my hands ran up and down the length of her.

"Legally speaking, they're advocates for trafficking victims."

"Shiny little euphemism, there."

"One leads to prison time. The other doesn't."

She blew out a breath, and my world tilted as she leaned a knee onto the mattress, the promise of her wet heat hovering an inch from where I needed her. "Pragmatic of you. So are the crypto keys. I'm assuming none of that can be traced." I certainly didn't need her approval or affirmation, but that didn't mean I wasn't loving being on the receiving end of it. "How much is on there, Grey?"

"Enough." In a world where the government owned our resources and could freeze them at the drop of a hat, where banks bordered on bankruptcy, diversifying our reserves had become necessary. Crypto was one of several—the security and anonymity unmatched. I'd loaded Alice's necklace with enough to help her vanish, trusting she was clever enough to do it should the need arise.

"*Greyson,*" she scolded.

"Enough to start over."

"Because this is dangerous—what you're doing?"

"Yes," I answered honestly. "Nobody likes someone threatening their supply chain."

A chill ran down her body, but when I removed my hands, she snatched one, bringing it to her face. Her remarkable, mesmerizing face.

I ran my thumb over her full bottom lip this time. The tiny scar just below it.

Fuck me, this woman was bold when she was authentic. I allowed my other hand to settle at her waist again, mesmerized by the alien warmth in my chest.

Wanted. I couldn't remember the last time I felt sincerely wanted. Let alone by someone that could give a shit less about my influence or the number of commas in my net worth.

Had I ever known desire like that?

I didn't think so. Which was why my attention was categorically divided when she kept pressing for information when all I wanted to do was press into her.

"You saw something. Found something when you were over there?" When I just nodded, she huffed a pouty little breath. "You're not supposed to talk about it?" I shook my head, and she swallowed harder than before. "But it's why you do this."

Snatching her hand, I brought it to my face, mirroring how she'd placed mine. She braced her weight on my shoulder and eased the rest of her body onto the mattress, straddling me properly now with her heaving breasts directly below my eyeline. I wrapped my free arm around the small of her back, pinning her against me as the last of my blood headed south. It was impossible to breathe, knowing a towel was the only barrier between me and all of her. The heat of her body robbed all my senses, cock straining against the zipper of my pants.

"Do you go out on these ops?" she asked, though the punch of demand was lost with her breathlessness.

"Not usually," I admitted. "My back is a liability. Too easy to be rendered useless by the pain—if I move wrong or take a nasty impact, or we're in the cold."

She nodded, gaze analytical as she studied my face. No pity. No sympathy. Just facts.

More confidently than I felt, I asked, "Are you in?"

"I'm just beginning to grasp what that entails."

"But you're not running for the hills," I pointed out. She studied me for a long beat before shaking her head once.

"No, Grey. I'm not running," she said, giving my hair a little tug for emphasis.

God damn, this woman was mine. Maybe she didn't know it yet. Maybe I couldn't wrap my head around how the fuck I felt any right to claim her. But she was.

It was that understanding that sent me flipping her onto her back, holding myself over her as I breathed her in. "There is no going back," I reiterated, no longer just discussing *Thunderstrike*.

"No," she agreed. "There's not." Her words solidified a bond to Alice Rhodes—*Hart*, I corrected myself—I never anticipated experiencing.

For the first time in my life, I felt *seen*. Seen by a woman who wasn't screaming as she bolted. By a woman who'd been witness to the worst of me for two years straight and was still choosing me now.

We were only just beginning to get to know each other—the *real us*—but it was enough.

Alice's fingers finding the buttons of my shirt gave me all the permission I needed. Mouths colliding, hands roaming, I memorized her lines as she worked the buttons free. Her body fit perfectly in my grasp, and fuck, if I didn't need her skin on mine.

ALICE

IF I FUCK SOMEONE, *it will mean something to me...*

For two years, I shared air with this man. The entire time believing I was some pawn he viewed as below him—easily discarded and easier to forget.

But he'd stated his feelings around sex quite bluntly that first day, which meant that the monster erection pressed against my belly would either be forgotten or very intentionally put to use. A shiver of anticipation worked down my spine, my body shuddering into him.

Now, I was *physically* below him and absolutely relishing the hard planes of his body ranging over mine. His gorgeous hazel greens ignited, the pupils blown wide, before Greyson dove for my neck. Nothing about the way this man touched or kissed me said I was anything shy of royalty. Neither did his satisfied rumble as I raked my fingers over his shoulders, loathing the suit still between us.

Princess, he'd once called me. *I felt like his queen now.*

Like the king he was always born to be, Greyson shifted seamlessly from conversing to conquering.

Mouth rough on the tender skin of my neck, he kissed a bruising line up the column.

So much need. So much demand in each forceful suck that rendered me speechless as I arched, dropping my head back to grant him access to every inch of skin.

This wasn't some casual carnal craving—not by what I knew of him or the way he rocked his hips against mine like I was his for the taking. Not in the way he came up for air, only to chuck off his jacket and loose button-up like a man unleashed.

In the next motion, he gently seized my arms, smoothly guiding them above my head and locking them in one hand as the other roughly scraped over my body like he couldn't mark enough of me.

No, this was a full-scale possession.

And I hadn't realized how deeply I needed it. To be owned like this. To be desired and used and pleasured by a man who only took what he wanted.

By a man who wanted *me*.

Propped up on the forearm still pinning my wrists—as if they weren't even a hindrance—he pulled back to look at me, wetting his lips as a cocky smile quirked one side of his mouth. I thought he'd kiss me again as he leaned down. Instead, he just hovered, swapping breath as those fiery eyes studied my own.

Sliding his free hand down to where I'd knotted the towel around my chest, Greyson breathed, "I've dreamed of doing this since the moment you walked into my office wearing that little black dress and blue blazer."

That was my first day. The cobalt blazer had been a gift from Elora—*a power color*. That's what she said. Apparently, that was an accurate marketing pitch.

"Oh, bullshit," I breathed. "Save your flattery, Grey."

"You still don't get it, do you?" he growled, robbing my breath in the next motion as he jerked the towel free. Baring all of me to him. Satisfied in the wake of my silence, his eyes scraped down to my heaving chest, his nostrils flaring and jaw clenching, before he snarled, "*Fuck.*"

He almost sounded *annoyed*. I wanted to say something snarky, to shove against the hold he had on my arms and take back some ounce of control, but Greyson was already moving.

It was the hard, wet pull of his mouth on my breast that permanently silenced me.

Whatever contents my brain once possessed liquefied and spilled free under the hands and mouth of Greyson Hart.

He swirled my nipple in his harsh mouth, a delicious pull of pain and pleasure fanning the inferno of lust, turning my body into a rag doll at this man's absolute disposal.

The moment he released my wrists, I threw my hands into his hair with a whimper of relief. I needed to feel him. To commit this moment to memory and hold it for rainy days. With that soul-igniting intensity I knew in all other aspects of his life, Greyson's hands moved to my body, scraping over my ribs and seizing my hips as he lowered himself off the bed and to his knees. With one forceful movement, he parted my thighs, muttering a curse as he revealed my weeping center.

Seriously. All it took was this man's brute force, expertly distributed over my desperate skin, and my vagina was begging for him to fill me.

"You're so wet, and I haven't even started."

Before I could produce what I'm sure would have been a very witty comeback about the size of the tent in his pants, he dove into my pussy. I thanked every deity that I'd taken El and Hadlee's advice and kept up a consistent wax schedule. Because he didn't hesitate to bury his face in my soaked center and lick straight through the middle, sending my spine bowing off the mattress.

"*Grey*," I whimpered, earning an approving hum before he *inhaled* deeply. *Damn, no pressure.*

"Never thought I'd get to taste you," he breathed, coming up for air with my juices glistening on his stubbled face. I leaned up on an elbow, reaching out my other hand to haul him up to me by his perfectly disheveled hair. The bastard wouldn't budge. "Not yet," he breathed. "I need to feel you come on my tongue, baby."

I'd never come from oral, truth be told. The thought alone made me squirm as he returned to his ministrations. Apparently, I was not, in fact, done squirming for Greyson Hart.

"Grey," I said again, this time as a protest that earned a gentle nip of his teeth against my clit.

"Is this our house, my clever Belle?"

"Yes," I breathed, simultaneously confused, so turned on, and terrified my brain was turning into a smoothie of warring hormones and logic.

"Good. And this *is* our bed?" he asked before leisurely sliding the flat of his tongue right up my center, the subtle scratch of stubble against my skin stinging in a delicious bite. All I could manage this time was a nod. "And aren't you *my* wife?"

"Yes," I panted. Okay, maybe it was more of a whimper as his lips wrapped around my clit and gave a hard pull.

"Then when we play, we do it by my rules."

"Rules?" I repeated stupidly. Half a question, half an answer. Half a brain cell clinging to life inside my head.

"The first time my wife comes, it will be on my tongue." If he kept up that steady stroke between sentences, that was going to happen embarrassingly quickly. "So when I take you with my cock, you can taste yourself on my lips." Another unforgiving drag of his tongue, only this time he slipped a finger inside my throbbing core, pulling a cry from my lungs. "So you know exactly who this pussy belongs to."

His words combined with an expert curl of his finger against a place hitherto untouched and just the right amount of pressure from his lips, and I detonated like a warhead. Stars burst behind my eyelids as two years of pent-up tension exploded through every synapse in my brain. As though he could feel every ripple and wave of pleasure my body kept serving, Grey held his position even as my thighs spasmed around his face.

That wasn't an orgasm.

That was some kind of magical, spiritual, soul-altering ascension. My very essence departed the human plane for a dimension where every muscle in my body could relax into the bed beneath me —well, every muscle except those in my throat, which were suddenly *aching*.

Like everything Greyson did, he wrecked me with unmatched efficiency.

Eyes half hooded, I breathlessly watched as he eased his fingers from my channel, then stood, reaching for his belt as his eyes scraped over my now languid body with wolfish satisfaction. But there was something else buried there. A kind of…approbation?

That look of wonder remained in his eyes as he ran a thumb over his lip and popped it into his mouth as though he'd gathered a bit of my pleasure to savor.

Filthy.

Animalistic.

Delicious.

My attention was diverted by a different sight, however. Because his cock was, indeed, pitching an impressive tent in his fancy slacks as he slid a condom from his back pocket. Right up until he freed it in one smooth motion that left him bare and intimidatingly beautiful before he rolled the condom right over the vascular, thick rod he'd been hiding between his legs. My mouth watered as he prowled forward, all thick muscles and a smattering of glorious, dark hair.

Perfect.

If you had asked me to draw my ideal man, he wouldn't have held a candle to Grey as he lowered over me with some shaken cocktail of adoration and lust in his eyes. "You about made me come just by screaming my name," he breathed, reverently lining himself up with my entrance.

Had I done that? I mean, that tracked with the raw ache in my throat. I'd evidently carved the letters of his name into my vocal cords. G-r-e-y-s-o-n.

With a devious smirk, he ordered, "Do that again."

And I did. Because in the next breath, he slid home. There was no warning, no cautious transition. Just a vicious, delicious claiming as he filled me entirely before stilling as he glared skyward.

"God, Grey!" My hands wrapped around his body, clinging to him like a lusty little lemur on its favorite tree. "Oh my god, *oh god,* oh god."

"Fuck," he muttered again, jaw flexing. "Dammit, Alice."

"What?" I breathed, evidently finding my lost second brain cell. The one that did the wording.

"You were made for me, beautiful. I knew you'd squeeze my cock like you needed to pump it for every last damn drop. Your pretty little cunt is as ruthless as the rest of you."

Too many compliments. Claimings. Filthy words.

System overload.

Luckily for me, he seemed to regain his impeccable control because he shifted, robbing my breath as he set a pace hellbent on destroying me. Each slide and snap of his hips shoved me closer and closer to that edge again, and I clung onto him. My life vest in a tempest sea. Like he was the only thing between me and the abyss determined to swallow us.

My fingers hesitated when I scraped over the puckered skin of scar tissue down his spine. Inexplicably, tears welled in my eyes, my mouth popping open as I felt the evidence of that pain. The reality was that he very nearly hadn't survived.

He smiled—a little too stiffly, but still authentically—before whispering, "It's alright."

"How?" I breathed, thinking of what he must've gone through. Thinking of that agony and hating the man that caused it. Something so simple, so often overlooked, and so unspeakably selfish.

"It brought me here. It brought me to you."

"Grey," I breathed for what must've been the millionth time.

"God, I love the way you say my name. Don't stop."

With that final demand, he returned to that ruthless pace, and I flattened my palms against the warm, broad plains of his back, needing him closer.

Pleasure overwhelmed my nervous system, made more intense as he wrapped a hand around my neck, thumb forcing my chin up so our eyes met. He captured me in the intensity of those dark hazels, like a butterfly in a spider's web.

My mouth popped open, the pleasure screwing up my face as victory curved his parted lips in an endearing open-mouthed grin.

I'd expected sex, but Greyson was taking more than I'd prepared to give him. In true Hart form, he was seizing what he wanted and doing it without remorse.

My pleasure.

My body.

My sanity.

With every thrust, he carved a part of me out I'd never meant to let go of. Seeming to see or sense the fear tainting this nirvana, he ran his thumb over my jawline, still holding me captive as he panted, "I've got you, Alice."

Nodding was all I could manage because the truth was, I didn't know how to articulate the war in my body.

He smiled softly, thrusts deepening as he demanded, "So give me what I want, baby. *Let go.*"

The next snap of his hips sent me hurdling right over the edge again. Hell, nobody had ever made me come *twice*. They certainly hadn't told me I was a good girl or beautiful or to give them more—all kinds of dirty promises pouring from his lips until my pleasure finally claimed his.

His body went rigid a beat before he slid free, straightening abruptly so that he towered over me. Pulling the condom off, he fisted his cock, and my eyes went wide with surprise.

Scrambling, I reached for him, knocking his hand out of the way to replace it with my own.

One, two, three firm pulls were all it took before he painted my belly and chest in thick ropes of cum. Spurt after spurt, he came as hard as I had, body seizing with jerky little movements as he dropped his head back with a guttural groan.

Tears filled my eyes again, but in the next beat, his mouth was on mine, his hands cradling my face like something precious. And I was once again consumed by Greyson Hart.

16

Are We Running a Marathon?

ALICE

"Leigh?" I yelped, dumping my bag by the front door and rushing across the condo as it slammed behind me. At some point, it stopped feeling like *my* condo and started feeling like hers, but that was a problem to think about later. Like. When I wasn't smack-dab in the middle of a midlife crisis. "*Leighton!*" Glaring at the empty pot of coffee and the obnoxiously bright red seven o'clock on the stove beside it, I rushed for the kitchen. "Leighton Alexandra, I know you are *not* still sleeping at seven am on a Tuesday!"

In the next four seconds flat, I dumped the coffee grounds with the finesse of an NBA player making a shot, slammed the basket back in, replaced the liner, and rotated for the grinds container. The suction on the lid had just broken when I heard her shuffling feet and a mumbled, "Fuck. Right. Off."

"I will not," I retorted as I scooped in more than the advisable amount of magic ground beans.

"The *last* thing you need is coffee," Leighton croaked, collapsing into the bar stool by the island, hair unkempt, pajama shirt askew, drool stain smearing her cheek. She was almost enough of a hot mess for me to forget that was the stool I sat on when Greyson proposed to me. But not quite.

"Ohhh yes, I do," I yipped back, jamming the 'on' button. "This is a double shot, triple shot, *quadruple* shot kind of morning. A coffee straight from a keg with the tap open, kind of morning."

"Are we running a marathon?"

"Kind of did," I blurted before slapping my hands over my mouth. When I turned to face her, two Rhodes gray-blues reduced to slits, focused on me. "Kind of alllllll-ready did," I reiterated, voice a high, squeaky, singsong. I sounded like Ross Gellar insisting he's fine, for Christ's sake.

Those narrowed eyes tracked my progress as my suddenly obnoxiously long legs gobbled up the kitchen. I scooped two mugs out of their cabinet and returned to my spot by the island as the machine percolated loudly behind me before turning to the fridge to fish out the creamer.

"You didn't," she accused, flipping her legs up into the bar stool so she could rest her chin on her knees as her eyes sparkled to life. Inevitably, the promise of juicy, ridiculous decisions made by her stupid big sister was enough to wake her.

I pursed my lips, nodding as I poured cream into our cups. "I did. I really did, Leigh."

"Alliiiiice," she groaned, jerking her body around like I exasperated her. "What are you *dooing*?"

In my most pathetic, mousiest tone, I confessed, "I don't know."

"I told you this was a bad idea," she whined. "*Platonic* partnership, remember? A business arrangement. We talked about this."

"We did."

"He set boundaries."

"He did."

"And you just jumped them like a drunk over a parking meter?"

"I mean, the jumping was mutual. It was mutual stupidity."

"Duh."

"Don't *duh* me. This wasn't just *my* idiocy; there was mutual idiocy. Mutual, toe-curling, throat scarring because you screamed so loudly, idiocy."

A smug little smile curled her lips. "So, was it at least a good marathon? If you're gonna blow your life up, it better be a good marathon."

I slammed the heels of my palms into my eye sockets like they could massage away my life choices. Couldn't watch my life fall apart if I couldn't see. "Uhhhhhhhhhg," I groaned, dropping my hands and whirling back to the coffeepot as the ensuing little white sparkles fell across my vision like those raining gold fireworks. Hoisting the carafe from the burner, I turned and filled both mugs as I complained, "This was the end of all good things. The Everest of orgasms. The *nirvana* of chemistry."

Snickering as she took her mug, Leighton said, "Sissy, you just haven't gotten laid in a few years. It's just sex."

GREYSON

"IT WAS *NOT* JUST SEX. That was…I don't know what the fuck that was, but it wasn't just sex. *What the fuck*, man?" I palmed my face before massaging the ache in my temples.

Still irritated at being woken at an hour *any* grown ass man *should* be awake at, Ollie smirked over his cup of coffee. He looked like he'd been electrocuted or like one of those troll things Beau was always playing with. "Sure this isn't just a bad case of blue balls?"

"Fuck off," I barked, snapping my head up.

His snort made me rather violent. "I'm just saying. It's been a while."

"So?!"

"*So,* maybe you just needed to get some," he suggested, nonplussed as he obnoxiously sipped the steaming liquid. "It's a basic human need, big brother."

"You would say that, man whore."

"Jealous?" he drawled with an obnoxious eyebrow wiggle. "But, for real. That Maslow guy put it on the same level as shelter for men. Food, water, shelter, pussy."

"That's the official ranking?" I jabbed with a glare.

"Obviously. You've been starving, and somebody slid over a filet minion with all the trimmings. Of course, you're freaking out; you forgot what it tasted like."

He certainly would not get the details on *that*. The woman was delectable. Pure, undiluted, unfragranced perfection. If a man is going to eat a girl out, he wants to savor *pussy*, not some chemical concoction they sell them with promises of rose-tainted cunt.

She was bare and beautiful and entirely at my mercy.

She was…Alice was *a vision*. A figment of my imagination brought to life. Even as I stared holes into my brother's counter, it was her body in my mind. The pale, peaked arch of her breasts, the bow of her spine as she came undone under my hands, her ass in the air for me as I buried myself to the hilt, the cry of *my* name off her lips.

In one night, she'd robbed more of me than I'd ever cared to share. She looked like she was going to cry after I came that first time, and I couldn't have that. Couldn't let her down like that. So, I'd done the only thing a man can do—I served her pleasure until her body went limp and sated, her breathtaking face relaxed as she willingly curled into my side. Even the focus line between her brows melted away, and I counted that as a victory. Some primal piece of me wanted to throw caution to the wind, my body begging to feel her bare. It took all my control to think clearly. To remember why that could never happen.

But the entire time…all I could think as I ravaged her was *mine*.

"I can't explain it," I growled, resuming my pacing. "It's never been like that."

"So, you connected," Ollie said with a shrug. "The chemistry was on point. Don't have a stroke over it."

"She's *my wife*," I breathed as panic rooted deeper.

This time, a coughing fit accompanied his snort, like he'd attempted to inhale the scalding liquid in his hand. *Good.* Karma was a bitch, and sometimes that bitch was instant. Unamused, I arched a brow and watched him laugh-choke-splutter back into coherent words.

"Right. She's *your wife.* If you were going to experience some spiritual connection with a woman, isn't that who it's *supposed* to be?"

"In ordinary circumstances? Maybe. But this isn't that, and you know it."

"You lusted after the woman for two years. In close ass proximity, at that. Couldn't escape each other," he said, shaking his head for emphasis. "Are you really shocked it was good?"

"It wasn't like that." *It was.* It was like that. I just didn't think it was so fucking obvious.

"Bullshit. You forget yourself, big brother. You kept her close; you refused to even lend her out to other departments. She's the *only* PA you let travel with you."

"She doesn't annoy me like the others," I grumbled, but it just made his punch-able face smugger.

"Who was on your arm for every gala?"

"That's beside the point—"

"Who did you drag to *assist you* on family trips?"

"She's like a walking encyclopedia of—"

He cut me off again, looking all too self-satisfied for my liking, as he slid off his chair and leaned an elbow on the back of it. "Trouble comes down the pipeline, and it's *her* you consult, *her* you allow to run damage control even with Tiffany still on board, and *her* you propose to for an elaborate coverup of a media mess."

"She knew too much—"

"And was the only woman in the photos? Yeah, I know how you justified it. But this isn't a *new* attraction."

"You don't know what you're talking about."

ALICE

"*DON'T I?* You're seriously telling me that your irritation over the last few years wasn't fueled by the fact that you wanted to do the horizontal cha-cha but couldn't?" Leighton pursed her lips in that know-it-all way of hers, cocking her head to the side. My wide-eyed silence had a feline smile lifting her cheeks as she kicked her feet back on the barstool beside her. "Sissy, I mean this with a great deal of love, but you're being ridiculous. Attraction, once buried, seems to manifest as irritation, and you let that man call all your shots for years while whining about it the entire time."

"He was *my boss*," I complained, "that's kind of the name of the job."

"Hating his guts wasn't in the job description, but you managed. Hell, you built him up to be some abominable monster when, in reality, he's actually a very considerate, very protective, very kind man." She bounced her head from side to side, her mess of hair swaying as she weighed her words. "Albeit a little bossy, he is a billionaire. It's to be expected." The last words came out the side of her mouth before she pursed it.

"He called me—"

"*A country bumpkin.* Yes. I know. *Your great-grandchildren* will know the tale because you immortalized it in all our brains while you painted him as the heartless dragon. Hell hath no fury like a Rhodes, scorned."

"He can be such an ass," I protested. "It's not like I *imagined it.* He could give frost giants frostbite."

"Sure, sure, sure, but I bet you were *looking* at his ass any time he left a room."

I shrugged. "Even pricks can fill out slacks well."

Leighton threw her head back and cackled so hard she nearly fell out of her chair. Through her wheeze-like giggles, she breathed, "Never seen a prick as impressive as a Hart brother." Her sporadic giggles had me coming apart at the seams like only sisters could do. Laughter-induced tears streaming from her eyes, she finally managed, "Is he as well-endowed as they look? Or is that some kind of rich guy crotch padding?"

Oh. Dear. Lord. "*You have no idea*," I admitted sheepishly, aware all the heat in my body had congregated in my face.

"Please," she scoffed. "Greyson drips big dick energy."

"Yes," I breathed, "he does."

"Damn, he *was* good," she observed.

"The end of all future sexual conquests good."

Leighton's delighted little wiggle did nothing to ease the nerves in my belly. Neither did her next words. "Well, at least you know you're compatible. That should make this whole arrangement better. I wonder if you'll fight less now that you can screw like bunnies."

"Leigh," I scolded, simply because it was easier than acknowledging we were in this marriage for the next three years, regardless of how this conversation went. "Don't be so crass."

"Don't be such a prude," she scoffed. "Stop holding out. Give me details on the fun stuff."

"Big words for a woman still hanging onto her V-card."

She shrugged like that didn't bug her at all. Honestly, I shouldn't tease her about it, but we were all a little perplexed about what she was waiting for. "All the more reason for you to take pity on me and let me live vicariously through you." She smacked her hands down on the marble, abruptly leaning forward. I sighed and melted onto the stool beside her. "Seriously. Tell me. What was he like? Soft and sweet doesn't really scream Greyson. He's so serious all the time. Was he bossy? *Oooh, I bet he's a dirty talker.*"

"He is," I mumbled weakly, sliding my coffee across the island. Chewing on my lower lip, I stirred the little gold heart spoon in circles as she waited with bated breath. "Book boyfriend level dirty talker. At one point, he told me to come like his dirty little slut, and I *exploded* on command. Like. *Sir.* Excuse you?" I shook my head, blinking the lusty haze away. "I don't even understand what happened last night," I admitted. But I could remember the harsh feel of his fingers on my skin, the delicious bruises where he'd held on for dear life while he gave me what we both so desperately wanted. "I almost cried, but it was like he…sensed it. He cradled my face, kissed away my fear, and held me until my breathing evened out. The next time, he was so gentle. It was like he used his body to soothe mine. He kept telling me he had me and wasn't going anywhere." Dropping the hand that hovered in front of my lips, I widened my eyes, blowing the air from my lungs into my cheeks before slowly releasing it. "The next three were…more physical."

"*That's* why you're walking funny?" She flashed a Cheshire smirk.

"Piss off," I laughed. "Just surprised I can stand."

Her laughter gave way to a pensive expression as she studied me. Sucking in a deep breath, Leighton hedged, "He cares for you, sissy. More than I think you realize. Certainly more than *I* realized. I thought I'd have to kill him and call Jameson to hide the body." My watery laugh made her smile as she added, "I swear when that migraine hit, you would've thought he was ready to kill that photographer. I'm not saying it's love yet, but it certainly isn't apathy."

"That's what freaked me out last night, I think. I was ready for physical, but it got—"

"Emotional?"

"*Spiritual,*" I said uncertainly. "I have experienced nothing like that, so it's hard to articulate. But this morning," I huffed a heavy breath, sliding off the stool to cross to the doorway. "It would've been easy to blow off as some physical attraction, but when I went to find toothpaste, I saw this in his linen cabinet." Reaching inside my discarded bag, I pulled out the kindest thing anyone had ever done for me and held it aloft for her to see. Leighton narrowed her eyes in confusion.

"You're…going to space?" She teased.

Laughing, I shook my head. "When that migraine hit, I'd asked if any of the staff had a cold cap, and he ordered me some. *Not one* —which would've been kind enough—but three, like he was afraid the first wouldn't work or something." I looked at the ridiculous blue hat and smiled, sucking down a breath. "He's…surprisingly kind, this beast of mine."

"What?"

"Never mind," I laughed, shaking my head.

"Did you call him a beast!?"

"I made a joke the first week that I'm Belle in his castle. It kinda stuck."

"Oh, now *shut up*—that's too cute."

"He calls me his Belle," I admitted, smiling softly.

"*His beautiful,*" Leighton swooned dreamily, clutching at her chest. "Alice, if you don't start dating your husband, we're going to have problems." Laughing, I buried my face in my hands as she asked, "Is he already in the office this morning? He's an early bird like you, right?"

"I don't know," I said, staring at the sweet gesture hanging from my fingers. There'd been an entire basket in there—essential oils, smelling salts, a business card for an acupuncturist, migraine-specific medication. He'd bought the internet's go-to solutions like he was stocking a me-focused apothecary.

"What do you mean you don't know? Was he still in bed this morning?" Leighton's questions drew my focus up, and I chewed on my lip as my nerves took over. Her swooniness gave way to judgment as she glared at me. *"Tell me you didn't."*

GREYSON

"SHE JUST LEFT?!"

"Yeah," I groused, collapsing into the armchair in the living room as my brother followed. "She was gone when I woke up. That's why I came here, fucker."

"*Oh fuck, man.*"

"That sums it up."

"This sucks."

"I was afraid you'd say that."

"I mean, it's one of two things," he said, shaking his head as he crossed his arms.

"Do either of them end with a sniper putting me out of my misery in your living room?"

"*Uh.* No." He sat on the coffee table across from me. "You either misread it, or she's freaking out."

"So, I'm a limp dick piece of shit that just slept with my assistant. Or she's also panicking?"

"Pretty much." He sat staring at our feet for a long beat before hopefully asking, "Maybe she's in the office?"

"Nah," I shook my head. "Jax tailed her—because she left without him, *which is a whole other conversation*—and she's at her old condo."

"Leighton still lives there."

"I guess."

"We dropped her off the other day. She's there," he insisted.

"What the fuck are you doing dropping off my sister-in-law?"

"She came over to paint Mattie's nails," he said simply. I scowled at him until he added, "They really hit it off, and the nanny was busy, so she babysat. Am I not allowed to make friends with our new in-laws?"

"The feral one?"

"She's not fucking feral," he snapped defensively. "She's *protective.* If anybody can respect that, it's you, motherfucker."

Begrudgingly, I agreed, "Fair."

"Besides. It's not my doghouse we're analyzing right now. It's yours. If she's with Leighton, that's probably good, right? She probably needed to talk."

"If she was going to get rid of me, I assume she'd go to Paxton," I mused. But the look on his face said the sister was more of a concern than I wanted to acknowledge. "Outstanding," I growled.

"Look. There's not a lot you can do here. Really, your only option is to go to work and pretend all is normal until you have time to talk to her."

"Talk."

"Yes, you dipshit. Talk. Like this. Tell her what you're thinking."

"Not my forte."

"Nope," he agreed amicably as he rose to his feet. "But if you can come over here with your tail between your legs, you can go face your wife in the office."

17

Not At All Conspicuous
ALICE

Alessandra Hart: America's New Sweetheart

Emerald Bay Titan Slaps Local Paper With Defamation Suit

An Exclusive Look at Emerald Bay's Very Own Cinderella Story

From Honeymoon to Hot Seat: Greyson Hart Speaks Out Against False Allegations

"How's it looking?"

God, just the sound of Greyson's voice raked fingernails down my nervous system, not unlike the marks I'm sure his back bore after last night. A flush heating my neck and face, I looked up to find him leaning against the doorframe of my office, hands nonchalantly stuffed in his pockets, with the top of a vicious hickey peeking out from his crisp collar. I'd had to layer on cover-up like my life depended on it in an attempt to conceal the one hovering just above the neckline of my dress.

Fighting my smile was futile, so I bit my bottom lip as I focused on the screen in a pathetic attempt to center myself. "Still a little more print time than I was hoping, but we're headed in the right direction, and public opinion weighs heavily in our favor."

"Think I can do anything better?" he asked cockily, sauntering over until he could lean on the corner of my desk.

Smirking up at him, I said, "I think we could humanize you a bit, and they'd eat it up."

The man actually wrinkled his nose like I waved something rancid below it. "What does that mean? I'm human."

"No," I argued, shaking my head. "You're stunning. But you're not human. Not to them. Hell, I worked twenty feet from your desk for two years, and I thought you were a robot."

"I like to keep things professional."

"I know." Not that the same could be said for the two of us now.

"And *private*," he emphasized, looking at me with some mix of endearment and amusement.

"*I know*," I repeated, leaning back in my chair to study him for a moment. "A little goes a long way, Grey. You're set on not making appearances with the kids?"

"You know why that's a terrible idea."

Kind of. We hadn't really gotten into the nitty gritty of it last night—just that he funded a mercenary group called *Thunderstrike* in an effort to fight modern slavery, freeing trafficking victims. *Obsidian*, the group Max had dug out of our system, was an insidious circle Marcom had been attempting to shut down for years.

Nonetheless, I nodded.

Their existence made them targets, whether or not he emphasized that. But I understood not wanting to illustrate the value they held to him if someone had traced his involvement.

Jax, who was currently filling his tumbler with crappy office coffee, was Greyson's partner. Only, he didn't have an injury keeping him from putting his boots to the ground when needed.

I have four people on the planet I actually trust. Three, if minors are eliminated.

All three of Greyson's confidants stood in the same building, divided by glass walls and staircases.

I'm not going to lie; that was a kind of praise I wouldn't be tossing aside anytime soon.

"So we start simpler. With us," I supplied.

"I think you've done quite enough, Mrs. Hart."

I shrugged, shaking my head as I glanced back over the software we used to gauge public opinion based on interactions. The algorithm was complicated, but the results were pretty easy. "Getting more involved with causes that mean something to us, you on a date night, slow down at the next gala and take the time to answer questions. These are easy things."

"I loathe the media."

"Yes, but we need them, Grey. We need them on our side for this."

"I need *you* on my side for this."

My cheeks split in a bashful smile as the heat intensified in them. "You have me."

"Do I?" he asked simply, but the fire in those hazels told me we weren't talking about the media anymore. I wiped my suddenly sweaty palms on my dress before meeting his gaze and nodding. "Come to lunch with me?"

"My pleasure," I answered softly, noting that Jax was heading across the fishbowl for those twin stair sets. I gently shut my laptop as I found my feet.

"Was it?" he pressed.

Rolling my eyes, I said, "You know it was."

"Then, why'd you leave?" he asked softly, eyes only for me. It was like the rest of the world ceased to exist beneath the heat of that stare.

"I may have panicked," I confessed, looking at my feet, my bag on the floor. His warm hands came to both of my arms. I hadn't even heard him close the distance, but suddenly Greyson was sucking the air from my tiny space, his frame inches from mine, forcing my eyes up to his.

"Panic begets panic. How do you think I felt waking up without you after...*that*?"

Swallowing hard, I studied the undeniable sincerity in his eyes. "I'm sorry if I hurt you—" Warm lips swallowed my sentence a beat before his hands came to my face.

"Did *I* hurt *you*?" he breathed against my mouth. When I shook my head, he jerked his chin up, lips tapping mine so, so briefly. Five orgasms, and I wasn't done. Needed more of him—*from* him. "Do you...regret it? Me?" Another head shake, this time earning the softest brush of his lips. "Then next time you panic, do it with me. We can't climb mountains on opposite peaks and expect this to work."

"So there is a *this*?"

"Unless I'm hallucinating."

"Uh...am I interrupting something?" Jax asked as he knocked on the doorframe.

"No," I blurted, but Greyson had other plans.

"Yeah, buddy, I got her for a while."

"I'm sure you do," Jax chuckled. "I'll pick up lunch. What do you two lovebirds want?"

"Whatever sounds good to you," Grey said simply, his eyes never leaving mine. "Do me a favor?"

"I'll just add it to the list." Jax's sarcasm might very well be my favorite quality in the man.

"Good deal. Close the door on your way out."

With a laugh, Jax did. To my surprise, he also hit the switch that deployed the electronic privacy screen across the glass of my office.

Gaping, I declared, "That's not at all conspicuous."

"My wife. My business," Greyson stated simply.

"You really like saying that, don't you?"

"I really do," he agreed smugly before claiming my mouth in a bruising collision. Strobes of memory flashed through my mind—his face buried against my center, his hands gripping my hips as he took me from behind, the way he threw his head back as he came in my mouth. We had devoured each other for hours until we collapsed into sleep. Judging by the unforgiving crash of his lips on mine, he had every intention of tearing a sixth release from my exhausted body right here in the office.

Peeling away, I staggered back a step, trying to keep him at arm's length as he stalked my movements. "*Stay*," I barked, earning a laugh. "Talk. *Words*. Words are good."

"What do you want to talk about?" he asked as his hand found mine, the other coming to grip my hip possessively. There was nothing hotter than being pursued by Greyson Hart, I decided. A freaking inferno had ignited in my office, threatening to sear the clothes right off my body.

"This. *Us*. Thunder—" his lips cut off my protest, and the next thing I knew, he'd lifted me onto my desk, a devilish glint in his eyes as he ran kisses down my neckline, savagely sucking at the spot above my collarbone.

"Words are overrated," he purred against my skin. "But I have four to ask you."

"Oh?" I squeaked.

"Go out with me? Please," he added with a chuckle. "*Five*. I had five, but you are unspeakably distracting."

My gulp was humiliatingly audible. "Like, dinner and a movie?"

"I can do better than that," he promised without hesitating.

"You want to...*date* me?"

"I want to do a lot of things to you, Belle. But now that you're legally mine, I think dating is an acceptable place to start," he said before returning to tasting every inch of my neck and collar.

"Grey, I..."

"Yes?" he breathed against my clavicle.

"About last night."

"Please, baby, *please* don't backpedal."

"When I almost..."

Brows raised, he reared back to study my face before gently finishing my sentence. "Cried?"

"Yeah. I, um, that was intense for me."

"Me too," he agreed bluntly.

"Why do you…um. Why did you…" My eyes fell but only made it as far as his pecs, where they strained against the fabric of his fitted shirt, my fingers lifting to fiddle with a button. Some mindless carnal corner of my body wanted to tear it clean off, never mind the fact that my vagina was crying from its sudden overuse. Desperately, I tried to cling to the words I needed to say.

Why wasn't I different? Why didn't he trust me? Why couldn't he finish with me?

But the more his hands roamed, the less coherent I became. "I know with other women you…*Reggie*."

"I promise Reggie never crossed my mind, and neither did anyone else," he swore, a seriousness in his eyes. "I can't explain what this is, what we have, or if it's going anywhere. For now, can we just see how this evolves? Because you were resplendent, Mrs. Hart. A fantasy I never dared to hope for."

God, I loved the way he called me that. Loved the way he talked. Perhaps that fancy private school education was good for something after all.

The intensity in his gaze and the seriousness in his tone sent me babbling like an imbecile. "Thank you. You as well. *I mean,* you were beautiful. *Are* beautiful. *Handsome.*" The more idiotically I spluttered, the broader his cocky smile grew. I palmed my forehead as his hands slipped beneath my dress. The instant his blunt fingers found the wet spot on my panties, that grin turned wolfish.

"Bent over your desk." He stroked up my aching center, pressing the fabric into my arousal. "Bent over *my* desk." One finger hooked my panties aside, trapping the breath in my throat. I glanced over my shoulder, but the privacy screen kept us concealed. His free hand wrapped around my jaw, victory in his eyes when he brought me back to face him. "Pinned against that thick wood door." One finger slid into my center, and my head fell back as pleasure captured me wholly. Greyson seized that opportunity to graze his teeth over my jugular before breathing, "On your knees, sucking me off in one of these damn office chairs."

"What?" I breathed like some ditsy airhead, my hands coming to rake through his hair. Had he hit me over the head with a stupid stick? Anyone could walk through that door right now. We were in *my* office, *not his*. There was no invisible barrier of terrifying CEO rules forbidding intruders.

"I'm thinking of all the ways I pictured taking you and trying to decide what comes first. Do you have a preference, *wife*?"

"Grey, someone could walk in."

With that hesitation voiced, he scooped me off the desk and set me in said office chair before lowering himself onto all fours.

Greyson Hart.

Was on the floor.

Crawling between my thighs. In his outrageously expensive suit.

Dead. I was dead. This was the last fantasy my final electric impulses would gift me with before I met my maker.

Grey yanked my chair closer to the desk, where this madness would be at least somewhat concealed. With a devilish smile, he threw my leg over his shoulder. All the while, those smoldering hazels drilled into my face, savoring my speechless reaction.

"Still feel like talking, Mrs. Hart?" he asked as he hooked my panties aside with his thumb, lowering until he could breathe in my sex.

"Words are overrated," I panted back, entirely mesmerized by the man below me, earning a satisfied hum of approval.

"Good girl." In the next heartbeat, his lips found my clit, a finger plunged inside, and the world around us vanished in a swirl of pleasure.

GREYSON

"AND THIS WILL *HUMANIZE* ME?" I asked Friday evening as Alice took a step back to admire her handiwork—her *ridiculous* handiwork.

"You never know; you might like it," she said smugly, tilting her head to one side as she surveyed me.

"They're jeans. It's not rocket science."

"You look good in denim," she noted, motioning for me to turn around.

"Let's go," I complained, but she just widened her eyes pointedly. With a huff, I rotated, glaring down at the three-buttoned shirt she'd stuffed me into. My suspicion was her choice had more to do with how absurdly tight it was than humanizing me in the eyes of the public, especially as she ran her warm palms over the width of my chest. "I don't see how this will help."

"Girls love Henley shirts. Don't try to make sense of it, just accept it."

"I *have* a woman. I don't need girls to like my clothing."

"You do if this summer press tour is going to work. You agreed to this," she pointed out for the umpteenth time. Though our plan was working, rumors of foul play were still circulating frequently enough that Alice decided it was time to ramp it up.

"And a Henley, beach shoes, and eating out of a *trailer* will help?" I repeated as she rolled her eyes and sauntered away with a flip of her gorgeous hair. I was still in disbelief that I no longer had to hide what the sway of her hips did to me.

"It's a taco truck, smart ass. *And it looks delicious!*"

"It *looks* like a listeria outbreak waiting to happen," I grumbled under my breath.

"Okay, drama queen. Don't you ever get sick of *tiny little portions* for *gigantic* price tags?" she teased as she hooked her handbag over her shoulder. A new one for her birthday was inevitable, although how much she'd allow me to spend on her had yet to be determined.

I decided that the best part of having a driver was that it allowed Alice to straddle my lap in the back of the limo, rocking her hips under those flimsy sundresses she was so partial to.

The worst part of having a driver was inarguably the fact that my wife seemed to enjoy provoking a raging erection, only to flash a coy smile as she slipped off my lap and out of the car, leaving me stranded on the bench seat until it reduced to a respectable size.

Still at half mast, I sighed as I eased out into the summer heat, glaring at her where she had plunked down beside Max in the sand. My brother was already here as well—waving like an idiot—as was Leighton, who was playing an aggressive game of tag with my niece and nephew. To his giggling delight, she appeared to be using Beau like a tiny human shield.

I just reached the first line of sand when someone sidled up next to me. Turning, I found a blonde ponytail and a reserved smile. Stacy, our best ally in this mess, was watching them with a melancholic smile on her face. "Sure makes a pretty picture," she said, lifting her camera to show me the back of it. Alice was sandwiched between Max and Ollie, and both the kids' faces split into open-mouthed giggles with Leighton on their tails. "Sure we can't post these?"

Chuckling, I shook my head. "You're nearly as relentless as my wife. But, no. And you'll never get a release signed for him, either," I explained, tapping on Max on the screen.

"Mind if we join?"

I glanced up to find the source of that familiar voice was a very sweaty Paxton Rhodes, alongside Dallas, one of our best receivers. Both were shirtless, wearing basketball shorts and running shoes.

"Pax!" Alice yelped, sprinting for him. He chuckled as he caught her, but she wriggled free quickly, wrinkling her nose. "I love you, but you're *ripe*."

"It's ninety degrees out, Menace," he pointed out.

"Isn't it the off-season?" she complained.

"Getting old, sis," Paxton supplied. I was about to tell him that the owner of the team just *loved* to hear that when he added, "Gotta stay on top of my game. Can't just bounce back like the young guys these days."

"Good man," I mumbled, grateful he took Ollie's investment seriously. "Are tacos on the off-season plan?"

"One cheat day won't kill us," Dallas pushed, looking more eager than his new quarterback.

"Carb, protein, veggies, I think it counts," Paxton said, grinning when his little sister beamed up at him. And just like that, our outing grew by two.

By the end of our meal, Stacy's 'paparazzi' images were finally up to Alice's standard—she'd cuffed my damn jeans and insisted on bare feet in the sand. Paxton had even been on board for a few beach football images because, naturally, Ollie just so happened to have one in his truck.

My reluctance gave way as Stacy flipped through her SD card on the back of the DSLR. I hated to admit it, but the media would eat this up. One big, happy, Emerald Bay family.

Drowsy from one too many tacos and hours in the sun, Alice laid her warm cheek on my shoulder the moment the car door closed behind us. Her happy little sigh had me relaxing into her, stroking lazy lines up her sun-kissed arm. A man could get used to this. This…community. The girl nestled into my side. I didn't want to think too hard about how we'd gotten here or where it was going because that's when the panic set in. But…for now, at least, she was mine.

I'd just closed my eyes, at peace with that reality, when she jack-knifed upright with a yelp. "Arthur, pull over! Pull over!"

"What the hell!?" I barked as Arthur calmly said, "Yes, Mrs. Hart."

"*Oh god, ohgodohgod,*" she breathed in a panic, brows pinched in the center.

"Alice. What's going on."

"I saw something!" she yelped, throwing herself out the car door onto the shoulder of the fucking highway.

"Jesus Christ," I growled, lunging after her. "Alice! Get in the car! Have you lost your mind?"

Cars rushed by, honking angrily as their wakes shook the town car. Emergency blinkers or not, this felt like a terrible idea. Especially as she bolted down the shoulder in her sandals, dress flapping in the breeze.

"Baby!" I barked, finally catching up to her. She could fucking move when she was motivated.

"Please don't be what I think you are. *Please,*" she pled as she… bent down to a *moving* trash bag.

"What the fuck?" I barked, snatching her arm and pulling her back. Then, I heard the whimper, my heart aching as my eyes closed. Kneeling, I opened the bag and wanted to be sick. Humanity's ability to discard life would forever rattle me to my core.

"Is that what I think it is?" she asked like she was praying to be wrong as tears welled in her eyes. I wanted to say no but lifted the bag to move us back toward the car. "Greyson!" she barked. "Please tell me I'm wrong."

Was bringing a trash bag puppy directly into my car a terrible idea? Probably. Was I about to do it anyway? Yep.

"Come on, Alice. We'll check him out when we're off the road."

"Oh god, dammit," she breathed, jamming her eyes closed before she rushed to stay by my side.

Door secured behind us, I opened the bag and, clenching my jaw so tight it could crack, fished out the surviving puppy.

His little cries would stick with me for the rest of my damn life.

18

Dogs Don't Just Trust Willy-Nilly

GREYSON

"People suck! *People suck!* I don't understand! How do people have this kind of capacity for cruelty?" Alice hissed under her breath as she stroked long lines down the puppy's now-white back. She promptly dubbed him *Chip* once we had him cleaned up and nestled into her lap. The vet came and went after we had the little guy bathed, and my beautiful wife had been a rollercoaster of pissed-off and panicked the entire time.

Aside from needing some help getting his calories back up, Chip was otherwise in miraculous form, and according to my vet, would have a wonderful future, to Alice's teary relief.

I'd never been a lapdog kind of guy—if the breed couldn't protect you or complete a task, sharing your space with a slobbering fur-ball wasn't really that appealing until I had Cap. But Chip would stay about this little. The mess of mud and mats was now gone, and he had stark white hair that told Doctor Melligan he was at least part Maltese.

Didn't mean much to me, but Alice lost her shit. As I scrolled through information online, I began to understand *why*. These weren't some mutts that filled up shelter kennels. They were designer dogs—highly sought after for their intelligence and endless adoration of their humans.

"You did well today," I noted, tangling my fingers in her long ponytail. "Making him feel safe. That was quite the ordeal."

"Thanks. *You* were incredible," she added, still stroking long, soothing lines from the crown of his little head to his tail. Captain was still tentatively sprawled over the end of the bed, his big snout pointing toward the newcomer curiously. He'd been about as displeased as his new mama with the situation and only stopped whining when Chip did. "It was like he knew you'd help him. That says a lot, Greyson. Dogs don't just trust willy-nilly, especially when they're scared."

Studying the trace of regret in her eyes, I softly assured her, "I never meant to be the monster in your story, Belle. I'm sorry you ever saw me that way."

"Hell hath no fury like a Rhodes scorned," she said, aiming for a joke, but her tone was too heavy with history to hit the mark.

I leaned up on my forearm so I could reach her chin, guiding her up and over to me. I pressed a kiss to her forehead, my eyes closing as I soaked up her sweet chai scent.

"I didn't exactly give you much to run with outside of asshole boss."

"I saw pieces, though," she admitted. "With Mattie and Beau and with other people around the office. With the little things you did for me—guiding me around, helping me out of the car. I was just too busy being mad at you to acknowledge them."

"Wanting you wasn't an option," I admitted, tucking a stray strand of silky hair behind her ear. My phone buzzed, and I pulled it out in case it was Doctor Melligan. The name on the screen made me hesitate. "Odd."

"What?"

"It's Royce," I said, forwarding the call to voicemail. This was Alice's time. The rest of the world could bugger off. A few seconds later, a text bounced onto my screen, his persistence piquing my interest.

ROYCE

Hey, Hart? How's newlywed life?

GREYSON

Better than I imagined. I think we're adopting a puppy.

ROYCE

laughing emoji That didn't take long. Happy wife, happy life, right?

GREYSON

Right.

ROYCE

That's why I'm reaching out, actually. Miranda and I
were chatting, and she just adores Alice. She hasn't
made a lot of friends in our circle, which has been
pretty isolating. I'd love to facilitate a get-together for
our ladies. We'd love to have you both over for dinner,
or we could spoil a good walk on the green. Sundays
are best for us. Run it by your bride and let me know
what you have open.

"WHAT'S UP?" Alice asked softly, intently studying my perplexed expression.

"They're inviting us for dinner. Or a round of golf. Evidently, Miranda adores you."

"Yes, well, I *am* adorable," she teased flatly, tossing her ponytail over her shoulder.

"Well, I'm aware of that," I said, pressing another kiss to her forehead and freezing when Chip stirred inside the cocoon of her crossed legs.

"What, you two never hang out?"

"Hang. *Out?*" I questioned sardonically, earning the most impressive eye roll known to man.

"Yes, Heartless, hang out. Get together. Enjoy a friendship."

"No," I answered honestly. "People value what I can give them more than my conversation." My phone buzzed again, and I glanced down at another message.

ROYCE

Miranda would like me to relay that if weekdays are
easier, the kids go down by seven, and we have the
patio to ourselves.

I've told her the nanny can put them down, but she
insists on doing it herself. Let me know.

"I CERTAINLY DON'T ENVY HAVING your schedule dictated by a tiny person's sleep schedule."

"What?" She leaned over my shoulder to glance at the screen.

"Coordinating bedtimes," I explained, turning the phone so she could thumb through the exchange.

"Don't ever want your own kids?" she hedged before her breath caught. Scrambling to explain, she said, "I mean, with the right person. Not that we need to think about that. We're just…"

"Alice."

"I didn't mean—"

"*Alice*," I chuckled, leaning over to shut her up. "I know what you meant. And no. It's not in the cards for me."

"Oh, Greyson," she breathed, but confusion marred her features when I looked down to study her reaction. "I don't understand," she admitted. "I thought you, um…"

"Pulled out on purpose?"

"Yeah," she admitted sheepishly, a pretty flush coloring her cheeks. I wanted to lick the color from her skin. If we were discussing any other topic, I would've.

"I did." Uncomfortable silence settled between us, weighing my chest down with the burden of history. So many factors influenced my decision on the subject, and none of them were pleasant. It wasn't a conversation I ever intended to have with another living soul, but her quiet patience wrapped around me like a physical tug.

We hadn't talked about *us*.

We'd had mind-blowing sex. Enjoyed each other's laughter. Merged our families, at least legally speaking. But we hadn't hedged the *what are we* subject since she'd climbed into my bed after reminding me she didn't want my fucking money—not even the untraceable insurance I'd provided for the worst-case scenarios. With a deep sigh, I breathed a truth I'd never thought would surface. "Life behind closed doors was very different from the Hart family's public appearance. You've met Reggie."

"Sure have," she muttered, not hiding her irritation.

"Dad was…worse. By the time Ollie was five, I knew I didn't want him to grow up like I did. He became my responsibility."

"You're not even four years older," she protested, no longer shielding her emotions from me.

Shrugging, I let out the air in my lungs before straightening, carefully thinking that one through. "It was enough. Enough to step between him and Dad. Enough to keep Carlisle's focus on me. I wanted to influence our mother to keep Ollie preoccupied with activities—book clubs, jump rope, soccer, football, swimming, and anything else that kept him out of the house. When we got older, I made sure Dad gave me both the pressure of our name and the punishment his anger doled out. I became his next in line so Ollie could be…free."

"I'm sorry," she breathed, but I shook my head when Alice turned to study me.

"It was what it was. I am who I am because of it, but so is

Ollie," I said, smiling. "He's a pain in my ass, but at least he's a happy pain in the ass, even after Carly."

"I do believe that's a prerequisite of brotherhood," she deduced, smiling tentatively. "I have six, and they're all varying degrees of asshole."

"Maybe," I agreed.

"Why do I sense a 'but' in this story?"

"Because you know me," I guessed with a shrug. "By the time I was a teenager, I'd decided I wouldn't be falling in line anymore. I partied. I did what teenage boys do."

"Get drunk and chase skirts," she guessed, unfortunately correctly.

"Something like that," I admitted, resisting the urge to reach out and take her hand. Whatever was happening between us, this was information she needed to ingest with a clear head. "As you so aptly summarized, Jenilee and I spent our junior year in high school together being idiots. We went our separate ways at the end of the summer, and I fell into mutual mischief with Selene." She nodded as I confirmed that dossier she'd memorized. Clearing my throat, I admitted what no other soul knew. "I met with a recruiter during my senior year, knowing I didn't want to fall in line with Dad and Reggie's plan for my life. My 'fuck you' of sorts was enlisting in the one organization our name couldn't overpower."

"The Navy was your *escape plan*?"

"Yeah," I admitted. "Pretty desperate, I know. I just needed to show them I wouldn't be their pawn."

"So, you became the United States Government's?" Was that concern or confusion in her eyes? I wasn't sure which, but the question seemed sincere enough.

"Desperate times, I guess." A heaviness settled in my stomach. "I hadn't told Selene yet—wasn't sure how to approach it. But uh… she got pregnant."

"Were you scared?" There wasn't any judgment in her tone. Curiosity, perhaps. An aggravatingly adorable note of trepidation.

"Of course," I scoffed. "What seventeen-year-old isn't scared of being a parent? But I told her we'd do it together. Obviously, money wasn't an issue. She'd have what she needed."

"Why do I feel like I'm going to cry by the end of this?"

"Because you're smart enough to know I don't have any children wandering around in the world." I said it like it didn't affect me, like my heart wasn't aching all these years later.

"Can I ask what happened?" she breathed, reaching out to lace her fingers through mine as I nodded, shifting my weight.

"She wasn't thrilled to hear about the Navy. But we agreed, once I got through RTC and NSW back east, that Coronado wasn't the worst option for the duration of her pregnancy while I kept training. Only," I shook my head, wishing my throat didn't still get tight all these years later. It was bullshit to care. "When I got back, there was no baby. She aborted, changed her mind, and said she never signed up to be a military wife. She wanted a Hart's life, and I gave her scraps instead."

My aching forehead made me reach up to smooth out the furrow. "I couldn't...blame her exactly. Her body, and all." My shrug felt forced, even to me. "But I would've done anything for her. *For them*. My world flipped upside down the day I heard that tiny heartbeat. She had to know that my trust would provide no matter what I did with my body or my time." I sucked down a breath, blinking away the burning at the bridge of my nose.

"You're human, Greyson. It's okay to grieve that. All the what ifs. That doesn't make you weak," Alice promised, rubbing gentle lines over my hand. The contact drew my focus before I glanced up to see her eyes welling with tears.

"Harts believe it does. At least, my father did. Selene...vanished. I actually poured a decent chunk of change into trying to find her, only to run into dead ends. It never settled right with me. It was so out of character for the girl I fell in love with that some part of me was in denial for years. When dad died, and I was scouring through his office, I found a record of a wire transfer to one Selene Adler."

"*No,*" she breathed, shoulders curling in on themselves as her mouth fell open in horror, free hand flying to cover her lips.

"Dad paid her *six figures* to abort my child and disappear. He buried their communications pretty thoroughly, but it wasn't *better than Jackson Reynolds* secure. When I inherited, I brought Jackson in to scrub our system, and he found the list of contingencies. It included a name change and instructions for her to move at least three hundred miles away from Emerald Bay."

"Jesus," she breathed, her fingers fluttering over her lips. "Greyson, I'm so sorry."

"It was a long time ago," I responded on autopilot, reaching for that wall of numbness I'd placed between me and the world decades ago.

"Does Ollie know?"

"No," I said firmly, turning to lock eyes with her before blinking away the ache of that past. "You're the only one. Well. Aside from Selene—or whatever her name is now. I suspected Reggie knew, but when I confronted him, he acted as appalled as I was. Believe it or not, he tried to look after us after Dad died. He's not...great at it," I admitted, tugging at the back of my aching neck. That was a generous description, if I was honest. "But he loves the way he was taught to love."

"That's not love," she countered softly, dislodging Chip from where he slept in her lap and gingerly setting him against Captain's side, where he promptly curled into a ball and closed his dark, watery eyes. Alice tucked the strands of hair away from her face to remove any barrier between us as she studied me, slowly easing over my lap and settling over my groin. "You hurting now. You hurting *then*—looking for her. *That* was love."

"Maybe." I turned away, needing to be done with this conversation, but Alice wasn't having it. Her dainty hands squished either side of my face, forcing me back to her.

"After all this time, you haven't ever…wondered? Wanted a family of your own with the right person?"

"Got a vasectomy."

A little smirk twisted her lips, and I knew before she opened them I wouldn't like what she had to say next. "Double birth control wasn't enough for you? Gotta pull out three."

"There's a failure rate for everything."

"Yeah, but like a one-percent—" Cutting her off with my mouth on hers had gradually become less effective. Evidenced by the fact that the instant I wasn't kissing her, she was fucking talking again. Relentless. Like a dog with a bone. "—chance, per kind of birth control. That's taking thorough to a whole new level."

"Kids are a liability. Collateral," I explained gruffly. "Having Mattie and Beau in the world—*and tied to me*—is bad enough. Love is a liability when you run in the circles I choose to." Pain bounced through her eyes, but she nodded slowly in understanding, shifting back to look down at me, although what she thought she'd find written over my face, I didn't know. Suddenly, her answer to my next question held more weight than I ever should've allowed it to. So much that my chest felt like she'd crush it should she pull out of my grasp. Tightening my hands where they'd settled on her hips, I traced the tip of her nose with mine. "Does that change anything?"

She pressed a kiss to my head, and I didn't mean to let her touch lull me, but my eyes slid closed when her hands found my jaw. This woman had a way of liquefying the pain of life and leaving only her scent in my lungs. She kissed each eyelid slowly before leaning back and stroking her chilled thumbs over my cheeks. Her touch was startlingly soothing. Thoughtfully, she studied me before shaking her head once.

What in the hell had I done to earn her affection?

Not taking the time to worry about that, I melted into her as she wrapped her arms around me. Refusing to be left out, my cock made its proximity known with a little jerk that earned a deliciously breathy laugh and a rock of her hips.

"Grey, you and I may not be…conventional," she hedged carefully before huffing a laugh that dispelled a bit of tension. "But as far as my family is concerned, you're one of us now. They're loud and dysfunctional," she said with a shake of her head, smiling down at me endearingly. "Meddlesome as fuck, and *thirteen kinds of overwhelming*, but…they're yours now, too. Milo will always lend an ear if you want a man in your life with an emotional capacity beyond a thimble. Jameson is terrified of emotions, but Rhyett and Paxton like to talk. You don't have to carry everything alone, Greyson."

Slowly, her words settled into my bones. The sincerity in them rattled my grasp on what the hell this was supposed to be as she forked her fingers through my hair, brushing it away from my face. Her disarming caress sent warmth swelling in my ribs, cock now straining against the zipper of my jeans.

Barely clinging to the leash on my emotions, I lifted my chin and demanded, "Come here," pleased when she eagerly obeyed.

This kiss was soft. Tentative. Embodying our confusion as the lines in our dynamic blurred into a smear of chalk on wet cement. I couldn't find it in me to care. For the first time in my life, I wanted to be exactly where I was. A sensation that amplified as she rocked over my dick, her supple lips brushing over mine.

"You told me we do this at my pace," she breathed between unsettled kisses. "But I need you to know that you matter too, Grey. If we're calling a shot that affects both of us, we do it together."

Nodding, I wrapped my arms around her back, straightening to claim her mouth with mine. Her hands fell to the hem of my Henley, stripping it up and over my head, as I raised my arms for her. Mouths colliding, my body demanded hers while my mind processed that promise.

Together.

I'd never known a true *together*. My parents and Reggie wanted to pull our strings like a taut marionette, ensuring each movement was their desired performance. My need to protect Ollie and his kids still influenced our friendship to some extent. Selene had bowed down to the power of Carlisle Hart without so much as telling me what she was up against. My military career reinforced that I was to yield to a superior's beck and call—property of the US government.

Together was a foreign thing. Something other men experienced. It was either me against the world. Or me beneath the boot of my latest ruler.

Alice's giggle broke the trance of allure her body offered beneath my hands, and I smiled against her lips before she leaned back and said, "We smell like wet dogs."

Head thrown back, my laugh reverberated off the ceiling. "Way to set the mood, baby."

"Just being honest."

"I'll show you honest," I growled, rotating us for the edge of the bed. "If I don't get inside you in about thirty seconds, I think I might die."

"How do you feel about shower sex?" she quipped cheerfully, a smug curl to those beautiful lips.

Standing with her in my arms, I answered, "Like you better hold on, my Belle."

She did as she was told, and I lumbered into the ensuite with my woman in my arms. I may have unearthed the past, but I could bury its ache in Alessandra Rhodes-Hart.

UNCLE REGGIE

Seriously, Greyson? Banning me from Hart House's approved list is below you. I'm leaving for Paris tomorrow, and we need to talk.

UNCLE REGGIE

Greyson, call me.

REGINALD HART

I know you're unhappy with me, but you need to put your ego aside and call me back.

It's becoming urgent.

REGINALD HART

You know I can see that you read my messages, don't you?

Stop being a child about this.

REGINALD HART

Call me now.

"IT'S nice to see her like this," Royce said under his breath as he elbowed me in the ribs on Sunday morning. After the most relaxed weekend of my life—in no small part thanks to the intentional absence of my phone—the four of us met up for a Sunday brunch. It was Alice's idea, thinking it wouldn't feel so formal, in case we got uncomfortable. It had been a surprisingly pleasant experience. Mostly because Alice seemed the most comfortable I'd seen her with someone in our circle.

Royce's jerked chin directed my gaze to our wives, where they walked several paces ahead, arm-in-arm, through the street festival Alice spotted on our drive into the city. Her dark hair fell to her lower back, swaying with each step, while Miranda spun her dirty blonde into some fancy clip.

Irritated, I pulled out my incessant cell phone and glanced at the screen in a poor attempt at discretion.

A bit disgruntled, I scowled as I pocketed the damn thing. With the utmost disrespect, my uncle could get fucked after the way he'd spoken about Alice. But his persistence was disarming if nothing else.

"Need to get that?" Royce asked, nodding to the insipid device.

"No, I'm sorry for interrupting," I said, clearing my throat. "I haven't really seen much about your bride," I admitted as my phone buzzed for what must've been the dozenth time that morning. Royce shook his head in answer.

"She's not like Alice—the way she grabs those fuckers by the balls and bends them into submission—she's stayed as far from the spotlight as humanly possible. It's all a bit much, you know?"

"I've been…impressed, to say the least, with how Alice has handled this transition."

"It probably helps that she ran the PR team for a while. She knew what being with a man like us entailed."

A man like us. What an intriguing concept. Royce owned a media company uptown. Technically, he was a competitor, but we'd formed a casual alliance at a charity golf tournament a few years back and would connect for a round every now and then. His father was still alive and well, an active member of their board of directors, despite his attempted retirement a few years back. We'd briefly considered acquiring the Ashcroft group but ultimately decided against it.

"She never really seemed to care what they had to say about her. Doesn't pay much attention unless it's a client they're blasting."

"All the better," he said. "They can be vicious when they want to be. Miranda let her guard down once with one of our chefs, who took pertinent information to the press. We pressed charges since she had violated her NDA. But…it didn't erase the damage done, and she's kind of stuck to herself since. Can't really trust anyone these days."

"Brutal," I noted. "Alice is a good woman. Salt of the earth. I would be beyond shocked if she ever did anything to hurt a moth, much less a mother."

"That's what Miranda said. She just has this gut instinct that we're all supposed to do something together, although she can't place her finger on what."

"You should have seen her with the puppy Friday. I don't think I've ever seen someone so distraught over an animal."

"My girl's the same way. We have six rescues."

"Six?!" I balked, barely reeling in exactly how appalling that concept was. Two was more than plenty. To my relief, Royce laughed.

"Yep. Got a whole pack. Listen, Greyson——" He tugged on his neck, and I braced for the inevitable. Usually, when someone initiates contact, they need something, especially when they pull out my first name. Like they knew me when they didn't. I just hadn't heard *what* yet. "I bought a table at the Performing Arts silent auction next month, and I've got four seats still sitting open. I haven't run it by the wife, but judging by that," he motioned toward where our girls were now enamored with a spoon art jewelry vendor. All the money for the finest accessories in the world, and these two wanted warped spoons. "I think it's safe to say we'd love for the two of you to join. Already paid for——you'd just be saving my pride by filling the seats."

Chuckling, I said, "I'll have to run it by her, but I'll take a wild guess and say as long as the calendar is open, she would enjoy that."

"I'll send you the details," he promised.

"Sounds good."

"I hope this is the beginning of a wonderful friendship."

"The sentiment is shared," I agreed amicably. The strange part was that it felt authentic.

IT WASN'T until we were home, and Alice tucked herself into her art room, that I finally fished my phone from my pocket and dialed

Reggie's number. Grinding my teeth, I counted all four rings before his gruff answer.

"Christ, it's about time."

"Is Emmaline okay?" I asked flatly. No doubt Ellington would tell me if anything was actually wrong.

"What?"

"Answer the question. Is Emma okay?"

"Yes, but—"

I cut him off, unwilling to entertain whatever scheme he'd concocted to re-enter our lives. "What about Ellington? Was he in a life-altering accident I don't know about?"

"No. Don't be rid—"

"Aunt Viv?" I snapped. "Gwen or the babies?" I pressed. My cousin and his wife were due with twins any day now. It's why the old fucker flew to France in the first place.

"All fine," he ground out. "But, Grey—"

"It's *Greyson* to you."

"You can't be serious." His snarl was deeply satisfying, accompanied by the mental image of that vein in his forehead pulsing.

"And yet, here I am. Listen, Reginald. We've said all we need to say to each other at this point. Obviously, this isn't about business, or you would've sent it over official channels."

"I have information you might find beneficial," he declared snootily. I just laughed.

"Then I look forward to hearing it when you present it to the board next month."

"Greyson, you are being *played*, my boy. Our circle is riddled with vipers—that detective always sniffing around, for starters. But you're so busy playing house with your little *girlfriend*, you're ignoring what's right in front of you—"

"I'll let you save your breath, *old man*," I bit back, ready to hear him call me his boy for the last goddamned time. "I'll ask for your opinions if you decide to show Alice and I the same level of respect you expect to be shown yourself. Unless you've been calling to apologize for the way you spoke about my *wife*—or apologizing *to her* for said disrespect—this conversation is over. Tell you what, you call back if either of those are on the agenda." Hanging up a phone hadn't been that satisfying since I could slam one back into the cradle to prove a point.

19

Why Is Axel Trying To Yeet Himself Off The Thread?
ALICE

New Hart Family Takes First Vacation

Summer in the Hamptons: Greyson Hart and Wife Spotted At 4th of July Cookout

From Navy Seal to Neighborhood Hero: What You Never Knew About the Philanthropic Greyson Hart

New Cutting-Edge Animal Foster Program at Emerald Bay Humane Society

Paxton Rhodes' Aggressive Routine Three Weeks Before Season Kickoff

Billionaire on the Bering Sea: Greyson Hart Visits Wife's Hometown

Giggling at the last headline we'd compiled into our media folder, I snapped a screenshot, cropped it in on Greyson's attempt at a smile, and fired it off to the family text thread. Never in my life had I seen a man look so uncomfortable holding a fish, but Greyson's expression was more of a bearing of teeth. The bright yellow rain slicker and waders looked so unspeakably out of place on his lean frame— boat, and mountainous island setting the scene or not. Seeing Greyson out of his element was more satisfying than it probably should have been, but I couldn't help myself.

He was beaming down at me in the article where we presented the first foster dogs to their new families, who would now receive scholarships to aid in veterinary care and individualized training. The program was called Chip's Clips, since they all got groomed and snipped, and it was the first initiative I got to push through since the wedding.

Naturally, that was the picture they all added hearts to before the texts started bouncing in. Still waiting for Miranda's SUV to pull up before I went into the spa, I decided to indulge in a moment of family shenanigans.

The Sibs:

NOEL

Do you just...drop an egg any time that man is in the room? Gotta pull out your wet floor sign?

MAX

I would fold like a damn lawn chair if a man looked at me the way Grey looks at Alice.

ALICE

I do. Regularly.

HADLEE

Suit Daddy shouldn't be allowed to hold puppies. That is now illegal.

ELORA

Happily married and still inclined to agree.

HADLEE

Happily single, but if I find one of those, I'd forget I owned shoes and don an apron for the rest of my life.

AXEL

1st: Ew. JFC. TMFI.

2nd: Yeah, right, Hads. You can't stay in one place for more than three weeks. Like you'd last.

MAVERICK

He has a point.

JAMESON

Know a lot about wet floor signs, baby?

NOEL

Winking emoji You tell me, Captain.

MAVERICK

Ew, guys, gross, stop.

PAXTON

Stop defiling the family text thread. All of you.

JAMESON

No can do, buddy. No can do.

ALICE

James, you in the harbor?

JAMESON

On our way now. Close enough we've got a cell signal
without the sat phone.

From May to October, our house had always been quiet while
Dad tackled the most lucrative season of the year. By the time I was
big enough to have any awareness, the boys were fishing with him all
summer. Now, I just wondered if giving Mom a peaceful house had
been just as much of a goal as training them into the family
business.

With Rhyett off building his own entrepreneurial dreams,
Jameson had been the one to step up and preserve our family legacy.
Had I not landed in a literal piece of heaven, I would've felt bad
that he and Noel pretty much only had Axel for company these
days. Our parents made a trip home for the bulk of summer, but
since Paxton's first game was the first week of September this year,
they were just going to make a road trip of being premature snow-
birds and migrate south a month sooner than usual.

On the rare occasion Jameson was on the text thread this time
of year, it meant he was either in the harbor or very near it. Which
meant it was the perfect time to grill them both. They'd gotten
engaged more than eight months ago, so it was time to start
prodding.

ALICE

Excellent. Did you two dumbasses set a date?

NOEL

Yes, actually! March 22nd!

ALICE

Still thinking Florida?

JAMESON

Yep.

NOEL

Perfect window before Salmon season, and Pax will
have a few weeks to recover. Brex and El are due
around Christmas, so it'll work for them too. Plus, El
and Brod should be on spring break.

ELORA

Very well thought out. I approve.

NOEL

Thought you might *winking emoji*

BREXLEY

I agree. Perfect pick, guys.

FINN

Finally. Thanks for the heads up, guys. Some of us
have to make arrangements.

ELORA

Road trip?

FINN

With a three-month-old? I love you, sis, but hell no.

BRODERICK

Smart man.

I grinned like an imbecile when Greyson's name popped up, a
flush warming my cheeks as I glanced up at Jax, who sat in the
driver's seat.

GREYSON

Just had to share that one, did you, babe?

ALICE

What?! You look cute.

GREYSON

I look like I shit my pants.

MAVERICK

LMFAO

I mean...

He's not wrong.

AXEL

#accurate

GREYSON

You're going to pay for that later, Mrs. Hart.

ALICE

Promise? *smirking emoji*

AXEL

gagging gif

FOR FUCK'S SAKE.

AXEL RHODES HAS LEFT THE CONVERSATION

PAXTON

HEATHENS.

RHYETT RHODES HAS ADDED AXEL RHODES TO THE CONVERSATION

RHYETT

Oh, deal, Ax. Not like we didn't all see the sock on your door in high school.

AXEL

Right. Discreet.

FINN

About as discreet as Yogi Bear in Manhattan.

AXEL RHODES HAS LEFT THE CONVERSATION
GREYSON HART HAS ADDED AXEL RHODES TO THE CONVERSATION

LEIGHTON

Sorry, guys, just got off work. Can anybody recap?

KAIA

Hey! Funny. Me too! Thousands of miles apart, and nothing stops twin telepathy.

Why is Axel trying to yeet himself off the thread?

LAUGHING, I set my phone in my bag and muddled through the contents on the bottom, pulling out my new lipstick and reapplying it in my compact mirror. Unexpected perk of being Mrs. Hart: in addition to having more than I could ever need, brands would do just about anything to send free products for me to try in hopes of a photo landing on Instagram.

How ironic was it that the people who didn't need freebies were the people who received them?

A gentle knock had me turning from my mauve lip stain and grinning when I spotted Miranda, who lingered in the car window. I knocked on the divider so they knew I was getting out and lunged for the door. We'd been getting together every two weeks like clock-work to get our nails done together and exchange books with our mini club—comprised entirely of us and our cosmetologists.

"Hiiiiiiiiii!!!" We squealed together, wrapping each other up before my hands flew adoringly to her round belly.

"How's baby bump?"

"They're good. Been using mommy's bladder as a punching bag, so that's not optimal, but what are you gonna do?"

"Miss ma'am," I exclaimed, immediately animating my voice as I bent down to talk at her belly like a lunatic. "You have to be nice to your mama, you hear me?"

"Still convinced it's a girl?"

"Just got a feeling," I supplied for the dozenth time as I straightened. "You look beautiful. Got that mama glow going for you."

"That's just sweat, darling."

"It has been insanely warm."

"How your brother plays in this, I'll never understand," she said as she hooked her arm through mine, and we headed toward the spa. Only Jax's sigh alerted me to the fact that he was out of the car, and I grinned over my shoulder. Much to my surprise, having a constant tail was probably my least favorite part of this whole arrangement. His cute, grumpy presence was like a storm cloud in the corner of every building I inhabited, no matter how briefly. Nail days were Jax's least favorite and the moment I most looked forward to.

So. Take that, Reynolds. Maybe he'd tell Greyson things were calm enough for him to leave, finally.

The picture-perfect front desk man with pearly teeth and a freakishly wrinkle-free tan greeted us. Seriously, how does one avoid aging while also worshipping the sun?

Cucumber waters in hand, we followed him back to our usual spots with our nail techs, Nikki and Katie. Like we'd synchronized it, all four of us whipped novels out of our bags, tabbed within an inch of their lives, and passed them around to whoever hadn't had a turn with them yet.

Greetings were exchanged, and swatches were selected. We all fell into the easy chatter of familiar company.

"You're both attending that auction tonight, aren't you?"

"Yep," Miranda chirped. The woman was easy to love, even without the adorable basketball baby in her belly. Her dirty-blonde hair was pulled back into an elegant twisty bun, and the sundress she'd picked gave her this whimsical, fairy-core vibe without stepping out of approved fashion trends.

She was the breath of fresh air I hadn't realized I desperately needed until we'd met up for brunch back in June and been attached at the hip ever since.

Community, aside from my family, has always been grueling for me. A love of soul-crushing conversation and hatred for small talk made finding people who wanted to connect a bit of a challenge in the age of surface-level Facebook 'friends.' Miranda was the first person who made it feel easy.

"Some art thing?" Nikki asked as she carefully filed down my old set of dip nails.

"I thought the art museum gala was in the spring," Katie interjected.

"It was. It was so insufferably stuffy," Miranda explained with an eye roll that had me smirking. Maybe that's what I loved about her. She had no more love for the soirees and formalities than I did.

"Glad we missed it."

"Heck, that was right before you and Grey finally launched your relationship to the media," Miranda pointed out.

"It was," I said with a laugh, hoping it was natural. Grey and I had come a long way in the last few months. If you'd told me I would end up catching feelings for my asshole boss, I would've asked what you were on and why you weren't sharing. But a friendship had bloomed around a stream of strange circumstances and an endless supply of vagina-destroying orgasms. Crazy to think just a few months ago, I was sprinting towards a Hart-free life.

And now? Now, I wasn't sure what we were or weren't, but I couldn't fathom a life where Greyson didn't wake me up in the morning with Italian espresso, and that was enough to make a girl nauseous.

Per my strategy, the allegations were finally dying out, successfully overwhelmed by our strategically placed interviews, articles, and donations. Swallowing my nerves, I added, "Long overdue."

"I still don't know how you managed that."

"Witchcraft," I responded, dead serious. Her slow smile had me breaking character like *Deadpool* breaks the fourth wall.

"If you love me, you'll teach me how to do that. Those assholes keep speculating I'm having twins, which makes me feel like Shamu."

"No orca in sight, just a beautiful, very healthy, adequately baby-fied mama-to-be," I assured.

"Regardless," she grumbled, blue eyes mesmerized by the file working over her nails. "I could use some of that. Hell, Royce didn't even know until he got the invite to the engagement party."

"Greyson is an unwaveringly private person."

"Oh, I know. Speaking of, I heard he's been working super late. Big project?"

"Oh," I sighed. Of course. He always had a big project. This month's had been a rather sizable merger, and then he played *Batman* at night, helping Jax strategize an op. While I understood the low-level semantics, I was nowhere near grasping the big picture. Of course, I couldn't say any of that and just led with, "Always."

"I know how that feels. Royce is always at the office. Even when he's home, he's glued to his phone unless we're on a date night or at one of the kids' activities. He does his best, but sometimes even those get interrupted."

"Grey…he likes to clock off at some point, you know? Turns his phone off so he can decompress at the end of the night. Or when we're with Mattie and Beau."

"The secret to having staff for everything."

"And two dogs with very limited bladder capacity," I teased, earning a laugh.

"How are those troublemakers?"

"Cap is done with Chip's shit, and Chip worships the ground he walks on."

"That's about right," she laughed. "Gosh, I'm glad all that media drama has blown over."

"I have a feeling it'll be a while yet before Grey lets Jax go."

"Oh, I just meant those bullshit allegations. You know how it is. With all those rumors flying, were you ever freaked out? I feel like I would've been so anxious."

Wouldn't you like to know? Shrugging, I said, "Not really. Bottom feeders doing what they do."

"They really are the worst."

"Parasites," I lamented.

"Agreed. Gosh, when they've gone after Royce, I've been in knots. All it takes is one nasty rumor, and people lose their shit, you know? I'm always worried some crazy person is going to believe those rags and hurt him or me and the kids. I hate it here."

"Awe, well, I get that. But don't let it all get too far in your head." I gave her a sympathetic smile before adding, "If there'd been any validity, that would've been different, but I know my husband."

She smiled, wiggling in her seat and sending her sunny chiffon dress swaying around her legs. "You're still so cute when you say that. That beautiful newlywed bliss."

"It really is," I agreed.

"Alright," Nikki interrupted. "We're doing something fun this week, yeah?"

"Yeah," I agreed. "I'm feeling lavender. It'll complement my dress tonight."

"Wanna try something new?"

"What kind of new?" Miranda pressed, leaning over our way nosily.

"We have a glow-in-the-dark base that can go under about any color. Sounds crazy, but I'm obsessed, and guys love it."

Grinning over at the pretty little blonde across the table, I thought that one over. "The guys like it?" I questioned. That could be just secretly rebellious enough without pissing off my stylists.

"Don't think too hard, it's pretty obvious," Miranda teased with a flirtatious wink. Shrugging, I rationalized that the press couldn't tell if my nails glowed in the dark. But the idea of Greyson watching my fingers wrapped around his shaft after our evening out had my toes curling in my shoes. "Why the hell not?"

THE AUCTION WAS AS to be expected. A spectacularly wealthy family opened their palatial, historical estate for us to ogle while enjoying a gallery-style display through gothic stone arches and looming hallways. The rich and famous did rich and famous things, most notably, mingling in dresses they'd been sewn into and eating tiny portions of pretentious food, more dog treat than substance. The women passive-aggressively fought to keep their name at the top of the hypothetical totem pole, while men flirted with women who certainly weren't their glittering, waifish wives.

Only this time, I spent most of the hours laughing. I just needed a fellow fish out of water to fit right in.

"Why yes, good sir, I would very much enjoy throwing away all my years of education to be at thy beck and call," Miranda intoned in her best English accent—which came out more cockney than The Queen's English, sending me snickering into my martini glass. "Do remind me what a colossal waste of time my degree was."

"Of course, you can build in stipulations around my required weight in our prenup."

She splayed her hand across her chest dramatically. "So long as I may counter with required erection size."

"Jesus," I barked, nearly spewing my drink out of my nose as I bent over laughing, shielding my face behind our table centerpiece.

"Would likely not approve of this conversation," Greyson's wry voice wrapped around me like a hug after a week apart. He'd been at the office from sunup to sundown, our meetings rarely overlapping. Sneaking downstairs to sit at the kitchen island to hear him talk about his day had become the highlight of my week. He'd pull out the prepared meals the chef stored in the fridge and eat them cold right out of the container, and I'd sit and commiserate the endless expectations of his role. But I'd missed being out with him.

Perhaps pigs had actually learned to fly.

Still in stitches, I turned to find him and Royce with mirroring cat-like smirks as they both held up our respective drinks. A fresh martini for me and a strawberry lemonade for my human-incubating companion.

"I mean, consummation is a biblical event," Miranda countered with a sly smile.

"She would know," I pointed out, staring at her belly. Royce burst out laughing as Grey shook his head, a satisfied humor slanting his lips as he leaned down to press a kiss to my cheek.

"I'd like to get biblical tonight," he whispered, the heat of his breath sending goosebumps down my neck as my face flushed.

"What do you think I bought this dress for?" I breathed back.

He was still smiling as he slid into his seat, clearing his throat. "Glad everyone is having fun."

"But not too much fun," Miranda said, lifting her strawberry lemonade.

"Alas, the limitations of motherhood," Royce lamented playfully. "You ladies spy anything worth bidding on?"

"An Irish getaway for four, or the session with Miley Cyrus' photographer," Miranda supplied.

"I'm with you on the getaway," I said, wrinkling my nose at the idea of yet another voluntary photo shoot. Personally, I was shuttered out for a hot minute. Our server arrived, pouring water refills as she made her way around the table, but her eyes kept going to Greyson. I'm not generally a possessive alpha-woman, but *my god, woman, I'm right here*. She was pretty, too. Kinky chocolate curls draped over her slender back, fair skin, and dark brown eyes.

My phone buzzed inside my clutch, but I ignored it, opting to set my arm across the back of his chair, playing with the ends of his hair as she looked between him and me. That's about the point at which she fumbled Royce's glass, sending it careening into his merlot and subsequently across the table. I'd just rocketed upright as it poured onto my lap.

"Oh my god! Oh my god, I'm so sorry!" In her haste to help, the woman set down the pitcher of water but managed to knock the entire thing over when she rushed to sop up the spilled wine. "Oh!" she yelped. Royce set his hand on her frantic one as she rushed to mop up the disaster.

"You're alright," he assured, which would have been sweet, except he made it awkward hanging onto her hand a beat longer than comfortable. Still looking terrified, she slowly removed herself from his grasp before glancing between me and Greyson.

"Mistakes happen," Greyson added, dipping his chin to meet her terrified eyes. She smiled weakly, nodding as she hurried to clean up. More staff arrived to assist, and her trepidation seemed to increase as she looked up to me.

"Mrs. Hart, I apologize; if you come with me, I'll help you save your dress."

I glanced at Greyson, and when he nodded, sucked down a breath, and moved to follow. "Thank you." Irritated with myself, I realized I'd been so swept up in Miranda and Royce and finally not feeling so alone that I hadn't taken note of her name. I didn't have a chance to ask as she wove us between tables and out the side room before we walked down a long hallway. I motioned to the bathroom, and she shook her head.

"A water line burst in that one," she explained. "The staff bathroom is open, though."

Glancing over my shoulder, I memorized the way back as the chatter of the auction faded. This place was a gothic-era labyrinth full of stone and stretching shadows, complete with beautiful golden faux torch lights jutting from the walls.

"It's really okay," I reassured, glancing down to the Burgundy staining my bold gold gown. Unless she was a secret sorceress, there wasn't any saving this.

"I'm probably getting fired either way, so I might as well make it right," she murmured, a waver in her voice as we hurried around a corner.

"I assure you, if it comes to that, Greyson will speak with your employer and make sure your position is secure."

"That won't be necessary, Mrs. Hart. Thank you, though." Petrified, flecked coffee-brown eyes found me over her shoulder. What in the hell had her so spooked? Her anxiety was palpable, and somehow, my instincts said it was way worse than the prospect of losing a job. She held open the door to a two-stall bathroom, and I stepped in, looking around. She rushed to fetch a rag from the cabinet and wet it. "Oh, this isn't working," she muttered so quietly I barely heard her, shaking her head as she dabbed away at the inevitable disaster of Burgundy. "I have a stain remover in the other room. Give me a moment, Mrs. Hart, and I swear I'll work miracles."

With a sympathetic smile, I nodded and said, "I needed to escape to a restroom anyway." The moment the door closed behind her, I sighed, studying the ridiculous space. It really was an exceptional imitation of ancient castles. The only thing out of place was the modern ventilation.

I hurried to use the restroom and wash my hands, sadly glancing down at my ruined dress. Not that it would have survived Greyson tearing it off me tonight. Anticipatory jitters rocked through my belly. We'd yet to decide what it meant, but my mind was in no rush to disrupt a dynamic we both seemed to think was working. I rotated to study the art hung against the stone walls, running my fingers over the dark wood trim dividing rock from wood. I'm not sure how long she intended to have me wait, but I didn't want to worry Greyson with an extended absence.

Hushed voices pulled my attention from the intricate painting of the Italian countryside—what looked like a field of poppy flowers hedged by slender towering trees—and I turned, scowling, until I realized they were coming from the air vent.

Ears straining, I heard a male timbre say, "He has no idea. I promise we're secure."

Chills ghosted down my spine, and my intuition prickled as I stepped into the stall below the vent, attempting to get closer.

"The wife?" A low, sardonic laugh. "His diversion tactic is clueless. I said I'll take care of it."

What the actual fuck? Interest more than a little piqued, I scrambled up onto the back of the industrial toilet, praying my pointed heels wouldn't lead to my untimely demise as I scaled higher, using my hands on the stall wall to balance. My phone buzzed in my clutch, and I hurried to silence it, precariously teetering on the porcelain. "It's sent." A brief pause, followed by a word that sent my stomach sinking with confirmed suspicion. "Passcode—Trah."

Trah. Like T-R-A-H? Hart…backward? Had I heard him correctly? That couldn't be a coincidence. Simultaneously, it felt idiotically obvious.

Oh shit. Glancing down to my phone, I had no less than fifteen texts and five missed calls from Max. Scrambling, I climbed off the toilet and headed for the door with no regard for my dress. Only, as I turned back the way we'd come, I heard the men's bathroom door creak open on squeaky hinges. Seriously, did they have the creepy castle vibes installed on purpose?

Ducking into an alcove, I pressed myself into the wall, praying the room behind me wasn't the one they were headed for, as two sets of male footsteps softly filled the hallway. Muttered voices culminated, and the three paths branched off before one set of footsteps continued on the path, and the other grew closer. Heart in my throat, I held my breath, praying the concealment of shadows hid me where I stood. My hand flew to cover my mouth as though that would silence my panic as I watched the distinct figure of Reggie Hart rush past me back toward the auction. The sound of the second pair of footsteps faded down the opposite hallway.

Son of a bitch.

20

Count Alice and I In For Pepperoni

GREYSON

Anxiety ate at my gut when the lights dimmed, and the auctioneer took his place at the podium. *Where in the hell was Alice?*

"If you'll excuse me, I have to take this," Royce said, kissing Miranda's cheek as he held up his illuminated phone. I nodded as she smiled endearingly, clinging to his fingers for one extra beat before releasing him to answer. Their oblivious nonchalance didn't ease my growing sense of unease. The dress was likely past redemption, and my only explanation was that our server knew where the hostess had spares, and they were looking for one. But that seemed awfully presumptuous for my wife and even more so for our waitress. Shifting in my seat, I glanced back toward the open double-door archway, hoping to spot long dark hair and that delectable gold dress.

Nothing. Just the security guards at their posts. *God damn it.*

Perhaps I'd grown paranoid in my years of service or in the short stretch since we'd started *Thunderstrike*. But I couldn't shake it. This is why my phone lighting up where I'd discarded it on the table had me following in Royce's wake without a preamble. Alice.

"Hey," I breathed once I was in the hallway. "Are you okay?"

"Yes and no," she answered breathlessly, a quiver in her tone sending me walking definitively down the hardwood floor past the ridiculous mounted torches.

"What does that mean?" Surveying the empty hall, I strained to hear anything that could lead me to her, coming up empty. "Where are you?"

"About that…"

"Baby, if your goal was to set me on pins and needles, you've been more than successful."

"I, um…I think I found something. But I'm stuck."

"Stuck?" Clearing my throat, I put some distance between myself and the security personnel. "You're going to have to elaborate. Your *zipper* is stuck?"

The sound of her swallow was audible over the line. "Are you alone?"

"About to be."

"If you know who owns this monstrosity of a house, tell me I'll be fine and order pizza."

The Gilbert family was new money but no less known in our circle than my own. Neal and Odessa were the hosts of this evening's auction. Where was she going with this, and why was my stomach plummeting like an elevator without a cable?

"That's fine with me. Count Alice and I in for pepperoni."

"Okay," she panted, something like excitement in her tone. "Good. Have you ever suspected they were tied to *Obsidian* or something similar? Tell me to make it two if you have or to hold the cheese if not."

"Make that one dairy-free." Now, my heart was hammering. Pinning my cell between my ear and shoulder, I lifted my wrist to type a message to Jax on my smartwatch. What in God's name had she stumbled into? "But I'm going to need it to the house before we get there."

"I'm hurrying," she assured. "But I think I'm locked in here."

"That's not what I want to hear. Where were you going to order it to?" *Please understand. Please, please understand.*

"His office, I think?" *That's my girl.* My air left in a rush of relief. "Maybe there's more than one. But it's down the hall, south of the staff bathroom at the back of the building." Casually picking up my pace, I pushed for the end of the hallway, not liking a bit of this. What the hell was she thinking, snooping around a place like this? With security crawling around like ants. "Listen, Grey, I think it's connected. I overheard two men talking about them being secure and someone not knowing anything and a wife as a *diversion tactic* and I don't think it was coincidence."

"Why?"

"Max called. He intercepted some kind of communication via the device he added to my phone."

"A *what*?"

"Never mind that. *Focus.* If they get to me before I get out of here, you need to hear this." Never in my life had my heart fallen out my ass as quickly as it did now. Taking fire from enemy combatants didn't make me feel the kind of terror that Alice in harm's way did. Only discipline kept me silent as I glanced over my shoulder to ensure I wasn't followed. "There's a code. A code on the server. Max has it, but something didn't sit right. The men in the bathroom said Passcode—Trah. Trah. Like t-r-a-h. Simple enough to deduce, they just flipped our last name. Stupid to so easily confirm my suspicions. If we apply it as a keyword on a cipher code, maybe it will mean something, but Max isn't through the numbers yet. He needed me to get closer to the computer, so I followed the second man down the long hallway, which is how I got locked in here."

"I really, really *hate* anchovies," I ground out, wanting to throttle her more than anything. What was she thinking? Worse. *What if she was right?* Were we sitting in the spider's nest?

She huffed a nervous little laugh, and I clung to the sound as I looked back one last time before ducking down the long, shadowed corridor. The subtle sound of my shoes settling on the hardwood had my body bristling.

Could I likely defend us if I needed to? *Yeah.*

Would my back hold up for the duration of a conflict? Only god knew the answer to that. I hadn't tested it. Jax was prepared to be a backup, but we were seriously outnumbered, and the entire grand hall was full of witnesses. This was *not* how things were done. Suspicions or not. We didn't just barge in blind. This is why civilians belonged far, far away from this life. *Jax's* life. She grunted like she was putting in a tremendous deal of effort before her panicked little sigh had my ribs constricting.

"The windows are sealed shut," she breathed. "Dammit."

Confident I was finally well and truly alone, I hissed, "Baby, I'm in the back hallway. Where the hell are you? And what do you mean the windows are sealed shut?"

"Third door on the right."

Reaching it, I turned the handle to no avail. No deadbolt, so we just needed to pick it. Kneeling, I pulled my government-issued set from my back pocket. Could never be too prepared, though Alice locking herself in our host's office certainly hadn't come to mind.

"Please tell me that's you."

"I'm here. I've got you," I assured, glancing around to ensure I wasn't on a security camera. "Dammit, baby, *what were you thinking?*"

"That some asshole thought my husband was clueless and I didn't care for that."

"While I appreciate your need to defend my intelligence, doing it at your own expense was never in my plan."

"I know."

"And yet here we are," I grumbled, selecting my tools and watching the end of the hallway. Oh, this was twelve kinds of not good. "I love you—r brain." *Oh, holy fuck,* now was not the time for declarations. We had many, many conversations to come before that one.

But the reality was…while I had no idea what the hell we were doing, I'd never had someone in my life who would come to *my* defense. Never had someone who'd witnessed all of my ugliness and chosen me, anyway. Maybe what we had wasn't love, but it was about as close as I'd gotten.

Clearing my throat, I growled. "You know I love *your brain*. But this was so damn boneheaded."

"Don't convince yourself I didn't think this through or assess the risks."

"You got *locked* in an *office*," I pointed out.

"Okay. Well. *Yeah*. I didn't expect the damn door to seal when it closed."

"*Yeah*, well," I mimicked, "think real hard on that one, because we'll be discussing this when we get home."

"Punish me later, suit daddy, but for now, just get me the hell out of here."

Suit daddy? Suddenly, I was glad she couldn't see the smirk on my face, because only Alice could put us in a pinch like this and still shoot for innuendos. "Don't you know bad girls get punished?"

"Don't you know they *like* it?"

I huffed a laugh as I worked the pins. "I'll test your theory later and you can tell me how much you like my bright red handprint on your ass, but for now, shut up and let your *suit daddy* listen."

Her breathless laugh preceded an alarmingly disciplined silence, save for the subtle shift and click of pins. Distantly, my mind registered applause from the auction, but I kept my head down, straining for those telltale metallic teeth. And just like I'd practiced a million times, it finally gave way. Quickly, I used my sleeve to wipe the door handle as thoroughly as I could without the proper supplies. Rushing through the door, I scanned the space before swallowing her body in my arms. Relief crashed through me like the surf.

She was okay. *I had her*, and she was okay.

"Christ, baby, what the fuck?" I huffed as I caught my breath. Hadn't realized I'd held it captive as I worked the lock open.

"Look, I got what he needed, okay? The signal had to be closer to the hard drive or something. When Max says jump, I just say how high, I don't ask other questions. But, we have to get back."

Nodding, I pulled away, surveying the space. "Did you touch anything?"

"Just the door handle," she said, panic in her eyes.

"Easy enough, I already got it," I promised, grabbing her hand as I stepped for the hallway. Alice rammed into me when I came up short, catching movement at the fork in the corridor. The sound of footsteps reverberating off the walls had me cursing under my breath as I shoved her back inside.

"*Hey!*" a distinctly male voice barked as footsteps sped up.

"Jiggs up, baby." Eyeing the windows, I debated between fleeing or laying her out on the floor and going with 'We got drunk and carried away.'

Certainly wouldn't help the scandal side of things, would it? An inebriated fall from glory. However, neither would getting caught breaking the Gilbert's office window.

Without prompting, Alice raised her phone to her ear, and I swore as the door clicked closed behind us. "You have their security cameras?" A bated breath. Meanwhile, I was making a beeline for the windows. "Anything in the south corridor, the windows outside, or the office?" Another pause. "Well, the alternative is starring in a live-action porno with an improvised script and praying they don't question us. I think those odds are firmly stacked against us, so yeah, I need to know. *Yes*. Good. Thanks." She shot me an animated grimace before jerking her chin at the window I was fighting open.

Damn archaic swollen frames.

Her expression would've been hilarious if I wasn't so livid I could spit. Rushing to help, Alice threw her entire body into it, both of us straining to get the wood to budge as someone banged on the door, demanding we open it.

Joke's on you, fucker.

But there was just enough room, and I had to bite back my need to slap her fucking perfect ass as she bent down to squeeze between the frame. There would be time for that later.

Unceremoniously, Alice crashed into the bush outside, popping up scraped, with leaves and twigs in her hair. Sucking my lips between my teeth, I nodded as she righted herself, both of us torn between laughter and running for our fucking lives. Hurriedly, I wiped down the window frame with my jacket, praying I fucked up any fingerprints we left behind.

The best thing about criminals? They're highly unlikely to call the police. In a fucked up way, I hoped what Alice found was as bad as she thought it was.

That was our only prayer in this fucking mess.

Careful to keep my palms off the bottom of the frame, I wedged myself through as she held it open with her forearms. She let gravity do the rest the moment I was on my feet, and the thing *thunked* back into place.

"Keep your face down," I demanded, snatching her hand as we bolted toward the front corner of the estate.

"Max'll scrub them!" she panted as she followed my lead. But a flash of neon caught my attention, and I looked down to see where her nails were *glowing* in the dark.

"What. The fuck. Is *that*?" I growled, raising her hand in front of us as we made a beeline through the grass.

"Oh," she giggled breathlessly. "They glow."

"I see that. Do you have pockets?"

"In couture?! No, Grey, I don't have pockets."

"Well—*fuck*." I laughed, shaking my head. "Tuck them into fists or something."

"We just broke out of a castle, and you're worried about *my nails*."

"Little glowing ghosts on the security feed?"

"I told you, Max is on it."

"Fucking ridiculous. Goes on an unapproved stealth op with glowing nails."

"It wasn't exactly *planned*," she protested, but humor slanted those pillowy lips a beat before she dragged her teeth over the bottom one. "My nail lady said guys love them."

"Your nail lady is *ridiculous*."

"I don't exactly think she had breaking and entering in mind when she made the suggestion."

Nothing about this should've been funny. Or entertaining.

And yet, I found myself electrified with the rush of adrenaline and morbid humor. Maybe it was truly too close a call, but it was also the closest thing I'd had to fun in a long damn time.

We stopped behind the cover of a couple of maple trees so I could look her over. I plucked the twigs and leaves from her hair, running my thumb over the scrape across her cheek and grimacing when I saw the accompanying cuts over her bare arms. Quickly, I slipped out of my jacket and draped it over her shoulders before she snaked her arm around my waist. We casually strolled out of the goddamn hedges and onto the driveway, making eyes at each other like nothing out of the ordinary was happening.

"What do I do about Miranda?" she asked as I helped her into the back of the SUV while Jax watched with open concern.

I swore, closing my eyes. "Leave it to me." It took approximately three minutes for me to wander back in the front entrance—trusting Max to scrub the footage after us—and find Royce, who was still on the phone, pacing the hallway.

"You okay?" he asked with a hand over the receiver.

"So sorry to bail, but Alice had too much to drink, so I'm taking her home," I supplied simply. He gave me a sympathetic smile, tossing up a casual wave before directing his attention back to his receiver.

· · ·

"DON'T LOOK at me like that," Alice said through a petulant scowl once Jax had us on the road. *Fuck, she was cute.* Especially in trouble. Shrugging, she protested, "I followed my gut, okay?"

"And where'd that get you?"

"Face first in a rosebush?"

Scoffing, I grumbled, "At least you're honest."

"And *right*, might I add." Triumphantly, she turned her phone in my direction. "Jax took a look. Every fifth letter was a fraction of a point smaller than those around it."

"It looks like gibberish," I admitted.

"Correct. But we tried an anagram. Then a shift. Still nothing, so we applied the keyword Trah, but got nothing. Flipped it to apply Hart, and ran it through again. It's a *Vigenère cipher,* Greyson."

"How the fuck do you know so much about codes?"

"Bored teenager on a perpetually rainy island, what the fuck else do you do but hit the library?" she supplied, nonplussed. I wasn't positive, but I was pretty sure there were a great many things she could have filled her time with, short of becoming a spy kid. Not that I was complaining. Her brilliance was as tantalizing as her beauty. "Beside the point. Look at the translation."

I did. And right there, in plain English, were the words *Transfer complete. Obsidian Secure.*

"What the fuck?"

"That's what we have to figure out. But, Greyson…?" When I just locked our gazes, she swallowed *hard.* I couldn't help but watch the muscles work, wishing it was for a much more satisfying reason. "Reggie came out of the bathroom I heard them talking in."

THE CONCEPT that my uncle was potentially embedded in the *Obsidian* web rendered me silent until we got home. The man had a daughter, for Christ's sake. I couldn't refute it in good conscience. But my mind couldn't quite compute the obvious as a potential reality, either. There were too many red flags to toss aside. As far as we were concerned, he was now a suspect and Jax would be launching an immediate investigation. My skin was left crawling, eclipsing my promises of punishment for my naughty, brilliant, reckless girl and our *biblical* evening, instead leading me directly to our room and into the shower.

Water frigid as a polar plunge, I submerged myself under the steady streams and jammed my eyes closed. But it was the idea that my own blood would profit off sex slaves that sent my fists slamming into the tile wall.

21

Feminism, Who?

ALICE

"*Fuck!*"

Heart heavy, I stepped into the bathroom, where I found Grey bare, leaning his forehead on his fists where they clenched against the shower wall. I couldn't even fathom what must be going through his head right now. Not that either of us were shocked that Reggie made shit choices, but this seemed...*extreme*, even for his Royal Dickness.

Grey's shoulders rose and fell in labored breaths as the water sluiced down his magnificent body. He truly was an unfairly gorgeous specimen. Equal parts honed muscle and just enough give to make him cuddleable. But that ass just never quit—a pert bubble butt, if I'd ever seen one. Watching streams of water pour over those tight glutes had me *salivating*. If he didn't look so distraught, I'd get on my knees and sink my teeth into it.

Maybe getting on my knees was a good idea, regardless. Distract him from the hell inside his head.

It was the rustle of fabric as I slowly unzipped my dress, which had tortured hazels flicking to me, my chest still heaving. Grey's mouth opened and closed twice, and I slowly slipped free, the gown hissing as it hit the floor. He looked me up and down, tracking my movement as I unclipped my strapless bra and let it follow suit, all too pleased with his sudden, intense focus on my peaked, desperate nipples.

While I still assert there's no graceful way to slink out of under-wear, I did my best before standing at my full height, waiting for a cue.

Tonight had my blood roaring in my ears, and there had never been a sweeter sound than his voice when he came through that door. It was safety and comfort, and surety that we would find a way out, all at once. Our playful promises exchanged on the phone kept my head on straight until he had me in his arms.

I needed them again. Those capable muscles wrapped around my body. His strong hands on my skin. Maybe it was bolder than I had a right to be, but I needed Greyson like the air in my lungs. Needed him to pull my mind into the moment and away from the idea that I'd shared air with a man who sold humans for profit. Away from the idea that the troubled creature before me would have to destroy his own uncle. Monster though he may be.

Lifting my chin, I let my hands settle by my side as his hungry gaze scraped over my body.

My ego purred as he gave me a curt nod, but something in me broke when he stretched a hand toward me, as though he'd wait for mine to fill his palm. As though he was as desperate to touch me as I was to be touched. When I reached up to take off the gaudy, amethyst-jeweled necklace our stylists paired with my gown, he shook his head.

"Leave it. You look royal."

"But won't it—"

"Leave it," he repeated over my concern, a bit out of breath. *Right.* Because thousands of dollars in jewels were disposable in this world. Nodding, I closed the gap, stepping over the tile divide and into water so jarringly cold it yanked my breath away. "Breathe," he ordered, snaking an icy hand around my middle and pulling my ass to his groin. Shakily, I fought to comply. "Own your fear. You're not dying. Tell your body that."

"E-easier to do when you-re n-not at risk of h-hypother-mia," I chattered as tears burned in my eyes.

He was torturing himself like he should be punished for Reginald's transgressions.

"Breathe," he repeated. "Control your mind. Learning control will keep you alive, baby. You never should've bolted into a situation without knowing it inside and out."

Fighting to comply, I jammed my eyes closed as every inch of my body *screamed* for relief. How in the fuck was he *talking* right now?

"My back seizes in this kind of cold," he explained. "I've been working to master it for years. I assure you, you can breathe through it." I wanted to argue that I wasn't capable of that. Greyson had always been motivated by control. It didn't surprise me that it extended to his own body. But...then his hands were sliding over my skin, rough and desperate.

He slipped them up to my breasts, kneading them urgently before giving my nipples a demanding tweak that sent desperate need blooming across my body.

A ravenous caress warred with the cold as one palm slid down my body until his fingers found my clit, where he began a steady circle of pressure.

"I need you," he admitted with a jagged exhale. Somehow, it was all the more vulnerable. My own oxygen now came in broken inhales as pleasure and cold warred for my focus. "Need to feel you. Know you're safe."

Nodding. Nodding, I could still do.

His responding chuckle was a desperately needed warmth, although I wished it could spread as my body shook against his, mind fighting to control the response. "You're crazy," I mumbled, finally about to call it quits when he increased the pressure on my clit, drawing my focus to the waves of pleasure his fingertips delivered.

Cold-pleasure-cold-pleasure.

My brain was short-firing, unsure of what the hell to focus on.

"That adrenaline rush heightens your awareness, doesn't it?" Greyson whispered coyly in my ear, fingers working so deftly my legs were shaking from something other than the frigid temperature. I nodded and a pleased growl rumbled in his chest as he dipped his fingers into my entrance, pleasure sending my head flying back to land on his shoulder as he pinned my body against his with the opposite arm. "I'm not sure I can be gentle," he warned as he leaned into my back, his pecs flexing against my shoulder blades.

With my eyes still jammed closed and my breath coming in desperate pants, I gasped, "So don't try."

His palm flattened against my low belly as he yanked me back into him. "You scared me today."

"I'm s-sorry."

"Are you?" he scoffed. "I don't think you understand what I would do to keep you safe, my Belle."

Those words wrapped me up just as much as his arms did, as he traded his forearm across the necklace on my chest for a palm wrapped around my throat, keeping my chin tipped up where I rested on his shoulder.

"I won't be s-so reckless."

"You're freezing, princess," he noted with some trace of amusement.

"Y-*yeah*," I said with all the tact of a 'duh.'

Greyson's opposite hand reached for the shower handle, flicking it to the left. By the time his fingers were back on my clit, the water was warming up, my entire body sighing with relief.

"You're my *wife*. My *world*, Alessandra Hart. Don't forget that."

Nodding, I managed to catch my breath as he gently worked his hands over my body. It was only the involuntary burning at the bridge of my nose that made me process what he'd just declared. Why was I always crying around this man? Did he mean that? In some small part? Or was that just lust steering his words?

"Did you mean what you said at the manor or was that the adrenaline talking?"

"Which part?" I asked, still trying to wade through his prior declarations.

"That you want to be *punished?*" he asked playfully, giving my clit a tap. What little air I'd managed to gather rushed out of my lungs in one blow, heat coursing through my entire body like he'd dropped a match into gasoline.

"Yes," I admitted, not hiding any ounce of the desperate need consuming my body.

Maybe I was fucked in the head, but I needed this man to *use me* for his pleasure. To possess every inch of me like he owned it. After years of fighting for his respect, I wanted nothing more than for him to fill me, to make this body serve his need to fuck and rut and cum. Some equally primal part of me wanted it to be *him*. Just us.

I'd never wanted a man like I *needed* every inch of Greyson Hart.

"Don't be such a gentleman, for once in your life. Sometimes I just need you to disrespect me a little."

"You like being my little whore?" Just those words, paired with his fingers working against my sex with unforgiving circles, and that pleased smile in his voice had my knees buckling. His chuckle as he supported my weight brought me more pleasure than it should've, but it wasn't enough. I needed more. "You will always be my princess, Alice. But just for tonight, you get to see what happens when little sluts think they can put themselves in danger." With no other explanation, he turned off the water, and held his hand up to steady me as he ordered, "Walk over to the counter, Alice."

Stomach in my throat, I nodded, accepting his steadying hand. Water still sliding down every inch of my body, I elatedly complied. Unwilling to think about the part of me rebelling against his demand, I followed the fire of lust over to his counter, watching as all six-foot-two-inches of *my husband* prowled up behind me in his naked, soaked glory. Eyes dark with need, a sly smile slanted his mouth as he came up behind me, gently running his fingers over my hips.

My god, the man was a deity. A carnal sex god made flesh, and I was the mortal maiden somehow blessed by his desire. My pussy gave a desperate pulse, needing him to fill me. Needing to feel him against all my walls.

Holding my eyes in our reflection, he ordered, "Lay over the counter." Swallowing my mouthful of butterflies, I did as he said, both loving and loathing the way his demands set my veins on fire.

Feminism, who?

The solid expanse of his still-chilled thighs met my backside as he closed the gap, broad hands digging into each cheek. "That's my good girl." The following slap against my ass made me yip in surprise, his smile sending an anticipatory shiver down my spine. "Mmmm," he purred before giving me another firm slap and then soothing the skin with a caress. "Pick a safe word, Alice."

Studying the face of the avenging warrior in the mirror above me, I whispered, "*Thunderstrike.*"

Smack.

Oh, fuck me—could you climax from being spanked?! Was that a thing? Because *my god*, my walls were trembling with as much need as the rest of me.

"Good. Does my girl want to be punished for scaring me today?"

That part of my brain in charge of the wording was entirely offline, so, lips parted as I panted for air, I nodded. Frantically. Pathetically. Begging for the sweet sting of his skin on mine. His smirk was roguish and delicious and made my pussy clench a beat before he slapped my ass again. The sound was as startling as that impact, then he soothed it away with his warm palm as we dripped shower water all over the floor.

"Spread your legs, baby," he demanded, nudging my thighs wider with his knee. In the next heartbeat, he sheathed what had to be at least two fingers inside me, based on that incredible aching stretch.

Bending over my body so he could reach around and rub my clit, he whispered, "You need to come, baby?" Another frantic nod. "Then hang onto the counter."

I did. God, I did. Evidently pleased, Greyson took up an unforgiving pace as he fucked me with his hands. Hard and relentless, he fingered me with expert precision, rubbing at my clit until the pleasure had me writhing beneath him.

"This is mine," he growled. "This pussy, your pleasure, that beautiful body. *Mine.*" A whimper escaped me, but evidently, that wasn't the response he was looking for because he stopped, sliding his fingers out as I panted against the cold stone of his sleek counter. *Smack.* "I want to hear you say it, baby, because my wife doesn't get to put herself at risk. Certainly not on *my* behalf."

"Y-yours," I stammered, rising on shaky legs.

"Mmmm, good," he growled, wrapping me up and peppering my neck in kisses. With his cheek against mine, one hand straightening my neck, he said, "Look how beautiful you are, Alice."

My eyes flew to our reflection. To his half-hooded eyes, dark with desire, to the way his broad hands spanned over my belly and bracketed my neck…to *me*.

Hair a mess of dark, wet tendrils dripping water down my naked body, soft with curves. The necklace he insisted I leave on shimmered even in low light. Some combination of his princess and his plaything.

That devilish smirk curving his mouth said Greyson saw it, too. Saw it and relished in it.

Voice low enough to smatter goosebumps over my skin, he breathed, "Mine should get on the bed so I can finish her," before nipping at that sensitive spot where my neck met my shoulder.

Rushing to comply, I made a beeline for the enormous, modern bed, ignoring the fact that I dripped water all over the floor on the way. When we got there, I turned to face him, smirking as I waited for instructions. Much to my pleasure, he bent to kiss me. Urgent. Needy. Bruising. I loved every moment of it. Then he was scooping me up, tossing me onto my back as he prowled onto the plush mattress after me. One hand pinned my chest to the mattress as he spread my legs with his own. The other lowered to my pussy, resuming his rotation on my clit before —*smack*—slapping right across my pulsing center. My breath hitched out of surprise, but his smile accompanied another soothing rotation before another gentle slap sent a jolt of shock through the ecstasy.

"Touch yourself, Alice, keep that pussy wet for me," he ordered after another rotation of pain and pleasure.

"What?" I breathed, surprised when he grabbed my hand and guided my fingers to my clit.

"Rub your clit while I grab a condom."

Nodding, I took over. The smile he showered over me was so beautiful it was nearly blinding. Proud and ravenous.

I'd earned that. Couldn't help but notice I'd certainly never seen an expression so radiant on his face before.

He snagged a condom and turned off the light in the next motion before coming back to join me on the bed. A low chuckle warmed the space over the crinkle of foil, making me grin a beat before he said, "Well, *now* they're sexy."

"What?" I breathed.

"Your nail lady wasn't entirely wrong."

"*Oh*," I gasped in surprise, glancing down my body to where my nails glowed, my fingers still working in a tight circle over my clit. Shit, that *was* fun. "Oh!" A little thrill ran through me at the idea of him enjoying watching me, and in one breath, I dipped my fingers into my soaked entrance, splayed the opposite hand over my belly, and slid it up to massage a breast.

Greyson *growled*.

That one sound was possessively demanding, and if I hadn't already been dripping for him, that certainly would have done it.

In the next breath, he knocked my hand aside and sheathed himself inside me in three shallow thrusts before he met bottom. Head thrown back, I gasped for air, but it was his name on my lips. My body had just adapted when he hooked a hand under my thigh, rolling me onto my side as he pinned my leg up to my chest, those shallow thrusts growing deeper with each movement until he robbed me of breath.

Ecstasy. Mind spinning, body tingling, unspeakable fullness that consumed every single last brain cell I'd come in here with. My hands grappled for purchase—his shoulders, his biceps, his hands, the sheets. Whatever they could reach. Like I could stay on the planet if I held on tight enough.

"Your cock...*incredible*...So big," I panted as he thrust in relentlessly.

"Damn straight," he snarled, sliding into the hilt, pinning my leg back so he could get deeper. Every muscle in his body rippled in the low light, a dark silhouette on a mission to destroy me.

It was working. With every rock of his hips, every flex of those gorgeous glutes and shift of those shoulders, he shoved me toward the edge. But he knocked me clean over when he growled, "Come for me, Alice."

I *detonated*, my channel clamping down around him. Greyson's body went rigid, and with a muttered curse, he stiffly slid out, fingers reaching down to grip his cock, giving it one yank before he poured himself into the condom.

GREYSON

THE GOLDEN BLADE of morning light slicing across our bed woke me the following morning. But it was the heat of my wife's decadent body curved against mine that nearly lulled me back to sleep. There had never been a peace like this woman safe in my bed. In my arms.

"You're exquisite," I breathed against her skin, groggily pressing a kiss to the back of her neck as she hummed her approval. Every time she gave me her body, I felt this tie between us strengthen. My need for her deepened. It was indescribable. Like an addict, I'd do about anything to get my fix. Beyond the sex, I craved her laugh and her sage words when we were apart. Her sarcasm when things got tense. "You sleep well, baby?"

"Mmmm," she purred contentedly. One joint at a time, she

straightened, popping her back and neck, followed by her ankles. "Like the dead."

"Good. I did my job, then."

"Is a vagina strain a thing?" She winced before giggling softly. "I think it's a thing."

Chuckling, I noted, "My dick feels bruised."

"That third round was one too many."

"Is there such a thing?" I argued, pulling her tighter against my body, taking way too much pleasure in the way she melted back into me.

"If I can walk without looking like John Wayne, you'll win, but prospects aren't high." A deeply satisfied yawn cut off her joke. Rubbing languid palms against her eyes, Alice rotated in my grasp until we were face to face. I pressed a kiss to her forehead, earning another contented sigh. "Gotta get up."

"Mmmm—*no.*"

She giggled before saying, "It's Sunday."

"And for the first time in weeks, I have no meetings to drag my carcass to." I buried myself in her mess of wavy hair. Hell, I hadn't even realized her hair was wavy until this morning. Had she never let it dry on its own before? "Bed. *Stay.*"

"I would if we could," she assured. "But it's family breakfast today."

"Fuck," I sighed.

"No, we already did that. Bruised dick, remember?"

"Very funny."

"Come on, sleepy."

"Don't leave," I protested, fingers grappling for purchase as she slipped away. Some part of my brain heard the pathetic lovesick puppy I'd become, but I couldn't find it in myself to care. I needed this woman. Needed to soak her up today. Looking more than a little amused, she bent down to press kisses across my chest. Never in my life had productivity been as unappealing as it was with the heat of her against my skin. Still wearing only the jewels from last night, her pert pink nipples peaked with cold or arousal; Alice was a vision. There was something like adoration in her gaze as she stroked her fingers through my chest hair with a soft smile on her lips.

"You are so damn beautiful, Grey. Like a sculpture." She traced the lines of my pecs, my abs. Every inch of my existence zeroed in on the feel of her against me. Would it ever be enough? "I want to memorize you."

"That sounds much more appealing than breakfast with my brother."

"And your niece and nephew.'

With a sigh, I righted myself, tossing the sheets off our laps.

Dammit. I promised Mattie we'd finish that insane puzzle she'd ordered ages ago. "Yeah, okay, I'm up."

"Yeah, you are," she teased with a brow wiggle as her eyes dropped to my dick, where it stood at attention.

"What happened to the vagina sprain?"

She shrugged playfully. "She'll be fine," she reached for me, my cock straining under her focus. "Come on, big guy. One quickie. But then we gotta get ready."

ALICE WASN'T KIDDING when she said the Rhodes knew how to do *family time*. There wasn't anything formal or practiced about our weekly breakfasts. They made it seem like this was a perfectly regular occurrence—as though they were entirely at home in my house.

Waltzing right in, Leighton and Paxton unceremoniously plopped down at the counter for coffee like her space was their space.

Like *my* space was their space.

It was somehow simultaneously irritating and endearing. But the three of them played with Mattie and Beau after meals like they were their own. And for that, I was eternally grateful.

"You two seem to have…settled," Ollie noted playfully as he emptied his third cup of coffee.

"Is that really shocking?"

"Well…*yeah*," he snorted, rising to stand and belatedly clear his place. Sundays had always been *our* days, on the rare occasion we were both free of meetings. No staff. Just us and the kids on the beach. Beau's giggles told me he'd likely lost their most recent hide-and-seek round and was now being tickled by one of the girls. If you'd told me my brother would trade America's best quarterback, and a few months later he'd be hiding behind my curtains like a six-foot-three *Big Bird*, I would've declared your idiocy for the world to hear. But that was the position that kept Beau and Alice hunting the longest. Ollie's voice brought my mind back into the kitchen. "My money was on her murdering you in your sleep."

"You underestimate me." My nonchalance did not beget the fact that the fear had certainly crossed my mind.

"Apparently."

"How's the feral one?"

The glare he leveled me with had me smirking into my Americano as he bit out, "*Leighton* seems to be doing great. She picks up a lot of shifts down at the restaurant. Seems to enjoy it."

"Good. That's good," I assured as I downed the last of my espresso.

"Asshole," he grumbled, rounding the corner of the island to put his dishes in the sink.

"Who's an asshole?" Paxton asked as he came into the kitchen, finding his way over to the barstool beside mine.

"My brother," Ollie groused.

"Certainly had us fooled for a while there—no offense," Pax said with a shrug. "But we only had Alice's spin on those stories, and nobody can hold a grudge quite like my sister. I still don't think she's forgiven me for an unfortunate *Barbie* beheading incident."

I winced before saying, "Maybe a bit more time on that one."

"What's your secret?" he quipped playfully.

Oh, my friend, if you only knew.

"Mind-blowing orgasms seem to work well for me," I responded with a smirk.

He groaned before shooting a look at Ollie like he could somehow help him. "That's my sister, man. Happy for you guys, but *gross.*" When I just grinned, he shook his head, adding, "I think what means the most to Alice is you didn't try to use your money to catch her attention, you know?" *Ouch.* "Taking care of her. Getting the supplies for her headaches, meeting up with our insane family— that's what matters to her, you know?"

"So I've learned," I said, smiling. But our lightheartedness was cut off by Alice's shaking voice. One word, and my heart dropped, fear slicing through my chest.

"*Grey!?*"

Ollie and I exchanged concerned glances as Paxton's brow furrowed at her tone, and in the next beat, all three of us were moving for the living room. My wife stood in her loose-fitting tank, tucked into casual shorts, but the ease stopped there. Her skin had gone terrifyingly pale, eyes rimmed in silver as a shaking hand rubbed at her mouth.

"Grey," she repeated, more a broken cry than my name. Rushing for her, I pulled her against me, terrified I couldn't make whatever this was go away. "It's *her*," she breathed.

"What happened, baby? It's who?"

Trembling, she rotated for the television, pointing a shaky hand. My heart dropped. I didn't have to unmute the local news in order to see the headline about the body dredged out of the river. Or for me to scour the flat brown eyes, fair skin, and dark, kinky hair of the victim.

I knew her. Had seen her only last night, fumbling to fix our table—

"Our server. The one who…" She gulped, hard.

The one who'd spilled wine over her dress and then escorted her past the perfectly functional guest bathroom to the staff facility.

The staff restroom *connected* to the men's room, where Alice believed she heard a man talking about *me*. Us. The man that led her to an office, where Max could access a buried code about *Obsidian*.

With her family surrounding us with worried faces, all I could do was wrap her tighter in my arms, pressing my lips to her hair.

They knew.

Izzie Medina
ALICE

From time to time, music reaches into my soul to meld a glimmering fragment of the artist into the fabric of my very being. Hozier was one of those artists for me. Especially so when I had too many emotions to grapple with and no safe space to grapple in.

To the serenade of his Gaelic lyrics, tears streaming down my cheeks, *I drew.*

My fingers ached with how long I'd whisked charcoal across paper.

Again and again, I started the piece only to throw it in the trash bin.

There was no perfection. Nothing adequate enough for Izzie Medina of Yuma, Arizona. The server whose name I hadn't bothered to learn.

Nothing was lifelike enough to capture the fear in those shallow eyes or how she rolled her lips between her teeth when she looked over her shoulder. Nothing could do justice to the woman who I was convinced had somehow…*known.* Known what I would overhear if she just got me to that bathroom. Known I'd put it together and fight to protect Greyson.

That palpable anxiety in her fidgeting fingers had nothing to do with a catering gig and everything to do with what she needed me to know.

"Why didn't you say anything?" I breathed, running my thumb across her lips to blend the shades. I knew better, but fuck anybody who limits your tools to pretentious store-bought items when skin works just fine. "Why didn't you tell me?" I muttered, replaying the fear pouring from her in waves. *She'd known.* Somehow, she'd known. Had she been a victim herself? Tucked in plain sight? I couldn't wrap my head around that idea, though. Not any better than I could erase the picture of her they'd plastered over the news the last few days.

Grey, Jackson, and Max were all hunting for answers. Attempting to find a very small needle in a very large haystack for any connection or correlation.

Izzie didn't have much known family.

She grew up in the south of Arizona.

Had no local relatives.

No easily identified features like tattoos on her skin.

Which, from what I'd read, made her…well, the perfect target. This meant if her body hadn't turned up, it might have been months before anybody knew she was gone.

And I very well may have been the last person that saw her alive.

Greyson had doubled our security at the house and the office, and Jax's men were on a rampage to find answers.

"It's beautiful," Greyson said, startling me as he came up behind me, wrapping me up in a hug and nuzzling into my neck. "*She's* beautiful," he amended, resting his chin on my shoulder as he looked up to the portrait of Izzie clamped onto my easel. All I could do was nod.

"Anything?" I breathed.

"*Obsidian* has gone to ground, according to tech. Nothing on the Izzie front for us or EBPD."

"It wasn't a coincidence."

"I know," he breathed matter-of-factly. Grey never doubted me once. Never pressed back on my suspicions.

"I can't shake the feeling she was warning us."

"*I know.*" He pressed a quick kiss to my cheek before straightening and stepping in front of my stool to cup my face in his hands, forcing me to meet those fiery hazels. "But you have to come downstairs and eat. I didn't see you stop for lunch today. Or yesterday, for that matter. And a banana hardly constitutes as breakfast."

"I'm fine."

"Alice, baby. I know this weighs heavy—believe me, I do. But it is not your fault. Hell, it isn't my fault. *Thunderstrike* is in full-scale counterattack mode, and we don't even have proof she understood what she'd stumbled into. Not everyone is convinced the two are related." My phone buzzed, cutting off the music, and we both turned to see Max's name across the screen. Greyson glanced at me and then stretched over to accept the call. "Evening, Max, what do you have?"

"Well, how do you do to you too, Hart."

A watery laugh cracked my face into a smile. "Hey, Maxi. How's it going?"

"Pretty good, thanks, *manners*. Work has been chaotic; big Jake has gone mic-happy with the town arm wrestling match again this year, Luca Morretti asked me to dinner, and your accounts still appear secure."

Brow furrowed, Greyson clarified, "So, whatever transfer occurred at the auction didn't touch us directly?"

"Or it wasn't monetary," Max agreed. "From what I can tell, still no movement on the dark web, although if they've caught onto us, I might start from scratch in the next day or so."

"What about Izzy?" Grey pressed, his eyes roving over my drawing.

"She was a ghost, man. No detectable ties, although if she was a victim, there wouldn't be."

"Keep me apprised of any changes."

"Obviously," Max said in his best impression of Alan Rickman.

"Wait," I interjected as Grey went pensive. "Max, did you say you're going out with Luca Moretti?"

"I may have slipped that under the radar."

Well, that at least made me smile. He'd had a crush on the kid back in high school, but his older brother stood Elora up for prom, and then they became public enemy number one. He'd never taken his chance at happiness. "Wow, long time coming." Even my ears could tell the words were flatter than he deserved. "Hope you have a great night. Don't take any of that Moretti bullshit."

"Never," he said triumphantly. "Alright, love birds, I gotta run. Just wanted to keep you posted on the whole lot of nothing on my end."

"Thanks, Max," we responded in unison.

"Love you," I added sadly. I missed him. Missed home. Everything suddenly felt glaringly out of place. Predominantly, this small-town Alaska girl with her nose in mercenary business and murder.

"Love you, too, menace. Keep your chin up. But...be safe, okay?" He took a long breath, and if it was anybody but Max, I'd be suspicious that he was hiding something. "Night guys."

When the line disconnected, Greyson tugged me off my stool and to my feet, promptly whisking me into his arms. "Come on, beautiful, let me make you something to eat."

I raised a teasing brow as I reared back. "*You're* going to make me something to eat?"

"Hey, dumping prepped food in a saucepan counts."

"Just impressed you know the word saucepan, though I assure you it wasn't designed to reheat entire meals." Giggling, I let him tuck me under his arm and lead me downstairs. Commotion caught my attention as we stepped off the bottom step and I glanced toward his office—which had transformed into an impromptu war room—where Jax was leading a meeting with a handful of their guys. All ex-military, all tragically good-looking if you were into scars, tattoos, and militantly tight hair. The idea of the *Obsidian* web moving this close to their home turf had the guys up in arms. Literally.

My dumb ass thought I could handle this. Loving him when I knew he was tangled in something dangerous. But knowing he was *funding* a campaign against traffickers and seeing him bent over the desk, glaring at the white boards littered with information with death in his eyes, surrounded by beefy mercenaries, certainly put my assumptions into perspective and—

Loving…him?

Breath filling my ribs in a rapid pump, I glanced up at Greyson as he led me to the kitchen island. Did I…did I love him? Of all the humans on the planet, had I run off and fallen in love with *my boss?*

Stunned stupid by that terrifying realization, I slunk into the bar stool when he prompted me to. I watched him walk around the corner to pull out pre-portioned meals to prepare for us. An unlikely warmth swelled in my chest, and I found myself melting into my chair back with a hand pressed to my lips as I watched him.

Certainly didn't have this one on my bingo card.

T-Minus Two Weeks To The Kickoff of Emerald Bay Bomber Season

THE NEXT WEEK went by in a blur of endless meetings and long hours at work, which, to my eternal gratitude, now included Grey and I sitting side-by-side in the corner office. If our hours were going to be astronomical, at least we could spend them lusting after each other while we both paced on our phone calls or muttered curses at our keyboards. The influx of end-of-summer projects provided a mind-numbing distraction, at the very least. Q-four was always packed to the gills for us, and this was no different. The *only* difference was my title, and the fact that Tiffany, our COO, was basically treating me like a mentee after Greyson groomed me for the position without my knowing.

To my simultaneous elation and horror, the vast majority of the Rhodes dirty dozen would be arriving by the middle of next week so that we could all spend some time together before watching Paxton break in his new stadium. While I wanted nothing more than to wrap them all up and listen to the familiar cacophony of too many voices in one space, the idea of them being here if *Obsidian* was operating inside our city made me nauseous.

Grey had—not at all helpfully—let me know *Obsidian* and the networks like them operate out of most major cities, along with some smaller ones. I guess he was trying to reassure me we'd just been oblivious and had all been fine, but it had the opposite effect. By Friday, at least the war room meetings had dwindled enough for my adrenaline not to spike every time I walked in the front door, which is why I finally felt free enough to soak up some evening blue hour on the beach when I got home. Grey had a few calls left, but a moment of solitude sounded ideal. Well…solitude plus Chip, and our forever-shadow, Jax. Our little rescue was sweet as pie, and seemed to like the beach as much as I did, although not if the waves had the audacity to get him wet.

My phone buzzed and, muttering curses that I hadn't silenced the damn thing, I fished it out of my denim short pockets.

MAX

You know that episode of Friends where Monica gets to dump that douche from high school?

ALICE

Yeah?

MAX

Me=Monica. Luca=Douche from high school.

ALICE

Nooooooo

SITTING UP STRAIGHTER, I stared down at the screen, shaking my head as his texts rolled in.

MAX

Twelve years later, and he's exactly the way I remember him.

ALICE

I mean… didn't you like him?

MAX

He never bothered to grow up.

His parents still house the little shit, and he's still working at the damn roller rink.

THE ROLLER RINK, ALICE.

All I could think is I wasted my high school years pining after this boy, only to get to know him at thirty and wonder what floor balcony his mother dropped him from.

I give up. Kaia is right; men are stupid.

ALICE

Men are stupid, but there are occasionally the Greysons of the world.

MAX

He's stupid too.

ALICE

Rude.

MAX

Took him two years to make a move. I don't have two years.

I IGNORED the pang of bitterness that if we hadn't been cornered, he wouldn't have even made a move now.

ALICE

Your ovaries are shriveling?

MAX

Har har har. I'm just...

...

Ready to settle down.

ALICE

gasping gif

Did you just...

MAX

I just.

CHIP WIGGLED his way up onto my lap, licking my chin as he stared up into my eyes expectantly. "Weird times, Chip," I muttered, encasing his entire head in my palm and giving him a little ruffle before stroking each ear, much to his tail-wagging delight. "*Weird times.*" Returning my focus to the screen, I tapped out a response.

ALICE

I'm in love with Greyson Hart, and my Maximus is all grown up and ready to plant roots. Hell really did freeze over. Okay, so let's look at the stats. What are you looking for?

MAX

My soul mate.

ALICE

Yes. I got that part.

What qualities are you hoping he'll possess?

MAX

Oh. That. Please hold. The bar has lowered, and I need to evaluate.

I WATCHED the three dots appear and vanish twice before tossing my phone down on the blanket I'd laid out. Much to Chip's pleasure, it freed up my other hand to commence obligatory pets, squishes, and tiny belly rubs. The blue gloom of approaching night made it hard to spot much beyond the white froth of the surf, but the sound lulled me into a sense of peace for the first time all week.

Quiet.

When in doubt, quiet is the answer. Absentmindedly stroking over Chip's fur, I wondered if Grey ever would have said something about that *maddening attraction*. Wondered if I hadn't quit, if the allegations hadn't hit…if he ever would have made a move.

Unlikely, I supposed. Perhaps years down the road, once I was an executive and there was less paperwork involved?

Somehow, the thought was immensely disappointing. Especially as images of his smile, the ringing of his laugh, the feel of his stubble against my thighs all ran through my mind. With a sigh, I traded Chip for the pen and notebook I'd tucked into my tote bag, and he harrumphed into a tight little ball against my thigh.

Elora was a huge proponent of journaling, and while I wasn't nearly as enthusiastic as she was, I had to admit it helped the last few weeks.

A tiny, cold nose booped my wrist as I finished filling the second page, sending the ink off the edge. He gave a little shiver as the breeze kicked up, rotating to sit and stare back at the house. By the time I'd turned my attention to my miniature-sized furry companion, the last of the light had vanished.

Without warning, Chip leaped from my side, bristling as he growled at the waves in that compact voice of his. Every hair on my skin rose before I could assess whatever had him ticked off.

But Jax's bellowed warning had me rocketing upright, sending sand flying.

"Alice, *run!*"

Greyson

BETWEEN BEING A MUCH MORE active participant with *Thunderstrike* since Izzie's murder, and tackling a massive merger at work, my shoulders and head were both aching by the time I got home Friday evening. The house was mellow, and while I couldn't wait to hold her, Alice looked entirely at peace on our beach with Chip in her lap and Jax keeping eyes out behind them.

Better to let her be and catch up once my head wasn't throbbing so adamantly. Like a hammer between the eyes. Captain glued himself to my thigh, quirking his head as I deliberated going to her or clearing my head, following when I decided on the latter.

Upstairs, stripped, and under the deluge of water, I took a minute to breathe. Captain dramatically collapsed onto the tile floor with a series of thuds, huffs and sighs that ultimately landed with him watching me through the glass. His obligation to lay on the tile was obviously deeply ailing.

Linking the Gilberts to *Obsidian* wasn't so much surprising as disheartening but only marginally less horrifying than our suspicions about Reggie—though his connection was yet to be verified. If money and power came with responsibility, why did so many of my peers collapse into evil? Some part of my mind said it was because money doesn't change people, it simply magnifies them. The selfish, desperate, and cruel remain that way. They just have more influence after clawing their way into the upper echelon of society. My uncle, father, and grandfather were cruel, scared, and spineless as children and became bullies who hid behind their wealth. On the opposite end of the spectrum were people like Alice, who suddenly had access to and influence over more money than most people saw in a lifetime and used it to fund scholarships for foster dog-parents and provide aid to families affected by wars in countries we would never see. She was loving before wealth. The money just gave that love a reach more people could feel.

It was the low rumble in Captain's chest, his enormous head lifting from where it rested on his paws and staring at the far wall that drew my focus.

"Cap?" I demanded as I stepped out of the shower, snatching a towel from the rack. Instincts rearing to life as I watched his muzzle twitch, I forgot about drying off and rushed into boxers, but before I'd yanked on sweatpants, Captain's growl spiked, and he bolted from the room, barking his damn head off.

Alice.

Panic hit like a SWAT team battering ram. I couldn't remember the last time my dog alerted.

Bypassing a shirt and shoes, I made my way to my bedside table to retrieve the firearm concealed within the lockbox beneath it and bolted after him.

My usually mellow canine was feral at the back door, jaw snapping, saliva flying, bark more of a desperate cry. *"Defend!"* I ordered as I wrenched the handle and threw it wide. Outside was a calamity of noises all at once—Jax's bellowed demand for my wife to run, Alice's scream and the keening wail of what I assumed was Chip. My feet were flying before I had the luxury of my eyes adjusting to the darkness. By the time I crested the beach, I could see enough.

Two assailants.

One intercepted by Jax, the other chasing Alice, where she was fighting gravity and the dunes of sand to get back to me.

Chip flew by my ankles in a screeching blur of white.

The second assailant lunged for Alice, my shout of warning too late as he lifted her off her now-kicking feet. A curtain of sand flew as she screamed, and he expertly positioned her between us, still pulling her away from me.

I dropped the gun I'd raised on instinct, barreling after Captain's streak of shadow slicing through the night. That ferocious growl came to a crescendo a beat before he collided with her attacker, and all three tumbled into the sand.

"Alice!" I bellowed, more so she knew I was coming for her than anything. A male voice wailed in agony as she sobbed my name back, and my heart broke in two. I had to move faster. Had to reach her. Had to get there in time.

A corner of my mind registered the house alarm finally screeching to life, floodlights powering on to illuminate the yard, enough falling onto the skirmish to make more sense of what I was seeing. The alarm system would send security responding like a fleet of pissed-off wasps and notify the police. But the entire world ceased to exist beyond Alice.

My wife was scrambling to her feet by the time I reached her—the yard expanse suddenly an eternity of torture—and it took all my training to keep my head on a swivel, to make sure there weren't more men coming for us as Captain's livid snarls and the attacker's cries of pain clouded my head.

Determining these two were alone, I scooped her into my arms before hoisting her behind me. Rotating to follow, determined to get her out of harm's way, I shoved her up the sand onto our grass and demanded, "*Run!*"

My girl ran, but only for a breath before Captain's bark turned into a desperate cry of pain. His growls returned, but the next whine had me whirling. Yip after yip, snarl after snarl, as the assailant jammed his fist into my dog.

My Cap.

My heart crashed as I saw the hold of his fist and the glint of metal in the floodlights.

Alice was screaming for Captain now, my mind rioting along with her as I pushed her toward the house. "*Run, baby*! Get inside!"

I raised my firearm, taking aim as the coward hit him again. With a pained whine, Cap fell to the earth this time.

Two consecutive gunshots cleaved the night.

23

I Think What Your Hulking Friend Meant Was Justice

GREYSON

A lethal kind of calm anchored me into the floor when I closed the door behind the last police officer. Only Detective Rivera remained, alongside Jax. A few of our *Thunderstrike* buddies were on their way over now that the chaos died down. Thankfully, Ollie and the kids were out at the cinema, but I'd sent both my team and city brass through to sweep his property, as well as Emmaline's, though she was two states away.

It wasn't the first time I took a life. Just the first on United States soil.

I had a sinking suspicion it wouldn't be the last.

Though I felt him wander up, I still flinched when Jax set his hand on my shoulder. "You alright, Pinman?"

"They put hands on *my wife*," I ground out.

"She's alright," Luke reassured from where he hovered, leaning against the archway to the living room. But they hadn't just laid hands on her. The whole ploy had been for Alice. Targeting Alice. At least according to a candid photo of her at *DeLuca's*—the one they'd pinned to the front door with a blade through her throat, splitting the wood beneath. We hadn't bothered to bring that bit to her attention. Seemed an unnecessary burden.

"There will be time for retribution later," Jax promised.

"*Justice*," Luke corrected. "I think what your hulking friend meant was justice."

"Same thing," Jax insisted. "We're in touch with MARSOC and FBI, Grey. The team has prepped everything we have on the Gilberts, and that's at least a start. They're inside our borders. They've got to deal with this."

"We have a hole in our security," I growled. I didn't want to talk about internal terrorism defense for the nation. I wanted to spill the blood of any motherfucker who thought they'd come up *my beach* to take *my girl* right out from under my nose. They'd come out of the goddamned water—like *Seals*.

"I know," Jax said gruffly. "We'll find it. The guys are on their way."

"You hear from the vet yet?" The sound of Luke's footsteps had me turning.

I didn't want to be touched.

Not by anyone but Alice.

Alice, who they'd bruised and shaken but was respectively okay.

Alice, who'd seen two men killed tonight. Who'd seen *me* kill a man tonight. Jax had dropped the other after the bastard successfully gashed open his side. EMTs had stitched him up, but he refused to leave Hart House to go to the hospital.

If I were Wyatt Earp, Jackson Reynolds would be my Doc. He wasn't going anywhere. Certainly wouldn't be leaving our side unless we exterminated every spider in that web. Ride or die took on a very different meaning in our world. But...a threat against my woman and my best friend in doggy ICU made this a code red.

The detective seemed to sense my need for space because he wisely kept his, instead stuffing his hands in his pockets as he assessed me.

"Cap's in surgery," Jax explained when the silence stretched. "She'll call us when we know more."

"He did good," I said lamely, my throat tight as I stared at the floor, trying to pace my breathing. "Went right for her."

"He's a good boy. He'll be alright, Hart," Luke said with a lot more confidence than I felt. The fucker I'd shot had stabbed my Shepard six times. *Six* blunt knife wounds. But Cap saved her. Wouldn't let up until he had to. Bought me time to catch up. "You should go check on your girl. Medics okayed her, but she wouldn't let us call her siblings—didn't want them here for this."

Alone. My Alice was sitting all alone.

The shake had only left my hands once the adrenaline trickled out of my system, replaced with a deluge of questions and a long string of law enforcement. Lucky for me, our night vision cameras had caught the conflict and triggered the alarms. Pretty irrefutable evidence we'd done what we had to do. Between that and Captain's injuries, we had Emerald Bay's finest planted firmly on our side. Their investigation would be focused on identifying the assailants and looking into their motives.

They'd find nothing. We hadn't had to tell each other as much.

My eyes found hard navy-blues, and Jax nodded.

"We've got some retired battle buddies headed over to reassess our security setup and team," I pointed out, though now that I was thinking about her—what this must have done to her—I wanted nothing more than to go to her and wrap her up. Count every finger, toe, and hair on her gorgeous head to ensure all was well.

"I've got the guys," Jax argued, squeezing the shoulder he still had a hand on. "You do what's important, do you hear me? Only you can be what she needs right now."

"Yeah," I said numbly, my mouth suddenly sandpaper dry. Guilt tore at my insides. She'd known I was affiliated with something dicey, but she was never supposed to be in the crosshairs. Never supposed to see what that world looked like. I'd assured her I wasn't an active pair of boots on the ground and that should have bought her some protection.

But it hadn't.

I hadn't.

A bodyguard hadn't.

Yet again, the best wasn't enough. Nodding, I repeated, "Yeah." I patted his hand where it rested on my shoulder, his hard gaze tracking my face as I slowly lowered his arm away and walked toward Luke, to whom I extended a hand. "Thanks for being here."

"Anytime. Let's not do it twice."

Forcing a chuckle, I said, "Sounds like a plan."

Their dulcet tones continued on as Jax saw Detective Rivera to his car, but my ears were straining for signs of Alice as I took the steps two at a time. Upstairs was auspiciously calm. However, that somehow made my nerves worse. I'd just…clung to her in the sand until police arrived. If *Obsidian* had infiltrated our local law enforcement, tonight could have gone a very different direction, with me in the back of a patrol car and Alice left here alone. That concept had tortured me from the moment his body hit the sand, slowly staining it crimson.

When I finally reached our room, I crept inside with the same care as that first night we'd finally given this thing a chance. The light was off this time, and the entire space was silent. The only similarity was that the bed was empty, where it sat in the faint stream of window light.

"Baby?" A floorboard creaked beneath me as I edged into the space. "Alice?" When no response came, my heart hammered harder, but then a soft throat cleared, and I heard her voice crack from the bathroom.

"*Grey?*"

On tentative feet, I crept into the ensuite and found her sitting with Chip, her back against a still-draining tub, wearing a blue nightgown I would normally die to strip off her. Not tonight.

Tonight, my eyes fell to the bruises blooming across her biceps, and the desire to rain down hell consumed my vision.

The gurgle of the last swirl of water filled the space as she turned to me, the numbness fading from her face as she looked me over, her lips trembling.

"Baby," I breathed, rushing for her. I gingerly set Chip aside and scooped her up onto her feet, pulling her against me. She finally released all the fear from the night into my T-shirt. Security had brought me a change of clothes after everything had been ruled self-defense. My sweats were stained with Captain's blood, and it took two hand towels to clean it off my skin. She'd held it together so well, but it was only a matter of time before it caught up with us. All I wanted to do was touch her. Memorize the way she felt beneath my hands, commit the lines of her exquisite face to the deepest part of my mind. She buried herself in my chest, and all I could think to say was, "I've got you."

But she was sobbing. Sobbing and clawing at the hem of my shirt, pulling it over my head. Her dress went next, leaving nothing between us. Something about our skin contact finally seemed to soothe her, and she just breathed against my chest. Slowly, I leaned down to scoop up her thighs, and she wrapped herself around my neck, clinging on for dear life as I got her to bed.

"You're safe," I whispered, pulling the covers back and setting her down before clamoring over her into my spot. "I've got you, baby."

With her cocooned inside my arms, my heart finally seemed to settle. *Safe.* She was safe. For now, at least, the threat had been mitigated, and we would sort this out and dismantle these motherfuckers from the top down, even if it was the last thing I ever did. "Did you take your migraine medicine?" I asked into her hair. If paparazzi had been high-stress enough to trigger one that severe, I didn't want to know what this could do to her. She nodded. "That's my good girl." Stroking long lines through her hair, I just held her. Skin on skin, we just steadied ourselves in the safe harbor of each other. Alice offered me a kind of sanctuary I'd never known existed. And I'd almost lost her. I would make this right. Come hell and high water, I would make this right for her.

My fingers came to a halt in her hair when she whispered a broken, "I love you." Every single inch of my body went rigid, the bridge of my nose stinging as I blinked away what her words did to me. "You don't have to say it back. I just...all I could think was that I was going to die, and after all of this, you'd never know that I love you."

It took longer than I'm proud of to steady my breathing and choke back the emotion of her declaration. Longer than she deserved for me to slowly ease her onto her back so that I could reposition myself, ranging over her, studying the sincerity in her eyes that carved the lines beside them into a timid, terrified little smile. Silver-lined gray-blues studied my face as frantically as I studied hers, her hand coming up to cup my jaw, even as I said nothing. Even as I fought to level my breathing and not crawl out of my skin.

I was never supposed to have anything or anyone worth taking. But she was here. Looking at me like I was the anchor in a tempest.

Easing onto my forearms while I held her gaze, I cupped both of her beautiful cheeks, studying her eager vulnerability. Gently, I pressed a soft kiss to her lips before finally brushing the hair away from her forehead and admitting, "That's a relief, Mrs. Hart. Because I love you, too."

ALICE

I DIDN'T HIDE my tears this time. My surprise at him saying it back gave way to some cosmically overwhelming, soul-deep relief when he gently pressed his lips to mine. Reverent strokes across my face gave way to desperate fingers twining in my hair as he shifted to cradle my head in his broad palms. The man looked nervous, out of his depth, which was likely the first time I'd ever seen him make a decision with any ounce of uncertainty.

Kisses growing harsher by the breath, he worked his way over my face, like he would dab all the tears from my cheeks with his lips. I melted beneath his palms as they roamed, caressing my ribs, palming at my breast and then my neck. Greyson's hands were frantic—as if he was still reassuring himself that I was with him, his eyes surveying each inch of skin.

Confirming my suspicions, he muttered, "I almost fucking lost you."

"But you didn't."

"Too damn close."

"*You* saved me, Grey. You, and Jax and Cap."

"You never should have needed saving," he argued, pressing kisses down my jaw until he could nuzzle into my neck. I felt it then, the damp heat of *tears* on my skin. "I finally have you, and they nearly took you from me."

"Baby," I breathed, my hands giving up the deathtrap I'd had on his arms to grab his face instead, forcing his eyes to mine. "You put Jax with me a lifetime before they got anywhere near me. You knew

I needed him, even when I was a petulant child about it. *He* warned me. He saw them come out of the water."

"Shouldn't have been so far away," he growled, pressing an open-mouthed kiss to my neck before latching on and giving the skin a good suck. "Should kick his ass for that."

"Life can't be lived like an animal in a cage, Grey. I have to have room to breathe."

"I know," he growled begrudgingly before moving down an inch, stealing my breath as he sucked at my skin again. Marking, tasting, claiming. He wanted to eat me whole, I decided. I didn't have any complaints to speak of.

"He was quick to react," I breathed, struggling to keep any train of thought with his skin on mine. "You and Cap got to me so fast."

"I can't bear to think about the alternative."

"There is no alternative," I insisted, "I'm right here, handsome."

Bowing his forehead against mine, Grey returned his gentle hands to frame my face, softer kisses pressing my mouth apart. This was...*different*. Reverent in his demand. Savoring as his tongue invaded.

I was desperate to memorize every inch of him. The taste of him in my mouth, the weight of his scent filling my lungs, the feel of his body over mine. Perhaps he was doing the same. Shoving the comforter away, he worked down my body, luxuriating in each inch of skin as he showered it in affection. Hesitating over the bruises on my arms and ribs, he spent an extra moment with his lips pressed against the blooming, livid red and purple.

Serving penance or giving thanks, I wasn't sure.

"I need you," I breathed, parroting what he'd said to me the night of the auction. Nodding against my belly, Grey raked his hands over my sides, determined to press his lips to every inch of my torso, down to my sex, before showering my thighs with his attention.

"You're the only person who's seen it all. My ugly. My laughter. And you're not running."

"I'm not running," I repeated, earning a relieved huff of breath from the man paying homage to my body.

"Be my forever, Mrs. Hart?"

The ragged vulnerability in his voice sent my eyes burning all over again. Nodding, I managed, "Please, Grey."

"You should rest."

"I need to know that you're real," I admitted on a needy exhale.

"*My* pace," he said, tone both a warning and an order. I simply nodded in response. I'd take whatever he was willing to give me.

He wriggled out of his sweats a beat before bringing his mouth back to mine, leisurely running his palm down the length of my body, gaze endearingly tracking the wake of his touch as though he left a visible trail to follow. My fingers found his hair, weaving between strands, holding his face to mine as I memorized his scent. Memorized the man I never thought I'd willingly die for.

This man who'd just killed for me.

With the care of worship, he settled his hips between my thighs, which parted to make room for him. Mouths sealed together as though we'd cease to exist if we separated, Grey positioned himself, running the crown of his dick over my slick sex before lining up with my entrance. With the briefest lock of our gazes, he rocked into me, filling me with life and my lungs with air. Surprise gave way to adoration, and then he slid his hands beneath me, gripping my shoulders and setting the pace.

More of a steady rock than the fierce thrusts I'd grown accustomed to, our bodies connected deeper and deeper. Connected in a way I couldn't describe.

Nobody had ever held me so closely.

Kissing me until my head was spinning, Greyson *made love* to me. We'd done sweet sex, but nothing like this.

Raw and real and just us.

Slow and steady, he rocked his hips, grinding up and in, dick hitting the depths of me with each roll until, together, we crested that edge. With a groan, his body went rigid, the telltale pulse and swell of his cock inside me, stealing my oxygen as my walls clamped around him. He held his position, even when his muscles relaxed, head bowing to mine, our breaths synchronized as we exchanged them like currency.

At last, he pulled back to look at me, but there was a shadow of something familiar—the same trace of panic I'd seen at the wedding. Softly, I said, "I've seen that look before. What are you thinking?"

His breath was a huff of disbelief as he stroked a hot palm down my face. "That I don't deserve you, baby."

"Why would you say that?"

"Because it's true. Forgive me, my love, for taking you anyway."

24

Holy Fucking Shit Balls, I Found It

GREYSON

Two Armed Attackers Dead After Attempt On Alessandra Hart

"Holy fucking shit balls, I found it."

Amused, I pried myself away from my work Tuesday morning to raise a brow at Max, where he'd set up camp beside Alice at her desk.

"The transfer wasn't monetary," he deduced, shaking his head, "it was purely informational."

"Those two sentences should not come out of the same human two seconds apart," I decided, earning a smirk from Alice as her fingers continued to fly across her keyboard.

To our chagrin—but no one's surprise—news of what happened Friday night had been picked up in the media by the following morning. While Alice had spent the bulk of Saturday notifying her family, she hadn't seemed even remotely shocked when Leighton, Paxton, *and Max* materialized in our living room by that afternoon.

Leighton hovered around like a frantic bumblebee, making coffee, filling teapots, compulsively wiping down counters, and making sure Alice ate. She ranted at the top of her lungs about the audacity of psychopathic sycophants before bursting into tears the instant we were alone together and hugging me while sobbing her thanks for saving her.

Paxton was less enthusiastic, as he *correctly* assumed she wouldn't have needed saving in the first place had she not married a Hart. He proceeded to interrogate every staff member who crossed his path and every security guard about their credentials—including Jax—and scowled at anyone in her proximity.

Leighton insisted it could be worse and informed me I should be thanking all the powers that be their big brother, Jameson, was out at sea and not able to ship his 'grumpy ass' down here.

This was, evidently, Rhodes' crisis protocol. The only reason the rest hadn't arrived was Alice literally begged them not to and insisted she needed the week of quiet to recover before they all rallied to support Paxton at his first game.

To his credit, Max arrived ready to do actual battle. He began Saturday evening in our living room, did a full weekend sweep of the house to hunt for bugs my 'suit buddies' would miss, worked beside us from home yesterday, and was already in Arthur's back seat by the time Alice and I slid into the car this morning.

My wife was a fucking warrior, more determined than ever to do whatever she had to do to serve not only me and our company but *Thunderstrike* in their mission to eradicate the fuckers.

I was positive *Obsidian* had no idea who they'd just unleashed when they made it personal. If scaring the daylights out of her hadn't been enough, Captain being held for post-op recovery certainly was. The vet had reclassified his condition as "stable but critical," but assured me they were administering pain meds and antibiotics and watching for any signs of complication or infection. Due to keeping him sedated, we hadn't been able to see him, but the vet assured us we could visit soon, as our company might aid the healing process.

"Oh, bite me, suit daddy," Max quipped back, clicking a rapid-fire sequence of keys.

"Maybe later," I said evenly, leaning back in my chair to see whatever he was about to show us. "What'd you find?"

"Don't tease me; it's not kind," he grumbled before whipping his laptop toward Alice and me like a weapon. "They're on your server. I mean, the files are encrypted, but—"

Eyes zipping back and forth over the screen, Alice finished, "These are financial transactions and *extensive* communications. They…they weren't just framing Greyson for embezzlement. If *Thunderstrike* went after *Obsidian* before these were discovered, he'd be implicated in…" She blew out a heavy breath, and Max picked up where she left off.

"All manner of illegal activities. Beyond the trafficking, there's money laundering, extortion, and…well, it might be faster to discuss the crimes not on the list."

"Grey, their counter move was to set you up to take the fall," Alice said as she scrolled down through the file Max had compiled.

He frowned at me before deducing, "Their attempt on Alice was likely to—"

"Blackmail me," I finished. "Into either defunding *Thunderstrike* or conspiring with *Obsidian*." My deduction earned a solemn nod.

"So, what was at the auction that the Gilberts needed?" Alice rubbed at her eyes. Tough as she was, I wasn't positive she'd actually gotten any sleep over the weekend. Couldn't blame her—I hadn't either.

"Reggie," Max and I answered in unison.

"But you said you found nothing linking him to this," she pointed out.

"I haven't," he agreed.

"Doesn't mean he's innocent," I scoffed, biting back a growl.

"No." Max shook his head. "What it means is if he's involved knowingly, he's covered his trail well."

"I don't think he's that bright," I huffed. Temper threatening my composure, I straightened, fiddling with a cuff link before I stood, buttoned my jacket, and tidied the lapel. Slowly, I paced around the desks to brace my hands on theirs.

"As much of a monster as I think Reggie is, I agree," Alice said, reaching forward to settle her hand over mine reassuringly. "But he's somehow involved. Could it have been an ISMI catcher?"

To me, Max explained, "That's like a cell phone interceptor. Essentially, they trick phones into thinking they're towers, so they connect with them, and from there—"

Cutting him off, I deadpanned, "Yes, I know what they are, thank you." Like I hadn't spent my life working toward being a Tier One operator *before* stepping into the role of CEO in one of the globe's largest corporate empires. *Christ.*

"Not just a pretty face. Very good, Mr. Hart." Max spun his laptop back toward him and narrowed his eyes pensively. *"Perhaps?* That would explain the stupid keyword and where these hooks are planted."

"Reggie *would* use our last name backward as a password," I grumbled, smirking to myself. Maybe I'd go to hell for finding humor in any of this, but it would be worth the satisfaction of knowing the old man was an idiot. Keeping myself focused, I asked, "Got any new names for me?"

"Working to decrypt more data…or rather, my software is in the background at the moment."

"Thanks, Max."

"I need to go for a run," Alice ground out by the time seven o'clock came around that evening. She pressed her palms to her forehead, blinking away what I assumed was the same layer of screen fog I had in my vision, popping her jaw as though she'd clenched it all afternoon.

Tensions had only gotten higher the deeper into the web we spiraled.

"My ass feels bruised," I groused, leaning into my chair to stretch my sore back. As though our agendas weren't already at their maximum capacity, every would-be break was filled with updates from Max and Jackson or a file that Alice wanted me to review with her.

We'd barely consumed any calories, and those we had gotten down were entirely to my assistant's credit. Paul surreptitiously slid into the room during a conference call and set thirty-two-ounce protein shakes in front of all three of us before slipping back out the door and closing it behind him.

As it turned out, Alice got exceedingly cranky subsisting on coffee and smoothies alone.

"My *eyes* feel bruised," Max muttered from where he was lying on my office floor with his arms draped over his face, dark hair fanning out like we'd electrocuted him. He'd compulsively run his fingers through it as our findings worsened, and I was fairly certain he'd managed to rub all the product out with his irritation.

"El swears by kickboxing," Alice noted, voice distorted by the extension of her throat as she leaned her head onto the back of her chair with her eyes closed. "But I just want to run the beach until I hit the cliffs."

My heart sank.

The glaring now-yellow and deep purple splotches on her arm had me grinding my teeth all day—a reminder of why we were bruising our asses until we could ensure a resolution.

What we needed was an inter-department sting spanning at least two states, but very likely three or four. Luckily for me, coordinating *that* fell on Jackson's plate. Even then…would I ever *not* panic at the idea of Alice out alone after a call that close? In current circumstances, that privilege would entail bringing a handful of security with her, *which she would hate.*

My fault. This need for security. This crushing sense of confinement she'd never signed up for. I'd plucked a girl from her free-range life in the Mistyvale mountains of a remote Alaskan island and put her in a cage. How long would it be before she hated me for it?

Gears churning, I thumbed through my mental files for a solution—something secure that would still let her blow off steam. As I studied the muscle definition in her bruised arms, I sat up straighter. Why did every Rhodes I'd met thus far look like they could knock a motherfucker out? I guess Paxton wasn't the only one born to be an athlete.

A plan began to solidify in my mind, a smile gradually creeping across my face as it did.

Okay. Not every aspect of being a Hart was a burden. As a matter of fact, it bought us some pretty cool privileges from time to time.

"I have a better idea."

ALICE

MY FACE *HURT*. As in, *physically* hurt from laughing so much.

Reasoning that the team was rarely in the training facility after about six, Greyson took full advantage of our status as owner, and the family—minus Max, who had no interest in sweating while the case was unsolved—convened on the indoor field after another smoothie for dinner.

Paxton brought Dallas, both still in their gear from training and what started as make-shift drills rapidly disintegrated into a chaotic game of tag when Ollie and the kids showed up.

"That's *cheating*!!" Leighton screeched as she sprinted, hips first, for the end zone, only for Ollie to 'tag' her long ponytail. "Hair doesn't count."

"Better than your ass," I mumbled, bending over to brace myself on my knees and catch my breath.

Play. Grey had realized what I needed wasn't to sprint head-strong in the opposite direction of our problems. It was to play. Maybe having the family in town for a few days wouldn't be such a bad thing after all. They helped me unwind like only siblings could.

"We need those red football tape things," she panted petulantly. "The Velcro screechy belt things."

"Flags?" Ollie asked, grinning like a child as he sucked down air, hands on his hips as he walked in a circle.

"Flags!" Leighton growled enthusiastically. "Yes, flag football! Duh. I need them," she demanded, snapping her fingers like a genie would appear to grant her request.

"We don't play with flags. We're not children," Paxton scolded as he sidled up between his two team owners. His statement was ironically punctuated by Dallas unceremoniously pegging him in the side of the face with a foam ball.

"*No concussing the quarterback*," Greyson complained to a round of laughter as Pax nailed a fleeing Dallas in the back of the head with said ball. "Or any of the fucking merchandise," he grumbled. It was adorably forlorn.

"*Boys*," I sighed theatrically.

"Man-children," he countered. "I pay millions of dollars a year to a seven-foot-tall fleet of man children."

"I think our tallest player is six foot seven," I pointed out, my knowledge on the subject sending his and Ollie's brows arching. I shrugged, "Seemed like something an owner's wife should know."

"Most of the wives know nothing."

"They don't have brothers on the field," Pax pointed out, grinning as he looped a sweaty arm around my shoulders.

"True," Greyson said snootily, flashing a proud smile down at me. The man was *spectacularly* good-looking. How I'd ever worked three feet from him under the delusion he was nothing but a heartless cyborg, I would never understand. Choleric? Sure. Could he probably practice affirming his employees a bit more frequently so they didn't constantly think they weren't doing enough? Probably. But *Captain Hartless* possessed one of the most heroic *hearts* I'd ever seen under all the pretense of being Emerald Bay's Titan.

Hair disheveled, sweat gleaming across his tan, bare chest, a rare smile on his face, Greyson truly was the living embodiment of Adonis, a reigning immortal trapped among laymen. *My* Adonis. I yearned to trail my fingers through that glorious smattering of chest hair, to slip under the loose band of his gym pants and cup that god-sized weapon he loved destroying me with.

"Don't look at me like that," Greyson murmured as he snaked an arm around my waist, pulling me into him and startling me out of my pathetic ogling. The others had dispersed to the bench for a water break, and I'd been so trained on him that I hadn't noticed. "You'll make me do something the media would absolutely love to get their hands on."

"Oh yeah?" I teased, rising on my tiptoes to steal a kiss but wincing when I went to wrap my arms around his neck. Concern flickered in his eyes, but he did his best to conceal it, to keep playing. God, I loved the man.

"Yeah."

"Like what?"

"Like fucking you right here on this field until our knees are raw."

"Might cause quite a tizzy," I agreed, glancing around at the security he had stationed throughout the enormous arena.

"Or commandeering the locker room and bending you over every solid surface until you're screaming my name."

"Nothing says team spirit like a raw throat."

"*Mmmm*," he purred, smile giving way to feline satisfaction.

"Thinking about my throat?" I guessed knowingly.

"And the way you smile around my cock when you're looking up at me."

"Dirty man," I teased.

"Filthy," he agreed before crashing his lips to mine. When he finally pulled back to take a breath, he studied me intently. "Feeling better?"

I released all the air in my lungs with the same level of enthusiasm as the tension he'd eradicated from my body with our field trip. "Yes," I sighed contentedly. "Much, thanks to you."

"Least I could do," he assured before silencing any remaining worries with another kiss.

By the time our limo was crossing the Emerald Bay Bridge toward home, he was putting those lips to an even better use.

I'D JUST STRAIGHTENED my shirt and hair when we pulled up to the Hart House gate with an unexpected visitor outside it.

Arthur pulled the car safely onto the driveway before rolling to a stop so Grey and I could open the doors and greet Miranda, where she stood with mascara-streaked cheeks, hovering uncertainly by the gate.

"Come in," I yelped, rushing for her. She gave a shuddering sob, collapsing into my open arms. "Sweetie, *what happened?*"

"You—I—*two of them*?! Oh my god, I just heard. With *daggers*?! Royce says Cap is in the hospital, and you—" Her hysterics cracked in two as she studied me with tears streaming down her cheeks. *Stunned,* I just held onto her as she commenced our awkward, over-belly hug.

She was breaking down *over me*?!

"Miranda?" I questioned. She frenetically disentangled our limbs before wiping at her face, lips still trembling.

"I'm sorry, I shouldn't have—I just—you're okay?"

"I'm okay," I assured, feeling like the biggest pile of shit on the planet for not calling her. "We tried to keep it from the media, but you know how that goes."

"Bloodthirsty savages," she sobbed.

"With police blotters, evidently."

"I'm so sorry, honey. So, so sorry."

I chuckled morbidly. "It's not your fault."

"You're just so wonderful, and you don't deserve any of this and—"

"Woah there, hormones," I teased. "I'm okay."

"Really?" she asked, looking me over like she didn't believe me.

"I mean, *no*," I admitted, glancing over my shoulder and locking on Grey, swallowing hard before explaining. "But he's making sure I'll get there."

"You should have called," she said with a sniffle that was just as vicious as a knife to the chest.

"I see that. I'm so sorry. I was on the phone all day with my siblings, and by the time I got through them, I was exhausted, and the story leaked, and then Max showed up."

"Max is here?!"

"Somewhere. He didn't cross the bay with us; said he had stuff to take care of."

"I want to meet him," she murmured with a little hiccup. Apparently, I sold the man well.

"Come on in," I offered, but her eyes widened.

"Oh! Not like this," she clarified, motioning to her face, but then down her entire body. She'd come here in maternity sweatpants and a t-shirt with what appeared to be a coffee stain on it. "I don't know what I was thinking," she admitted. "I saw the article, and I was in the car before I could explain it, and then called Royce, and he couldn't reach Grey, and I just…panicked."

Was it possible for a heart to mend and break simultaneously? Aside from my siblings and Max, I didn't really have friends who would bother worrying about me. I mean, I hadn't ever really had *friends*. The smart, quiet teacher's pets rarely do.

"I'm so sorry I didn't call."

"You can't be the one comforting me. That's not how this works," she protested.

"I'm not used to having someone to worry about me outside of family," I admitted anxiously. Vulnerability was about as comfortable as a lemon bath after rolling in rosebushes. "Please come inside. We can make tea?"

But right as she looked between me and Grey, a wolf-whistle sounded from the house, and I spotted Max with Detective Rivera with his arms crossed, looking less than pleased. Max made his way toward us with a laptop under his arm.

"Maybe another time," Miranda placated, eyeing the leather-clad Lucas where he loomed from the doorway. He looked distinctly pissed off, the more I evaluated him. For a squat little guy, he did *brooding hero* well.

"Yeah," I breathed, more disappointed than I should've been.

"I'm sorry I just dropped in like this," she said, finally getting a little volume back in her voice, a hint of color in her cheeks.

"Don't be," I countered apologetically, leaning forward to scoop her up. "Thank you for caring."

"You'd be there for me," she said without hesitating, and I couldn't help but smile.

"Yeah. But since you're here—Miranda, this is my Max. Maxi, this is our friend, Miranda," I offered as he sidled up beside me, Grey closing the distance as well. They shook hands before we all bid my very pregnant, very teary friend goodnight.

It was only as we were walking away from her toward the house that Max asked, "Do you remember Eric Connely?"

"Noel's shitbag ex? The Florida senator's kid? Yeah. I think I do." Max helped Noel get rid of her stalker boyfriend once and for all after Jameson nearly killed him for laying hands on her. She'd been clever enough to collect all manner of evidence when she realized she was in danger. They'd even taken down the family company's board of directors—the whole corporation nearly went belly up.

The whole fiasco was kind of hard to forget.

"Detective Rivera here brought us some interesting intel to add to the intrigue. Eric was moved to a low-security facility this week. *Coincidental?*"

"Based on your tone, I'm thinking not."

"You're thinking correctly. Wanna know who came up in *Obsidian*'s list of in-pocket politicians and crooked cops?"

"*No way,*" I breathed as Luke quietly opened the front door for us.

"Daddy Connely is the tree from which that rotten apple fell."

"I think I need to hear this story," Greyson said as he locked the door behind us.

25

We've Been Invaded

ALICE

"I'm sorry, Alice, that's everything I had," Noel lamented, sounding more than a little bit crushed she hadn't somehow squirreled away more blackmail on the psychotic family her path had crossed with. "I've been gone for a few years now, but if you have someone in Florida, I can tell them what I remember, see if they can track anything down. I think they've mostly consolidated to Tampa now that they're 'retired' these days." I could hear the whoosh of her hands as she used literal air quotes. "Max and I didn't quite take *everything*—just what we could prove legally."

Tucked into a reclined armchair in the corner, Max harrumphed but didn't bother to open his eyes.

"That's plenty, thank you. Corroborating our theory about the Connely's association with the Gilberts was the best kernel of information you could've had tucked away in there."

"I hate to think they have anything to do with this. They were always so kind. Then again, so was Eric—at least to everyone else."

"Just let us know if you remember anything?"

"Of course! The fuckers still star in an occasional nightmare, so I'll let you know if anything pops up."

"Well, we don't want that. You've already been a tremendous help, Noel, thank you," Greyson said, from where he braced his hands on the desk to either side of my cell. Noel laughed in that uninhibited way of hers. It was infectious, my own cheeks lifting.

"*Of course.* I had no idea you still consulted for the government. How cool is that?"

I smirked as he did, but without missing a beat, he responded, "Luckily for me, my injuries didn't render me entirely useless. Happy to be appreciated for my expertise." I mean. Technically, it wasn't a lie. This takedown would involve local PD and the feds. Perhaps consulting was exactly what we were doing.

"Happy to help. Sorry I couldn't give you any more information. We'll see you guys in a couple of days."

"Looking forward to meeting in person." The first wave of Rhodes was due to arrive any minute, intent on an entire week of family time before Paxton's game. The rest would trickle in throughout the week. I'd offered to make them all postpone, but Grey insisted we get back into a routine. Fear would not be permitted to rule our lives, he promised. I prayed he was right.

"Love you, Noelie bear," Max said with a yawn. I wasn't actually certain he'd slept more than a few collective hours this week.

"Yeah, love you guys. I mean, mostly you, but when he gets back, tell Jameson I love him, too," I added.

She snorted indelicately and then, with a giggle, said, "Love all of you. You be safe now, okay?"

A round of agreement and prolonged farewells followed before we disconnected the call. I watched as Greyson processed our conversation, his breathing disciplined and steady as he walked over to the open window to stare out at the estate. Broad shoulders rose and fell incrementally as he did his best impression of a Greek statue. Slowly, not wanting to disturb his focus, I followed. Our landscapers were busy primping the hedgerow and mowing the grass while groceries were delivered to our iconically grumpy chef. You'd never know a storm was brewing inside these magnificent walls or that two lives had ended in the backyard just over a week ago.

I still couldn't get myself to go out back and noted Greyson had also abandoned his favorite routines on the terrace.

The low-hanging overcast sky turned that disconcerting reality a bit softer, the air slightly less suffocatingly arid, and Grey's eyes a bit more green than hazel. I found them mesmerizing, even in their frustrated furrow as he churned over all the information we'd gathered. We'd combed endlessly through the data Max and Luke had presented over the last few days. *So many names.* Connections. So many wrongs in this world, just begging to be righted.

Still more unanswered questions.

"How are you not overwhelmed right now?" I asked softly.

"What makes you think I'm not?" he countered, a gentle slant to his mouth.

"You've got this whole Zen master thing about you. I've always respected the way you keep your composure." A solitary brow arched skeptically. "Okay," I amended, "not *always*. Your control used to drive me bananas."

"Bananas?" he questioned dryly.

"That is the official terminology," I declared, nodding solemnly.

"It did earn me a rather unflattering assortment of nicknames."

Scoffing, I said, "That was probably the result of your inability to call me a good girl for working so hard for you."

"Affirmations belong in the bedroom."

"I mean," I shrugged, a smirk competing with a flush to dominate my face. "You don't hear me complaining."

"But I am," Max grumbled from where he still sat micro-napping like an angry, oversized cat in the corner. "You two are nauseating."

"Thank you," Grey gloated without missing a beat, shifting to scoop me into his arms. A breath after his lips brushed mine, the study door burst open.

Whirling, we came face to face with a fuming Reggie, Preston on his heels. Max slowly straightened in my peripheral.

The poor kid was rambling, his words squished together. *"I'm so sorry, sir,* I-couldn't-stop-him. Security waved him in. Says he has pertinent information regarding—"

Greyson's gently raised hand silenced him, his blond hair flopping as he bent over to catch his breath. The ire of Emerald Bay's titan turned on Reggie. I didn't miss the way he subtly positioned his body between mine and his uncle's. "Preston, send security in to speak with me." Our nineteen-year-old assistant nodded once before sprinting off like he was on a mission. "I do believe I've made my sentiments about your presence in our life perfectly clear, but if you can't comprehend the boundary lines, I'll dumb it down for you."

"Hear me out," Reggie growled, the sound of his voice like nails on a chalkboard. We hadn't found anything damning. No way to prove he was associated with the monsters in our city, aside from the timing of that conversation and his presence in that hallway.

Nonplussed, Greyson motioned to the chair across the desk, but when Reggie sat, Greyson simply loomed over the desk, staring down his nose at him with all the concern you'd show a slug. Wordlessly, Max rose to take his place, standing between me and them, with just enough room to watch around his slender shoulder.

"I have—"

"My house," Greyson spoke over him, leaning forward to brace himself on the desk. "You're chairman of nothing here. My rules of engagement were made clear."

What in the hell was he talking about? Perplexed, an ache formed between my brows as I glanced from Greyson's shoulder to Reggie's impassive face. Only the reddening of his skin revealed his anger. With a huff, the old man wet his lips before turning to me.

"I apologize for my words before the wedding." Evidently, that didn't meet the requirements because Greyson cleared his throat, and Reggie's eyes flicked to him before returning to my face. I would not squirm. I did, however, accept Max's strength when he gave my fingers a little squeeze by our sides. "I'm sorry I disrespected your place in my nephew's life as a future Mrs. Hart. I should have silenced my judgments. Which, as it turns out, were misguided." Greyson's huff of annoyance was the only approval he'd grant. As an afterthought, he added, "I'm sorry someone is trying to hurt you to get to my nephew." Returning his focus to said nephew, Reggie leaned forward to brace his forearms on the desk as he clasped his hands. "You have a hole in your security, son."

"Not your son," Greyson stated flatly, mask and tone impervious. It was the one and only time I saw a flicker of emotion in Reggie's eyes. But the declaration was redundant. Of course, there was a hole. Our head of security, Mike, had been working around the clock to figure out where it came from. Albeit, I certainly hadn't expected an ounce of concern from the man we suspected fed them the information in the first place. He was either a proficient performer, or we were missing a piece.

"What happened to Alessandra last week should be an impossibility," Reggie stated equally robotically. "I tried to warn you. Tried to tell you not to trust your circle." His measured words sent irritation boiling in my veins. *What had I missed?* "It's an affront to our very name."

Ope. There it was. His old faithful—their *reputation.* That made much more sense. Now, I did smirk. At least the muddy colors of his values were consistent. But I was still curious as to what conversation the two reigning Harts shared that I was clearly not privy to.

"I'm deeply moved by your level of concern."

I nearly snorted hearing those words drip from Greyson's lips in a perfectly practiced monotone. Forcing myself to poker up, I watched the exchange with the care of an irritated cat. One does not marry the Titan and not learn to stand like his queen.

"Mike, or Luke, or Mr. Reynolds—"

"Captain," Greyson deadpanned, earning a blink of confusion from his rapidly disgruntled uncle.

"Pardon?"

"*Captain* Reynolds."

"Yes, well, captain or not. Someone is leaking information outside these walls. How did they know your vulnerability was the beach?"

"It's. *The beach,*" he said dryly. "The vulnerability is implicit."

"Stalking through the water like Seals? You don't find that a rather pointed message?"

"Of course, it was a pointed message." His tone painted Reggie the town idiot, and I quite enjoyed it. "But my and Captain

Reynolds' roles in the navy are public knowledge. If you have evidence we have a mole, present it quickly."

Reggie's gaze flicked to me and Max before back to Greyson, his knee beginning to bounce beneath the desk. *Interesting.* I dug through my memory but wasn't sure I'd ever seen the man fidget.

"I trust them both implicitly," Greyson stated authoritatively before leaving the silence to linger as he turned to sit on the edge of his desk, still staring down at his uncle. The sound of boots filled the hallway, and Greyson looked to his watch with an irritated flick of his head. Countdown was ticking.

"You know," Reggie breathed. When Greyson arched a brow, Reggie furrowed his. "Someone is gunning for you, Greyson. First the embezzlement allegations, and now this. Are you in trouble?"

"It would appear so."

"Don't play with me. We have the resources to help you. What did you get yourself tangled up in?"

"I'll let you know when my investigators find out."

"Watch your back, my boy. You never know who you can trust in this life. Your circle should be tight, and should you find your enemy, keep them close until we can decide what to do with them."

Two armed security guards materialized in the doorway in their slick black-on-black shirts and slacks, and Greyson nodded his acknowledgment. "If that's all, these gentlemen will escort you to your car, as Alice and I have prior obligations."

"You can't be serious," he said, evidently appalled.

As Greyson gracefully slunk onto his feet, he smiled for the first time in the entire encounter. "Never know who you can trust, and all that."

With a huff reminiscent of a pissed-off bull, Reggie stood abruptly. More footsteps were audible in the hall beyond as he stared for a long moment, studying his nephew. My palms stung where my nails were biting into the skin to keep myself steady. We didn't know if he was dirty. Couldn't prove it. Saying something now would only tip him off. I was determined to have Greyson's back in this strategy, and speaking up would only undermine him.

"Watch your back. I would hate for a repeat incident to end with a less favorable outcome." As Reggie turned and walked through the gap between guards, the three of us stood as immobile sentinels, watching him step through the doorway just as Royce and Miranda cautiously edged around the corner, looking a bit ashen. Reggie paused, the security guards mimicking his halted movement. He stared Royce down for a beat before looking back to Greyson and muttering, "So much for a tight circle," before leading the guards down the hallway.

"Should we come back later?" Miranda hedged, anxiously

looking after what I assumed was a spectacularly pissed-off Reggie, then back to the three of us in the study.

"Everything okay?" Royce pressed, a protective hand coming to hover over her belly.

"All is well," Greyson reassured regally. "You're the first to arrive, but we're thrilled to have you."

"Brought you some brandy," Royce offered with a sympathetic shrug. "I intended it for coping with the in-laws, but it seems like you need it now."

With a chuckle, Greyson nodded, his shoulders relaxing as we funneled into the hallway to prepare for the onslaught.

GREYSON

WHO NEEDS a party when your family is *gigantic*?

The Rhodes arrived a chunk at a time, while Ollie, Mattie, and I hovered on the perimeter of my patio, observing the chaos.

Rhyett, Brex, and Quinn—all blond, tall, and blue-eyed like some Scandinavian advertisement—were the first in the door, bearing flowers for the house and a disarmingly thoughtful care package for Captain, for whenever we got to bring him home. Homemade peanut butter dog treats, chew toys and CBD gummies were all pointed out by a very concerned Brexley as she rubbed her hand over her growing belly.

Paxton arrived with both Finnegan—or *Finn*, as he preferred to be called—and Hadlee, who was a pint-sized duplicate of my wife, save for the golden hair in some fancy, skinny braid hanging around her shoulder. "Looks like a mermaid tail," Mattie had said before asking Hadlee to teach her how to do it. Much like Elora, Hadlee greeted me with an unnerving spider's smile and a handshake more intimidating than most men.

Jesus, it was definitely the women to fear in this family.

About two hours later, we all funneled outside to greet Leighton when she pulled in with her identical twin, Kaia. They earned a chorus of laughter as a rather gangly young man spooled himself from the back seat of her single-door Honda with no shortage of muttered epithets. He stood, looking rather pained as he popped his neck, and then his shoulders and hips, like he'd been stuffed in there involuntarily.

"Could be worse," the first twin quipped with a one-shoulder shrug.

"Could've been the trunk," Leighton—*I was about ninety percent positive*—finished as the mirror images vanished, arm-in-arm, into the house without further ado.

Clearing his throat, our newcomer gave an embarrassed, not-so-little wave. He had to be at least six-foot-four. As I studied the muscle mass on his lean body, I guessed, "You must be Maverick."

A goofy grin spread over his face as he sauntered forward to shake my hand. Ollie had been hovering beside me and canted his head, evaluating his lanky frame. "You're a little tall for a wide receiver."

Maverick grinned devilishly as he stretched an impressively long arm up vertically. Christ, his hands were nearly twice as wide as mine. "All about that reach, man."

"Yeah, but can you move that mammoth frame down the field?" my brother challenged. Of course, he was up to speed on what the baby of the family was doing in Washington. Maverick's stats were more than promising, but especially for a walk-on.

"Ran track from sixth grade through graduation," he supplied with a nonchalant shrug, as though he wasn't standing in front of the *owners* of the *Emerald Bay Bombers*. I liked him immediately. "Got roped onto the team for my speed and my reach."

"Players vie for spots on that team *for years* through high school. They're champing at the bit for a chance to red-shirt. What do you mean you got *roped* onto the team?"

Maverick shrugged. "Coaches always notice the giant kids. Back home, everybody wanted me just for my height. Very beginning of the year, I made friends with a cheerleader, and she caught video of me breaking up a fight on campus. Pulled them apart like a couple of chihuahuas," he explained with a cocky little smile that had me swallowing a laugh. "Apparently, coach liked what he saw and asked me to try out."

Oliver wrinkled his nose, narrowing his eyes in irritation. "Just like that?"

"Just like that," Maverick said, snapping his fingers. Now, his smile looked more than a little smug. I mean, his numbers backed up his ego, so good for him. "Red-shirting just made sense. I only played high school ball in Mistyvale, and it wasn't a career path or anything."

"Jesus," Ollie grumbled, shaking his head. "Well, nice to meet ya', you lucky son of a bitch."

"I'm sure the last name helped," Mav supplied, expression turning sheepish as he jerked his chin toward Paxton, who approached with a megawatt smile.

The afternoon was a blur of greetings and laughter as my house filled with a portion of our new in-laws. If the text thread had been overwhelming, it was nothing to the real-life chatter of this many voices.

"We've been invaded," Mattie noted astutely, while Beau

relished in the attention from so many pretty women cooing over his little bow tie. He was particularly smitten with the toddling Quinn, who bore a sparkling black bow in her spring-loaded blonde curls.

Chip, meanwhile, was running in frantic serpentine patterns, unsure of who would provide the best level of affection.

"This is only half of them," Oliver pointed out, a little bewildered from where we observed their conversations. Alice's decision to have us 'elope' had never felt more valid.

"*Yikes*," Mattie exhaled, still a little wide-eyed, her shoulders stiff under my hands where she leaned against my stomach. She'd planted herself in front of me well over an hour ago and refused to move since.

I chuckled, squeezing her shoulders and supplying a tentative, "More to love?"

"I guess," she said, sounding horrified.

"A little less love might've benefited their mother," Oliver muttered, bursting out laughing when I elbowed him in the ribs. Our levity was cut short by something that could only mean trouble, my stomach sinking as my face fell from the humor only a breath before.

Jax, Luke, and Mike were all barreling into the room like hounds on a trail. "Excuse me, sunshine," I murmured apologetically, guiding my niece to her daddy's quickly opened arms. Alice somehow picked up on the impending doom because she met me beside them and the group of us wordlessly tucked into the foyer.

"Mrs. and Mr. Hart, we have a situation," Mike said, looking stone-cold sober. A thin sheen of sweat coated his dark brown skin, eyes hard as stone.

"Things have escalated," Jax supplied with a growl.

Shaking his head, Luke muttered, "Understatement of the year award."

"*What?*" Alice demanded, a bit breathlessly as he glanced over her shoulder toward the house full of her siblings.

"The house is secure," Jax reassured. "But the office has been hit."

"Hit?" I bit out, my blood pressure making a dangerously abrupt climb.

"Arson, sir. The fire was put out, but the exterior was vandalized before responders got there."

"Was anyone inside?" I asked mechanically, trying to inventory who could've been harmed or targeted on a Saturday.

"Just the cleaning crew and weekend security. That's who called it in and scared them off."

"Arson?" Alice's voice cracked.

"They were just passing by—nothing unusual on the cameras

until they lunged, broke the downstairs windows, and tossed in Molotov cocktails," Mike supplied.

"Was anything taken?" Alice asked, that calculating cunning in the gray-blues I loved so much.

"No, Mrs. Hart. One of them managed to get inside, but security responded too quickly for it to be effective."

"Too sloppy," I pointed out as my mind rushed through the meaning of something so abrupt. "Just sending a message." It was pretty damn clear. *Back. Off.* I cracked my knuckles, followed by my aching neck.

Jax nodded, but his eyes flicked up as someone approached. I expected one of my in-laws but found Royce's light blue eyes heavy with concern. "You sure everything's okay, Greyson?"

"Just an incident at the office," I said quickly. "Security is just bringing us up to speed."

He turned over a shoulder toward where Miranda was chatting away with an enthusiastic Hadlee. "You'd tell me, if I needed to be worried, right?" He asked as he came back to face me, tone heavy.

I nodded before reassuring, "All is well, Ashcroft. Enjoy the party."

"Tell me if you need anything. There's been a lot going on, and I'm happy to lend a hand or my security if you need reinforcements," he offered, holding my gaze for a beat before heading back to his wife. Something heavy settled in my gut as I watched him cross the space. But my brain couldn't put it together before Luke was talking.

"One suspect in custody, and we're going to question him down at the station. I could bring you in with me."

Unease settled in my spine. God damn my uncle. Suddenly, my paranoia was flaring, distorting my reality as everyone became suspect. Reggie. Royce. Luke. Even Jax suddenly set my nerves bristling.

I needed air. "Take Jax," I instructed before stepping between them and outside into the gray of a looming storm. Jax at least could handle himself.

It wasn't him. If we had a mole, it wasn't Jackson. We'd survived too much. Been beside each other for too many damn years. What the fuck would he even gain? *Thunderstrike* was his damn idea.

Resolved that he wouldn't turn his back on us, I nodded to myself. He'd note all the same information I would if I went in person. It was my old Captain to follow me outside, however.

"They're coming for us, Grey. Two of our guys were involved in *accidents* this morning. Brakes went out on one vehicle. The steering on another."

"Both okay?"

"Yeah, gratefully. But…there's something else you should know. Mike found this, pinned to the door like last time."

Turning to see whatever new horror his words promised, ice crept into my veins. The singed paper in his leather-gloved hand was some fucked up movie poster of a woman on her knees in chains. Only…it was Alice's face hastily taped over the photograph. Judging by the gaping hole through the torso, they'd stuck it to the door with a knife again. When he flipped it over between his fingers, however, it was a very real photo of my wife.

In a gold gown stained red, looking over her shoulder in the Gilbert's damn hallway outside that office door. Eyes meeting Jax's fierce navy blue, I nodded before glancing around to ensure we were alone.

"Have you and Max found anything to link my uncle to this?" The grim resignation in Jax's eyes was emphasized by how hard his jaw flexed before he spoke.

"Nah, man. He looks clean."

Nodding as I chewed that over, I declared, "I want Neal Gilbert in a grave or a cell by tomorrow morning. Don't care how it happens. Find me a team that won't ask questions."

26

In a Grave Or In a Cell

JACKSON

There is nothing quite like the eerie silence in the heartbeat before you give a command to launch an op. To the predatory focus of my mind evaluating the dozen screens on the wall of the command center.

In a grave or in a cell, that was my mission for Grey. Unfortunately for us, federal involvement made the latter much more likely.

Beyond the lives of innocents and justice for the shit bags holding them, this sting was personal. *Obsidian* made it personal when they targeted my best friend's girl. When they left that fucked-up reminder that there were worse fates than death for those in their path.

With one last steadying breath, I cracked my neck, stretched my fingers, and then tapped my earpiece in an ancient routine. Meaningless, of course. Our tech was state of the art and our connections clear, but it was like muscle memory. An automatic reflex.

Everything was accounted for. The briefing had been short and to the point. Neal and Odessa Gilbert were our primary targets, with a secondary mission to capture or incapacitate the *Obsidian* operatives we could, both within the warehouse and throughout the city.

Our timing had to be precise. With this many organizations involved, not a team could be so much as thirty seconds off, or this whole thing would go to shit. The feds looked at apprehending these sleaze bags as a perk, but they were here to collect the last bits of evidence we needed to build the federal case against the rest of their damn network.

Disciplined breaths held steady as I scanned each aspect of the plan. Rivera's local brass had the perimeter secured. My screens reflected our body cams and the drone footage for *Thunderstrike*, EBPD, and the fleet of suits waiting for their signal. Their security footage had been hacked and looped, so they couldn't see us coming.

My men were broken into two smaller groups—one for frontal assault and one for infiltration through a side entrance.

Everything was in place. And a lot more people than Greyson were counting on me to execute this efficiently.

Now or never.

I said my prayers silently before tapping the sign of the cross, cleared my throat, and began. "All units, report status," I commanded, voice steady as I braced one arm over the other, resting my fist against my chin.

"Alpha team in position," Viper's hushed response sent me nodding at their screens. The man had been my second in command ever since Grey's accident.

"Bravo team, ready on your go."

"Perimeter secure," Rivera came through next.

With one last deep breath, I embraced the addicting cocktail of adrenaline and predatory calm and ordered, "Green light. Alpha team, breach the entrance. Bravo team, prepare for entrance. Execute on my mark." A final scan of the feeds showed everything where I needed it. Alpha was stacked up and waiting for command. Bravo was still a line of sculptures, their movements synchronized and precise. Out of habit, I adjusted the leather band on my watch, double-checking the face to make sure our timing was exact. My heart picked up as I watched the seconds tick by. Accuracy was critical as our other teams moved in around the city. There could be no gap between breaches—no chance for them to warn each other, where crucial players could escape.

Three, two, one. "Mark."

In a synchronized flurry of motion, my screens erupted as our infiltration team silently slipped through their side entrance to disable interior security systems with practiced efficiency. These men stood shoulder to shoulder under enemy fire in the Middle East. This would feel like a fucking drill for them. Problem was, *it wasn't.* The motherfuckers hunkered down inside that metal shell would be just as eager to spill their blood as any enemy combatant on the outside.

Right on cue, a thunderous explosion marked bravo team's breach, a handful of our camera feeds shaking with the aftershocks as their internal security rushed like disoriented bees to respond. "Flashbangs out. Secure the entry point." Not a moment later, a quarter of my screens were momentarily blinded, and I leaned forward to brace myself on the desk.

Like clockwork, our guys picked off shell-shocked *Obsidian* operatives like ants in a pile. "Alpha, proceed down the main corridor and clear each sector. Bravo, head to the server room and disable systems."

Agent Mitchell's voice came over comms. I wasn't a tremendous fan of sharing space with feds, but in this case, I could begrudgingly agree they were needed. "I've got eyes on the server room. Confirming heavy encryption. Bravo, prepare for digital extraction once we're inside."

A grim kind of satisfaction settled in my chest as I watched our teams sweep through what, up until now, had been headquarters for the Emerald Bay division of *Obsidian*. Not over till it's over, I reminded myself, releasing my hold on the edge of the desk, where my fingers had somehow tightly clenched around the rim. Flexing my hands, my focus sharpened on my alpha team as they cleared the corridor.

One by one, we checked the boxes as Bravo headed for the servers. It was the smooth operations that made me nervous.

In my experience, all it took was one moment of a dropped guard to throw an entire squad six feet into the ground.

Movement caught my attention, and I narrowed my eyes on the small line of *Obsidian* operatives as they poured into the space to engage the front of team one. "Alpha, contact left. Suppress and flank. Bravo, cover Alpha's advance."

Team two pivoted on command, the rapid percussion of cover fire forcing me to suck down a breath as our guys flanked the attackers.

Agent Mitchell drew my attention to my top right monitor as he announced, "I'm seeing movement on the north side. Reinforcements incoming. Delta team, position to intercept."

One by one, I cracked my knuckles, monitoring the chaos. Some days, running command was its own kind of high. But in moments like this—moments where my guys were under fire—I ground my teeth to keep from snarling because being shoulder to shoulder on the ground was somehow less helpless feeling. All I could do now was trust their training and do my damndest to give the right commands.

Greyson refused to leave Alice unattended during our attacks. Not that I could blame him. The bastard would be snarling by now if he was here anyway, demanding I let him march in there himself. It was better this way. Better that he wasn't fighting this sense of uselessness.

And just as quickly as they'd encountered trouble, our teams neutralized the resistance. Blowing out a breath, I tapped my earpiece, like somehow that kept me connected to my men. "Tango down. Secure the perimeter. Sweep for additional hostiles." Relief had me straightening, cracking my knuckles all over again.

Yeah. Grey would fucking hate this.

Room by room, I watched our men sweep through the warehouse, my eyes rotating through the screens, searching for any more enemies in hiding. Vigilance was the lifeblood of this position, and I wasn't about to let mine drop.

Lord willing, every aspect of this op was clicking into place, and we'd end the evening with at least sixty suspects in FBI custody. The count would've been higher if they hadn't forced our hand. In my opinion, some evils deserved fifty cents of lead, not a plush cell and three meals a day. *Alas.* Checks and balances and all that shit.

Nodding as they moved through the plan, I confirmed the next step. From what I could see, Neal and Odessa had unsuccessfully attempted to flee out a back window. My concern was whomever they had inside that room with them. "Primary targets located in the back office. Alpha, hold positions. Bravo, shift to support. Watch for crossfire."

As if I'd prompted the confirmation, Mitchell came through next, and our lines were blessedly clear. "Confirmed visuals on Neal and Odessa Gilbert. Proceed with caution. There are hostages."

With a few tapped keys, I changed my display. My new visual confirmed a woman held like a shield in front of Neal, with a gun to her head. Fucking coward. What was the end goal here? He'd already fucking lost. The question was *who* he held.

"Run this through facial recognition and get me an ID," I demanded as I watched the Gilbert's back into a literal corner like rabid fucking animals.

They both needed a bullet between the eyes, and as long as we got the innocents out of there, I kinda wished that's how this ended. If the information in their minds wasn't as valuable as it was, that's likely *exactly* how their story would end.

Pulse hammering in my ears, I watched, rapt, as Bravo adjusted their formation, and my mind ran through the million and one ways this could play out poorly.

Mitchell was barking commands about a negotiator as Viper ordered Neal to release the hostages and surrender. I did my best to keep eyes on the others, but my focus kept coming back to the confrontation in that back room.

"Sniper team, I want a clean shot if necessary."

"Negative," Bullseye responded, and I watched him scramble to shift his position and re-aim, blowing out a breath when he confirmed, "I've got the shot." The man could shoot a shadow off a horsefly. Pretty sure he had a gun in his hand by age six. If he said he had it, he fucking had it.

"Wait for my command," I ordered as a familiar chill of determination stilled my hand. But it wasn't needed. I watched in disbelief as Neal put his hands up and backed away from the woman before slowly lowering his weapon onto the floor.

It was only once they were both cuffed on the slick, unforgiving concrete—too kindly, if you ask me—that I finally inhaled, scanning the screens again for any other threats. "Alpha, secure hostages and sweep for intel. Bravo, regroup at the side entrance and prepare for exfil."

With my hands laced behind my head, I focused on my breathing as our team executed the plan bit by bit. But it was when my tablet screen lit up with that first green light that I finally threw my hands up in victory. Because this warehouse was one of six targets today.

The second was secure.

Pacing, I watched as the building was cleared and evidence was collected.

Grey and Alice were probably losing their fucking minds. Couldn't blame them if they were. I had eyes on the progress, and I was getting frantic. *So close.* We were so close to dismantling a ring of fucking monsters, and I couldn't afford to hope until every one of them was in custody. The problem with having our hand forced today was that now the rest would know we were coming, making our long-term goal infinitely more complicated. It didn't matter, I supposed. I'd still shred them to pieces before my time was up.

Even as I watched more green lights mark targets five, three, four, and eventually, six, as secure, my gut twisted like I was forgetting something. *Missing* something.

Brick by brick, we robbed these fuckers of the empire they'd built on the suffering of innocents, and it wasn't enough.

I watched as our teams regrouped and finally marked our op as complete on the tally board. Feds rolled in to collect their prizes and I watched for what must've been hours, but felt like days, until every one of our men was accounted for.

"Nice work, everybody. Stay alert. All units stand by for debrief." Even saying the words and watching them eventually exit did little to ease the sense of trepidation. By the time we debriefed, and I looked over our next steps—irritated this was now a federal issue and I wouldn't be getting the goddamned resolution—I decided it was just the fact that I was handing it off that had a knot tying my guts up.

The hum of my now empty monitors lulled me into complacency as I watched reports roll in, and only once I had all six, did I reach for my phone. Time to update the boss.

27

Persistent Pain In My Ass

ALICE

With an irritable huff, I rolled over and tossed my head onto the pillow for what had to be the hundredth time in the last few hours. Every inch of my body was restless with the need to act—to do *some-thing* of value—which made attempting sleep a unique form of torture. This is why so many people live to run. Hell, if my mind didn't settle, the treadmill downstairs was sounding more and more appealing. It could at least provide the momentary illusion of forward progress where there was none.

After their very direct attack on our family's legacy, *Thunderstrike* was moving on *Obsidian* in a matter of hours. Their primary focus would be homed in on the Gilbert family within our city. I might not have been privy to every scrap of information Greyson's men had on Neal and Odessa Gilbert, but I had enough to fear this going very wrong. What they'd shared with me was damning evidence of their involvement in laundering *Obsidian*'s capital and ongoing connections with the organization's higher-ups, the least of which was Noel's ex's family. I'd never imagined living a life where a man who nearly kills his partner in a scramble to keep control is the least of the evils. But they were all right there—under our noses, plastered over tabloids the people salivated to get their hands on. The devil in plain sight.

"*Breathe*, beautiful," Greyson ordered huskily. The man was even bossy about how I should rest. Somehow, that was annoying, adorable, and entirely on brand for him. "I've got you. Get some sleep."

"*You're* awake," I pointed out, earning a snort of amusement a beat before the mattress silently shifted below his weight as he rolled over to scoop me into his arms, dragging my body into the warm cocoon of his. With a sigh, I relaxed into the muscled embrace of my husband as he peppered kisses over my shoulder.

"My men are running point to keep my family safe when I can't," he said bitterly. "Of course, I'm awake."

"What's yours is mine, handsome."

"Evidently, that includes apprehension."

"It would seem so."

"You need to rest."

"*You* need to rest," I retorted petulantly. "Your strength was always your mind, Grey. Not your muscle. Your guys need you thinking clearly."

"My part in this is done now that the feds are involved. Max doesn't waste time when it counts. I like that about him."

Did I preen a little knowing that my best friend had been an invaluable tool in dismantling the Gilbert's fortress of stone? *Duh.* The man was about as brilliant as my husband. The two of them, plus Jax, had compiled a list that was concerning enough to demand that their contacts in the FBI take immediate action.

"They're going in tonight?" I confirmed, chest tight with the idea of my storm cloud of a bodyguard out there risking his life to bring down a web of psychopaths alongside a handful of his guys, Detective Rivera, and local brass.

"Just waiting for the call that it's done." He shifted his weight a little, ribs nearly still against mine.

"Jax will be fine," I assured, and he nodded against my back before pressing another kiss to my bare skin. "He'll be back here glaring at us over morning coffee."

"Yeah," he agreed curtly, voice too tight to lend me any sense of comfort. I couldn't shake the feeling that there was more to say, but he was holding it close to his chest instead. For a moment, my selfish bitch of a heart was just unspeakably grateful I didn't have to wait at home praying to get a call from Greyson. Then my stomach climbed up to lodge in my throat, because odds were there *were* partners waiting in this city. Waiting for loved ones that may or may not make it home. Judging by their assassination attempt, *Obsidian* was no less equipped than we were.

Eyes burning, I rotated in his arms so I could bury my face against his chest, inhaling his musk, soaking up his warmth as I reassured myself he was here. That we'd done everything we could to give our men the best chance at a clean sting and quick wrap-up. I just couldn't shake this niggling sensation that we'd missed something critical. Like a worm burrowing its way into my brain, I fought back the discordant voices in my mind. This late in the game, all I could do was trust the process, give thanks my man was safely wrapped around me, and pray everyone fighting for us made it home safely.

"I can think of more enjoyable ways to pass the time," he promised as his hands roamed south, earning a disbelieving giggle.

"You can't be serious," I teased.

"Am I ever *not?*" he countered. I was about to say point taken, but his warm palm reached my clit, and I sucked down a breath instead.

"What do you want to do when this whole operation is over?" I breathed, laughing when he groaned and clamped his teeth down on my shoulder before answering.

"My Belle, I have my hand on your pussy, and you think I'm giving a single fucking thought to anything else?"

Grinning, I shook my head. "You're trouble."

"Undoubtedly."

"Now, answer the question."

"Persistent pain in my ass," he growled.

"Always. But you knew that when you married me."

"Fantastic point. When this is over, I'm taking you back to our island," he said, a delightful smile lacing promise through his voice. He moved his mouth closer to my ear, my neck tickling with the heat of his words. "I'm finally going to fuck you on that beach and again in the shower with the glass wall overlooking the ocean—I'll press you up against that window and make you scream my name." Leisurely, he pressed a finger inside me and began a steady pump, arousal stirring in my center. "Make you come in every corner I've fantasized about since that first day I tasted you."

"And then?" I pressed, already more breathless than I cared to admit. The idea of him hammering home with my breasts against the cold glass as I watched those cerulean waves was ridiculously tantalizing. Something about being pinned beneath the strength of this man undid me quicker than anything else.

In answer, he ground his palm over my clit as he curled his finger. "Then, I'm cracking open a bottle of Macallan and your favorite Riesling—what was that little Vineyard you loved so much in Massachusetts?"

"*Marion Cline?*" I gasped like an imbecile, thighs shaking with the pleasure he wrung from me as they clamped over his hand. A satisfied hum rumbled in his chest.

"Ahhh, yes. The one with the turret. We'll open a *Marion Cline* Riesling. And then watch the sun go down until I can bend you over that sofa and memorize the sounds you make as you shatter under the night sky. Maybe we'll sleep under the stars and pretend this world doesn't exist."

"S-sounds good," I stammered, grinding against his palm in a desperate hunt for friction when he slipped his finger free to add a second. Greyson trailed his free hand up my thigh and under my silky nightgown until his hand found my breast, kneading it before giving the nipple a little tweak. He just clamped his teeth over the junction between my neck and shoulder when his phone rang, and we both sucked down a breath.

"Don't go anywhere," he ordered, unwinding our limbs and bringing his fingers to his mouth to suck my juices from them before turning to grab his cell. He blew out a breath before confirming who was calling with his curt greeting. "Reynolds?" He was quiet for a long beat before blowing out a relieved-sounding sigh. "Casualties?" There was another pause as my ears strained to pick up every other word Jax rattled off in a blunt procession, but this time, he buried his face in my neck as he listened. "*Thank fuck.*" His entire body relaxed into mine; that one sign finally allowed me to inhale properly. "Well done, Jax. This is *huge*…That's our biggest bust yet. Now, give the feds what they need and get your asses home." His chuckle followed a very *Peanuts'* teacher version of what I was ninety percent positive was *I don't take orders from you.* "Fuck off. Get over here, and we'll pour a drink to victory." The instant they disconnected, he tossed his phone onto the floor and a peal of laughter tore from my throat as he flipped me onto my back.

GREYSON

ALICE'S squeal of laughter was better than music to my ears. Both Neal and Odessa were in custody, along with a lengthy list of their security personnel and a handful of executives. Better yet, nearly thirty victims had been recovered through various points in our city.

Alice was safe. At least from the immediate threat. The others would fall like dominoes if Jax and I had a say in it.

Safe.

My bride was safe.

"Greyson!" she yelped as I nipped my way down her neck, hands firm on her belly, making her squirm as I worked my way over her frame.

"We're safe, baby. Jax gave the all-clear."

"So, I don't need my grumpy shadow anymore?"

Smirking, I bit down a little harder and growled, "Nice try, princess."

"Dammit," she breathed, but she was arching her spine, dropping her head to the mattress to expose her throat. *Fucking hell.* Cock growing painfully hard, I reached a hand up to bracket her neck, relishing in the little whimper the simple sign of ownership earned.

Mine.

This woman was mine. She showed it in her relentless pursuit of excellence and in her steadfast, righteous support through the trials *Thunderstrike* brought into our lives, right down to her vulnerability here in our room. She watched with bright doe eyes as I reared back to shuck off my pajamas, quick to comply when I told her, "Up on your knees for me, baby."

Crushing her lips with mine, I beat back the fear, the questions, the absolute terror of the last week and relished in the feeling of her in my palms. Her soft waist, generous hips, and strong thighs. The breathy hitch of her inhale as my fingers found her slick pussy. "Always so responsive," I noted.

It was as though her body was forged for me—quick to meld into my touch and just as apt to let me know when she was wanting. "That's my good girl, *my* beautiful *wife*."

A whimper escaped her, and I settled my hands on her waist, turning her around. Alice was always so quick to shift gears, to allow my hands to lead her where I wanted her. It was as though she got off on pleasing me, and that idea was enough to destroy even the strongest man. In tune with what I needed, she bent at the waist, quickly on her hands and knees for me as I closed the distance, bringing the creamy skin of her ass and thighs flush against me as I bunched the silk dress up around her waist.

Her damn nightgowns would be the death of me. It was all I could imagine any moment my schedule had a brief gap. One minute, I was dismissing a meeting or hanging up the phone, but when my eyes closed, it was Alice on her knees for me in that deep blue V-neck. *Alice*, splayed across our bed, gold silk draped over her chest as her lips parted. *Alice*, one blush strap askew, her pert breast and dusky nipple entirely erect as she threw her head back, and I dove to suck her peaked flesh into my mouth.

She was my obsession. And someone thought they could threaten her to get to me. There was a creeping sense of terror that Neal Gilbert wouldn't be the last motherfucker to set their sights on my wife. That fear crashed against the stubborn determination that we'd always keep her safe. But for now, I just needed to worship the woman who'd stolen my focus as she robbed me of my heart.

I reached down to run the head of my dick over her slick entrance, teasing her clit and relishing in the sound of her mewled response. She leaned back into me, and I didn't hesitate. In one harsh thrust, I bottomed out inside her wet heat, holding her hips as I fought to keep control of my impending release. Her tight channel had barely gripped my cock, and I was already dripping pre-cum inside her. The sensation of Alice riding me bare would never lose its novelty. The woman gripped my dick tighter with every desperate claiming thrust. With every squeeze of her hips.

"*Greyson*," she gasped as my hips snapped forward again. She could say my name like a plea a million times in this life, and it would never be enough.

Safe. She was safe. And she was mine.

Collapsing onto her forearms, Alice bowed her head into her hands, her silky chocolate strands melting into a pool in her palms as my pace increased. The soft window light cast shadows over her delectable curves—an incendiary beauty, like she'd combust, and I'd thank her as she took me to the next life.

"Please," she begged, although she didn't specify what she needed. More friction? For me to drive into her harder? Some combination of the two?

With my broad palms on her ass, I squeezed into her soft flesh, snapping my hips deeper with each movement. Bit by bit, piece by piece, I would dismantle the walls she'd built around herself, demanding she let me in. Some animal need to possess every inch of her, to know every curve and wall took over my body, urging me to deliver a kind of pleasure she'd never known before me. Would *only* know with me.

Alice's cry had my dick weeping against her walls, but it still wasn't enough. I slid free of her channel to gather her arousal, sliding it up to the pleated rim of her perfect ass. Sliding my cock back into her center, I circled that forbidden temptation with my thumb, lubing the skin before hesitantly pressing against that ring of resistance.

Alice *moaned*. The sound alone nearly had me spraying my load inside her.

Head thrown back, she sucked down breath like her life depended on it, and then arched her back, leaning into me and lifting that delectable ass in offering.

"You are so fucking sexy," I snarled, stilling inside her. I gently pressed into her tight ring of muscle, hesitating when she gasped. Her walls nearly yanked my orgasm free as they clamped down around my dick. Before I could ask her anything, she was arching into me again, urging me on, begging for more.

"*Please*, Greyson," she mewled, nodding her head in encouragement.

"Damn, baby. You want me to fill you up?"

"Please," she begged again, more desperately this time. Gingerly, I slunk deeper inside her tight little ass, a shudder rocking through me, my dick twitching eagerly as her ravenous moan encouraged my newfound exploration. I slid my other hand down her spine and back to her hip. God damn, she was fucking perfect for me.

Returning to our previous pace, I savored every thrust, every moan and cry of ecstasy as she filled our room with her pleasure. Her walls fluttered around my cock, ass tight as I slowly eased my thumb in and out at a gentle rhythm. Mine. Alice was mine. And I would destroy any motherfucker stupid enough to set sights on her.

None of it mattered in the end. Not the business. Not the operation. Not the life I'd known for thirty-five years before she said yes to my insane proposition in her kitchen.

Just this.

Us.

Her.

In the end, the only thing that I would take to my grave was my memory of Alessandra Hart.

My wife.

When she shattered around me, the heat beneath my skin became an inferno, and I followed her over the edge with a roar.

THE ROOM at the end of the hall had long collected dust, painfully vacant, like a reminder of my life. Not anymore. Never again, if I had anything to say about it.

The walls were now covered in mounted charcoal sketches and splashes of color over canvas. Alice spent her evenings unwinding in a collection of acrylics and pastels, and sketches she swore were trash, but that had me mesmerized. One piece at a time, she'd made the room hers—her easel and stool by the windows overlooking the ocean. The oversized fuzzy chair in the corner with an equally fluffy blanket and her books now filling the wall of shelves.

Our week was full of end-of-summer wrap-ups and the beginning of fourth-quarter clients, in addition to the clean-up after *Thunderstrike* delivered retribution on my behalf. As satisfying as it likely would have been to pay a visit to the Gilbert's in their new cinderblock home, I didn't need to validate why their threats had been effective.

They knew. Just as they knew who'd put them in there, and if they had a fraction as many brain cells as dollars seized by the U.S. government, they also knew I'd put them down if it came to that, without hesitation.

We'd filled our evenings with entertaining the Rhodes—boating, touring the city, and a match of football on the Emerald Bay field.

So, it was more than a little heartwarming to follow a comedic trail of her possessions through the foyer and down the hallway when I got back Friday evening. Like a nod to our normal routine, her shoes were halfheartedly discarded feet apart, followed by her blazer draped over an armchair beside the one painting she'd purchased for the hallway. By the time I crept through the cracked open door, I'd collected her discarded jewelry from a sofa table my assistant acquired at an auction a few years back.

With her music blaring—Hozier, if my memory served me well —and her eyes trained on the canvas on its stand, she focused with a statue's stillness. With a firefly's grace, she flitted forward to swirl a brush across the blue before stepping back and canting her head. She almost moved to the melody, like a well-rehearsed dance, as she nonchalantly added more color to the painting. I studied it then, smiling as I recognized the undeniable beginning of our island. The beach where our lives were irreparably altered.

"It's perfect," I said softly, smirking as she jumped and faced me.

"Christ, Grey. *Make a noise.*"

"I did. Several, actually. You just didn't hear me."

"In the zone, I guess."

"Our beach?" When she nodded her confirmation, color flushed her cheeks. I would never tire of seeing her blush for me. "You ready for tomorrow?"

"Yeah," she sighed, the sound a bit jittery. "I don't know why I'm nervous; it's not *me* playing on that field."

"Because you want your brother to be successful. That's admirable if you ask me."

"Pax has fought so hard for this."

"I know."

"The *Wolves* got him two Super Bowl rings."

"Doesn't mean he can't lead the Bombers to their first in decades."

She smiled at that, rubbing the back of her hand over her face and leaving a smear of teal across her cheek. Laughing, I closed the distance to wipe her face clean.

"That's for you," she said, nodding to the painting.

"Yeah?"

"Yeah. I thought it could go in our room."

"Finally get rid of that heartless, modern catastrophe you hate so much?"

This smile she didn't bother to hide. "*Maybe,*" she replied, her arched brow and spark of challenge in her eyes making me laugh.

"Thank you. The other bores me to tears, anyway."

"As it should," she declared snootily before raising a hand to cup my face, stroking her thumb over my cheekbone and leaving a damp trail in her wake. Her eyes widened as I deadpanned, a nervous giggle rising up her throat as I lunged.

PAXTON RHODES THREW for five hundred and nine passing yards his first game on the Emerald Bay field, and the packed arena lost their minds. And with good reason—another fifty yards would've made history.

With each throw, the fans grew more feral. By the time he shot a canon of a pass to none other than Dallas Miller for the game-winning touchdown, the team was just as ecstatic, rushing the field in celebration.

Royce, who'd spent most of the game shooting concerned daggers at his phone as he checked on Miranda, actually leaped to his feet beside me as Miller crossed the end zone. He turned to me with his hands up for dual high-fives.

"Holy shit, man!"

"Is it too soon to say we're back?" I boasted. He shook his head, blond hair swaying. But there was a disconnect in his eyes as if he wasn't really with us. Worry creased his brow.

I didn't get to ask any questions, because Alice and her siblings instantly reduced to hysteria—hugging and bouncing about.

Oliver's grin met mine over her shoulder as she rocked back and forth in an Elora-Leighton sandwich. The girls yelled with more ferocity than the cruelest of coaches the entire game, and Elora had the mouth of a sailor on her. Hell, all six of them did.

Fitting, I supposed.

"I hate that Miranda missed this," he lamented, shaking his head. His wife had stayed home, not feeling well. This close to her due date, they'd decided it was better to get some rest. I couldn't blame them.

"She doing any better?" I asked as Rhyett and Maverick both patted my back when they stepped behind me, making a beeline for the doorway. This was certainly the busiest the Hart family box had ever been, shy of the occasional corporate networking event.

Concern lined Royce's eyes as he shook his head. "She said she was going to try and nap, but I haven't heard from her since."

"Get your ass home," I barked. "Go check on your girls."

"Still determined it's a girl?"

"If I've learned anything in the last few months, it's that Alice is always right."

"Hold on," that familiar voice had me grinning as my eyes closed. Alice was miming a whiteboard eraser, complete with squeaking sound effects, when I turned to face her sly smirk. "Back up and say that again; I didn't have a recorder going."

"*Busted*," Royce muttered, looking greener by the minute.

Tucking Alice under my arm, I pressed a kiss to her forehead. "Love you, baby. You know you're brilliant; don't pretend otherwise. Congratulations today, by the way."

"Congratulations to *you*, Mr. Owner," she countered playfully. "My brothers are gonna hang back with Ollie for the press conference, but me and the girls were thinking about heading home to make sure everything is ready for the afterparty. You wanna come with?"

"I'm actually gonna head home too," Royce said, anxious eyes flicking between the two of us. His pallor had sympathy nausea unsettling my gut.

"You look a little seasick," Alice noted. "Which is rather unfortunate on solid land."

He grunted an attempt at a laugh before grimacing and admitting, "I feel like shit. Would it be a terrible inconvenience if I caught a ride home? I'll have somebody come grab the G-wagon."

My wife wrinkled her nose but shook her head. "You're on the way, anyways. I'm sure my brothers can handle your car."

Nodding, he fished his keys from his pocket and tossed them to her. "Just…not the kid. He scares me." We both smirked, eyeing Maverick. "Thanks, Alice. I uhh…" He swallowed like that muscle was all that kept the bile down.

"Why don't you go wait by the car?" my wife suggested. Royce just nodded, holding a hand up to keep us at bay as he backed away.

"*Yeah*," he managed to grunt. "Good plan."

"See you in a few." A sympathetic smile crept over her beautiful features as she watched him exit in a hurry. Wrapping her arms around my waist, she muttered, "*Yikes*. You going to come with, Mr. Hart?"

Before I could answer, Mattie threw her arms around Alice's waist and buried her face against her stomach. "*Please* take me with you!!" Their nanny had no-showed after Carly made sure to stake her baseless claim to Oliver and their kids last night. The only time *Cruella* bothered to show up was if someone deigned to give the three of them attention befitting any creature larger than a flea.

Ollie had brought them both along, and while Beau seemed ecstatic at the prospect of going out on the field, four hours of football and pre-game was evidently more than our Mattie could tolerate, based on the desperation in her voice and her little arms locking around my wife. "Please! Leigh says she'll paint my nails for the party."

"Oh, will she now?" Oliver grumbled, arching a brow at Leighton, who just flashed a mischievous smile, daring him to challenge her. My brother obviously valued his balls intact and was wise enough not to take the bait.

"Oh, come on, Dad, I'm *ten*," she stated with a teenager's scowl on her face.

"Just for tonight," he allotted. "*If* your aunt is okay taking you home."

Grinning, Alice's amused eyes met mine. "Fine by me. Can you convince Uncle Grey to join us?"

"*Please*, Uncle Grey?" Mattie begged, batting her eyes in an adorably awkward attempt to win me over. Before I could answer, I spotted Luke, who leaned against the threshold. He dipped his chin, and I sighed.

Squeezing Mattie and Alice each in one arm, I said, "You three go. I'll be right behind you. I've just got something to take care of."

Narrowing her eyes with comedic accusation, Alice teased, "Nothing too exciting, I hope."

"Nah, just a friend," I assured, nodding to Luke as he moved into the space, weaving through Rhodes siblings as they funneled out into the hallway. She sighed theatrically but pressed a kiss to my cheek.

"Five minutes, *max*, Mr. Hart," she demanded, tone mimicking scolding.

Laughing, I kissed the top of her head before unwinding my hold on her, then tracking the three of them as they headed out hand-in-hand, turning sideways dramatically to fit through the doorway. A smirking Jax stalked after them.

"Hart," Luke said by way of greeting.

"Rivera," I returned, studying the cautious purse to his lips. He seemed to sense my scrutiny, quick to poker up. "What can I do for you?"

"I got a question for you, and I don't think you're going to like it."

"Fuck," I growled. "*What now?*"

"How well do you know Royce Ashcroft?"

28

Stay With Me

GREYSON

I blinked at a deeply concerned detective. His jaw set, Luke furrowed his brow.

"*Royce?*" I shook my head as the blood in my veins turned to ice. "*Just* left with *my wife*, Royce? We're friends with him and Miranda."

"Has he ever spoken about his mother?"

"Haven't exactly delved into family history." When his expression gave nothing away, my brows pinched.

"I was a little worried about that. Royce results from an affair, Greyson. Mrs. Ashcroft adopted him legally, but it has always been a point of contention for their family, according to his father."

"I don't understand," I admitted, although some rabid animal was burrowing into my gut.

"I was afraid of that," Luke said, palming at his jaw. "Grey, we're unearthing a lot of history in this interrogation, and Odessa said something the first day that tipped me off. *She's* his *mother*, Greyson. Neal covered the whole thing up to save face on his climb for power, but his newlywed bride was out of the public eye for nearly *a year* right after the wedding. Ashcroft announced the birth of his son before she returned."

"That proves nothing," I countered. Although it would give her just enough time to deliver her baby and get back into normal clothes if she wasn't preoccupied with a newborn.

"No. But my interview with Daniel Ashcroft today does. He and Royce are recently estranged. Did he tell you that? Said Royce was resentful of being pried away from his biological mother."

"Why didn't I know about any of this?" I growled more to myself than to him, making a beeline for the exit as he rushed to follow.

The fucker was a friend. Or the closest thing I had to one, aside from Jax and my brother. His mild-mannered wife had been *hysterical* when Alice was attacked. It made little sense.

"Where are you going?" Luke barked as I rushed out the door.

"He *just* left," I growled over my shoulder. "I need to catch up to Alice and Mattie."

"We don't know if he even knows anything about *Obsidian*, Grey. I got to you before anyone got to him or Miranda to question them. Thought you said he'd be here."

"He knows," I growled.

"What? How do—"

"I just...*call it a gut instinct*," I snapped, rapidly stabbing the elevator button as if that would make the cables work faster. Dialing Alice, I pulled my phone to my ear.

He'd been on the phone that night. That night at the auction.

Gotten us there in the first place—and...*for what?*

Then our server *just so happened* to spill on Alice and led her to that bathroom only to turn up dead in the river?

No. That wasn't happenstance.

Alice heard a one-sided conversation with someone talking about a situation too eerily similar to ours to be tossed aside, using our last name as a goddamn keyword, and assumed the second party was Reggie, but...Royce had been on the phone when I left and still pacing outside the ballroom when I came back to cover our asses.

When the elevator opened, my assistant Preston stepped out, looking perplexed. "Mr. Hart, this just arrived for you," he announced, hoisting up a gift basket with two bottles inside. "The note said, 'To a game well played'."

My heart...plummeted, stomach flipping as I eyed the contents. "What the fuck?" I extended a hand to the *gift*. Bile rose in my throat as my fingers traced the label on the bottle of white wine.

Marion Cline Riesling.

It was carefully placed beside a bottle of Macallan.

White hot rage consumed my vision, my chest constricting.

Then, I'm cracking open a bottle of Macallan and your favorite Riesling— what was that little Vineyard you loved so much in Massachusetts?

"They're in my house," I snarled as Luke stuck an arm out to hold the elevator. My gaze snapped to his. "Luke. *They've been in my fucking house. They're in my fucking bedroom.*" Luke fumbled to catch the basket as I hurled it into his arms.

Oliver chose that moment to slip out of the family box with a very heavily lidded Beau in his arms.

"*Greyson,*" he said simply, all the questions buried in his eyes.

"I've got to go," was all I managed to get out, my heart sinking as I dialed Alice's number on muscle memory, jamming the first-floor button. The doors pinged open, and before they could close behind me, my brother and nephew were on the damn thing with us.

"Royce is a Gilbert," I barked by way of explanation as Alice's voicemail clicked on. "*Fuck!*"

"I don't understand," Oliver said, blinking away his confusion. Seemed to be a theme for the Hart brothers today. His knowledge of our most recent sting was low-level, at best. Just a vague overview, so he didn't go responding to the wrong invitations with the wrong kind of people. "*Ashcroft.* Ashcroft is Odessa Gilbert's bastard son."

"You're kidding," Ollie scoffed like he was waiting for a punch line. One that would never come because the elevator doors were opening, and I slipped between the stainless-steel door and wall and bolted for the exit. The throng of people was nothing but immobile obstacles between me and my damn car. Weaving between them, I forced a path outside.

"Greyson?!" A concerned, familiar female voice caught my attention, and I whirled, praying it was Alice, although my gut knew it wasn't. It wouldn't be that easy.

Elora and Hadlee were staring at me from their spot on the curb, brows furrowed with concern above eyes so eerily similar to Alice's that it nearly brought me to my knees. God dammit, I would kill to have her there between them.

"Where's Alice?" I barked. "Leighton and Mattie. They all came down together…" but my words drifted when Elora shook her head, fear entering those familiar eyes as Hadlee rose on her toes as if she could gain a better vantage point to scan the crowd.

"I'm coming with you!" My brother's pissed-off demand had me turning, but I was shaking my head before he caught up to us with Luke by his side.

"Not with Beau, you're fucking not."

"You don't get to bark orders at me. Mattie is with them!" Ollie snapped back.

"What's *going on?*" Elora demanded, straightening. Broderick's husband-radar was thoroughly tuned because he descended on our huddle within a heartbeat. A quick survey placed five of their six brothers within twenty yards. *Good enough for me.* In the next breath, I scooped Beau out of Oliver's arms and handed him to Broderick, who was quick to wrap him up. The tall brother—*Jameson?*—was scowling at me before scanning the crowd expectantly. It was his eyes I held before rotating to the professor.

"Take Ollie's car. Preston will drive you home. Guard him with your fucking life. Do you hear me?"

Wide brown eyes blinked twice, and then he nodded, seeming

to clear his confusion. The others were closing in, sensing or hearing our tension, I wasn't sure. Elora yelled something after us, but my eyes trained on our target. Mind rushing through our response.

I needed to notify my security.

Needed Luke to call for backup.

Needed to get ahead of this.

By the time Oliver's and my dead sprint for the car ended, I'd already reached Alice's voicemail for a second time and dialed her again.

Her GPS showed her getting on the highway home. It *should* be comforting, knowing where she was. But I couldn't shake my trepidation. Home wasn't any safer. Not with them inside it. Not with the Ashcrofts still categorized as *a friend* in her mind.

A concerned-looking Arthur was stepping out of the idling SUV as I pinned my phone to my shoulder.

"Ride with Preston," I ordered, slipping past him into the driver's seat. We were already rolling, Arthur jumping away from the car when Ollie's door slammed closed. "*Pick up, baby.* Please, pick up."

ALICE

MATTIE AND LEIGHTON were belting out the lyrics to "Another Brick in the Wall" by Pink Floyd when Jax merged our SUV onto the highway. His amused eyes found mine in the rearview mirror, and I laughed as he slowly pressed the accelerator, the engine thrumming to life.

Royce awkwardly cleared his throat from where he swayed in the passenger seat, his cell clutched in his hand. "Thanks for the ride, Rhodes."

Scowling, I muttered, "God, that sounds weird now."

"Like being a Hart?" he questioned softly. My smile set my chest heating, a hand coming to rub over my sternum.

"Yeah," I breathed. I really did. Thoughts of Greyson wrapped around me—glimpses of his laugh on the patio, or his palpably intense focus as we worked. The memory of his finger in my ass as he hammered into my pussy, breaking me apart on his dick, suddenly was all-consuming. The man had taken me captive in both body and soul, and I wouldn't have it any other way. "I do love being a Hart. Well," I amended, thinking of Reggie the Dick, "I love being Greyson's."

He nodded, throat bobbing as he grabbed the oh-shit handle, and Jax rolled the passenger window down with a revolted-looking glower. "If you're gonna hurl, you do it *out* of the fucking car. Understand?"

"Yeah," Royce grunted, looking worse for wear. *Poor bastard.*

Smirking, I shook my head at my cranky ass bodyguard. The volume with which the girls were serenading us had decreased, though Leighton was still crisscrossed and twisted so she could see Mattie in the back.

We had just reached the Emerald Bay Bridge to the opening cords of Rolling Stones' *Beast of Burden* when I heard the distant buzz of a phone. When Leighton glanced at hers and shook her head, I mumbled an *oops* and bent to fish mine from my bag.

Seven missed calls from Grey glared back at me. My first worry was Paxton, but when I brought the receiver to my ear, his frantic, "*Where are you?*" had me second guessing that. I straightened and looked around us, making sure all was well.

"We're on the bridge," I said, voice mirroring his anxiety.

"Watch your surroundings. Do you understand me?"

"Yeah," I breathed, the panic in my tone catching Jax's attention in the mirror. He turned the music down a notch but kept bobbing his head as though determined to keep it a good day. As though the oldies station could preserve our joviality.

"Royce is one of them." The world stopped, my eyes flicking to the back of Royce's coifed blond hair before thinking better of it and holding Jax's eyes in the mirror instead.

"What?" I breathed, fighting to keep my voice even. Leighton's concern landed on me like a physical weight, but I shook my head, waving her off. She kept singing, but now she was looking around us, a little too obvious in her alarm for anyone to miss it.

"Odessa Gilbert had an affair with Daniel Ashcroft that resulted in Royce."

"But that doesn't mean——"

"Until I know otherwise, we treat him like an enemy. Understood?"

Eyes darting between Jax in the mirror, who was subtly tracking my conversation, and Royce, where he leaned against the door frame, fingers tapping out a message on his phone, I scrambled, brain going blank. "Yeah, we're almost home. We're almost to Miranda and Royce's house."

"*Cocksucker*," he snarled, an engine revving in the background.

Heart ratcheting up, I did my best to keep my tone casual. "You right behind us, baby?"

"Five minutes at most."

Nodding, I forced myself to breathe. "Good deal. So, we'll get home around the same time. Caterers are setting up as we speak."

"Do you remember what I told you?"

My mind emptied entirely. "Um, about the menu?"

"About our security protocols?"

"Yeah, I got it," I said, trying to reach back into those first months of summer as he gave me the layout of the house and the vehicles. Mostly, I just prayed if it was true, this wasn't the day he'd make his move.

"Stay on the phone with me," Greyson ordered. "I fucking love you, Alessandra Hart. I fucking love you so goddamn much." *Why did he sound like he was saying goodbye?* The blade of terror in his voice had my heart accelerating, the bridge of my nose burning.

"I love and miss you too, you big—" I was in the middle of my thought when Jax glared into the mirror, silently rolling up Royce's window, startling him away from the door. He turned down the music as the song swapped to *California Dreamin'* by The Mamas & The Papas, and without hitting his blinker, swerved into the far right lane, cutting between two rows of traffic.

Leighton was whirling for the back window as I pointed toward Royce, my attempt at a subtle head's up lost on a very focused Jackson.

"I mean it, Alice," Grey snarled as rubber squealed. "*Stay with me.*"

But Leighton was *screaming*.

Leighton was screaming words I couldn't make sense of.

Greyson was barking orders in my other ear.

Royce was turning, looking more irritated than concerned.

I whirled right as a tinted black SUV slammed into our bumper, sending us jolting forward as Jax slammed on the gas, and Mattie screamed in terror. My neck gave a pang of protest, and I turned, wide-eyed, to Jax's reflection as he methodically glanced between our mirrors.

"What's happening?" Greyson demanded, but I was preoccupied with the *second* vehicle snaking up beside us—some sporty black thing—and the *man* with the black barrel of a gun pointed at our window.

"Get down!" I yelled. Before I could make sense of her motions, Leighton had ripped her buckle off and was throwing herself over Mattie as Jax swore.

Oh god, *Mattie*.

Without hesitating, Jax cranked the wheel to the left and slammed into the black Charger, sending it spinning out, where—at least judging from the horrible sounds behind us as he fought to control the vehicle—traffic T-boned it.

I released a paradoxical breath of relief as I thanked whatever benevolent being was watching out for us and prayed that nobody innocent had been hurt in the wreck.

"Get fucking buckled," Jax barked as he hit the center lane and slammed on the gas. Leighton, breathing haggard, rushed to follow his order. And just in time, too, because without warning, Jax slammed on our brakes, the SUV behind us smashing into the back with enough momentum to send my phone flying as Mattie broke into sobs in the third row. The screeching of rubber on asphalt and metal on metal tore through the air a beat before Jax pulled some insane circle maneuver that sent our assailant flying as he cut back across the lanes of traffic to the chorus of horns blaring.

Jax hit the inside shoulder of the bridge and floored it, our rearview mirror snapping off to the scream of the vehicle scraping over the concrete barrier.

"Holy shit!" Royce barked, looking more than a little green around the gills.

He couldn't be one of them.

I couldn't reconcile the concept with the sweet couple I'd spent my summer with. The preening parents. Or the bloodless-looking face staring wide-eyed at Jax as he invented a lane for us. Spotting an opening, Jax swerved through a gap between vehicles and put us right in the center lane ahead of the line of traffic.

"Alice, I could use some backup."

"Jesus fucking Christ, do I look like I know how to call for backup?" I screeched as I contorted in my seat to check our left side. But Leighton was tossing me her phone, and I dialed 911 before the words came out of my mouth.

Think, Alice, think. There had to be a way out of this that kept Leighton and Mattie safe.

"They were going to shoot at us! *What the fuck is going on!?*" Leighton hissed, her hands clamped over Mattie's ears like our language or volume was what the tiny, sassy super genius would be concerned with. Tears streaked down her little wan cheeks, and I vowed to deliver retribution on her behalf. I'd find a way.

"They're trying to kill us or capture us," Jax noted helpfully.

"I fucking see that, but *why?!*" Leighton demanded as the engine roared and Jax barreled toward our side of the bridge. My shoulders pressed into the leather with our increased speed.

"Because your sister stuck her nose where it didn't belong."

Every muscle in my body went rigid, but it wasn't Royce's words that held me captive—it was the pistol, now trained on Jax in the front seat. In the same breath, Jax lunged for the dash, where I knew he held his firearm in a magnetic holster below the wheel. Royce didn't get closer, instead turning the gun toward me as he demanded, "*Hands on the wheel, Reynolds.*"

Jax froze, those dark eyes flicking to me in the rearview mirror as my gaze rotated between the threat and the man hellbent on mitigating it. Jaw flexing, Jax raised his other hand before setting it on the wheel.

"Royce," I panted, tone desperate, "don't do this. You don't have to do this."

"Didn't want to," he said, the words tight. While his gun stayed on me, his eyes were on Jax—he'd decided who the threat was.

Slowly, trying not to gain his attention, I glanced at Leighton. Nostrils flared, chest heaving, the anger in her eyes trumped the fear there as she sucked down air. Determination set her jaw when our eyes locked. We didn't need *words*. We had twenty-three years of sisterhood and decades of surviving six brothers together. I glanced down at Mattie's untied combat boots before returning my focus to the psychopath now yelling at Jax as he revved the engine.

"*Slow down!*" Royce barked, turning the pistol on Jax.

"You're gonna kill us either way. I'll take you with us," Jax promised flatly as the engine roared, towering bridge posts flying by us at a terrifying speed. His words pulled another sob from Mattie, and my heart cracked. Throat tight, I fought to swallow the terror pushing bile up my throat.

Fear served no one.

Fear clouded your judgment.

Killed your focus.

My peripheral vision caught the subtle movement of Leighton unlacing Mattie's black boots.

"Royce, don't do this," I pled, voice infinitely calmer than the shit storm roaring inside my head. "You have a *baby* on the way. A *wife* waiting for you at home. Put the gun down."

"I don't have a choice—they *took* them."

My stomach bottomed out as fear wrapped around my windpipe. "Who?"

"All of them, Alice."

"The kids?" I asked, voice cracking as his petrified eyes landed on my face.

"When we didn't turn you over, they—they took Miranda today."

"Who?" I demanded, equally horrified and hopeful as the end of the bridge crept closer. "I—it wasn't supposed to go this way," he said in a near-sob, light blue eyes watering as he wielded the weapon between me and Jax. "*I* let them in, Alice. I let *her* in. It's my fault. If something happens to them, it's *my*—"

"Who took them?" I repeated. "Royce, if your family is in trouble, we can help you. Greyson can help you."

"You're all dead men walking," he argued, shaking his head. His hand trembled, the pistol along with it. I wasn't the only one to notice—Jax's eyes flicking from the threat to the road. "We all are. You in exchange for them. *That's the price.*"

"Get fucked," Leighton spat, but I was shaking my head.

"I'll go," I barked, hands raised. "Just let everyone go, Royce. Let them get out of this, and I'll come with you." We were almost there. Almost across the metal monstrosity—certainly past the tallest point. If we could just get to solid land, Leighton and I could make our move.

But we wouldn't get a chance. Because all at once, Jax shot a warning glare into the mirror and slammed on the brakes, sending everyone lurching forward. Royce's face smashed into the dash as Mattie screamed, but it was the sound of the gunshot that reverberated inside my skull before the car veered violently sideways.

They say you see your life flash before your eyes when death has you in its claws, but that's a lie. At least, it was for me.

Time *stopped.* Ceased to exist as we careened through the metal edging and hurtled toward the dark expanse of water. It suspended as the SUV hung over the bay, as blood splattered across the ceiling and dash.

It wasn't my *life* replaying as the scream tore up my throat.

It was the sound of Greyson begging me to stay with him.

29

If You Get Us Killed, I Will Beat You to Death

ALICE

"Baby, I need you to breathe, okay?"

Radiant pain tugged me into consciousness, my mind scrambling to make sense of what I was hearing.

Leighton. That was Leighton's voice beyond the sobs. Beyond the steady trickle of water and radio. All of the stimulus was contained behind a sponge—some bizarre absorbent buffer between the world and the steadily throbbing pain in my head. My neck and chest. *Ba-boom, ba-boom, ba-boom,* it echoed with each rapid thump of my heart.

Fuck me, it was hard to breathe.

Searing agony crept from my spine to my skull, needling at the back of my eyes.

"I can't!" A hysterical, childlike voice cried. *What the hell was the water? Where was it coming from?*

"Listen to me. I'm going to get us out of here. But you have to stop screaming and let me think. Can you do that for me?"

"Mm-hmm," came a shaky reply.

The pieces started to filter back into my mind as Leighton's forced calm permeated the fog filling it. Copper saturated my tastebuds and I winced, blinking my eyes open to find myself suspended crookedly in the SUV, the pain in my chest actually a thick belt across my sternum.

Seatbelt.

Oh, god. *No!*

Mattie.

Mattie was going home with us.

Choking on some combination of blood, panic, and saliva, I startled upright, bringing a hand to my hammering head and finding my skin warm and sticky. *Ouch.*

We'd crashed off the bridge.

We'd *crashed* off the Emerald Bay bridge.

Blood splatters were everywhere as my eyes scanned ahead, where both Jax and Royce were unconscious or dead; I wasn't sure which.

"Jax," I croaked, throat aching.

"Thank fuck," Leighton gasped, the first hint of panic slicing through her facade of calm. "Jesus Christ, can you move?"

Blinking away the spots in my vision, I shifted my hands… wiggled my toes. "Yeah."

"Can you unbuckle? Mine is jammed."

I pulled—tugging against that pressure on my chest, and found the belt tightly locked into place. When I pressed against the band of fabric, panic latched around my windpipe when it wouldn't release. Again and again, I jammed against the red button, but it wouldn't give.

"No," I panted. Wincing, I shifted my weight, trying to keep the belt extended but ease the weight off the mechanism.

Breathe, Alice.

Think, dammit.

My vision was slightly blurred, making me blink as if that could clear the film.

Concussion? Probably.

There was light in the cab, but not what I expected.

We were nose down in the water—dark navy creeping up the windshield. So, we hadn't submerged entirely. Not yet. Which meant I hadn't been out long—just got my bell rung. The source of water was obvious: a steady stream pouring through the vents and around the front doors.

The urge to hyperventilate was overwhelming, and I forced myself to fight it, to suck down long, steady breaths of air despite the protest in my ribs.

Breathe. Control your mind. Learning control will keep you alive, baby. Naturally, Greyson's voice would be the anchor my mind would cast. Breathe. Control. I could do this. Had to do this.

"Jax," I croaked again. "*Jackson!*"

Nothing. Not a stir of movement. Eyes burning, I forced myself to breathe and looked around. How in the hell did you get out of a belt like this?

Jax.

He always carried an assortment of blades. "Mattie?"

"I'm here," she squeaked, voice warbling.

"Hi, sweet girl. We're going to figure this out, okay?"

"Okay," she breathed back bravely.

"That's my girl. Are you in your belt, or did yours release?"

"I'm out," she said, seeming to steady as I talked to her. But the water was climbing, more than halfway up the windshield, my heart rate along with it.

"Good," I rasped, the strain in my voice arguing with the certainty I put into that word. "That's good. Listen to me and do exactly what Leigh and I say, okay?"

"Okay," she squeaked.

"I need you to climb down to Jax. He has knives in his pockets. I need you to get them for us."

"I can't," she breathed, the tremor in that word breaking my heart.

"You can," Leigh whispered. There was a moment of silence— just the rush of water through the vents and the crackle of the radio dying as my mind sprinted, panic creeping through my aching bones as I tried to calculate how long we had before this behemoth of a vehicle submerged entirely. A minute, maybe two at best. The windshield was cracked but seemed to be holding steady. Incredible for now, but breaking the glass to get out would be another issue…

One thing at a time, or my impending meltdown would win. I huffed out a breath in an attempt to stay centered.

"Quickly, Mattie," I encouraged, holding my hand out so she could grab it. The angle wasn't too severe, but she was just a peanut. A very smart, very shy little peanut. I was a grown woman, and my heart was racing so frantically it was almost impossible to steady my breathing. Mattie had to be losing it. And god, I had no idea what she'd see if she got down there. If I had any other option, I'd take it.

Her warm little fingers landed in mine, and a breath of relief whooshed out of me as she scampered down the center between the captain's chairs.

"Good, Mattie, just like that, sweetie," Leighton encouraged. I could hear her shifting—no doubt assessing our best escape routes just as frenetically as I was. The water was steadily soaking Royce's still lap.

"I don't want you looking around up there, okay? Stay focused. Eyes on the middle console and then Jax's pockets—no detours, alright? We just need the knives. Nothing else."

"But Captain Reynolds—"

"I'll take care of him, okay? Just get us out of these so we can get us all out of here."

Nodding, she blew out a shaky breath and did as I'd asked, keeping her eyes down, although her breathing grew concerningly shallow as she crept over the console and fumbled for the blades as the water poured over his seat, hitting my ankles like a wall of ice. My eyes flicked up to Royce, where he slumped against the corner of the window and dash.

"Got 'em," she breathed, rushing to scramble back to me and hand me the first of two prizes.

"Good, Mattie. Now I need you to carefully climb to the back, okay?"

"But—"

"No buts. I need you to climb to the back of the car."

"*Now*, Tillie," Leighton ordered, tone firm. Reluctantly, Matilda scrambled back and over the third row of seats.

That would buy her the most time. Buy *us* the most time.

To my relief, Jax's knives were meticulously cared for. Even so, it took considerable effort to saw through the damn seatbelt, eyes flicking between my task and the encroaching water as it crept higher. If that cold wasn't waking Jax…

"Jax, I swear to god," I snarled, not finishing the empty threat, though it hung in the air to the grunts of Leighton and I both fighting the serrated edges through thick fabric.

God damn you, Royce. Bile climbed up my throat, a rush of saliva filling my mouth as my head pounded. I forced it back. Forced the panic back as a sudden surge of water rushed inside, the last hum of the engine flickering out. Oh god, *ohgodohgod.*

I needed to move faster.

Needed to *think* faster.

Needed to see Greyson, just one more time. Tell him I loved him. That it was wholehearted and unconditional. That one person in his life loved him, not for what he could give me, but for the courageous, self-sacrificing hero that he was and would always be.

My hand was screaming by the time the threads finally snapped free, a rush of relief filling my lungs.

I caught myself on the driver's seat, turning to see Leighton snapping out of hers. *Thank fuck.* She turned immediately for her seat, freeing the headrest in one adrenaline-charged motion before handing it to Mattie. Eyes on me, she yelled, "*What now?*"

"Jax," I breathed, scrambling forward. Hands trembling, I eased onto the center console, somehow warring with the idea that my movement would send us sinking faster. Unsteady breaths miraculously got me close enough to see the blood across his chest.

Royce *shot* him. Shot the man keeping me safe. The only friend Greyson truly had.

One of his four.

First, they put Cap in the hospital, and now *three of* those four were trapped with a traitor in a sinking car.

Biting back the sob bubbling in my throat, I reached up to his pale neck, pressing my fingers against his pulse point and raptly watching the subtle rise and fall of his chest.

"Is he…" Leighton hedged, unwilling to finish the thought.

"Alive," I said. "He's alive." But my relief was short-lived because we were sinking faster. Too much air was being displaced. Which is why it was a damn miracle when I plunged my hand into the icy water and Jax's buckle clicked open on my first damn try. "Jax!" I barked, smacking my cold, wet hands on his cheeks. "Jax! You have to wake up. *Please*," I croaked. The man was six-two and at least two hundred pounds of muscle. There was no way I could *move* him. But I couldn't leave him either. "*Jax!*"

"*Sissy*," Leighton warned, and I looked down to see the water pouring in more aggressively now, about to reach my feet on the center console.

"God dammit. *Jackson!*" Nothing. Not a god damned flutter of lashes or twitch of a muscle.

"These will help!" If it was any other ten-year-old, I probably wouldn't have looked, but it was Matilda's little voice snapping my attention up. She was waving two yellow life vests in her hands. We'd used them on the boat this week, and never in my life had I been so grateful some wonderful idiot failed to do their job and left them in the car.

"Yes!" I cried, holding a hand out for one. Leighton tossed one my way, and then immediately busied herself strapping Mattie into the other.

By the time I'd heaved Jax's muscled limbs through the damn thing, the water was hitting his chest, my knees soaked, and tears were burning down my cheeks. As I surveyed the navy, climbing up the window, a memory tugged like a thread pulled tight.

Window breakers in every car. That's what Greyson said during his endless security briefing. I must've said it aloud because Leighton gasped, "*Yes!*"

I whirled, lunging for the keys and yanking them from the ignition. My shaky movements sent them flying, and I cried out as they splashed into the rising water. "No!"

"*Sissy*," Leighton screeched as the back windows started leaking in a steady stream. Panic clawed up my throat. Hands trembling, breaths serrating, I threw myself down, water soaking my shirt, and reached into the icy water, trying not to panic, not to let the cold send my logic soaring. "*Alice*," she said, her voice shaking now. She started slamming the metal tips of the headrest bars into the window. Again and again, she swung with every ounce of her strength.

"I know!" I snapped, fishing through the dark water with frantic fingers. "I love you. I love you, Leigh."

"Stop that bullshit right the fuck now—" *slam*, "and find the goddamn keys—" *slam*, "so help me if you get us killed, I will beat you to death—"

A morbid laugh caught in my throat right as my fingers hit the familiar handful of keys and pepper gel. Yanking them back, I rotated, cursing my shaking hands as I found the damn tool. "Thank you, Greyson. *Leigh*," I barked. "I can't get him up there on my own." It wasn't supposed to come out so hysterical. I wasn't supposed to sound like I was being crushed. But the water was climbing, the cold inching onto my belly, and fear was beginning to riddle away any sense left in my head.

I assure you; you can breathe through it. Inhale-exhale, inhale-exhale. Like the desperate flutter of a caged bird, my lungs fought for air. For control.

With an unceremonious whoosh, Leighton flipped the back seat down flat, sending the water parting, and scrambled over it before doing the same to the one I'd occupied a moment ago. Together, we hauled a bleeding Jax over one hurdle after the other, dragging his body through the dark water, both sucking down gulps of air between whimpers of pain.

"He's going to bleed out," she brokenly sobbed as we pulled him into the damn trunk.

"Can't leave him," I panted, too terrified to argue but too broken not to try.

"Sinking now," she noted, tears in her eyes. I nodded as Mattie started to cry, the water reaching us in the back.

"No tears, Mattie. Save your breath, baby girl," I instructed, nodding as she did the same. "I need you to focus."

"Breathe," Leighton coached, grabbing both of Mattie's arms. "*Breathe.*"

"We're all going to take one big breath together, right before I break the window, okay?"

Nodding frantically, Mattie said, "'Kay."

"The water is going to rush in. It's going to be really fucking cold. No matter what, you hang on to me unless I'm pulling you down, understand?" Leighton instructed. This time Mattie just gave a nod, her eyes flicking to the blackness filling the cab, only Royce's head bobbing above the water.

God dammit, Royce. I unconsciously shifted back toward his motionless form in the front seat. His beautiful babies and Miranda's bright smile flashed through my mind. He said they'd *taken her*. The image of his bloodless face collided with his words. *When we didn't turn you over…*

When those men failed on the beach, and Miranda showed up hysterical…were their children at risk *then*? Was he innocent in this? Forced into it with his family on the line?

Leighton's words yanked me back to the task at hand as she grabbed Mattie's face in her palms and pressed a kiss to her forehead. "Eyes on me. I've got you." When they wound their hands together, Mattie gripped on so tight her knuckles bleached white. Our breaths reduced to rapid-fire pants as the water hit our ribs.

"Ready?" I asked, looping my hand through Jax's vest strap. It would be a damn miracle if I could haul Jax to shore. *Two grown men?* I'd just die trying. And if that icy water climbing up his chest hadn't jolted Royce awake, perhaps there wasn't a man left to save.

Leighton's only response was a curt dip of her chin.

"On the count of three." They both nodded, and I gripped the window breaker in my fist, praying the thing worked. "One," I breathed, positioning the device against the top corner, where the glass would be weakest. "Two." Leighton shifted her body so her feet were braced against the seat instead of the floor. "Three." With a press of the button, the thing punched a hole through the glass, sending a stream of water pouring in as vicious cracks spiderwebbed across the broad panel. "Big breath," I instructed, forcing my shallow, panicked gulps of air to deepen.

With one last glance at Leighton, we both raised our arms to break it free, and the water rushed in.

GREYSON

"JESUS CHRIST," Ollie cried as he came up beside me, hands gripping his hair as tears welled in his eyes.

It was the gaping wound at the end of the bridge that had my heart slamming against my rib cage as we sped across the bay and down to the bank below.

No.

It wasn't possible. Wasn't… couldn't be…

My brother seemed to be in shock. His mouth was unhinged, disbelief prying his eyes open wide.

I was frantic. Eyes scraping from one horrible thing to another.

Red and blue lights tore right past the wreck.

The hole in the wall of the bridge.

The taillights of a black SUV bobbing out of the water, nose, and windows already swallowed by the darkness. Fifty yards out. Maybe more.

I was waist-deep in freezing water before a familiar voice barked, "Hart!" I didn't turn, eyes prodding the rippling waves for any sign of life. Of survivors. "Let first responders do their job. You'll get yourself killed."

Luke's voice sent my eyes slamming closed. By the time those cops and EMTs reached the bank, the girls would be out of air if they weren't already. Fuck that. If the option was going home alone or not at all, I'd take the latter.

"You won't make it out there in time," he warned, voice closer. "They're gone, man."

No.

Not my Mattie.

Not my wife.

I would know. Somehow, I'd know if she was gone.

Would have felt the universe dull in her absence.

No.

But they *were* gone—the taillights vanished, swallowed by depthless inky black. My fingers flexed at my side—once, twice, *three* times—and I pictured Alice's smile, the warmth of her body on mine, the unforgiving heat of that Caribbean sun I'd said my vows beneath, and dove.

Muscle memory took over—slow, deliberate breaths and precise strokes—as I fought to keep my back from seizing from the shock of it.

Not today.

Today, I would be what she needed me to be.

Today, I would breathe through it.

Alice strong.

That was the mantra I clung to.

It was wild that in all those brutal training sessions, my body had never been more numb than it was in that bay. Never been as ruthless as I cut through the water in disciplined strokes.

Alice strong. Alice strong.

With each pump of my heart, each rotation of my arms, the words repeated.

Her laugh. The way she rolled her eyes when I pushed her buttons. Her body shattering beneath me…the look of wide-eyed panic on that beach after I sealed our marriage with the kiss to end them all. All three of them piled on the couch, watching movies with the dogs. With every pull of my arms, pieces of us flashed in my mind. Hell, I even saw all the beautiful moments with Leighton as my heart begged a god who'd forgotten me to save them.

Never in my life had the sound of a scream been so sweet. I reared out of the water as that piercing cry broke the air, eyes stinging as I spotted Mattie in a life vest, bobbing in the water.

I think I yelled her name, changing my trajectory toward her a beat before Leighton broke the surface. She immediately orientated herself and latched onto the vest's strap, hauling my niece toward shore.

I decided I fucking loved the feral one.

"Alice!" I bellowed, treading water and frantically doing a one-eighty, searching the depths. But she wasn't there. She wasn't bobbing to the surface like her sister. My stomach sank. "Leighton!" I barked. Her wide eyes found mine as she pinned Mattie to her side, hauling her along in a side stroke. "Where is my wife?!"

"She was…" Leighton's eyes went frantic with terror as she flipped her gaze back over her shoulder. "She was right there. She was *right there*!" The last words were a hysterical scream, her focus now split between her sister and my niece. But Ollie was cutting through the water, not twenty yards behind us. And Mattie was shaking her head when our eyes locked.

"I'm okay!" she sobbed as shivers wracked her tiny body. "*Go, Uncle Grey!*"

With that, I dove toward the place where the car had just vanished. I didn't swim for long before bright yellow caught my stinging vision in the blur of depthless black. Diving deeper, I wrapped my hands around the vest and powered upward. A sound of absolute desperation left my lips as I blinked away the water to find Alice, towed behind the vest clipped around Jax. He coughed, eyes fluttering open as he hacked up water, only to drift closed again.

Alice cleared the water from her lungs, but waved me off, flipping onto her back to let the bay hold her up.

"Jesus Christ," I croaked. Tears cut through the icy water clinging to my skin. "Are you hurt?" I barked, staring at the rapidly blooming red that spread on her face. She shook her head.

Alive. They were alive.

More blood was spreading over Jax's vest, and my brain drifted to secondary concerns in the water. "We have to get to shore!"

She nodded, but said nothing as she sucked down air as she tried to catch her breath. Thank god. Thank fucking god. Thank any power that brought her back to me.

My relief was short-lived, as Jax's quick inhales caught my attention—too fucking shallow.

When I reached for her, she shook her head, rotating onto her belly. "I'm okay," she panted. "But he's not."

30

A Family Matter
GREYSON

Beep.

Mattie, curling into Leighton's lap on the soaked sand and holding on for dear life. A silently sobbing Oliver wrapping them up in his arms.

Beep.

Leighton, looking more likely to kill the EMT than let him take her.

Beep.

Alice swaying as she fought to stay vertical where she kneeled in the sand, applying pressure to Jax's chest. The sound of her screaming for help as first responders tore onto the bank.

Beep.

My wife loaded into an ambulance while Mattie, Leighton, and Ollie were stuffed into another. The first tearing onto the road with sirens blaring and Jax inside.

Beep.

The bruising crack of my knees as they hit the tile floor when they took Alice behind double doors, I couldn't follow through.

"Grey?" Something warm that smelled like an ashtray was under my nose, jerking me awake. My brother's stony expression was locked on my face, and I blinked into the gloom of the hospital room. The obnoxious beeping sound clicking memories like slides through my mind was Mattie's monitor. I'd nodded off in the stiff, pleather armchair in the corner, my neck protesting the awkward angle. Sucking down a breath, I straightened, eyes darting to where my niece slept, still hooked to the IV with Leighton cocooning her little body.

"What is it?" I demanded, reluctantly accepting the offered cup of hospital coffee he was wielding in my direction.

"Come on," he whispered, glancing back at the girls like he was afraid to wake them.

My stomach sunk. Throat tightening. Eyes burning.

I couldn't… couldn't follow. Couldn't endure anything else.

Jax had miraculously survived a very tedious surgery and many transfusions. They were now treating him for infection, but he'd yet to wake. As if the gunshot wasn't enough, he'd sustained a concussion and broken ribs in the wreck.

Leighton—the endearingly feral honey badger that she was—had discharged herself against medical advice because they wouldn't let her stay beside my niece as a patient. In her words, there wasn't shit they could do for her broken ribs or collar bone, anyway. The moment the papers were signed, she'd allegedly scowled at the front desk lady like the policy was her fault before stomping to the elevator to go back to Mattie. She'd slithered into a gap between Matilda and the bed frame that was much too small for a full-grown woman, and yet she managed. Although I'm sure an abundance of pain medication helped her settle in there.

My Alice had been the last priority—her jaw set, and eyes ignited with white-hot rage—as the others were tended to.

Right up until she passed out in the bathroom.

I watched in silent terror as the staff rushed in with a crash cart, maneuvered her onto the flat stretcher, and wheeled her behind double doors. Unforgiving white tiles hit my knees when they gave out, and I prayed to any deity that would listen to bring her back to me.

Evidently, the tears burning my cheeks hadn't been silent, because before I could catch my breath, a little blonde with Alice's eyes was kneeling in front of me with her hands on my face, her chin trembling before she scooped me into a standing hug with alarming strength.

Hadlee, I distantly remembered.

In the next breath, another set of arms wrapped around us. Another. *Another.* One after the other, her siblings lent me their strength, heads bowed together until a football-sized huddle consumed the hallway.

Someone prayed.

Everyone murmured their assent and amen.

The next hours were the worst of my life.

Brexley, Max, and Quinn reluctantly left the waiting room huddle to go to Oliver's so the baby could sleep. Broderick attempted to get Elora to follow suit, to no avail.

Drips of information were leaked to us by nurses that came and left just as quickly.

Broken collar bone, sternum, and ribs.

Internal bleeding.

Surgery.

Each face was more grim than the last as I paced the hallway until Mattie asked for me, and my heart broke all over again.

Alice had agreed to help me out of scandal, to save my skin for no reason beyond a bone-deep sense of justice, and my secrets hurled her to the cusp of death. In a matter of weeks, we'd made an enemy that nearly robbed me of my dog, and now three of my most beloved human beings on the planet were in these sterile papered walls. Two tiptoeing on the territory of the Grim Reaper.

I couldn't go in there and patch either of them back together. There wasn't anything all our fucking money could buy that could make this right. Nothing in my power to *fix this*.

When Ollie and I rounded the corner into the waiting room, her siblings all looked up at once. Jameson and Paxton both rose to their feet expectantly.

Even as they closed the distance to stand to either side of me, I knew I didn't deserve their solidarity.

My fault.

This was all my fucking fault.

I had a feeling that the ever-silent Jameson would put me out of my misery if this went belly up. Or at least he would if I told him the truth.

A flicker of surprise turned into a flame of outrage in my chest when I spotted Reggie off in the corner of the room. His balding head rested in his hands, elbows braced on his knees. I didn't have time to respond before Ollie was nudging me in the ribs.

It was the surgeon in black scrubs that came into the room and snapped me from worst-case scenarios and the anger of his pathetic, artificial presence.

"Mr. Hart?" When I nodded, she pulled her mask below her chin, a tentative smile on her face lending me an ounce of comfort. "Your wife is out of surgery, and it went as well as it could have. We stopped the bleeding and have no indication of any permanent damage. She's in for a long recovery, but I do expect her to make a full one."

A collective whoosh of breath left the room. Someone burst into sobs. Ollie palmed his jaw, eyes shooting skyward as his tears overflowed. Paxton slapped a hand between my shoulder blades as Jameson collapsed to kneel with his head in his hands, rocking on his heels. My uncle found his feet, his eyes locked on me and...*bloodshot*.

Tears seared my eyes as I watched the doctor's sympathetic expression. "She's awake in her room and asking for you."

My pulse slammed so hard against my ears that I couldn't make sense of the words hurled at me from *twelve* different angles. I couldn't find words as Reggie nodded solemnly, setting a hand on my shoulder as he walked past us and down the hallway.

I just numbly followed the doctor back to a room in a wing I had yet to wander. When I rounded the corner and stepped over the threshold, groggy gray-blue eyes found mine, a weak smile lining her lips as I cracked like an egg.

Collapsing to my knees by her bedside, I shakily grasped her hand in mine and brought it to my lips as relief washed through me. Alice thumbed away the tears on my cheek as she gave a little murmur.

"I don't think beasts are supposed to cry," she rasped before coughing a little laugh out.

"My Belle," I breathed, unable to meet her eyes, even as I felt them boring into the top of my head. Shame was a hideously consuming companion. She slipped her fingers from mine, and I let her. I'd deserve it if she left—deserve it if she fled to the far corners of the world and changed her name so not even Max could find her.

But the woman knew me well. Saw everything as I diverted my gaze, wiping my hand across my mouth, because she brought her fingers to my chin and tugged me back to her. "Grey." When my eyes stayed closed, she said, "Look at me." I did. How was she so beautiful, even with her skin wan and a cannula in her nose? Even nearly broken, Alice was the most radiant creature I'd ever beheld. The woman who saw everything smiled softly and shook her head. "I'm *not running.*"

ALICE

Eight months later…

"ARE YOU READY?"

"I think so."

"Are you *sure*?" Greyson pressed, with a devilish glint in his eyes that made my smirk deepen.

"Pretty certain."

"Cause it's not too late to change your mind," he insisted.

"I think that ship has sailed, Mr. Hart."

His low rumble of a laugh made me smile. "I dunno. Frankly, that crowd is *terrifying*. They all look so expectant."

Over the winter, we'd made Hart House our own, the walls now covered with paintings and splashes of color. We traded the sterile, magazine-worthy, Cape Cod-style furniture for eclectic, curated pieces we'd chosen together. If we were going to bring something home, it had to speak to us personally. None of the generic showroom bullshit. To Greyson's eternal amusement, he actually liked color more than the neutral pallet his designers had granted him over the years. Blue, in particular, held his fancy.

With a dramatic sigh, Captain rose from his plush bed beside my vanity as we found our feet. "Ready, big guy?" I asked, bending down to ruffle his ears and straighten his bow tie before scratching down his spine.

"Hey," Grey protested. "No calling the dog 'big guy' if I'm around. I resent that."

My laugh mixed with the enthusiastic tippy-tap of Cap's paws as he waggled back and forth between my hands. A jealous Chip came leaping from our bed like an albino flying squirrel. His little claws screeched across the hardwood as he slid up beside us to demand pets, too. Captain grumbled his displeasure before heading for the French doors to lead the three of us out to the inevitable chaos.

My family—yep, *all of them* in their loud, chaotic glory—and a handful of our friends were chattering just beyond the patio. Squeezing Greyson's hand in mine, I sucked down a steadying breath. Through the wall of glass, everyone we loved milled about. Bulb lights sparkled under the golden hour pastels of a Southern California sunset. White tents lined the perimeter of our property, and the sizzle of meat on the grill competed with the trail of music from the live band placed against the border of sand.

For our one-year anniversary, Greyson had insisted we finally celebrate our vows the way I 'deserved' to. Whatever the hell that meant.

But he'd known better than I did, because he kept it intimate and informal. A live acoustic band, beautiful view, the people we could count on—which was, admittedly, a lot more than just four of us now—and a Mistyvale-style fish fry.

Greyson kissed my temple before opening the door and motioning me through to a chorus of whoops, applause, and obnoxious wolf whistles.

"*Brothers*," I muttered.

"Tell me about it," he grumbled, jerking his chin toward the dance floor, where Oliver was twirling Mattie in one hand and Leighton—who had a giggling Beau wrapped around her back like a chimp—in the other. Paxton was just behind them and flashed me a wink over the shoulder of his intimidatingly gorgeous date. Her black curls swayed at her lower back.

Unabashedly, Max sidled up next to Grey with a shit-eating grin on his face and a slick button-up and slate gray vest wrapped over his lean frame.

"Suit Daddy," he said by way of greeting, complete with a signature Max eyebrow waggle.

"Christ," Grey muttered, an adorable little flush creeping into his cheeks. Max was entirely undeterred, to no one's surprise, and my eternal amusement. He'd been around a lot this year, making this place feel more like home than ever. As per usual, both work and his love of travel had him bouncing around the planet. Brexley and Elora had an eager mother's assistant after their births, and Hadlee called him up north for some help when she was house hunting. But aside from that and the occasional unavoidable work trip, he'd been here with me as we created a new sense of normal.

"About damn time, you two. I've got something I'm dying to show you—you're gonna *love it*, I promise."

I was still laughing as my *maddeningly attractive* husband was dragged over to Max's computer, where it sat on a patio table. Unwilling to snake my way through the party until Grey was beside me, I leaned onto the banister of the terrace and watched the commotion with a smile on my face.

"Looking awfully radiant, little Hart. Sure that old asshole is taking good care of you?"

Grinning at the familiar baritone, I turned to smirk up at the one and only Jackson Reynolds. *"Oh,* I'm fairly certain all my needs are accounted for." His cheeky little smile filled my chest with a warm sense of safety a beat before he pulled me into a bruising bear hug. Like me, Jax had a bit of a rocky road to recovery in the fall, but he'd spent it here with us. Together with Max, Luke, and a couple of trusted FBI contacts, we put our heads down and worked our asses off to bring *Thunderstrike* firmly above board. The road hadn't been easy, but after their rescue of Miranda Ashcroft and her children, and the ensuing unveiling of the city's seedy underbelly, stepping into the light became rather inevitable.

The part that stung even all these months later was the fact that Miranda had known. *My friend*—or who I thought was my friend. She'd known who was hunting me, and she hadn't told us. I mean… more than anyone, I was aware of what we'd do to protect those we loved, and with her unsuspecting children in *Obsidian's* crosshairs… maybe I couldn't understand what that felt like, but I don't think I would've protected my husband until I knew they were going to kill *her,* if our roles were reversed.

Even knowing she'd been under duress didn't ease that wound. She'd been on her way to deliver everything she knew to Detective Rivera when *Obsidian* tracked her down and forced her into an SUV at gunpoint. Royce's sudden onset of sickness had been in reaction to an image of the three of them with Odessa's head of security.

Royce.

The man used me as an in to get closer to Greyson and violated our home—used our friendship to get inside and plant bugs after

Max's sweep to provide his mother with the information she needed to blackmail us or back us into a corner, whichever it came to.

In the end, Royce was presumed dead in the bay, although his body was never recovered, and Miranda secured one hell of a plea bargain. Who wouldn't sympathize with a heavily pregnant mom of three who was protecting her children from her husband's psychotic blood family? Especially when she sang like a damn canary after *Thunderstrike* got her out.

As of this month, *Thunderstrike* was a known government initiative, with Jax at the helm. They still relied on retired vets for the bulk of their muscle, and their toys were admittedly a bit nicer due to Greyson's generous funding.

This time last year, if Grey had told me the big blond wall of muscle beside me would feel like family, I would've choked on saliva from snorting so hard. It wasn't like I *needed* an extra brother-figure with the six towering smartasses wandering around, but he'd become mine as much as Grey's. Well, a brother that made inappropriately flirtatious jokes just so he could laugh when I squirmed.

"I mean it though, kid," he added as we pulled apart. "You look good. Healthy. Happy."

"I am happy," I declared with a grin and a flush creeping up my neck. The best part was how deeply I meant it. There was nothing fake or forced—no mask I had to hide behind when the crowd thickened. Joy, while hard fought for, had become synonymous with *home* for me. This slice of peace Greyson carved out of the chaos for us.

"Good," he said with a grin, turning to look out over the people beneath the twinkling lights as he tucked me against his side. "You, of all people, deserve it. Enjoy that, you little warrior."

Okay, so Jax had made a much bigger deal out of me not leaving him for dead in the bottom of the bay than was strictly comfortable. He would've done the same for me.

"You deserve that too, you know?" I pressed, earning a side-eye and matching, incredulous smirk.

"I'm not like Grey."

"No?"

"No," he scoffed playfully. My growing smirk had him narrowing his eyes down at me. "No meddling," he barked.

I put my hands up and shook my head. "No idea what you're talking about, Reynolds. I'm too busy to meddle these days."

"Better be," he grumbled, shoving me playfully sideways. "Christ, woman. Grey and Ollie are bad enough. I don't need it from you, too. Some of us are better off alone."

"That's what Greyson said," I pointed out.

"Yeah, well, Grey's an idiot."

I burst out laughing a beat before Leighton scooted up beside me and handed me a martini. "The babies are conspiring against us," she declared.

"Excellent. Keep this one preoccupied so she can't be a menace," Jax grumbled. "Tiny dictators are right up her alley."

My retort was cut short as someone cut the sound to the live band, the beginning notes of *Ice Ice, Baby* by Vanilla Ice coming on over the built-in speakers as blue and purple lights began pulsating to the music. Brows merging with my hairline, I looked between Leigh and Jax before we all whirled to the sound of Greyson groaning, "*Max!*"

Max's evil laugh had us all busting at the seams by the time Greyson appeared, still shaking his head as the light show continued. But when his eyes found mine, his scowl splintered into a soft little smile.

"I have a surprise for you," he murmured, bypassing our company to wrap those glorious palms around my waist as people began to sing along.

"Another one?!" I balked. A cold nose booped my thigh, and I glanced down to see an expectant Cap, like he was in on his crazy daddy's secret.

"Yeah, baby, another one. Let me steal you for a moment."

"You get her all the time!" Leighton protested, a little slant to her lips. Whatever occurred in the hours I was out in that hospital, the two of them had forged an adorable friendship—albeit, it was full of sarcasm and friendly jabs they claimed as a love language.

"Just another moment," he promised, weaving our fingers together.

"Use protection," Jax barked after us, sending my skin flaming as I glared at Greyson like the fucker's big mouth was his fault.

"Come on, baby," he whispered, swallowing his humor.

Curious, I abandoned the chatter of the party and followed my husband into the blue glow of sunset.

31

Okay, Pavlov

ALICE

'

"Kinky," I teased as Greyson set his hands over my eyes.

"You have no idea," he said as he rocked his hips into my ass, nudging me forward.

"I think I'm beginning to," I insisted. "Surprised you didn't pull out one of our blindfolds." Sex with Greyson was still soul-shattering a few hundred times later. I would think I'd grow immune to his gloriously possessive hands, but that had certainly yet to happen. Some days, he worshipped me; others, we just needed to fuck. But it was always his wonderful affirmations poured over my needy little heart that made me melt.

"Thought about it, believe me. But they're like a trigger for me. I just look at one and go painfully hard."

"Okay, Pavlov."

"Maybe let's not refer to me as a slobbering dog when I'm thinking about your nipples in my mouth."

Laughing, we continued on to the soothing crash of waves that gradually swallowed the sound of the party as he guided my steps through shifting sand. "I still don't get any clues?"

"Shhh, just enjoy the waves."

In a futile attempt to nip at his wrist, I whipped my head to the side, but he just snickered and in the next motion, I was in his arms. "Be a good girl and keep your eyes closed," he ordered.

"You're bossy," I prodded.

"And you like it."

He wasn't wrong. "Is that what you're telling yourself?"

"That's what you tell me when you suck my cock to the back of your throat like my personal whore."

My cackle trailed away as the dulcet notes of piano tiptoed over the crash of surf, and I turned my head in an attempt to hear more of it. "What is that?"

"Not the response I was expecting," he noted lightly, and I pinched his chest through the slick material of his button-up. "That's *part of it*, princess."

When Grey set my feet back into the warm sand, I realized I was chewing my lip. Elegant piano music played, my ears straining to recognize the notes. "Can I open yet?" I demanded impatiently.

"Hang on," he said, but then he let go of me, and I threw my hands out in protest, earning a dark chuckle that sent heat climbing beneath my skin. The subtle whoosh of his feet through the sand held my attention until they silenced, leaving in their stead the most disarming combination of sound and caress of warm air on my cheeks. Anticipation sent butterflies flying through my chest, my teeth running over my bottom lip until at last, Grey breathed, "Now."

I opened my eyes to find Greyson Hart kneeling on a beautiful blue and gold Thai throw we'd found together. The corners were framed by flickering tea lights and taller candles, and a canopy of glimmering lights formed a peak in the center.

"Grey?" I breathed.

"A year ago, I took you as my wife without earning that title. Not long after, I asked you to date me, Mrs. Hart, and you agreed. In the year since, you've stood by my side through literal hell. You've had my back when the world came against us. You've chosen me time and again—your loyalty unmatched." He cleared his throat, shifting his weight on the blanket. "But something was missing—the theatrics of it all. The grand gesture a love like this deserves."

"Grey," I gasped as he reached into his vest pocket and pulled out a rather thick stack of papers. "What is this?"

"What I should have shown you then. Because before I had any right to call you mine, I knew you would be."

With nerves in my belly, and confusion throbbing in my mind, I stepped through the sand, careful not to kick any up onto his beautiful arrangement. Between two of the canopy poles was a string with photographs clipped to it. Some were Mattie's polaroids, others were prints off our phones, but none were those we'd paid a fortune to craft so strategically.

Me on Grey's back with him laughing, soaking wet from a water fight.

Greyson, looking like he shit his pants on the boat last summer, made me laugh.

Me, asleep on the back patio with the lights glimmering above, looking entirely at peace.

Grey and me dancing at a gala.

Hell, there was even one of us at Paxton's first Emerald Bay game, proudly wearing our jerseys and foam fingers before everything went to shit.

Me in that damn sling for my arm, glaring at him from the couch where he'd surrounded me in all manner of treats to choose from.

Me and Leighton covered in flour, sandwiching Ollie's laughing kids between our grinning faces at Christmas.

Eyes watering, I returned to his intense gaze where my real-life Adonis knelt in the sand. I took the stack but just stared at my husband as my breathing picked up tempo with the significance he'd so thoughtfully sown into each little detail. As if in confirmation, the piano gave way to the ethereal notes of *Borders* by Kalandra. The song I'd been singing the night we started this relationship authentically.

When I glanced to the papers, confusion settled in for a long moment as I read over the words so hastily written and scratched out. I'd know Greyson's handwriting anywhere.

~~Alessandra, you are the light of my life~~

~~Alessandra Rhodes, you have challenged me from the day you walked into my office~~

AND THEN A FAMILIAR paragraph sprawled at the bottom of the page stopped my breath. My gaze flicked to his, lungs tight in my chest as I looked back to the words he'd said last year on our beach.

To the most stubborn, ambitious, infuriating, and beautiful woman I've ever known. I am not a perfect man. You, of all people, have seen the ugliest parts of me, yet you stand here, declaring our lives united. Your grace and empathy inspire me beyond words—to be a better man, to be courageous enough to feel more deeply.

While I may never be flawless, I vow to dedicate my life to earning the loyalty you've given me. If any woman can push me to conquer impossibilities, it's you, Alessandra Lennon Rhodes.

My Nona always told me that the Hebrew phrase for partner—Ezer Kenegdo—translates to 'a helper opposite him', which I think perfectly reflects your unique ability to challenge me in ways no one else can. If you allow me, I vow to prove myself worthy of you. I may never fully deserve what you've given me, what you've sacrificed to stand beside me, but I promise to spend my life trying.

WHEN MY BURNING eyes pulled away from the text, he smiled softly as I poured flustered words between my lips. "These are...*you* wrote our vows?"

"Took a few dozen renditions, but they got there."

"I thought—"

"It seemed inauthentic to pay someone to write the words which would bind my life to yours."

"Greyson," I stammered, my voice breaking. "I had no idea. I—"

"Had every right to hate me, my Belle. But I *never* hated you." He gently swiped my left hand in his, and I scowled as he slipped the mammoth ring from my finger.

"What are you—"

But he was shaking his head and pulling a little blue box from his jacket. "That one was for *them*," he said pointedly, tucking it away in his breast pocket. *Them*. The world. The paparazzi. The psychopaths trying to skewer him. "This one is for *you*." When Greyson popped the box open, I sucked down a breath, the bridge of my nose stinging as tears demanded release. I'd done a remarkable amount of crying for Greyson Hart in the last twelve months. The ring inside the velvet cushion had two accompanying bands— all Art Deco, gold and diamonds surrounding an emerald fitting for the name of our city. "This time is just for the stars, the sea, you, and me...well, and Cap...and Chip." Captain, who'd unceremoniously plopped onto a large rock jutting from the beach, lifted his big noggin to turn it sideways when he heard his name. "I love you, *Mrs. Alessandra Hart*. I screwed up my chance to give you a proper proposal, so instead, I ask you this: stay with me. You know all there is to know—the good, the bad, and the ugly. And I'm asking you to stay with me."

Smirking to cover the tears blurring my vision, I pointed out, "That wasn't really said like a question, Grey."

"That wasn't really an answer, Alice."

"Yes," I breathed, losing the battle with my emotions as I beamed, and tears poured when he slid the new ring into its rightful place. Beautiful. And absolutely *me*. Not flashy. No gaudy camera bait to be seen. Just a piece that was a little quirky around the edges, but classic all the same. Grey rose to his feet and crushed me against him a beat before his mouth found mine.

"Thank fuck, because that party would be pretty awful if you said no," he teased, the smirk I loved so much twisting his words. "There's more."

"More!?" I croaked as he lifted me up, my dress bunching around my waist as he hoisted me onto his hips, expectation colliding with…*nerves* in his eyes?

"Read the next one."

Too much. The man was too much for me. Too sweet. Too… vulnerable to wrap my head around. No trace of the robot was left in sight. Wrapping my arms around his neck like a koala, I turned to the next page and hesitated, throat tightening as I saw *Emerald Bay Urology* printed at the top left corner. Blood turning to ice, heart in my belly, I asked, "Are you…are you *sick*?"

A dark rumble vibrated my ribs, but he pressed his lips to my shoulder and whispered, "No."

"Then what is this?"

"A gift. Should you choose to accept it?"

"Will this letter self-destruct before I make sense of it?"

Another chuckle, this time as he buried himself in my hair. "Stop panicking and read it, Alice."

Struggling to swallow, I did, and my confusion turned to shock, followed by a crushing wave of overwhelm. "I read it and I'm *still* panicking."

"Only if you want me to. It's just an appointment, and there's no guarantee I can—"

"You're *reversing* your vasectomy?"

"I'm still waiting for my wife to approve the procedure. But… that is the plan. Our decisions shouldn't be limited by choices I made out of fear, shame, or grief."

"What happened to kids being a liability?"

"*Love* is a liability," he said simply. "But you've shown me I can't live without it, either." With a gentle brush of his lips on mine, he sent my head spinning. "You found me as a broken man and salvaged the heart few people knew I still had beating. The greatest honor would be watching the love of my life mother my children."

"I love you," I breathed shakily. His answering smile was enough to light my soul on fire. Honestly, I never imagined the kind of love that would make me all warm and fuzzy once the initial jitters wore off—never imagined the all-consuming, sweep-you-off-your-feet kind of romance. And yeah, okay, ours certainly had an unconventional beginning, but what mattered in the end was that we'd found our way to each other in this insane world. The significance of this offer hit me square in the chest, and a wave of affection for Greyson Hart nearly took my legs out from under me.

"I love you, too. What do you say, baby?"

"You want a family."

"I want *our* family," he corrected.

"You're serious."

"As a heart attack."

"It's safe?"

"*Worried about me?*"

"*Obviously,*" I squeaked.

"Simple outpatient procedure. Sit on some frozen peas for a few days. The doctor comes highly recommended."

"And you've thought this through?" I asked, although even to me, it was obvious I was grasping at straws. My eyes stung as I imagined life with our own little Hart heiress or maybe a little prince our nephews could terrorize. Would they get Hart hazels or Rhodes blues? Would they be quiet like us, or would the universe have a sense of humor and send us an Elora or an Oliver? I suppose most women worry about whether or not their partner would be a good father, but…that never crossed my mind. Not with Grey. I didn't have to ask myself because I knew he'd be incredible. Our babies would have the world at their disposal. And yes, we had to live a life with an insane security force, but…there was nothing this man wouldn't do to protect our family. His guys included.

Sensing my need to process, he just nodded. After what had to be an uncomfortably long buffering period, he finally pressed, "So?"

I looked between those beautiful dark hazels, illuminated only by the glittering bulbs draped above us, and smirked. "Put a baby in me, Mr. Hart."

The warmth of his laughter would live in my mind for the rest of my life. Struggling to compose himself, he finally chuckled a light-hearted, "I don't think it works quite like that."

"Then, *practice,* dammit," I blurted before our lips collided. Still grinning against my kiss, he lowered us onto the blanket, hitched my dress around my hips with warm, ravenous hands, and did just that.

Thank you for reading!

<u>Want more Alice and Greyson?</u>

SNAG **your free copy of their Bonus Epilogue** (exclusive for my reader's list) and see what the Harts are up to eight years later!

Bonus points: you'll be the first to know about updates for Leighton's story, *Mended Hearts,* the second book in *The Hearts Of Emerald Bay.*

DOWNLOAD THE EPILOGUE HERE:
https://dl.bookfunnel.com/g9hkqoui06

LOVE THE RHODES? Applications for the street team are open! Apply here!

WANT someone to talk to about the books? We'd love to see you in the Grayshell Babes reader group on Facebook! Join here!

Afterword

Good golly, Miss Molly. Alice and Grey took me for a freaking ride, and I loved every damn minute of it. I don't know if there has ever been a couple that hit me so hard, fast, and distinctly, let alone a book that kept me in flow state as consistently as this one. I am *obsessed* with this book. And *yes*, I said that with all of the enthusiasm of David in *Schitt's Creek*.

But, for real. If I could write a series just for Grey and Alice, I would. 100%. As I wrapped up their story, I had tears in my eyes—not just because they're adorable, but because I was not anywhere near ready to say goodbye. Truth be told, I miss them already.

If you're still here reading, then I hope you loved them too. I mean, I assume so. That, or you have the determination of that lone survivor of a sock that just keeps resurfacing after every load of laundry. I gotta say, I appreciate your persistence! Please go feel some sunshine now though, friend. If, however, you're in the former group, I can't tell you how grateful I am that you're here, loving on these two with me. I always have an idea of what my books will look like, but leave room for my characters to move about as we go. These two were both game to follow the path I had sketched out but wanted to do it with a bit of their own flare—boy, isn't that in line with their characters?—and many (many, many) more words than I'd anticipated.

As heartbroken as I am to be saying farewell, I'm beyond relieved they'll be around for the remainder of the series. I hope we 'meet' again in the spring, when *Mended Hearts* picks up where these two left off!

Thank you so much for reading! If you wanna help shout it from the rooftops, every single review makes a gigantic impact, and I'm so, so grateful for every one of them.

Xoxo
　Sydne

Thank You!

My readers: You guys are my why!! Thank you for reading, for reviewing, for popping into my DMs to squeal or giggle or kick your feet with me. There's nothing like hearing someone fell in love with these fictional people I love so dearly.

The dream team: Sam, Heather and Jess, you guys keep me going on the bad days, and I know in my heart of hearts you're why I haven't thrown in the towel. Thank you for all of our chaotic spaghetti throwing, late night voice memo's, invaluable feedback, and for helping craft a book we absolutely love. Love you ladies!

My hubby: Baby, thank you for showing me a patient love. A love that makes space for quirks and mistakes. Thank you for your endless belief in me and these stories I write. Love you forever.

Shannon— Thank you for creating a gorgeous line of covers for THOEB!

About the Author

Sydne Barnett is a lover of spunky, badass heroines, and heroes that embrace their wild. She's an avid reader, never turns down a good cup of coffee, loves hiking with her hubby, and lives for finding their next adventure.

If she's not writing, you can probably find her behind her camera, swimming, or curled up with a homemade pastry, watching Friends, HIMYM, or Gilmore Girls.

Raised in the Treasure Valley, Idaho, Sydne has a love for one-light towns, and winding backroads, but refusing to ignore her soul's call for adventure, she hit the road with her family, and now they call the world their home.

Let's connect!

Reader's Group: https://www.facebook.com/groups/grayshellbabes

Tiktok: https://www.tiktok.com/@barnettbooktalk

Instagram: https://www.instagram.com/barnettbooktalk/

Newsletter: https://shorturl.at/acJSZ

Also by Sydne Barnett

Nomadic Rhodes

South of The Skyway (book 1)
Brewing Temptation (book 2)
Finding A Way Back Home (book 3)

The Hearts of Emerald Bay

(Rhodes universe continued, billionaire edition)
Salvaged Hearts <—you are here.
Mended Hearts (Coming Spring 2025, now available for pre-order)
Winning Hearts (Coming Summer 2025, now available for pre-order)
Catching Hearts (Coming Fall 2025, now available for pre-order)
Title TBD, **(surprise!** *book #5!)*

Romantic High/Urban Fantasy as S.J. Barnett

Commanding Flame And Shield (Grayshell Rising, book one)
Commanding Earth And Shadow (Grayshell Rising, book two)